Lovely, and gay, and charmingly innocent, Kitten was the most impressionable young lady ever to step into Regency London. Bundled off at only a moment's notice, she was transformed in an instant—from an orphan into the lovely Lady Sheringham.

Flushed with naivete and an eagerness to learn, Kitten soon found her way through the sophisticated paths of London, causing her elegant husband's face to pale.

GEORGETTE HEYER

FRIDAY'S CHILD

A BERKLEY MEDALLION BOOK
PUBLISHED BY
BERKLEY PUBLISHING CORPORATION

Copyright © 1946, by Georgette Heyer

All rights reserved

Published by arrangement with G.P. Putnam's Sons

SBN 425-02297-8

*BERKLEY MEDALLION BOOKS are published by
Berkley Publishing Corporation
200 Madison Avenue
New York, N.Y. 10016*

BERKLEY MEDALLION BOOKS ® TM 757,375

Printed in the United States of America

Berkley Medallion Edition, FEBRUARY, 1973

Monday's child is fair in face,
Tuesday's child is full of grace,
Wednesday's child is full of woe,
Thursday's child has far to go,
Friday's child is loving and giving,
Saturday's child works hard for its living;
And a child that's born on Christmas Day,
Is fair and wise, and good and gay.

FROM HALLIWELL'S *Popular Rhymes and Nursery Tales*

CHAPTER 1

"Do not, I beg of you, my lord, say more!" uttered Miss Milborne, in imploring accents, slightly averting her lovely countenance, and clasping both hands at her bosom.

Her companion, a tall young gentleman who had gone romantically down upon one knee before her chair, appeared put out by this faltered request. "Damn it—I mean, dash it, Isabella!" he expostulated, correcting himself somewhat impatiently as the lady turned reproachful brown eyes upon him, "I haven't started!"

"Do not!"

"But I'm about to offer for you!" said the Viscount, with more than a touch of asperity.

"I know," replied the lady. "It is useless! Say no more, my lord!"

The Viscount arose from his knee, much chagrined. "I must say, Isabella, I think you might let a fellow speak!" he said crossly.

"I would spare you pain, my lord."

"I wish you will stop talking in that damned

7

theatrical way!" said the Viscount. "And don't keep on calling me 'my lord', as though you hadn't known me all your life!"

Miss Milborne flushed, and stiffened a little. It was perfectly true, since their estates marched together that she had known the Viscount all her life, but a dazzling career as an acknowledged Beauty, with half the eligible young gentlemen in town at her feet, had accustomed her to a far more reverential mode of address than that favoured by her childhood's playmate. In some dudgeon, she gazed coldly out of the window, while her suitor took a few hasty turns about the room.

The prospect, which was of neat lawns, well-stocked flowerbeds, and trim hedges, was a pleasing one. but it was not from any love of sylvan settings that Miss Milborne was at present sojourning in the country. Her withdrawal from the Metropolis some weeks previously had been in consequence of her having contracted an odiously childish complaint which had made it necessary for her to disappear from the Polite World at a moment when she might have been pardoned for considering herself, if not its hub, at least its cynosure. Her Mama, quite as sensible as herself of the ridiculous nature of her indisposition, had announced her to be quite worn-down by the exigencies of fashionable life, and had whisked her off to Kent in a post-chaise-and-four, where, in a comfortable mansion suitably retired from the haunts of men, she was able not only to recover her health and looks in seclusion, but also to communicate her complaint to two abigails, and a youthful page-boy. She had emerged from her sick room some weeks earlier, but since she was still a trifle pale and out of looks, Mrs. Milborne, a lady distinguished by her admirable sense, had decided to keep her in the country until (she said) the roses should again bloom in her cheeks. Quite a number of ardent gentlemen had presented themselves at Milbourne House, having driven all the way from London in the hopes of being permitted a glimpse of the Incomparable, but the door remained shut against them, and they were obliged to relinquish their nosegays and passionate billets into the hands of an unresponsive butler, and to tool their various chariots back to town without having had even the refreshment of being allowed to press their lips to the fair hand of the Beauty.

Lord Sheringham would undoubtedly have met with the same reception had he not presumed in a very unhandsome way upon his long acquaintance with the family, by riding over from Sheringham Place, where he had been spending the night, leaving his horse at the stables, and walking up through the gardens to enter the house through one of the long windows that opened on to the lawn. Encountering an astonished footman, his lordship, very much at home, had tossed his whip and his gloves on to a table, laid his curly-brimmed beaver beside them, and demanded the master of the house.

Mr. Milborne, being quite unblessed by the worldly wisdom which characterized his spouse, had no sooner grasped the purpose of this visit than he suggested vaguely, and not very hopefully, that his lordship had better speak to Isabella himself. "For I'm sure I don't know, Anthony," he had said, looking doubtfully at the Viscount. "There's no saying what may be in their heads, no saying at all!"

Correctly divining this cryptic utterance to refer to

his wife and daughter, his lordship had said: "At all events, you've no objection, sir, have you?"

"No," replied Mr. Milborne. "That is—— Well, no, I suppose I don't object. But you had best see Isabella for yourself!"

So the Viscount was ushered into the Beauty's presence before she had time even to draw down the blind against the too-searching light of day, and had plunged without the slightest preamble into the first offer of marriage he had ever made.

Miss Milborne found herself in the unhappy predicament of not knowing her own mind. The Viscount had been one of her acknowledged suitors for the past year, and the fact of her having known him almost from the cradle did not blind her to his charms. He was a handsome young blade, wild enough to intrigue the female fancy, and if not as brilliant a match as the Duke of Severn, who had lately shown flattering symptoms of being on the verge of declaring himself, at least he was much more presentable—his grace being a stolid young man inclined to corpulency. On the other hand, the Viscount was by no means so devout a lover as his friend Lord Wrotham, who had several times offered to blow his brains out, if such a violent act would afford her pleasure. In fact, the suspicion had more than once crossed Miss Milborne's mind that the Viscount had joined the throng of her admirers for no better reason than that he was never one to be out of the mode. His professed adoration had not so far led him to abandon the pursuit of opera-dancers and Cyprians, or to rectify those faults of character to which Miss Milborne had more than once taken exception. She was a little piqued by him. If he would but display a few tangible signs of his devotion, such as reforming his way of life, which was shocking; growing slightly haggard, like poor Wrotham; turning pale at a snub; or being cast into rapture by a smile, she thought she would have been inclined to accept his proffered suit. But instead of behaving in a fashion which she had come to regard as her due, the Viscount continued on his reprehensible course, according her certainly a good deal of homage, but apparently deriving just as much pleasure as ever from a set of sports and pastimes which seemed to have been chosen by him with a view to causing his family the maximum amount of pain and anxiety.

She stole a look at him under her eyelashes. No, he was not as handsome as poor Wrotham, whose dark, stormy beauty troubled her dreams a little. Wrotham was a romantic figure, particularly when his black locks were dishevelled through his clutching them in despair. The Viscount's fair curls were dishevelled too, but there was nothing romantic about this, since the disorder was the result of careful combing, and Miss Milborne had a strong suspicion that his passion for herself was not of such a violent nature as to induce him to interfere with his valet's inspired handiwork. He was taller than Wrotham, rather loose-limbed, and inclined to be careless of his appearance. Not that this criticism could be levelled at him on this occasion, Miss Milborne was obliged to own. He had dressed himself with obvious care. Nothing could have been neater than the cravat he wore, nothing more rigorously starched than the high points of his shirt-collar. The long-tailed coat of blue cloth, made for him by no less a personage than the great Stultz, set without a crease across his shoulders; his breeches were of the fashionable pale yellow; and his top-boots were exquisitely polished. At the moment, as he paced about the room, his countenance was marred by something rather like a scowl, but his features were good, and if he lacked Wrotham's romantic expression it was an undeniable fact that he could, when he liked, smile in a way that lent a good deal of sweetness to his wilful, obstinate mouth. He had deceptively angelic blue eyes, at odd variance with the indefinable air of rakishness that sat upon his person. As Miss Milborne watched him, they chanced to encounter hers. For a moment they stared belligerently, then his lordship's good-humour reasserted itself, and he grinned. "Oh, deuce take it, Bella, you know I'm head over ears in love with you!"

"No, I don't," said Miss Milborne, with unexpected frankness.

The Viscount's jaw dropped. "But my dear girl ——! No, really, now, Bella! Most devoted slave! Word of a gentleman, I am! Good God, haven't I been dangling at your shoe-strings ever since I first knew you?"

"No," said Miss Milborne.

The Viscount blinked at her.

"When you first knew me," said Miss Milborne, not rancorously, but as one stating a plain truth, "you said all girls were plaguey nuisances, and you called me Foxy, because you said I had foxy-coloured hair."

"I did?" gasped his lordship, appalled at this heresy.

"Yes, you did Sherry; and, what is more, you locked me in the gardener's shed, and if it had not been for Cassy Bagshot I should have been left there all day!"

"No, no!" protested his lordship feebly. "Not all day!"

"Yes, I should, because you know very well you

12

went off to shoot pigeons with one of your father's fowling-pieces, and never gave me another thought!"

"Lord, if I hadn't forgotten that!" exclaimed Sherry. "Blew the hat off old Grimsby's head too! He was as mad as fire! Devilish bad-tempered fellow, Grimsby! Went straight off to tell my father. When I think of the floggings that old man got me—— Yes, and now you've put me in mind of it, Bella, how the deuce should I be giving you a thought with Father leading me off by the ear, and making me too curst sore to think of anything? Be reasonable, my dear girl, be reasonable!"

"It doesn't signify in the least," responded Miss Milborne. "But when you say that you have been dangling at my shoe-strings ever since you first saw me, it is the greatest untruth ever I heard!"

"At all events, I liked you better than any other girl I knew!" said the Viscount desperately.

Miss Milborne regarded him in a reminiscent way which he found singularly unnerving. "No, I don't think you did," she said at last. "In fact, if you had a preference, I think it was for Hero Wantage."

"Hero?" exclaimed the Viscount. "No, dash it all, Bella, I never thought of Hero in all my life. I swear I didn't!"

"No, I know that," said Miss Milborne impatiently, "but when we were children you did like her more than you liked me, or Cassy, or Eudora, or Sophy, because she used to fetch and carry for you, and pretend she didn't mind when she got hurt by your horrid cricket-balls. She was only a baby, or she would have seen what an odious boy you were. For you were, Sherry, you know you were!"

Roused, the Viscount said, with feeling; "I'll swear I

13

wasn't half as odious as the Bagshot girls! Lord, Bella, do you remember the way that little cat, Sophy, used to run and tell tales about the rest of us to her mother?"

"Not about me," said Miss Milborne coldly. "There was nothing to tell." She perceived that her reminiscent mood had infected the Viscount, the gleam in his eye warning her that some quite undesirable recollections were stirring in his memory, and made haste to recall him to the present. "Not that it signifies, I'm sure. The truth is we should not suit, Sherry. Indeed, I am deeply sensible of the honour you have done me, but——"

"Never mind that flummery!" interrupted her suitor. "I don't see why we shouldn't deal extremely. Here's me, madly in love with you, Bella—pining away, give you my word! No, really, my dear girl, I'm not bamming! When he measured me for this coat, Stultz found it out."

"I fancy," said Miss Milborne primly, "that it is the life you lead that is to blame for your being thin, my lord. I don't flatter myself it can be put to my account."

"Well, if that don't beat all!" exclaimed his lordship indignantly. "I should like to know who's been telling tales about me!"

"No one has been telling tales. I do not like to say it, but you must own that there is no secrecy about your conduct. And I must say, Sherry, I think if you really loved me as you say you do, you would take *some* pains to please me!"

"Take pains to please you! Take— No, by God, that's too much, Bella! When I think of the way I've been dancing attendance on you, wasting my time at Almack's night after night——"

"And leaving early to go to some horrid gaming-hell," interpolated Miss Milborne.

The Viscount had the grace to blush, but he regarded her with a kindling eye, and said grimly: "Pray what do you know of gaming-hells, miss?"

"I am thankful to say I know nothing at all of them, except that you are for ever in one, which all the world knows. It grieves me excessively."

"Oh, does it?" said his lordship, anything but gratified by this evidence of his adored's solicitude.

"Yes," said Miss Milborne. An agreeable vision of the Viscount's being reclaimed from a life of vice by his love for a good woman presented itself to her. She raised her lovely eyes to his face, and said; "Perhaps I ought not to speak of it, but—but you have shown an unsteadiness of character, Sherry, a—a want of delicacy of principle which makes it impossible for me to accept of your offer. I do not desire to give you pain, but the company you keep, your extravagance, the wildness of your conduct, must preclude any female of sensibility from bestowing her hand upon you."

"But, Bella!" protested his horrified lordship. "Good God, my dear girl, *that* will all be a thing of the past! I shall make a famous husband! I swear I shall! I never looked at another female——"

"Never looked at another female? Sherry, how can you? With my own eyes I saw you at Vauxhall with the most vulgar, hateful——"

"Not in the way of marriage, I mean!" said the Viscount hastily. "That was nothing—nothing in the world! If you hadn't driven me to distraction——"

"Fiddle!" snapped Miss Milborne.

"But I tell you I love you madly—devotedly! My whole life will be blighted if you won't marry me!"

"It won't. You will merely go on making stupid bets,

and racing, and gaming, and———"

"Well, you're out there," interrupted Sherry. "I shan't be able to, because if I don't get married I shall be all to pieces."

This blunt admission had the effect of making Miss Milborne stiffen quite alarmingly. "Indeed!" she said. "Am I to understand, my lord, that you have offered for my hand as a means of extricating yourself from your debts?"

"No, no, of course I haven't! If that had been my only reason I might have offered for a score of girls any time these past three years!" replied his lordship ingenuously. "Fact of the matter is, Bella, I've never been able to bring myself up to scratch before, though the lord knows I've tried! Never saw any female except you I could think of tieing myself up to for life—I'll take my oath I haven't! Ask Gil! Ask Ferdy! Ask George! Ask anyone you like! They'll all tell you it's true."

"I don't desire to ask them. I dare say you would never have thought of offering for me either if your father had not left his fortune in that stupid way!"

"No, I dare say I shouldn't," agreed the Viscount. "At least, yes, I should! of course I should! But only consider, my dear girl! The whole fortune left in trust until I'm twenty-five, unless I marry before that date! You must see what a devil of a fix I'm in!"

"Certainly," said Miss Milborne freezingly. "I cannot conceive why you do not immediately offer for one of the scores of females who would doubtless be glad to marry you!"

"But I don't want to marry anyone but you!" declared her harassed suitor. "Couldn't think of it! Damn it all, Isabella, I keep on telling you I love you!"

"Well, I do not return your love, my lord!" said Miss Milborne, much mortified. "I wonder you will not offer for Cassy instead, for I'm sure Mrs. Bagshot has positively thrown her at your head any time these past six months! Or if you are so squeamish as to object to poor Cassy's complexion, which I will own to be sadly freckled, I make no doubt Eudora would think herself honoured if you should throw your handkerchief in *her* direction! But as for me, my lord, though I'm sure I wish you very well, the thought of marriage with you has never entered my head, and I must tell you once more, and for the last time, that I cannot accept of your obliging offer!"

"Isabella!" pronounced Lord Sheringham, in boding accents, "don't try me too far! If you love Another— You know, Bella, if it's Severn you mean to have, I can tell you now you won't get him. *You* don't know the Duchess! Can't call his soul his own, poor old Severn, and she'll never let him marry you, take my word for it!"

Miss Milborne rose from her chair abruptly. "I think you are the most odious, abominable creature in the world!" she said angrily. "I never—— Oh, I wish you will go away!"

"If you send me away, I shall go straight to the devil!" threatened his lordship.

Miss Milborne tittered. "I dare say you will find yourself mightily at home, my lord!"

The Viscount ground his teeth. "You will be sorry for your cruelty, ma'am, when it is too late!"

"Really, my lord, if we are to talk of *play-acting*——!"

"Who's talking of play-acting?" demanded the Viscount."

17

"You did."

"Never talked of any such thing! You're enough to drive a man out of his senses, Isabella!"

She shrugged and turned away from him. The Viscount, feeling that he had perhaps not shown that lover-like ardour which, he was persuaded, consumed him, took two strides towards her and tried to take her in his arms. He received a box on the ear which made his eyes water, and for an instant was in danger of forgetting that he was no longer a schoolboy confronting a tiresome little girl. Miss Milborne, reading retaliation in his face, strategically retired behind a small table, and said tragically: "Go!"

The Viscount regarded her with a measuring eye. "By God, if I could get my hands on you, Bella, I'd——" He broke off as his incensed gaze absorbed her undeniable beauty. His face softened. "No, I wouldn't," he said. "Wouldn't hurt a hair on your head! Now, Bella, won't you——"

"No!" almost shrieked Miss Milborne. "And I wish you will not call me Bella!"

"Oh, very well, *Isabella,* then!" said his lordship, willing to make concessions. "But won't you——"

"No!" reiterated Miss Milborne. "Go away! I hate you!"

"No, you don't," said his lordship. "At least, you never did, and damme if I can see why you should suddenly change your mind!"

"Yes, I do! You are a gamester, and a libertine, and a——"

"If you say another word, I *will* box your ears!" said the Viscount furiously. "Libertine be damned! You ought to be ashamed of yourself, Bella!"

Miss Milborne, aware of having been betrayed into unmaidenly behaviour, burst into tears. Before the greatly discomposed Viscount could take appropriate action the door opened and Mrs. Milborne came into the room.

Mrs. Milborne's eye took in the situation at a glance, and she lost no time in hustling the discomfited young man out of the house. His protestations fell on inattentive ears. She said: "Yes, yes, Anthony, but you must go away, indeed you must! Isabella is not well enough to receive guests! I cannot imagine who can have let you into the house! It is most obliging in you to have called, and pray convey my respects to your dear Mama, but at this present we are not receiving visitors!"

She put his hat and his gloves into his hands and inexorably showed him out of the front door. By the time she had returned to the drawing-room, Isabella had dried her eyes and recovered her composure. Her mother looked at her with raised brows. "Did he make you an offer, my love?"

"Yes, he did," replied Isabella, sniffing into her handkerchief.

"Well, I see nothing to cry about in that," said Mrs. Milborne briskly. "You should bear in mind, my love, that the shedding of tears has the very disagreeable effect of reddening a female's eyes. I suppose you refused him?"

Her daughter nodded, sniffing rather more convulsively. "Yes, of course I did, Mama. And I said I could never marry anyone with so little d-delicacy of principle, or——"

"Quite unnecessary," said Mrs. Milborne. "I wonder

you should show so little delicacy yourself, Isabella, as to refer to those aspects of a gentleman's life which no well-bred female should know anything about."

"Well, but, Mama, I don't see how one is to help knowing about Sherry's excesses, when all the town is talking of them!"

"Nonsense! In any event, there is not the least need for you to mention such matters. Not that I blame you for refusing Sherry. At least, I own that in some ways it would be an ideal match, for he is extremely wealthy, and we have always been particular friends of—— But if Severn were to offer for you, of course there could be no comparison between them!"

Miss Milborne flushed. "Mama! How can you talk so? I am not so mercenary! It is just that I do not love Sherry, and I am persuaded he does not love me either, for all his protestations!"

"Well, I dare say it will do him no harm to have had a set-down," replied Mrs. Milborne comfortably. "Ten to one, it will bring him to a sense of position. But if you are thinking of George Wrotham, my love, I hope you will consider carefully before you cast yourself away upon a mere baron, and one whose estates, from all I can discover, are much encumbered. Besides, there is a lack of stability about Wrotham which I cannot like."

In face of the marked lack of stability which characterized Viscount Sheringham, this remark seemed unjust to Miss Milborne, and she said so, adding that poor Wrotham had not committed the half of Sherry's follies.

Mrs. Milborne did not deny it. She said that there was no need for Isabella to be in a hurry to make her choice, and recommended her to take a turn in the garden with a view to calming her spirits and cooling her reddened cheeks.

The Viscount, meanwhile, was riding back to Sheringham Place in high dudgeon. His self-esteem smarted intolerably; and, since he had been in the habit, during the past twelvemonth, of considering himself to be desperately enamoured of the Incomparable Isabella, and was not a young gentleman who was given to soul-searching, it was not long before he was in a fair way to thinking that his life had been blighted past curing. He entered the portals of his ancestral home in anything but a conciliatory mood, therefore, and was not in the least soothed by being informed by the butler that her ladyship, who was in the Blue Saloon, was desirous of seeing him. He felt strongly inclined to tell old Romsey to go to perdition, but as he supposed he would be obliged to visit his mother before returning to London, he refrained from uttering this natural retort, contenting himself with throwing the butler a darkling glance before striding off in the direction of the Blue Saloon.

Here he discovered not only his parent, a valetudinarian of quite amazing stamina, but also his uncle, Horace Paulett.

Since Mr. Paulett had taken up his residence at Sheringham Place some years previously, upon the death of the late Lord Sheringham, there was nothing in this circumstance to astonish the Viscount. He had, in fact, expected to find his uncle there, but this did not prevent his ejaculating in a goaded voice: "Good God, *you* here, uncle?"

Mr. Paulett, who was a plump gentleman with an invincible smile and very soft white hands, never permitted himself to be annoyed by his nephew's patent dislike and frequent incivility. He merely smiled more broadly than ever, and replied: "Yes, my boy, yes! As you see, I am here, at my post beside your dear mother."

Lady Sheringham, having provided herself with a smelling-bottle to fortify her nerves during an interview with her only child, removed the stopper and inhaled feebly. "I am sure I do not know what would become of me if I had not my good brother to support me in my lonely state," she said, in the faint, complaining tone which so admirably concealed a constitution of iron and a strong determination to have her own way.

Her son, who was quite as obstinate as his parent, and a good deal more forthright, replied with paralysing candour:"From what I know of you, ma'am, you would have done excellent well. What's more, I might have stayed at home every now and then. I don't say I would have, because I don't like the place, but I *might* have."

So far from evincing any gratification at this handsome admission, Lady Sheringham sought in her ridicule for a handkerchief, and applied this wisp of lace and muslin to the corners of her eyes. "Oh, Horace!" she said. "I knew how it would be! So like his father!"

The Viscount did not fall into the error of reading any complimentary meaning into this remark. He said: "Well, dash it, ma'am, there's no harm in that! Come to think of it, who else should I be like?"

"Whom, my boy, whom!" corrected his uncle gently. "We must not forget our grammar!"

"Never knew any," retorted the Viscount. "And don't keep on calling me your boy! I may have a lot of faults, but at least that's one thing no one can throw in my face!"

"Anthony, have you no consideration for my poor nerves?" quavered his mother, bringing the vinaigrette into play again.

"Well, tell that platter-faced old fidget to take himself off!" said the Viscount irritably. "Never can see when he's not wanted, and the lord knows I've given him a hint times without number!"

"Ah, my b—— But I must not call you that, must I? Then let it be Sherry, for that, I collect, is what your cronies, your boon companions, call you, is it not?"

"I don't see what that's got to do with it," responded his nephew. "If you hadn't taken it into your head to come and live here, you wouldn't have to call me anything, and that would suit me to a cow's thumb!"

Mr. Paulette shook a finger at him. "Sherry, Sherry, I fear your suit cannot have prospered! But never mind, dear boy! Persevere, and you will see how she will come about!"

The Viscount's cerulean eyes lit with sudden wrath, and a tide of red coloured his cheeks. "Hell and the devil confound it!" he exclaimed furiously. "So you're at that, are you? I'll thank you to be a little less busy about my affairs!"

Lady Sheringham abandoned tactics which appeared unlikely to succeed, and contrived to possess herself of one of his lordship's hands. This she held between both of hers, squeezing it eloquently, and saying in a low tone: "Dearest Anthony, remember I am your Mother, and do not keep me in suspense! Have you seen dear Isabella?"

"Yes, I have," growled the Viscount.

"Sit down, my love, beside me. Did you—did you make her an offer?"

"Yes, I did! She won't have me."

"Alas! The dearest wish of my heart!" sighed Lady Sheringham. "If I could but see you married to Isabella, I could go in peace!"

Her son looked at her in a bewildered way. "Go where?" he demanded. "If it's the Dower House you're thinking of, there's nothing that I know of to stop you going there any day you choose. What's more, you may take my uncle along with you, and I won't say a word against it," he added generously.

"Sometimes I think you wilfully misunderstand me!" complained Lady Sheringham. "You cannot be ignorant of the enfeebled state of my health!"

"What, you don't mean that you're going to die, do you?" said the Viscount incredulously. "No, no, you won't do that! Why, I remember you used to say the same to my father, but nothing came of it. Ten to one, it's having my uncle always hanging about the place that wears you down. Give you my word, it would kill me in a week, and there's never been a thing the matter with my nerves."

"Anthony, if you have no consideration for me, at least you might consider your uncle's sensibility!"

"Well, if he don't like it he can go away," replied his lordship incorrigibly.

"No, no, I am too old a hand to be offended by a young man crossed in love!" Mr. Paulette assured him. "I know too well the feelings of mortification you are labouring under. It is very distressing indeed. A sad disappointment to us all, I may say."

"In every way so eligible!" mourned Lady Sheringham. "The estate would round off yours so delight-

24

fully, Anthony, and dearest Isabella is so precisely the girl out of all others whom I would have chosen for my only son! Her father's sole heir, and although it cannot compare with yours, her fortune will not be contemptible!"

"Damme, ma'am, I don't want her fortune! All I want is my own fortune!" said his lordship.

"If she had accepted your hand you would have had it, and I am sure I would have been glad to see it in your hands, though heaven knows you would squander the entire principal before one had time to look about one! Oh, Anthony, if I could but prevail upon you to relinquish a way of life which fills my poor heart with terror for your future!"

His lordship disengaged himself hurriedly. "For the lord's sake, ma'am, don't put yourself in a taking over me!" he begged.

"I knew she would reject you!" said Lady Sheringham. "What delicately nurtured female, I ask of you, my son, would consent to marry one whose footsteps are set upon the path of Vice? Must she not shrink from those libertine propensities which——"

"Here, I say, ma'am!" protested the startled Viscount. "It's not as bad as that, 'pon my soul it's not!"

His uncle heaved a sigh. "You will allow, dear boy, that there is scarcely an extravagant folly you have not committed since you came of age."

"No, I won't," retorted the Viscount. "Dash it, a man can't be on the Town without kicking up a lark or so every now and then!"

"Anthony, can you tell your Mother that there is not a—a *Creature* (for I cannot bring myself to call her a Female!) with whom you are not ashamed to be seen in the most public of places? Hanging upon your arm, and caressing you in a manner which fills me with repugnance?"

"No, I can't," replied the Viscount. "But I'd give a monkey to know who told you about that little ladybird!"

He rolled a choleric eye towards his uncle as he spoke, but that gentleman's attention was fixed upon the opposite wall, and his thoughts appeared to be far removed from earthly considerations.

"You will break my heart!" declared Lady Sheringham, applying her handkerchief to her eyes again.

"No, I shan't, ma'am," said her son frankly. "You didn't break your heart over any of Father's fancies that ever I heard of! Or if you did you can't do it again. Stands to reason! Besides, when I'm married I shall hedge off, never fear!"

"But you are not going to be married!" Lady Sheringham pointed out. "And that is not all! Never in my life have I been so mortified as when I was obliged to apologize to General Ware for your abominable behaviour on the road to Kensington last month! I was ready to sink! Of course you were intoxicated!"

"I was no such thing!" cried his lordship, stung on the raw. "Good God, ma'am, you don't think I could graze the wheels of five coaches if I'd shot the cat, do you?"

His mother let her handkerchief drop from a suddenly nerveless hand. "Graze the wheels of *five coaches?*" she faltered, looking at him as though she feared for his sanity.

"Five of 'em, all in a row, and never checked!" asserted the Viscount. "Sheerest piece of curst ill-fortune that I overturned old Ware's phaeton! Must have misjudged it. Cost me the wager, too. Backed myself to graze the wheels of the first seven vehicles I met past the Hyde Park turnpike without oversetting any of 'em. Can't think how I came to bungle it. Must have been old Ware's driving. He never could keep the line: a mere whipster! No precision of eye at all!"

"Unhappy boy!" exclaimed his mother in throbbing accents. "Are you dead to all sense of shame? Horace, speak to him!"

"If he does," said the Viscount, his chin jutting dangerously, "he'll go out through that window, uncle or no uncle!"

"Oh!" moaned his afflicted parent, sinking back on her couch and putting a hand to her brow. "What, what, I ask of you, brother, have I done to deserve this?"

"Hush, my dear Valeria! Calm yourself, I beg!" said Mr. Paulett, clasping her other hand.

"No wonder poor Isabella rejected his suit! I cannot find it in me to blame her!"

"Alas, one cannot but feel that for the sake of the estate it may be for the best!" said Mr. Paulett, strategically retaining his clasp on that frail but protective hand. "Loth as I am to say it, I cannot consider poor Sherry fit to assume the control of his fortune. Well for him that it is held in trust for him!"

"Oh, is it well for me?" interjected poor Sherry wrathfully. "Much you know about it! And why my father ever took it into his head to make you a trustee beats me! I don't mind Uncle Prosper—at least, I dare say I could handle him, if it weren't for you, for ever putting a spoke in my wheel! And don't stand there bamming me that you're mighty sorry Bella wouldn't have me, because I know you're not! Once I get the confounded Trust wound up, out you'll go, and well

27

you know it! If my mother chooses to let you batten upon her, she may do it, but you won't batten on me any longer, by Jupiter you won't!"

"Ah!" said Mr. Paulett, smiling in a maddening way. "But there are two years to run before the Trust comes to an end, my dear boy, and we must hope that by that time you will have seen the error of your ways."

"Unless I get married!" the Viscount reminded him, his eyes very bright and sparkling.

"Certainly! But you are not, after all, going to get married, dear boy," his uncle pointed out.

"Oh, aren't I?" retorted his lordship, striding towards the door.

"Anthony!" shrieked Lady Sheringham. "What in heaven's name are you going to do?" She released her brother's hand, and sat up. "Where are you going? Answer me, I command you!"

"I'm going back to London!" answered the Viscount. "And I'm going to marry the first woman I see!"

CHAPTER 2

As might have been expected, the Viscount's Parthian
shot immediately prostrated his parent. She evinced
every sign of falling into a fit of the vapours, and was
only revived by the reflection that the Viscount was no
longer present to be chastened by the sight of his
mother suffering from strong hysterics. A little
hartshorn-and-water, tenderly administered by Mr.
Paulett, a few lavender , drops sprinkled upon a
handkerchief, and some gentle hand-slapping presently
made it possible for the afflicted lady to open her eyes,
and to straighten her turban. She at once confided to
Mr. Paulett her conviction that Anthony would bring
home some dreadful, vulgar creature from the opera-
ballet on his arm, if only to spite her, and expressed a
fervent longing for the quiet of the family tomb.

Mr. Paulett did not feel that there was much danger
of his nephew's marrying anyone in the immediate
future. He said that he would find Anthony, and repre-
sent to him that his unfilial behaviour was leading his
mother's tottering steps to the very brink of the grave,
but by the time he had restored the lady to such health

as remained to her, and had pointed out to her that a young gentleman desperately enamoured of a Beauty was not very likely to fall into matrimony with some other female, the Viscount was already upon the road to London.

He was driving his curricle. A pair of spirited bays were harnessed to it; a sharp-faced Tiger was perched up behind him; his portmanteau was strapped in its place; and the Viscount, with all the air of one shaking the dust of a loathed spot from his shoes, drove along at a spanking pace, and with very little regard for whatever other vehicles he might chance to meet on the road.

The Viscount had had many grooms, and several Tigers, but it required an iron nerve to drive out with him in one of his wild fits, and since these attacked him with alarming frequency, and very few grooms possessed the requisite amount of disregard for their lives and limbs, none of them had remained long in his service. By the greatest piece of good fortune he had chanced upon the individual at present hanging on to the curricle behind him. The acquaintanceship had begun with the picking of the Viscount's pocket, as he emerged from a jeweller's shop on Ludgate Hill. Jason, who had started life in a Foundling Hospital, passed by way of the streets of London to a racing-stable, and thence, through a series of disreputable circumstances, back to the streets of London, was an inexpert thief, but an inspired handler of horses. At the very moment when the Viscount, grappling his captive by the collar, was preparing to drag him off to the nearest Round-house, the prime bit of blood between the shafts of his lordship's phaeton took exception to a wagon which was advancing up the street, and reared suddenly, knocking the groom, who should have been holding his head but was gaping at the Viscount instead, off his feet. A commotion was at once set up, during which Jason wriggled out of the Viscount's slackened hold, and, instead of taking to his heels, leaped for the chestnut's head. In a very few moments, order had been restored, the chestnut apparently recognizing a master-mind in the dirty and ragged creature who had prevented him from bolting, and was now addressing uncouth blandishments to him. Since he was, with good reason, quite the most unpopular horse in the Viscount's stables, even having the reputation of being willing to savage anyone for the very moderate sum of a mag, or halfpenny, the circumstance of his dropping his head into the unsavoury bosom before him most forcibly struck his owner. The Viscount at once forgot the contretemps which had brought this wizard to his notice, and there and then engaged him to be his new Tiger. Jason—he had no other name, and no one, least of all himself, knew how he came by that one—never having encountered even such careless good-nature as the Viscount's in the unnumbered years of his life, emerged from the trance into which his unexpected luck had pitchforked him to find himself in the employment of a nobleman considered by his relations to be volatile past reclaim, but in whom he recognized, in that moment of blinding enlightenment, a god come down to earth.

The Viscount, who had never made the least attempt to reform himself, did much to reform his new Tiger, not, indeed, from any particular zeal, but because he felt the force of his friends' representations that continued intimacy with a man whose Tiger could be counted on to relieve one of one's purse, fobs, and seal, had certain grave drawbacks. The Viscount promised to mend matters, which he did by thrashing his Tiger soundly, and laying orders on him never to rob any of his master's friends again. Jason, who cared less for the thrashing than for the frown upon his deity's face, promised to thread a path of rectitude, and made such efforts to keep to this that in a very short time nothing more than a warning word to him, or, at the worst, a command to restore whatever he might have filched from some chance-met acquaintance, was necessary to preserve the utmost harmony between the Viscount and his cronies.

For the rest, although he might lack polish, he proved to be the most devoted servant the Viscount had ever hired. No slave could have been less critical of his owner's vagaries, or more tireless in his attentions. He had been overturned in his lordship's curricle five times; had had his leg fractured by a kick from a half-broken horse; had accompanied the Viscount on some of his more hazardous expeditions; and was generally supposed to be willing to engage on his behalf on any enterprise, inclusive of murder.

As he hung on to the straps of the curricle behind the Viscount, he observed dispassionately that he knew all along that they wouldn't stay above two days in that ken. Receiving no answer to this remark, he relapsed into silence, breaking it only at the end of a mile to recommend his master to pull in for the corner, unless he was wishful to throw them both out on to their bowsprits. His tone indicated that if the Viscount had any such wish he was prepared cheerfully to endure this fate.

However, the Viscount, having had time to work off the first heat of his rage, steadied his pair, and took the corner at no more than a canter. The main road to London lay a couple of miles farther on, the lane that led to it from Sheringham Place winding alongside the Viscount's acres for some way, and then curling abruptly away to serve a small hamlet, one or two scattered cottages, and the modest estate owned by Mr. Humphrey Bagshot. Mr. Bagshot's house was set back from the lane and screened by trees and a shrubbery, the whole being enclosed by a low stone wall. The Viscount, whose attention was pretty equally divided between his horses and his late disappointment, kept his moody gaze fixed on the road ahead, and would not have spared a glance for this wall had not his Tiger suddenly recommended him to cast his daylights to the left.

"There's a female a-wavin' at you, guv'nor," he informed his master.

The Viscount turned his head, and found that he was sweeping past a lady who was perched on top of the wall, somewhat wistfully regarding him. Recognizing this damsel, he reined in, backed his pair, and called out; "Hallo, brat!"

Miss Hero Wantage seemed to find nothing amiss in this form of salutation. A little flush mounted to her cheeks; she smiled shyly, and responded: "Hallo, Sherry!"

The Viscount looked her over. She was a very young lady, and she did not at this moment appear to advantage. The round gown she wore was of an unbecoming shade of pink, and had palpably come to her at second-hand, since it seemed to have been made originally for a larger lady, and had been inexpertly adapted to her diminutive size. A drab cloak was tied round her neck, its hood hanging down over her shoulders; and in her hand she held a crumpled and damp handkerchief. There were tear-stains on her cheeks, and her wide grey eyes were reddened and a little blurred. Her dusky ringlets, escaping from a frayed ribbon, were tumbled and very untidy.

"Hallo, what's the matter?" asked the Viscount suddenly, noticing the tear-stains.

Miss Wantage gave a convulsive sob. "Everything!" she said comprehensively.

The Viscount was a good-natured young man, and whenever he thought of Miss Wantage, which was not often, it was with mild affection. In his graceless teens he had made use of her willing services, had taught her to play cricket, and to toil after him with the game-bag when he went out for a little hedgerow shooting. He had bullied her, and tyrannized over her, lost his temper with her, boxed her ears, and forced her to engage in various sports and pastimes which terrified her; but he had permitted her to trot at his heels, and he had allowed no one else to tease or ill-treat her. Her situation was not a happy one. She was an orphan, taken out of charity when only eight years old to live in her cousin's house, and to be brought up with her three daughters, Cassandra, Eudora, and Sophronia. She had shared their lessons, and had worn their outgrown dresses, and had run their numerous errands—such services being, her Cousin Jane informed her, a very small return for all the generosity shown her. The Viscount, who disliked Cassandra, Eudora, and Sophronia only one degree less than he disliked their Mama, gave it as his considered opinion, when he was fifteen years

34

old, that they were brutes, and treated their poor little cousin like a dog. He had therefore no difficulty now, as he looked at Miss Wantage, in interpreting correctly her somewhat sweeping statement. "Those cats been bullying you?" he said.

Miss Wantage blew her nose. "I'm going to be a governess, Sherry," she informed him dolefully.

"Going to be a *what?*" demanded his lordship.

"A governess. Cousin Jane says so."

"Never heard such nonsense in my life!" said the Viscount, slightly irritated. "You aren't old enough!"

"Cousin Jane says I am. I shall be seventeen in a fortnight's time, you know."

"Well, you don't look it," said Sherry, disposing of the matter. "You always were a silly little chit, Hero. Shouldn't believe everything people say. Ten to one she didn't mean it."

"Oh yes!" said Miss Wantage sadly. "You see, I always knew I should have to be one, one day, because that's why I learned to play that horrid pianoforte, and to paint in water-colours, so that I could be a governess when I was grown-up. Only I don't want to be, Sherry! Not *yet!* Not before I have enjoyed myself just for a *little* while!"

The Viscount cast off the rug which covered his shapely legs. "Jason, get down and walk the horses!" he ordered, and sprang down from the curricle and advanced to the low wall. "Is that mossy?" he asked suspiciously. "I'm damned if I'll spoil these breeches for you or anyone else, Hero!"

"No, no, truly it's not!" Miss Wantage assured him. "You can sit on my cloak, Sherry, can't you?"

"Well, I can't stay for long," the Viscount warned

her. He hoisted himself up beside her and put a brotherly arm round her shoulders. "Now, don't go on crying, brat: it makes you look devilish ugly!" he said. "Besides, I don't like it. Why has that old cat suddenly taken it into her head to send you off? I suppose you've been doing something you shouldn't."

"No, it isn't that, though I did break one of the best teacups," said Hero, leaning gratefully against him. "It's partly because Edwin kissed me, I think."

"You're bamming me!" said his lordship incredulously. "Your wretched little cousin Edwin hasn't got enough bottom to kiss a chamber-maid!"

"Well, I don't know about that, Sherry, but he did kiss me, and it was the horridest thing imaginable. And Cousin Jane found out about it, and she said it was my fault, and I was a designing hussy, and that she had nourished a snake in her bosom. But I am *not* a snake, Sherry!"

"Never mind about that!" said Sherry. "I can't get over Edwin! If it don't beat all! He must have been foxed, and that's all there is to it."

"No, indeed he wasn't," said Hero earnestly.

"Then it just shows how you can be mistaken in a man. All the same, Hero, you shouldn't let a miserable, snivelling fellow like that kiss you. It's not the thing at all."

"But how could I prevent him, Sherry, when he caught me, and squeezed me so tightly that I could scarcely breathe?"

The Viscount gave a crow of laughter. "Lord, only to think of Edwin turning into such an out-and-outer! It seems to me I had best teach you a trick ot two to counter that kind of thing. Wonder I didn't do it before."

"Thank you, Sherry," said Hero, with real gratitude. "Only now that I am being sent to be a governess in a horrid school in Bath, I don't suppose I shall need any tricks."

"It's my believe that it's all a hum," declared Sherry. "You don't look like any governess I've ever seen, and I'll lay you odds no school would hire you. Do you *know* anything, Hero?"

"Well, I didn't *think* I did," replied Hero. "Only Miss Mundesley says I shall do very well, and it is her sister who has the school, so I dare say it has all been arranged between them. She is our governess, you know. At least, she used to be."

"I know," nodded Sherry. "Sour-faced old maid she was, too! I'll tell you what, brat: if you go to this precious school they'll make you a damned drudge, and so I warn you! Come to think of it, what the devil are they about, turning a chit like you upon the world?"

"Miss Mundesley says I shall be very strictly taken care of," said Hero. "They are not turning me upon the world, exactly."

"That's not the point. Damme, the more I come to think of it the worse it is! You're not a pauper-brat!"

Miss Wantage raised her innocent eyes to his face. "But that is what I am, Sherry. I haven't any money at all."

"That don't signify," said the Viscount impatiently. "What I mean is, females of your breeding aren't governesses! Never knew your father myself, but I know all about him. Very good family—a curst sight better than the Bagshots! What's more, you've got a lot of damned starchy relations. Norfolk, or some such place. Heard my mother speak of them. Sounded to me like a very dull set of gudgeons, but that's neither here nor there. You'd better write to them."

"It wouldn't be of any use," sighed Hero. "I think my father quarrelled with them, because they wouldn't do anything for me when he died. So I dare say they wouldn't object to my becoming a governess at all."

"Well, I do," said the Viscount. "In fact, I won't have it. You'll have to think of something else."

Miss Wantage saw nothing either arbitrary or unreasonable in this speech. She agreed to it, but a little doubtfully. "Marry the curate, do you mean, Sherry?" she asked, slightly wrinkling her short nose.

The Viscount stared at her in the liveliest astonishment. "Why the devil should I mean anything of the sort? Of course I don't! Of all the nonsensical girls, you're the worst, Hero!"

Miss Wantage accepted this rebuke meekly enough, but said: "Well, I think it's a nonsensical notion too, but Cousin Jane says it must be the curate, or that horrid school."

"You don't mean to tell me that the curate wants to marry you?" demanded Sherry.

Miss Wantage nodded. "He has *offered* for me," she said, not without pride.

"It seems to me," said his lordship severely, "that you have been getting devilish flighty since I saw you last! Marry the curate, indeed! I dare say he kissed you behind the door too?"

"Oh *no*, Sherry!" Miss Wantage assured him. "He has behaved with the greatest propriety, Cousin Jane says!"

"So I should hope!" said his lordship, rather spoiling the austerity of this remark, however, by adding reflectively, a moment later: "Sounds to me like another dull dog."

"Yes, he is," agreed Hero. "I quite think he may be very kind, but oh, Sherry, if you won't be offended with me, indeed I would rather be a governess, for I don't at all want to marry him!"

"What beats me," said his lordship, "is why he should want to marry you! He must be a curst rum touch, Hero. You'd never do for a parson's wife! You can't have told him how you glued the Bassenthwaites' pew that time everyone was in such a pucker."

"Well, no, I didn't," admitted Hero. "But it was you who did the gluing really, Sherry."

"If that isn't a female all over!" exclaimed Sherry. "Next you'll say you had nothing to do with it!"

Miss Wantage tucked a small, confiding hand into his arm. "I *did* help, didn't I, Anthony?"

"Yes, and spilled the glue over my new smalls because you thought you heard someone coming, silly chit!" said the Viscount, recalling this incident with a darkling look in his eye.

Miss Wantage gave a little chuckle. "Oh, how you did slap my cheek! It was red for hours and hours and I had to make up such a tale to account for it!"

"No, did I really?" said the Viscount, rather conscience-stricken, and giving the cheek a friendly rub. "What a deuced young brute I was! Not but what you'd have tried the patience of a saint, brat, often and often!"

"Yes, that is what my cousins say, and I can't but feel that I should try the curate's patience even more, Sherry, because I do seem always to be getting into a scrape, though indeed I don't mean to. At least, not every time."

"Don't keep harping on the curate!" ordered the Viscount. "The whole idea of your marrying him is the greatest piece of nonsense I ever heard! In fact, it's a very good thing I chanced to come down here, for the lord knows what silly trick you'd have tried to play off if I hadn't caught you in time!"

"No, and I am so glad to see you again, Anthony," she replied. "I thought perhaps you would come."

"Good God, did you? Why?"

"To wait on Isabella," she replied innocently.

"Ha!" uttered his lordship, with a harsh and bitter laugh.

Miss Wantage looked wonderingly up at him. "You don't sound very pleased, Sherry. Would she not see you?"

"Pleased!" ejaculated his lordship. "Much I have to be pleased about!"

"I know she wouldn't receive any of the other gentlemen, though they came all the way from London for the purpose, but I did think she would see you."

"Well, she did," said the Viscount shortly. "And for all the good I got by it, I might as well have stayed—— Here, who told you I wanted to marry Bella?"

"You did," answered Miss Wantage simply. "It was when you came down last year. Don't you remember?"

"No, I can't say that I do, but it don't signify. She won't have me."

"Sherry!" cried Miss Wantage, quite shocked. "You don't mean that you have offered, and she has refused you?"

"Yes, I do. And that's not all!" said the Viscount, his wrongs rising forcibly to his mind. "She said my character was unsteady, and I'd no delicacy of principle! That, from a girl I've known all my life!"

"It isn't true!" Hero said, warmly clasping his hand.

40

"I'm a gamester, and a libertine, and she don't like the company I keep. I'm————"

"Sherry," interrupted Hero anxiously, "can she have heard about your opera-dancer, do you think?"

"Well, upon my word!" gasped the Viscount. "What the devil do you know about my opera-dancer? And don't say I told you, because that I never did!"

"No, no, Edwin told me! That is, he told Cassy, because they had a quarrel, and it was really she who told me."

"You've no business to be talking of such things!" said his lordship sternly. He thought it over, his brow creasing. "Besides, it don't make sense! Edwin told Cassy, because they had a quarrel? Where's the sense in that?"

"Why, Sherry, because he said that before she set her cap at you, she might as well know————" Miss Wantage broke off, flushing deeply. "Oh, I *wish* I didn't say things I ought not to!" she said, much mortified. "Truly, I didn't mean to be such a cat!"

"Oh!" said his lordship. "So that's what's in the wind, is it? As a matter of fact, I knew it," he added, momentarily abandoning the grand manner. "And you may tell your cousin Cassy, with my compliments, that she may as well spare herself the trouble, for I haven't come to that yet! Now, don't go blurting that out at her the first time you see her again! And stop chattering about my opera-dancer! I've a very good mind to go up to the house and have a word with Edwin! Prating about my affairs all round the countryside! Now I know where my damned meddling uncle had it from! Pack of lies!"

"Haven't you got an opera-dancer after all?"

asked Miss Wantage. "Because if you haven't, I will tell Isabella so myself, and then perhaps you can be comfortable."

"You won't say anything about it at all!" said the harassed Viscount.

"Yes, but Sherry——"

"*No*, I tell you! For one thing, a pretty-behaved female don't mention such subjects: and for another—— Well, you wouldn't understand!" He encountered an enquiring look from the eyes which met his so frankly, and cast about in his brain for a suitable explanation. "Confound you, Hero, there's nothing in it! Everyone has a fancy-piece or two, but it don't signify a jot, take my word for it!"

Miss Wantage was perfectly ready to take his words, but she felt that the question had not been thoroughly thrashed out. "Well, but, Sherry, perhaps you did not explain it to Isabella quite well? Don't you think——"

"No, I don't," said his lordship hastily. "The long and the short of it is that Bella don't care a rap for me."

Miss Wantage, finding this hard to believe, suggested that poor Isabella must have had the headache.

"No, it wasn't that. Not but what she did look a trifle pale, now you put me in mind of it. But Incomparable as ever!" he added loyally.

"She *is* very pretty," said Miss Wantage. "She even looked pretty when she had spots."

"*Spots?*" repeated the Viscount, in a stunned voice. "She never had a spot in her life!"

"Well, not ordinary spots, like Sophy, but the ones you have with the measles, I mean."

"Isabella didn't have the measles!"

"Yes, she did," replied Hero. "That's why her Mama brought her home. She felt dreadfully poorly, and Mrs.

Milborne told Cousin Jane that the spots came all over her."

"*No!*" said the Viscount, revolted.

"They do, you know," explained Hero.

"Of course I know that! But Isabella can't have had the measles! They said she was worn-down by the gaieties of London!"

Hero looked surprised at this. "Well, I don't know why they should have said that, because they must have known it was the measles. Two of the abigails had it as well, besides Mrs. Milborne's page."

"Good God!" said the Viscount. A grin dispelled the look of shocked dismay on his face. "So that's why she wouldn't receive anyone! Poor girl! By Jove, I'd give a monkey to see Severn's face, if he knew! Deuced romantic fellow, Severn! Wouldn't like it at all!"

"Is he the Duke?" enquired Hero interestedly.

Gloom descended once more upon her companion. He nodded.

"Is—is she going to marry him, Sherry?"

"It's my belief he won't come up to scratch," replied the Viscount frankly. "Not that I care. *My* hopes are quite cut-up!"

"Oh, Sherry, do you mind very much?" asked Hero, her heart wrung.

"Of course I mind!" said his lordship testily. "My whole life is blighted! Might as well go to the devil without more ado. Which is what I very likely shall do, because if I don't get my hands on my fortune I shall be punting on tick before you know where you are, and we all know what that means!"

Hero nodded wisely. The Viscount laughed, and pinched her nose. "You haven't a notion what it means! Never heard of a cent-per-cent in your life, have you, brat? Or of a poor devil finding himself in the basket?"

"Yes, I have! That's on all the stage-coaches, and you ride in it if you are very poor!"

"Well, it may come to that yet," grimaced Sherry. "The thing is that my principal's tied up in the stupidest Trust anyone ever thought of. Would you believe it, I'm kept on a beggarly allowance until I reach the age of twenty-five, unless I'm married before then? A couple of my damned uncles manage everything—or they should, but Prosper's too curst lazy to keep an eye on the other old scoundrel! He can't stand the fellow any more than I can—none of my father's relatives can bear the sight of my mother's family, and God knows I don't blame them, for a bigger set of spongers I'll swear you never clapped eyes on!—but will he bestir himself to get rid of the fellow? Not he! There he sits, in *my* house, living at *my* expense, and ten to one feathering his nest with *my* money, not to mention putting a lot of nonsensical notions into my mother's head, and pretending he's disappointed Bella wouldn't have me! Disappointed! He was so glad he couldn't keep the smile off his greasy face! Damme if I know why I haven't napped him a rum 'un any time these past six years!" He broke off, the look of bewilderment on Hero's face recalling him to a sense of his company. "Here, don't you let me hear *you* using cant like that!" he admonished her. "If they hadn't made me as mad as Bedlam between the lot of them, I shouldn't have said it. At least, I should, but not to a female."

"No, I won't," said Miss Wantage obediently.

"That's what you say now," retorted the Viscount, "but I know you, Hero! I never could let my tongue go when you were within hearing but what, as sure as check, out you'd come with it, with never less than half a dozen tabbies in the room, too! 'But Anthony says it, Cousin Jane!' You can't be surprised I used to box your ears now and then!"

"Well, I truly won't this time," Hero assured him. "I couldn't very well, because I don't know what it means."

"No, and you are not going to know, so it's no use plaguing the life out of me to tell you! All that signifies is that there was no bearing it any longer. When it comes to being told—by my own mother, mark you! —that no woman of sensibility would accept of me, it's the outside of enough! All because I had the curst bad luck to upset old General Ware's phaeton! Anyone would have thought I'd murdered the fellow, but no such thing! He shot into the hedge, all right and tight, not a penny the worse for it! What's more, I pulled him out, and considering it was his devilish bad handling of the ribbons which lost me my wager there are plenty of fellows in my place who would have left him there! But was he grateful? No! Tottered straight off to write and complain of me to my mother!"

"Never mind, Sherry!" Miss Wantage said, squeezing his arm. "They are all horrid, and unkind! They always were. Only I did think that Isabella——"

"I'll not hear a word against her!" said the Viscount nobly. "She is, and will always be, the Incomparable! But if she thinks I'm going to wear the willow for her sake, she's mightily mistaken! And it wouldn't surprise me above half if that's just what she'd like me to do, for of all the heartless baggages I ever encountered——

But that's neither here nor there."

"What *are* you meaning to do, Sherry?" asked Miss Wantage solicitously.

"Just what I told my mother, and my platter-faced uncle! Marry the first female I see!"

Miss Wantage gave a giggle. "Silly! That's me!"

"Well, good God, there's no need to be so curst literal!" said his lordship. "I know it's you, as it turns out, but——" He stopped suddenly, and stared down into Miss Wantage's heart-shaped countenance. "Well, why not?" he said slowly. "Damme, that's exactly what I will do!"

CHAPTER 3

For one dazed moment Miss Wantage could only gaze blankly up at him. "M-marry *me*, Sherry?" she stammered.

"Yes, why not?" responded his lordship. "That is, unless you have some objection, and considering the way you were ready to marry the curate I can't for the life of me see why you should have!"

"No, no, I wasn't ready to marry the curate!" protested Hero. "I told you that I would prefer to be a governess!"

"Well, never mind about that," said his lordship. "It's no use your saying that you'd prefer to be a governess to marrying me, because it's absurd! No one would. Dash it, Hero, I don't want to talk like a coxcomb, and I dare say I may want for principle, and have libertine propensities, and spend all my time in gaming-hells, besides being the sort of ugly customer no woman of sensibility could stomach, but you can't pretend that you wouldn't be far more comfortable with me than at that curst school you keep on prosing about!"

47

Miss Wantage was far from wanting to pretend anything of the sort, but the notion of marrying one who had for a number of years appeared to her in much the same light as he appeared to his Tiger seemed so fantastic that she could neither credit him with any serious intentions, nor believe that such a dazzling change in her bleak future could really take place. "Oh, Sherry, don't, please!" she begged, a catch in her voice. "I know it's a hum, but, please, I wish you will not!"

"It's no such thing!" the Viscount said. "In fact, the more I think of it the more it seems to me an excellent plan."

"But, Sherry, you love Isabella!"

"Of course I love Isabella!" responded Sherry. "Though, mind you, I don't say I'd have offered for her if I hadn't been so deuced uncomfortably circumstanced, for to tell you the truth, Hero, I'd as lief not be married. However, it's no use thinking of that! Married I must be, and if I can't have the Incomparable I'd as soon have you as any other. Sooner," he added handsomely. "I'm devilish fond of you, Hero. It's my belief we should deal famously, for you don't take pets, or go off into odd humours, and you won't expect me to alter all my habits, and spend my time dancing attendance on you."

"Oh, no, no!"

"Of course, I know it ain't a love-match," pursued his lordship. "For my part, I've done with love, since Isabella cut up all my hopes. I dare say there is nothing that would please her more than to think that she had embittered my life, just as she seems like to do to poor George's, but I'll be damned if I mean to administer to her vanity by letting her know it!"

A sympathetic sigh from his companion brought his

attention round to her. He surveyed her somewhat doubtfully, as an unwelcome thought occurred to him. "I wish you weren't so devilish young!" he complained. "A pretty pickle we shall be in if you take it into your head to fall in love with some fellow or other after we're tied up! Come to think of it, you're too young to be married at all. Damme, you're nothing but a baby!"

"Augusta Yarford was married when she was only just seventeen, Sherry," offered Miss Wantage hopefully.

"That's a very different matter. She'd been out a couple of seasons, and if ever a girl was up to snuff it was Gussie Yarford! But you have never been into society at all, or met anyone besides your precious cousin Edwin, and some dab of a parson."

"And you, Sherry," she said, smiling shyly at him.

"Yes, but I don't signify, any more than if I had been your brother." A qualm seized him. "I suppose I ought not to do it," he said, with a vague feeling of chivalry. "I don't mind people calling me a libertine, but I'm damned if I'll have them saying I took advantage of a chit not out of the school-room!"

Miss Wantage clasped her hands together in her lap, and said rather breathlessly: "Sherry, if you think I might suit, please—please do marry me, for I know I should like it above all things!"

"Yes, but you've no more notion of what it means than that sparrow," said the Viscount bluntly. He thought this over for a moment, and added: "In fact, much less."

"But I should like very much always to be with you, Sherry, because you are never cross with me, and I should enjoy such fun, and go to London, and see all the things I've only heard of, and go to parties, and

49

balls, and not be scolded, or sent to that dreadful school, and—oh, Sherry, it wasn't k-kind in you to put it into my head if you d-didn't really mean it!"

The Viscount patted her shoulder in a perfunctory way, a slightly rueful grin quivering on his lips. Shatter-brained he might be, but the full implication of this artless speech was not lost on him. "Oh, lord!" he said.

Miss Wantage swallowed a sob, and said valiantly: "You were only funning. Of course I should have known that. I didn't mean to tease you."

"No, I wasn't," said his lordship. "Damme, why shouldn't I marry you? I know you haven't had time to fix your affections, but ten to one you never will, and in any event you won't find me the sort of husband who's for ever kicking up a dust over trifles. I shan't interfere with your pleasures, as long as you keep 'em discreet, my dear. And you needn't fear I shall be forcing my attentions on you. I told you I was done with love. A marriage of convenience, that's what it will be! Dash it, it may not be as romantic as I dare say you'd have liked, but you can't deny it will be more amusing than being a governess!"

Miss Wantage nodded fervently, her eyes like stars. "And I do think it is romantic," she said.

"That's because you know nothing about it," replied Sherry cynically. "Never mind! You'll enjoy cutting a dash in London, at all events."

Miss Wantage agreed to this with enthusiasm. But the next instant a thought occurred to her which quenched the sparkle in her eyes. "Oh, how I wish we could! But they will never, never let us, Sherry!"

"Who's to stop us?" he demanded. "that's one thing my father didn't put into the damned Trust! I can marry anyone I please, and no one can say a word."

"But they will," said Hero bodingly. "You know they will, Sherry! Your Mama wishes you to make a Brilliant Match, and she will do everything in her power to prevent your throwing yourself away upon me. I have no fortune, you see."

"I know that, but it don't signify in the least. Once the Trust ends, I shall have plenty for the pair of us."

"Lady Sheringham will not think so. And Cousin Jane would pack me off to Bath tomorrow if she knew!"

"Hang it, I don't see that, Hero, dashed if I do! She'll say it's a devilish good match: she's bound to!"

"That's just it, Sherry: she would say it was far too good for me! She would be so angry! Because, you know, she does hope that perhaps you might take a liking to Cassy, or even Eudora."

"Well, I shan't. Never could abide the sight of either of them, or of Sophy, for that matter, and it's not likely I shall change at my time of life. However, there's a good deal in what you say, Hero, and if there's one thing I detest more than another it's a parcel of women arguing at me, and having the vapours every five minutes, which is what would happen, sure as check! And if your cousin did pack you off to Bath I should be obliged to go there to rescue you, and I can't bear the place. There's only one thing for it; we must go off without saying a word about it to anyone. Once the knot's tied, and we can do that fast enough if I get a special licence, they won't say anything—or, at any rate, if they do, it won't be to us."

"Won't it?" Hero asked doubtfully.

"No, because for one thing there'd be no sense in it, and for another we can show them the door," said the Viscount.

"You don't think Cousin Jane will say that I am under age, and have it put at an end? People can, can't they, Sherry?"

The Viscount gave this his profound consideration. "No," he pronounced finally. "She won't do that. Don't see how she could. I mean, only think, Hero! I'm not a dashed adventurer, eloping with an heiress! I'm devilish eligible! She'll be obliged to swallow it with a good grace. Dare say she'll look to you to find husbands for those insipid girls."

"Well, if you think I could, I would try very hard to do so," said Hero seriously.

"No one could find husbands for such a parcel of dowdies," replied his lordship, with brutal candour. "Besides, I don't like them, and I won't have them in my house. Come along! We've wasted enough time. Someone will be bound to come looking for you, if we dawdle here much longer. Hi, Jason!"

"Come now?" gasped Miss Wantage. "But I have nothing with me, Sherry! Must I not pack a portmanteau, or at least a bandbox?"

"Now, will you have sense, Hero? Do you expect me to come driving up to the front door to pick you up? If you go back, and start packing a portmanteau you'll be discovered."

"Oh, yes, but—— You don't think I should creep out of the house when it is dark, and join you here?"

"No, I don't," replied his lordship. "I don't want to kick my heels in this damned dull place for the rest of the day! Besides, there's no moon, and if you think I'm going to drive up to town in the dark, you're mightily mistaken, my girl! I can't see what you want with a portmanteau. If the rest of your gowns are anything like the one you have on now, the sooner you're rid of them the better! I'll buy you everything you want when we get to London."

"Oh, Sherry, will you?" cried Miss Wantage, her cheeks in a glow. "Thank you! Let us go quickly!"

The Viscount sprang down into the lane, and held up his hands. "Jump, then!"

Miss Wantage obeyed him promptly. Jason, who had led the horses up to them, regarded her fixedly, and then turned an enquiring eye upon his master.

"I'm taking this lady up to London, Jason," announced the Viscount.

"Ho!" said the faithful henchman. "Ho, you are, are you, guv'nor?"

"Yes, and what's more, I don't want a word said about it. So no tattling in whatever boozing-ken you go to, mind that! And no tattling in the stables either!"

"I can keep me chaffer close," replied Jason, with dignity, "but it queers me what your lay is this time!"

The Viscount tossed Miss Wantage up into the curricle, gathered the reins in his hand, and prepared to mount beside her. "I'm going to be married."

"You, never!" gasped Jason. "But she ain't the right one, guv'nor! Lor', you must have had a shove in the mouth too many, and I never suspicioned you was lushy, so help me bob! Werry well you carries it, guv'nor! werry well, indeed! Gammoning me wot knows you, you was sober as a judge, and all the time as leaky as a sieve! But what'll you say when you comes about, me lord? A rare set-out that'll be, and you a-blamin' of me for letting you make off with the wrong gentry-mort!"

"Confound your impudence, of course I'm sober!"

said the Viscount wrathfully. "You keep your nose out of my affairs! What the devil are you laughing at, Hero?"

"I think he's so droll!" gurgled Miss Wantage. "What is a gentry-mort?"

"God knows! The fellow can't open his mouth without letting fall a lot of thieves' cant. Not fit for your ears at all. Stand away from their heads! all's right!"

The curricle moved forward. Jason sprang nimbly up behind, and said over the top of the lowered hood: "I'm not a-going to keep me sneezer out o' your affairs, guv'nor. Be you ee-loping?"

"Of course I'm not—Good God, so I am!" said his lordship, much struck.

"Because if you be," pursued Jason, "and if you don't wish no one to know nothing about it, that young gentry-mort didn't ought to be asettin' up there beside you like she is."

"By Jove, he's in the right of it!" exclaimed the Viscount, reining in suddenly. "We shall have half the countryside blabbing that they saw you driving off with me! There's nothing for it: you'll have to sit on the floor-boards, and keep yourself hidden under the rug, Hero."

Her experience of life not having engendered in Hero any expectation of having either her dignity or her comfort much regarded, she made no objection to this proposal, but curled up at the Viscount's feet, and allowed him to cast the rug over her. Since his method of driving was of the style known as neck-or-nothing, she was considerably jolted, but she made no complaint, merely clasping her arms round the Viscount's top-boots, and pressing her cheek against the side of his knee. In this fashion they covered the next few miles. The Viscount pulled up beyond the second toll-gate, giving it as his opinion that they were now reasonably safe from any chance encounter with persons who might recognize them.

"I don't mind staying where I am, if you think it would be better for me to do so, Sherry," Hero assured him.

"Yes, but you're giving me cramp in my left leg," said the single-minded Viscount. "Get up, brat, and for the lord's sake smooth your hair! You look the most complete romp!"

Miss Wantage did her best to comply with this direction, but without any marked degree of success. Fortunately, the exigencies of the particular mode of hairdressing affected by his lordship obliged him to carry a comb upon his person. He produced this, dragged it through the soft, tangled curls, tied the hood-strings under Hero's chin, and, after a critical survey, said that it would answer well enough. Miss Wantage smiled trustfully up at him, and the Viscount made a discovery. "You look just like a kitten!"

She laughed. "No, do I, Sherry?"

"Yes, you do. I think it's your silly little nose," said the Viscount, flicking it with a careless forefinger. "That, or the trick you have of staring at a fellow with your eyes wide open. I think I shall call you Kitten. It suits you better than Hero, which I always thought a nonsensical name for a girl."

"Oh, it is the greatest affliction to me!" she exclaimed. "You can have no notion, Sherry! I would much rather you should call me Kitten."

"Very well, that's settled," said Sherry, giving his horses the office to start again. "What we have to do now is to decide what the devil I'm to do with you when I get you to London."

"You said you would buy me some new clothes," Hero reminded him, not without a touch of anxiety.

"I'll do that, of course, but the thing that's worrying me a trifle is where you are to sleep tonight," confessed Sherry. "We shan't have time to be married today, you know."

"No, not if we are to go shopping," agreed Hero. "I could come home with you, couldn't I?"

"No, certainly not! Wouldn't do at all!" responded Sherry decidedly. "Besides, I haven't a home. I mean, I live in a lodging off St. James's Street, and it's not a situation that would suit you. What's more, there's no room for you. I suppose I could take you to Sheringham House, but I shouldn't think you'd be very comfortable there, with only old Varley and his wife in charge of the place, and everything under holland covers."

"Oh, no! Please don't take me there!" begged Hero, quite daunted by such a prospect.

Jason, who had been listening with the greatest interest to the conversation, interposed at this point to give it as his opinion that nothing could be more prejudicial to the smooth conduct of the elopement than for Varley, whom he described as a tattling old chub who could be counted on to whiddle the whole scrap, to get wind of the lay. The Viscount, who, in common with every other young blood, was fond of interlarding his conversation with cant terms, found no difficulty in understanding this dark warning. On the whole he agreed with it, but he said with some severity that these strictures on an old family retainer had their origin in Varley's discovery of an attempted theft of his

56

watch-and-chain, some months previously.

"And that puts me in mind of something I forgot!" he exclaimed, turning his head over his shoulder. "Dashed if I wasn't in such a pucker when I left home that it went clean out of my head! I don't know what you stole while we were there, but you can't have been two days in the place without biting something. Hand it over!"

"Keep your glims on the road, guv'nor, keep your glims on the road!" Jason besought him. "I never mills any ken of yours! I'll cap downright I never did, nor I never will!"

"Jason!" said his lordship, in minatory accents.

The Tiger gave a sniff. "I forked a couple of meggs from the tallow-faced old cull," he admitted sulkily. "He never tipped me a Jack, he didn't."

"Do you mean you filched a couple of guineas from my uncle?" demanded Sherry.

"Well, how was I to know you didn't want him forked?" asked Jason. "You never said nothing to me about it, guv'nor, nor I didn't think he was a friend o' yourn!"

"Oh, well, if that's all, there's no harm done!" said Sherry cheerfully. "Not but what it was probably my money, if we only knew."

"Does he always steal things, Sherry?" whispered Hero, round-eyed.

"Oh, yes, always! He can't help it, you know."

"But is it not very awkward?"

"No, it doesn't worry me," Sherry replied simply. "Never takes anything of mine. It used to be a devilish nuisance when he would keep on forking my friends—he had my cousin Ferdy's watch five times before I broke him of it—but he don't do that now, and

57

in any event most people know that if they lose anything when they've been with me they have only to tell me about it. Always hands over the booty if I ask him for it. That reminds me! Hi, Jason! Don't you dare steal anything from this lady! Mind, now! I'll turn you off without a character if she misses so much as a handkerchief!"

"You wouldn''t never, guv'nor!" gasped the Tiger, horrified.

"Well, no," admitted Sherry. "I dare say I wouldn't. But I'd break every bone in your body, so don't you forget it!"

This merciful mitigation of the threat appeared to relieve the Tiger's mind. He heaved a sigh, and very handsomely offered to allow himself to be nibbled to death by ducks if he should so far forget himself as to take even a pin from his prospective mistress.

The Viscount, accepting this assurance told Miss Wantage that she might rest at ease. "Matter of fact, I don't suppose he would think of robbing you," he confided. "Still, we may as well be on the safe side. Queer little fellow! Do anything in the world for me, and damme if I know why!"

"How old is he?" enquired Hero.

"Haven't a notion, my dear. Don't think he has either. Shouldn't think he can be more than eighteen or nineteen, though."

"He's so very small!"

"Oh, there's nothing in that! Trained for a jockey at one time, till they kicked him out of the stables for thieving. You know, I've been thinking, Kitten, and it's my belief I'd best take you to Grillon's."

"Had you, Sherry? Where is that?"

"Albemarle Street. It's a hotel. Devilish flat and respectable, but that can't be helped."

"Will you stay with me there?" Hero asked, a little nervously.

"Good God, no! That *would* mean the devil to pay! We shall have enough to do as it is, concocting some kind of a tale to account for a chit of your age jauntering about without a chaperon, or an abigail. Yes, by George, and you haven't any trunks either! We ought to have brought a cloak-bag, and a few bandboxes. Grillon's will never take you in without! Why didn't I think of that before?"

"That's just like you, Sherry," observed Miss Wantage patiently. "You never would pay the least heed to anything I said, and then you blamed me when things went awry! Always! You know very well I asked you to let me pack a portmanteau. Now what shall we do?"

"Well, it can't be helped. And I never said a word of blame, not one!"

"No, but you were just about to," replied Hero, with a mischievous look. "I know you, Sherry!"

He grinned. "Little cat! I'll tell you what we shall do. We'll drive straight to my lodging; send my man, Bootle, out to buy your trunks; take a hackney to Bond Street; purchase what you stand in need of for the night; take everything back to my lodging; pack 'em up; and drive off to Grillon's with 'em. I shall say you're my sister—no, that won't do: ten to one, they know I haven't got a sister! I'll say you're my cousin. Going back to school in Bath. Come up from Kent—that's true enough!—spending the night in London—I promised I'd meet you—abigail broke her leg getting out of the chaise—taken to hospital—no female
59

relative in town—what am I to do? Nothing for it, of course! Take you to a respectable hotel! Couldn't be better!"

Miss Wantage having no fault to find with this scheme, the rest of the journey was pleasantly beguiled by elaborating the Viscount's ingenious story, filling in a few details, and laughing heartily over the approaching discomfiture of their respective relations. When the metropolis was reached, a slight squabble arose between them through Miss Wantage's urgent desire to look about her, and the Viscount's determination that she should keep her hood drawn well forward to hide her face. This soon blew over, however, and nothing could have been sunnier than Miss Wantage's mood when she presently jumped down from the curricle outside the Viscount's lodging.

His lordship's valet, Bootle, was of necessity a long-suffering and phlegmatic personage, but the sudden arrival of his master, with a shabby young lady on his arm, palpably shook his iron calm. By the time he had grasped that he beheld his future mistress, he had schooled his countenance into an expression of one inured to calamity, and expectant of any outrage. When he learned that he was to sally forth immediately, to procure such baggage as was suited to a lady of quality, his feelings were only betrayed by the faintness of the voice in which he uttered the words: "Very good, my lord!"

But when the Viscount had swept Miss Wantage out again, he so far forgot himself as to confide to the interested proprietor of the lodgings that if Fate had not decreed that he should have a swollen jaw upon the day fixed for the Viscount's return to his ancestral home, and if the Viscount had been less obliging in granting him a holiday to have the offending tooth drawn, a chain of circumstances, which he foresaw could only end in disaster, would never have been set up. The proprietor, a literal-minded gentleman, said that he had never seen Mr. Bootle nor anyone else, for that matter, managing to check any of his lordship's starts. He apostrophised his lordship as a regular dash, turf or turnpike, a vulgarism which offended Bootle so much that he went off to execute the Viscount's commission without vouchsafing another word to his crony.

The Viscount, meanwhile, conveyed Miss Wantage to a certain mantua-maker's establishment in Bond Street, where he was not unknown. Here, after a few moments' brief and startlingly frank colloquy with the astonished proprietress, he handed Miss Wantage over, to be fitted out as became her station. Nothing occurred to disturb the harmony of these proceedings, except a slight contretemps arising out of Miss Wantage's burning desire for a very dashing confection of sea-green gauze, with silver ribbons, and the Viscount's flat refusal to permit her to wear any garment so outrageously unsuited to a young lady supposedly on her way to a select seminary in Bath. This trifling quarrel was adjusted by the mantua-maker, who, foreseeing a valuable customer in the future Lady Sheringham, spared no pains to exercise all the tact at her command. She suggested that his lordship should buy a demure (and extremely expensive) gown for Miss Wantage to wear in the immediate future, at the same time laying by, for a later occasion, the sea-green gauze which had so taken Miss's fancy. The Viscount agreed to this, and was at once obliged to call Miss Wantage to order for hugging him in public.

By the time these purchases, with a few other of a

more intimate nature, had been made; a hat to match the muslin dress chosen at a milliner's shop farther down the street; a pair of lavender kid gloves procured; such items as brushes, combs, and Joppa soap added to the list of necessities; and a faithful promise made to Miss Wantage that she should visit this entrancing thoroughfare again upon the morrow to make further purchases, dusk was falling. The betrothed couple returned to the Viscount's lodgings, Miss Wantage in a state of inarticulate bliss, and her cavalier divided between amusement at her pleasure in her first new gown, and a strong inclination for his dinner. Bootle having proved himself worthy of his trust, nothing further remained to do but to pack the various purchases in two neat trunks, and to summon another hackney to convey them to Grillon's Hotel.

Seated in this homely vehicle, Miss Wantage slipped a small, gloved hand into Sherry's, and said in a quivering voice: "*Thank you,* Sherry! Oh, I *wish* I could tell you——! You see, no one has ever given me anything before!"

"Poor little soul!" said his lordship, patting her in a friendly way. "There, don't cry! You may have anything you like now, you know. Anything except that shocking hat with the purple feathers, that is! Mind, you're not to buy that tomorrow, Kitten? I shall have it taken straight back, if you do!"

"No, Sherry, I promise I won't," said Miss Wantage submissively.

CHAPTER 4

Upon the following morning, not very much after ten o'clock, two young gentlemen sat at breakfast together in the front-parlour of a house in Stratton Street. The apartment, which was the lodging of Mr. Gilbert Ringwood, bore all the signs of being a bachelor abode, the furniture being old-fashioned, and designed rather for comfort than for elegance. A mahogany sideboard supported an array of bottles, rummers, tankards, and punch-bowls; a pair of foils was propped up in one corner of the room; several riding-whips hung on the wall, amongst a collection of sporting prints and engravings; three snuff-jars, a box of cigars, and a marble clock adorned the mantelpiece; and the imposing mirror hung above it had tucked into its rather loose frame various cards of invitation, and two advertisements: one of a forthcoming event at the Royal Cock-pit, and the other of a sparring-contest to be held under the auspices of Mr. John Jackson at the Fives-Court, Westminister. Further testimony to the sporting proclivites of the owner of this apartment was provided by a pile of *Weekly Dispatches*, and a copy of the

Racing Calendar, which reposed on the writing-desk by the window.

In the centre of the room stood an oblong table, spread with a white cloth, and laid with such dishes as might be supposed likely to tempt the appetites of Mr. Ringwood and his boon-companion, the Honourable Ferdinand Fakenham. These, however, were poor. Neither gentleman had been able to fancy the soused herrings, or the buttered eggs, and had done no more than toy with a few slices from the sirloin, and swallow the merest mouthful of a fine York ham. Rejecting the chocolate which had been made for them in a silver pot, they washed down such morsels as they selected for consumption with ale poured from a large brown jug into sizeable tankards.

Mr. Ringwood, who, as was proper, sat at the head of the board, was nattily attired in a coat of superfine cloth with pearl buttons; a pair of exquisite Unmentionables; and Hessian boots of startling cut and gloss; but Mr. Fakenham, from the circumstance of having slept in his coat, was at present arrayed in one of Mr. Ringwood's dressing-gowns. This was a resplendent garment of brocaded silk, whose rich purple sheen accorded extremely ill with the pallor of Mr. Fakenham's amiable, if slightly vacuous, countenance.

It had not been from any fixed design that the Honourable Ferdinand had spent the night on the sofa in his friend's lodging. An evening whiled away at the Castle Tavern, Holborn, had engendered in him an affection for Mr. Ringwood that led him to accompany this gentleman back to Stratton Street, in preference to directing his erratic footsteps in the direction of the parental home in Cavendish Square. Whether from a natural disinclination to proceed farther on his way, or from a hazy belief that he had reached his proper destination, he had entered the house, arm in arm with his friend, ambled towards the sofa, and stretched himself out upon it, wishing Mr. Ringwood—for he was the soul of politeness—a very good night. Mr. Ringwood, always a thoughtful host, had spread a carriage-rug over his willowy form, and had sent in his man to remove his boots. As an after-thought, he had himself taken a night-cap in to his guest, and had fitted it tenderly on to his head.

Since neither gentleman was of a loquacious disposition, and both were suffering in some slight degree from the aftermath of a convivial evening, few words were exchanged over the breakfast-table. Mr. Ringwood brooded gloomily over the racing news in the morning's paper, and Mr. Fakenham sat with his clouded gaze fixed on nothing in particular. The sound of a vehicle approaching at a smart pace up the street awoke no interest in either mind, but when it drew up outside the house, and a brisk knocking almost immediately fell upon the door, Mr. Fakenham palpably winced, and Mr. Ringwood closed his eyes with the air of one suffering exquisite discomfort. He opened them again a moment later, for an impatient footstep sounded in the passage, and the door burst open to admit Lord Sheringham, who came briskly in with all the objectionable appearance of one who had not only gone sober to bed, but had also risen betimes.

"Gil, I want a word with you!" he announced, tossing his hat and his gloves on to a chair. "Hallo, Ferdy!"

"It's Sherry," Mr. Fakenham somewhat unnecessarily informed his host.

"Yes, it's Sherry," agreed Mr. Ringwood, staring fixedly at the Viscount. "Thought you was in the country."

"So did I," confessed Ferdy. He looked at his cousin, and apparently feeling that something more was required of him, asked with friendly interest: "You back, Sherry?"

"Well, good God, you can see I am, can't you?" retorted his lordship. "What the deuce are you doing here at this hour, and in that devilish dressing-gown?"

"Spent the evening at the Daffy Club," explained Ferdy simply.

"Oh, cast-away again, were you? Damme if ever I saw such a fellow!" said Sherry, hunting on the sideboard for a clean tankard, and pouring himself out a liberal libation of ale. He drew up a chair, pushing various trifles which reposed on it on to the floor, and sat down. "Gil, you're a knowing one: I want your help!"

Mr. Ringwood was so much moved by this unexpected tribute that he blushed, and dropped the *Morning Chronicle*. "Anything in my power, Sherry! Know you've only to give it a name!" he said. A disturbing thought occurred to him; he added mistrustfully: "As long as it isn't to carry a message to George!"

"Carry a message to George?" repeated Sherry. "Why the deuce should I want a message carried to George?"

"Well, if it isn't, it don't matter. For I won't do it, Sherry, and it's no use asking me to."

Mr. Fakenham shook his head portentously. "Taken one of his pets," he said. "Came smash up to me in Boodles yesterday, asking where you was. If I'd had my wits about me I'd have said you'd gone off to Leicestershire. Deuced sorry, Sherry! Never at my best before noon!"

"Oh hang George!" said Sherry. "He needn't think he's going to blow a hole through me, because he ain't."

"Seemed very set on it," said Mr. Fakenham doubtfully.

"Tell him to take a damper! That's not what I came about. Gil, where does a fellow get hold of a special license?"

The effect of this question was to cast his lordship's two cronies into stunned silence. Mr. Fakenham's rather prominent eyes goggled alarmingly at his cousin; Mr. Ringwood's jaw visibly dropped.

"*Now* what's the matter?" demanded Sherry. "Don't tell me you've never heard of a special licence! Of course you have!"

Mr. Ringwood swallowed once or twice. "You don't mean a marriage-licence, do you, Sherry?"

"Yes, I do. What else should I mean? Thing you have to have if you want to get married in a hurry."

"Sherry, she's never accepted you?" gasped Mr. Ringwood, his brain tottering.

"She?" said the Viscount, frowning at him. "Oh, the Incomparable! Oh, lord, no! Wouldn't look at me! It's not she."

"Good God!" said Mr. Ringwood, relaxing. "I wish you will not burst in on a fellow with a shock like that, Sherry, dear old boy! Gave me such a turn——! Who wants this special licence?"

"I do. Don't I keep on telling you so? Seems to me you must have shot the cat about as badly as Ferdy last night!"

Mr. Ringwood stared at him, and then, as though

mutely seeking guidance, at Mr. Fakenham.

"But you said she wouldn't look at you!" said Mr. Fakenham. "Heard you distinctly. If she won't look at you, no sense in a special licence. No sense in it either way. Banns: that's what you want."

"No, I don't," replied Sherry. "Banns won't do for me at all. I must have a licence."

"Much cheaper to have banns," argued Mr. Fakenham. "Where's the use in laying out your blunt on a licence? Stupid things; much better stick to banns!"

"You're a fool, Ferdy," said his lordship, not mincing matters. "I'm getting married today, and I can't do that without a licence."

"Sherry, it's you who must have shot the cat!" exclaimed Mr. Ringwood, with a touch of severity. "How can you be married today, when you say she wouldn't look at you?"

"Lord, can't you think of any other female than Isabella Milborne?" demanded Sherry. "I'm going to marry someone else, of course!"

Mr. Ringwood blinked at him. "Someone else?" he said incredulously.

Mr. Fakenham, having thought it over, pronounced; "Oh! Someone else. No reason why he shouldn't do that, Gil."

"I don't say he *can't* do it," replied Mr. Ringwood. "What I say is that it sounds to me like a hum. He went off to Kent to offer for Isabella, didn't he? Very well, then! Now he walks in here and says he's going to marry someone else. Well, what I mean is, it's absurd! No other word for it: absurd!"

"You're right!" said Ferdy, forcibly struck by this presentation of the case. "He's bamming again. You shouldn't do it, Sherry. Not at this hour of the morning!"

"Confound you both, I'm in earnest!" Sherry said, setting his tankard down with a crash which made Ferdy jump like a startled deer. "I'm going to marry a girl I've known all my life! Damme, I must marry someone! I shan't have a feather to fly with if I don't."

"Who is she?" asked Mr. Ringwood. "You've never offered for the Stowe girl, Sherry, dear old boy? Not the rabbity-faced one?"

"No, of course I haven't. You don't know her; never been to London in her life! I ran off with her yesterday."

"But, Sherry!" expostulated Mr. Ringwood, a good deal shaken. "No, really dear boy! You can't do that sort of thing!"

"Well, I've done it," replied the Viscount, a shade sulkily.

Mr. Fakenham made a helpful suggestion. "You want Gretna Green, Sherry. Post-chaise-and-four."

"Good God, no! It's bad enough, without that!"

"You *can* get married in the Fleet," offered Mr. Fakenham.

The Viscount arose in his wrath. "I tell you it isn't that kind of an affair at all! I'm going to be married in a church, all right and tight, and I want a special licence!"

Mr. Fakenham begged pardon. Mr. Ringwood gave a slight cough. "Sherry, old boy—don't want to pry into your affairs—wouldn't offend you for the world! —You ain't thinking of marrying the lodge-keeper's daughter, or anything of that kind?"

"No, no! She's a Wantage—some sort of a cousin,

but they don't own her. Father went through all his blunt, and kicked up a dust of some kind. Before my time. The point is, she's as well born as you are. Mrs. Bagshot brought her up: she's another of her cousins. You must know the Bagshots!"

Mr. Fakenham was suddenly roused to animation. "If she's a Bagshot, Sherry, I wouldn't marry her! Now there's a horrible thing! Do you know that woman has brought out a third one? For anything we know she's got a string of 'em—and each one worse than the last! Cassandra was bad enough, but have you seen the new one? Tallow-faced girl called Sophy?"

"Lord, yes, I've known the Bagshots all my life! Hero's not like them, I give you my word!"

"Who?" asked Ferdy, his attention arrested.

"Hero. Girl I'm going to marry."

Ferdy was puzzled. "What do you call her Hero for?"

"It's her name," replied Sherry impatiently. "I know it's a silly name, but damme, it ain't as silly as Eudora! Besides, I call her Kitten, so what's the odds?"

"Sherry, where is this girl?" asked Mr. Ringwood.

"She's at Grillon's. Couldn't think of anywhere else to take her. Told 'em she was on her way to school, and her abigail broke her leg getting down from the chaise. Best I could think of."

"Did she, though?" said Ferdy, interested. "Dare say she didn't wait for the steps to be let down. I had an aunt—well, you remember her, Sherry! Old Aunt Charlotte, the one who———"

"For God's sake, Ferdy, will you go and put your head under the pump?" cried the exasperated Viscount. "There wasn't any abigail!"

"But you said———"

70

"He made it up out of his head," explained Mr. Ringwood kindly. "ought to have been an abigail."

"Yes, by Jove, and that's another thing I shall have to arrange!" exclaimed Sherry. " 'Pon my soul, there's no end to it! Where the deuce does one find abigails, Gil?"

"She'll find one," Mr. Ringwood said. "Bridegroom don't have to engage the abigails. Butler and footmen, yes. Not abigails."

His lordship shook his head. "Won't do at all. She wouldn't know how to go about it. I tell you, she's the veriest chit out of the schoolroom. Not up to snuff at all."

Mr. Ringwood eyed him uneasily. "Dear old boy, you haven't run off with a schoolgirl, have you?"

A rueful grin stole into the Viscount's eyes. "Well, she ain't quite seventeen yet," he admitted.

"Sherry, there'll be the devil of a dust kicked-up!"

"No, there won't. That old cat of a Bagshot woman don't care a rap for the poor little soul. If it hadn't been for me, she'd have packed her off to be a governess at some rubbishing school in Bath. Hero! Chit who used to go bird's-nesting with me! I couldn't have that, damme if I could! Besides, if I must marry someone, I'd as lief marry Hero as anyone."

This heresy was too much for his cousin, who uttered in shocked accents: "Isabella!"

"Oh, well, yes, of course!" said Sherry hastily: "But I can't marry her, so it might as well be Hero. But that's neither here nor there. Where do I get a special licence, Gil?"

Mr. Ringwood shook his head. "Damned if I know, Sherry!" he confessed.

The Viscount appeared much dashed by this reply.

Fortunately, the door opened at that moment, and Mr. Ringwood's man came in with the Honourable Ferdinand's coat, which he laid reverently across a chairback.

"Chilham will know!" said Mr. Ringwood triumphantly. "Extraordinary fellow, Chilham! Knows everything! Chilham, where may his lordship get a special licence?"

The valet betrayed not the smallest sign of surprise at this question, but bowed, and replied in refined accents: "I believe, sir, that the correct procedure will be for his lordship to apply to his Grace the Archbishop of Canterbury."

"But I don't know the fellow!" protested his lordship, looking very much alarmed.

The valet executed another of his prim bows. "I apprehend, my lord, that acquaintanceship with his grace need not be a requisite preliminary to the procuring of a licence from him."

"I'll tell you what, Sherry," said his cousin, with a good deal of decision, "I wouldn't go near him, if I were you."

"Should his lordship prefer it, I fancy, sir, that any bishop will answer his purpose as well," said Chilham. "Will there be anything further, sir?"

Mr. Ringwood waved him away, just as a violent knocking sounded on the street-door. "No, nothing! If that's anyone wanting to see me, I'm not at home!"

"Very good, sir. I will endeavour to intercept the gentleman," said Chilham, and withdrew.

His efforts at interception were not crowned with success. Sounds of an altercation penetrated to the parlour, to be followed an instant later by the eruption into the room of a startlingly handsome young man,

72

dressed in riding-breeches and top-boots, and a long-tailed blue coat, with a Belcher handkerchief carelessly knotted round his throat, and his luxuriant black locks in a state of disorder which allowed one ringlet to tumble across his brow. His fiery dark eyes swept the room, and singled out the Viscount. "I knew it!" he said, in a throbbing voice. "I saw your phaeton!"

"Did you?" said Sherry indifferently. "If Jason's forked your purse again, there's no need to get in such a taking. I'll tell him to hand it over."

"Don't try to trifle with me, Sherry!" the newcomer said warningly. "Don't try it, I say! I know where you have been! You have taken a damned advantage of me, by God!"

"No, he hasn't," said Mr. Ringwood. "Now, sit down, George, for God's sake, and don't put yourself in a pucker over nothing! I never saw such a fellow!"

"Nothing to be in a pucker about," said Mr. Fakenham, adding his helpful mite. "Sherry's going to be married."

"*What?*" gasped Lord Wrotham, turning a ghastly colour, and rolling his eyes towards the Viscount.

"No, no, not to Isabella!" Mr. Ringwood assured him, touched by the sight of such agony. "Really, Ferdy, how can you? Sherry's going to marry another female."

Lord Wrotham staggered to a chair, and sank into it. Anxious to make amends, Mr. Fakenham poured out some ale, and pushed the tankard towards him. He took a pull, and sighed deeply. "My God, I thought—Sherry, I have wronged you!"

"Well, I don't mind," said the Viscount handsomely. "Got too much else to think about. Besides, you're always doing it."

73

"Sherry," said Wrotham, fixing him with a hungry gaze, "I insulted you! If you want satisfaction, I will give it to you."

"If you think it would afford me satisfaction to stand up for you to blow a hole through my chest, you're mightily mistaken, George!" said Sherry frankly. "I'll tell you what: if you don't stop trying to pick quarrels with your best friends, you won't have any left to you!"

"I think I am going mad!" said Wrotham, with a groan, and dropping his head in his hands. "I thought you was gone into Kent to steal a march on me with the Incomparable!" He raised his head again, and directed one of his fiery stares at Mr. Fakenham. "It was you who told me so!" he cried accusingly. "Now, upon my soul, Ferdy——"

"All a mistake!" said Ferdy feebly. "Never at my best before noon!"

"Well, as a matter of fact, that's what I did do," said Sherry, with a candour bordering, in the opinion of his friends, on the foolhardy. "Only she wouldn't have me."

"She refused you!" Wrotham cried, his haggard countenance suddenly radiant.

"That's what I'm telling you. It's my belief she's got better game in view than either of us, George. If she can bring him up to scratch, she'll have Severn, you mark my words!"

"Sherry!" thundered the distraught lover, springing to his feet and clenching his fists, "one word of disparagement of the loveliest, the most divine, the most perfect of women, and I call you out to answer for it!"

"Well, you won't get me out," responded the Viscount.

"Am I to call you a coward?" demanded Wortham.

"No, no, George, don't do that!" begged Ferdy, much alarmed. "Can't call poor Sherry a coward because he don't want to go out with you! Be reasonable, old fellow!"

"Oh, lord, let him call me what he likes!" said the Viscount, quite disgusted. "If I weren't going to be married today, damned if I wouldn't draw your claret, George! It's time someone let a little of that hot blood of yours!"

"What's more," said Mr. Ringwood severely, "Sherry never said a word you could take amiss. Suppose she does mean to marry Severn? What of it? No harm in that, is there? Dare say she's taken a fancy to be a duchess. Anyone might!"

"I will not believe that she could be so worldly!" Wrotham said, striding over to the window, and staring out into the street.

His long-suffering friends, relieved to see that his rage had, for the moment, abated, returned to the consideration of the problem confronting Sherry. Their discussion presently attracted Lord Wrotham's attention, and he came away from the window, and quite mildly asked the Viscount to explain how he came to be marrying a totally unknown damsel. Sherry very obligingly favoured him with a brief resume of his elopement; and Lord Wrotham, convinced at last that he had relinquished all pretensions to the hand of the Incomparable Isabella, warmly shook him by the hand, and offered his his felicitations.

"Yes, that's all very well," said Mr. Ringwood, "but it don't help us find a likely bishop for this special licence."

"It'll have to be a Fleet marriage, Sherry," said Mr. Fakenham mournfully.

"No," said Mr. Ringwood. "Won't do at all. Not legal."

At this point, Lord Wrotham shocked the company into silence by saying that he was acquainted with a bishop. He explained this extraordinary lapse by adding apologetically that his mother had been as thick as thieves with the fellow any time these past ten years; and, being still under the revulsion of feeling brought about by the realization that the Viscount was no longer one of his rivals, offered to introduce him to this cleric.

The Viscount at once closed with the offer, and proceeded to enlist the services of Mr. Ringwood. Mr. Ringwood, learning that this task was to escort his friend's bride on a tour of the milliners' and mantua-makers's shop which graced the town, and to dissuade her from purchasing garments unsuited to her station, goggled at the Viscount in dismay. His expostulations went quite unheeded. The Viscount assured him that he would deal famously with Miss Wantage; and, after appointing a rendezvous with Lord Wrotham, bore him off in his phaeton to Grillon's Hotel.

CHAPTER 5

Miss Wantage, in spite of her natural terror at being left without support in such a formidable place as Grillon's Hotel, had passed a peaceful night, the unaccustomed excitement of the previous day having made her tired enough to sink into a sleep from which not all the strange noises of a London street had the power to rouse her. The Viscount had very kindly stayed to partake of dinner in her company before leaving the hotel for his own lodging; and since he had promised to visit her betimes next morning she was able to part from him with tolerable composure. But the high-bred stares of several dowagers sojourning in the hotel, coupled with the overt curiosity of the chambermaid who waited on her, made her feel very ill-at-ease, and it took all the comfort afforded by the knowledge of being dressed in a modish new gown to sustain her spirits until the arrival, at eleven o'clock, of the Viscount, with the shrinking Mr. Ringwood in tow.

Being blessed with the friendliest of natures, Miss Wantage accepted Mr. Ringwood with perfect complaisance. Upon being told that Gil would take care of her while his lordship was otherwise engaged, she smiled confidingly at him, and said: "Oh yes! Thank you! How kind it is in you! Will you take me to buy a hat for the wedding, please? Sherry made me buy this one I have on, because he told everyone I was going to school in Bath, but I will *not* wear it for my wedding!"

"Well, you need not," replied Sherry. "But mind, Kitten, you are not to choose what Gil don't like!"

"Oh no, indeed I won't!"

The horrified Mr. Ringwood made an inarticulate noise in his throat. It was not attended to. Sherry instructed him to be firm with Miss Wantage, and—in an under-voice—for God's sake not to let her buy a hat more suited to a *chere-amie* than to a lady of Quality!

Mr. Ringwood, no lady's man, was understood to say that really—no, really!—he knew nothing about such matters, but the Viscount summarily disposed of this objection and returned to the vexed question of abigails. Miss Wantage seemed surprised, but gratified, to learn that she was to have an abigail, but since she had no notion how to set about acquiring one, she was unable to help his lordship. Mr. Ringwood then had the brilliant idea of laying the matter before Chilham. This found instant favor with Sherry, who said that he would drive straight back to Stratton Street as soon as he had paid Miss Wantage's reckoning.

"And that reminds me!" he said suddenly. "Where the deuce are we going to stay?"

"Stay?" repeated Mr. Ringwood.

"Dash it, Gil, we shall have to put up somewhere until I decide where we are to live!"

"But—— Are you meaning to stay in town, Sherry?" asked Mr. Ringwood, with ideas of honey-moons chasing one another through his head.

"Of course we're going to stay in town! Where the devil else should we stay? But I won't stay at this place, and so I tell you! Of all the stuffy—— Besides, we couldn't stay here. They think Kitten's on her way to school."

"Well, you've got a house, dear old boy—very fine house! Best part of the town—excellent address—— Why not go there?"

"I suppose it will come to that in the end," agreed Sherry, with a marked lack of enthusiasm. "But I can't take possession of it before I've told my mother I want it. We shall have to put up at an hotel in the meantime. Only thing is, which hotel?"

"There's Limmer's," suggested Mr. Ringwood doubtfully.

"Limmer's!" ejaculated the Viscount. "With all the Pets of the Fancy for the chit to hob-nob with! As well take her to the Castle Tavern!"

Mr. Ringwood, much confused, begged pardon, and once more searched his brain. He bethought him of Ellis's; and after the Viscount had spurned this hostelry with a loathing engendered by his having once dined there with his mother, rejected a suggestion that Graham's was said to be comfortable, and, on the somewhat obscure grounds of having an aunt who used to stay there, refused to enter the portals of Symon's, it was decided that the young couple should take up their temporary abode at Fenton's, in St. James's Street.

"Well, now that we've settled that, I'd best be off to go with George to visit this curst Bishop of his," said his lordship. He added, not without a touch of disapproval; "Queer start, that: George being acquainted with a Bishop. Shouldn't have thought it of him."

"No, I shouldn't either," agreed Mr. Ringwood. "Of

course you do get 'em in the family sometimes. Thing that might happen to anyone."

"Yes, but you don't *know* 'em," Sherry pointed out. "Besides, he didn't say this one was a relation of his. Very odd fellow, George."

"You know what I think about George, Sherry?" Mr. Ringwood said, as one who had given much consideration to the subject. "It's a pity he's such a devil of a fellow with the pistols. Makes it deuced awkward, sometimes, being a friend of his, because there's no knowing when he'll take one of his pets, and then nothing will do for him but to call one out. At least, I don't mean that, precisely, because it stands to reason no one's going to go out with George, unless they can't help themselves, but the thing is he ain't happy. Pity!"

"Oh, I don't know!" said Sherry. "He was never as bad until the Incomparable came to town. Don't pay much heed to him, myself. How long will it take me to fork this Bishop of his for that licence, do you suppose? I mean, where are we to meet?"

Mr. Ringwood having no ideas to advance on the probable length of time this delicate operation would need, it was decided, after a good deal of argument, that as soon as Miss Wantage had accomplished her shopping, she should be escorted to the Viscount's lodging, where he engaged himself to meet her. The party then broke up, Sherry going off to pick up Lord Wrotham, who had returned home to change his Belcher handkerchief for a neckcloth more in keeping with the exalted company he was to seek; and Mr. Ringwood sallying forth with Miss Wantage in the direction of Bond Street.

Any idea he might have cherished of being able

within an hour or two to relinquish his charge into her betrothed's keeping was put an end to by the discovery, when they repaired to the Viscount's lodging shortly after noon, that his lordship proposed to meet his Hero only at the Church door. He had left a hastily scribbled note for Mr. Ringwood, informing that everything was in a way to being fixed right and tight; and that he relied upon his friend to bring the bride to St. George's, Hanover Square, not a moment later than half-past two o'clock.

Mr. Ringwood, who was by this time on very friendly terms with the most unexacting young lady he had so far encountered, communicated the contents of the note to her, and said; "Well, what would you care to do now, I wonder?"

"I *could* wait here," offered Miss Wantage, in a tone which indicated that she would consider such a course pretty flat.

"No, that won't do," Mr. Ringwood said, frowning. "I think I had best take you to eat a little luncheon. After that——" He paused, eyeing her speculatively. Miss Wantage returned his gaze with one of pleasurable expectation. "I know what you'd like!" he said. "You'd like to see the wild beasts at the Royal Exchange!"

Nothing could have appealed more strongly to Miss Wantage's youthful taste, so as soon as she had changed the chip-straw hat for an Angouleme bonnet of white thread-net trimmed with lace, she sallied forth once more with Mr. Ringwood, tripping beside him with all the assurance of one who knew herself to be dressed in the pink of fashion. The Angouleme bonnet most becomingly framed her face; she had taken great pains to comb her curls into modish ringlets; and if the figured muslin gown was less dashing than a certain pomona green silk which Mr. Ringwood had assured her, in some agitation, Sherry wouldn't like at all, no fault could be found with her little blue kid shoes, or her expensive gloves and ridicule, or with the sophisticated sun-shade which she carried to the imminent danger of the passers-by.

They were a trifle late in arriving at the Church, owing to Mr. Ringwood's having made an unfortunate reference during the course of the afternoon to the Pantheon Bazaar. Miss Wantage had immediately demanded to be taken to this mart, and had enjoyed herself hugely there, dragging Mr. Ringwood from shop to shop, and alarming him very much by developing a sudden desire to become the possessor of a canary in a gilded cage, which happened to catch her eye. Mr. Ringwood was as wax in her hands, but he had a very fair notion of what his friend's feelings would be on being met at the Church door by a bride carrying a bird in a cage, and he said desperately that Sherry wouldn't like it. He had very little hope of being attended to, but to his surprise he found that these simple words acted like a talisman on his volatile companion. So although the hackney which conveyed them from the Bazaar to Hanover Square might be rather full of packages and bandboxes, at least it contained no livestock, a circumstance upon which Mr. Ringwood considered he had reason to congratulate himself.

Not only Sherry was awaiting them in the Church porch, but the Honourable Ferdy Fakenham was well, whom he had brought along to support him on this momentous occasion. Both gentlemen were very nattily attired in blue coats, pale pantaloons, gleaming Hessians, uncomfortably high shirt-collars, and exquisitely arranged cravats, the Honourable Ferdy sporting, besides (for he was a very Tulip of Fashion), a long ebony cane, lavender gloves, and a most elegant buttonhole of clove-pinks. It was Ferdy who had procured a nosegay for the bride to carry, and the bow with which he presented it to her had made him famous in Polite Circles.

"Hallo, Kitten, that's a devilish fetching bonnet!" said the Viscount, by way of greeting. "But what the deuce made you late? You had best pay off the hack, Gil: no saying how long we shall be here."

"No, Sherry. Keep the hack!" said Mr. Ringwood firmly.

"Why? If we want a hack, we can call up another, can't we?"

"The thing is, Sherry, there are one or two packages in it," explained Mr. Ringwood, a little guiltily.

The Viscount stared at him, and then took a look inside the vehicle. "One or two packages!" he exclaimed. "Good God! What the deuce possessed you to bring a lot of bandboxes to a wedding?"

"Oh, Sherry, they are things I bought at the Pantheon Bazaar!" said Miss Wantage. "And we had no time to take them to your lodging, and I am very sorry if you do not like it, but I didn't buy the canary which I wanted!"

"My God!" said the Viscount, realizing his narrow escape.

"Told her you wouldn't like a canary," explained Mr. Ringwood, with a deprecatory cough.

"I should think you might well!" replied his lordship. "Oh, well, it can't be helped; the hack had best wait for us! Lord, if I haven't forgotten to present you, Ferdy! It's Ferdy Fakenham, Kitten. He's some sort of a cousin of mine, so you may as well call him Ferdy, like the rest of us. You're bound to see a lot of him. George Wrotham would have come along too, but we couldn't bring him up to scratch. Sent you his compliments, and wished us both happy, or some such flummery."

"Couldn't face a wedding," Ferdy said, shaking his head. "Comes too near the bone. Shook him badly, poor old boy, the mere sight of the licence! Gone off in the dumps again."

Mr. Ringwood fetched a sigh, but the Viscount was disinclined to dwell upon Lord Wrotham's troubles, and proposed that they should stop dawdling about for all the fools of London to gape at, step into the Church, and settle the business. They all went in, therefore, and the business was, in fact, soon settled, without any other hitch than the discovery by the bridegroom, midway through the ceremony, that he had forgotten to purchase a ring. He rolled a frantically enquiring eye upon his cousin Ferdy, who merely gazed at him with dropped jaw, and the eyes of a startled fawn; and then, rendered resourceful through alarm, tugged off the signet ring on his own finger, and handed it over to the waiting cleric. It was much too large for Hero's finger, but the glowing look she cast up at him seemed to indicate that she did not in the least resent his lack of foresight. It fell to Mr. Ringwood's lot to give the bride away, which he did with a somewhat self-conscious blush. Everyone signed the register; the Honourable Ferdy saluted the bride's cheek with rare grace; Mr. Ringwood kissed her hand; and the bridegroom confided in a relieved aside to his supporters that he thought they had brushed through it pretty well.

Once outside the Church again, the Viscount

handed his wife into the hackney, and turned to consult his friends on the best way in which to spend the evening. Mr. Ringwood stared at him very hard, and even Ferdy, who was not much given to the processes of reasoned thought, goggled a little at a suggestion that they should all foregather at Fenton's for an early dinner, pay a visit to the theatre, and wind up an eventful day by partaking of a snug little supper at the Piazza.

"But, Sherry, dear boy! Lady Sheringham—wedding night—won't want a party!" stammered Ferdy.

"Fudge! what the devil should we do, pray? Can't spend the whole evening looking at one another!" said the Viscount. "Kitten, you'd like to go to the play with us, wouldn't you?"

"Oh yes, do let us!" cried Hero at once. "I would like it of all things!"

"I knew you would. And you would like Gil and Ferdy to go along with us too, I dare say?"

"Yes," agreed Hero, smiling warmly upon these gentlemen.

"Then that's settled," said the Viscount, getting into the hackney. "Fenton's Hotel, coachman! Don't be late, Gil!"

The vehicle drove off, leaving the Honourable Ferdy and Mr. Ringwood to look fixedly at each other.

"Know what I think, Gil?" Ferdy asked portentously.

"No," replied Mr. Ringwood. "Damned if I know what *I* think!"

"Just what I was going to say!" said Ferdy. "Damned if I know *what* I think!"

Pleased to find themselves in such harmonious

agreement, they linked arms in a friendly fashion, and proceeded down the road in the direction of Conduit Street.

"Dear little soul, you know," presently remarked Mr. Ringwood. "Seems to think the devil of a lot of Sherry."

The slight uneasiness in his voice penetrated to Ferdy's intelligence. He stopped suddenly and said: "I'll tell you what, Gil!"

"Well, what?" asked Mr. Ringwood.

Ferdy considered the matter. "I don't know," he confessed. "Better look in at Limmer's, since we're so close, and have a third of daffy!"

The bridal couple, meanwhile, were rattling over the cobbles in the direction of St. James's Street. The groom put his arm around the bride's waist and said: "Devilish sorry I forgot the ring, Kitten! Buy you one to-morrow."

"I like this one," Hero said, looking down at it. "I like to have it because it is your very own."

He laughed. "You wouldn't keep it long! In fact, you'll very likely lose it before the night's out."

"Oh no! I shall hold my finger crooked, so that it can't drop off. Sherry, when your cousin said 'Lady Sheringham'—did he mean *me?*"

"Of course he did. Though to tell you the truth, it sounded very odd to me too," admitted his lordship.

Hero turned wide eyes upon him. "Sherry, I know I am Lady Sheringham, but it doesn't seem possible! I have the horridest feeling that I shall suddenly wake up and find that it has been all a dream!"

"I know what you mean," nodded his lordship, "though when I think of all the things I've had to do to-day it seems to me more like a nightmare." He encountered a dismayed look, and said hastily: "No, no, not being married! I didn't mean that! I dare say I shall like that very tolerably once I've grown used to it. But that Bishop of George's! Do you know, I had to swear an oath, or whatever they call it, that you had the consent of your guardians, Kitten?"

"But, Sherry, I haven't!"

"No, I know that, but you wouldn't have had me let a trifling circumstance like that stop me, would you? Besides, there's no harm done: your precious Cousin Jane ain't going to kick up a dust, you mark my words! She'll be thankful to be so well rid of you, I dare say."

Hero agreed to it, but a little doubtfully. The Viscount said in a bracing tone that what they both needed was a bottle of something to set them up.

They arrived presently at Fenton's Hotel, to find that Bootle was already installed there, and had not only unpacked his master's trunks, but had loftily instructed a chambermaid to perform the same office for my lady. As much to preserve his own dignity as Hero's, he let drop, in the most casual way possible, the information that her ladyship's maid had been smitten with the jaundice, leaving her mistress temporarily unattended. His grand manners, the slightly contemptuous glance he cast round the best suite of apartments in the hotel, and the nicety of taste which led him to rearrange the ornaments on the mantelpiece of the sitting-room which separated my lord's from my lady's bedchamber, quite over-awed the chambermaid and the boots, and inspired them with a belief in the propriety of Lord and Lady Sheringham which only the appearance upon the scene of this erratic couple would dispel.

His lordship's first act, on his arrival, was to ring for

a waiter to bring up a bottle of burgundy, and another of ratafia; his second was to produce from one pocket a small package, which he handed over to his bride, saying as he did so: "Almost slipped my mind! There's a wedding gift for you, brat: frippery things, but I'll buy you better ones, once the blunt's my own."

"*Oh!*" gasped Hero, gazing in incredulous delight at her first pair of diamond ear-rings. "Anthony, Anthony!"

"Good God, Kitten, they're only trifles!" he expostulated, as she cast herself on his chest. "My dear girl, do have a care to my neckcloth! You've no notion how long it took me to get it to set just so!"

"Oh, I'm so sorry, but how could I help it? Sherry, will you pierce my ears for me at once, so that I may wear them to-night?"

This, however, the Viscount did not feel himself competent to do. Hero's face fell so ludicrously that he suggested that the ear-rings might very well be tied on with a piece of silk for the time being. She cheered up immediately, and by the time the waiter came back with the required refreshment, had achieved a result which her husband assured her would defy any but the narrowest scrutiny. They then toasted one another, and the Viscount was moved to declare that he was dashed if he didn't believe that he had done a very good day's work.

Later, when she appeared before him in the sea-green gauze, he stared at her in great surprise, and said: By Jove, he had never thought she could look so well! Encouraged by this tribute, Hero showed him a cloak of green sarsnet trimmed with swansdown, which she had purchased that morning, and upon his expressing his unqualified approval of this garment, confided, a little nervously, that she feared he might, when he came to see the bill, think it a trifle dear. The Viscount waved aside such mundane considerations; and they then went downstairs in perfect amity to receive their dinner guests.

It was evident from the expressions on their countenances that Mr. Ringwood and the Honourable Ferdy thought that their friend's bride did him credit. Each of these gentlemen had brought with him a wedding gift, the results of an earnest discussion which had taken place between them over two glasses of daffy at Limmer's Hotel. The Honourable Ferdy had selected a charming bracelet for the bride; Mr. Ringwood had chosen an ormolu clock, which he thought might come in useful. Hero accepted both offerings with unaffected delight, clasping the bracelet round her arm immediately, and promising the clock an honourable position on her drawing-room mantelpiece. This put the Viscount in mind of the chief problem at present besetting him, and as they all took their seats round the table in the dining-room, he again raised the question of his future establishment.

Mr. Ringwood was firm in holding to it that the family mansion in Grosvenor Square was a good address, a circumstance by which he seemed to set great store; but Ferdy, while concurring in this pronouncement, gave it as his opinion that Sherry would have to throw all the existing furniture out into the road before embarking on the task of making the house fit to live in.

"Yes, by God, so I should!" exclaimed Sherry. "Most of the stuff has been there ever since Queen

Anne, and I dare say longer, if we only knew. Oh, well! Hero will like choosing some new furnishings, so it don't really signify."

The Honourable Ferdy, who had been pondering at intervals all day how his cousin's wife came by such a peculiar name, now introduced a new note into the conversation by saying suddenly: "Can't make it out at all! You're sure you've got that right, Sherry?"

"Got what right?"

"Hero," said Ferdy, frowning. "Look at it which way you like, it don't make sense. For one thing, a hero ain't a female, and for another it ain't a *name*. At least," he added cautiously, "it ain't one I ever heard of. Ten to one you've made one of your muffs, Sherry."

"Oh no, I truly am called Hero!" the lady assured him. "It's out of Shakespeare."

"Oh, out of *Shakespeare*, is it?" said Ferdy. "That accounts for my not having heard it before!"

"You're out of Shakespeare too," said Hero, helping herself liberally from a dish of green peas.

"I am?" Ferdy exclaimed, much struck.

"Yes, in the *Tempest*, I think."

"Well, if that don't beat all!" Ferdy said, looking round at his friends. "She says I'm out of Shakespeare! Must tell my father that. Shouldn't think he knows."

"Yes, and now I come to think of it, Sherry's out of Shakespeare too," said Hero, smiling warmly upon her spouse.

"No, I'm not," replied the Viscount, refusing to be dragged into these deep waters. "Named after my grandfather."

"Well, perhaps *he* was out of Shakespeare, and that would account for it."

90

"He might have been," said Ferdy fair-mindedly, "but I shouldn't think he was. Mind you, I never knew the old gentleman myself, but from what I've heard about him I don't think he ever had anything to do with Shakespeare."

"Very bad *ton,* my grandfather," remarked the Viscount dispassionately. "Regular loose-screw. *none* of the Verelsts ever had anything to do with Shakespeare."

"Well, I dare say you must know best, Sherry, but only think of *Anthony and Cleopatra!*" argued Hero.

"Anthony and who?" asked Ferdy anxiously.

"Cleopatra. You must know Cleopatra! She was a Queen of Egypt. At least, I *think* it was Egypt."

"Never been to Egypt," said Ferdy. "Accounts for it. But I know a fellow who was in Egypt once. Said it was a sad, rubbishing sort of a place. Wouldn't suit me at all."

Hero giggled. "Silly! Cleopatra is hundreds and hundreds of years old!"

"Hundreds of years old?" said Ferdy, astonished.

"Good God, you know what she means!" interpolated the Viscount.

Mr. Ringwood nodded. "She's a mummy," he said. "They have 'em in Egypt." He felt that this piece of erudition called for some explanation, and added: "Read about 'em somewhere."

"Yes, but the one I mean is in Shakespeare," said Hero. "I expect it's the same one, because he was for ever writing plays about real people."

A horrible suspicion crossed Ferdy's mind. He stared fixedly at her, and said; "You ain't a blue-stocking, are you?"

"Of course she's not a blue-stocking!" cried the Viscount, bristling in defence of his bride. "The thing is she's only just out of the schoolroom. She can't help but have her head crammed with all that stuff!"

"Anyone can see she's not a blue-stocking," said Mr. Ringwood severely. "Besides, you oughtn't to say things like that, Ferdy. Very bad *ton!*"

Mr. Fakenham begged pardon in some confusion, and said that he was devilish glad. A fresh bogey at once raised its head, and he demanded, in accents of extreme foreboding, whether the evening's entertainment was to consist of Shakespeare. Upon being reassured, he was able to relax again and to continue eating his dinner in tolerable composure.

The play to which the Viscount carried his guests was not of a nature to tax even the Honourable Ferdy's understanding. It was a merry, and not always very polite, comedy which all three young gentlemen pronounced to be very tolerable, and which cast Hero into a trance of ecstasy which would not allow her to withdraw her rapt gaze from the stage for an instant. She did not quite comprehend some of the witticisms which appeared heartily to amuse her companions, and at one point she threw Mr. Ringwood into acute discomfort by asking enlightenment of him. Fortunately, the Viscount overheard her, and rescued his friend from his dilemma by saying briefly that she wouldn't understand even if she were told.

During the interval it was soon made evident that the Viscount's box was attracting a good deal of attention from other parts of the house. His lordship, detecting various acquaintances amongst the audience, waved and bowed; and after a few minutes a knock fell on the door of the box and a fashionable-looking gentleman entered, glancing curiously at Hero from under rather drooping eyelids, and saying in a languid tone: "So you are come back again, my dear Sherry! And without a word! I begin to think I must have offended you."

"Hallo, Monty!" responded Sherry, getting up from his chair. "What a fellow you are for funning! No offence at all! I'm devilish glad to see you here to-night—want to present you to my wife! Hero, this is Sir Montagu Revesby—particular friend of mine!"

Hero felt a little shy of this elegant stranger, who looked to be some years older than Sherry. The slightly supercilious air that hung about him, and the irony of his smile, made her uncomfortable, but she was naturally prepared to like any friend of Sherry's, and she held out her hand at once.

Sir Montagu took it in his, but his brows had flown up in quick surprise, and he directed a half-laughing, half-startled glance at Sherry. "Is it so indeed?" he said. "You are quite sure it is not you who are funning, my dear boy?"

Sherry laughed. "No, no, we were married to-day! Ask Gil if we were not!"

"But this is most unexpected!" Sir Montagu said. "You must allow me to offer you my felicitations, Sherry." His cold eyes ran over Hero; his smile broadened. "Ah—my *deepest* felicitations, Sherry! And so you were married to-day? Dear me, yes! How very interesting! But why did you not send me a card for the wedding?"

Mr. Ringwood unexpectedly decided to bear his part in this interchange. He said rather shortly: "Private ceremony. St. George's, Hanover Square. Lady Sheringham desired it so. Don't care for a fuss."

"In deep mourning," corroborated Ferdy, feeling

93

that a little embroidery was needed.

"No, *not* in mourning," said Mr. Ringwood, annoyed. "Wouldn't be here if she was. Family reasons."

"Nonsense!" said Sherry, rejecting this kindly intervention. "To tell you the truth, Monty, we made a runaway match of it."

"Save trouble," murmured Ferdy, faint but pursuing.

"I understand perfectly," bowed Sir Montagu. "I must think myself fortunate to have been amongst the first to make Lady Sheringham's acquaintance. For I do not think——?"

"No, she's never been to town before," replied Sherry. "She's a cousin of the Bagshots: known her all my life."

"Indeed?" Sir Montagu's eyebrows seemed to indicate that he found this surprising. "Well, that is very delightful, to be sure. But I fancy the curtain is about to go up on the second act. I must not be lingering here."

"Join us at the Piazza for supper, Monty!" Sherry suggested.

Sir Montagu thanked him, but was obliged to excuse himself, since he was engaged with some friends. He bowed once more over Hero's hand, promised himself the pleasure of waiting upon her formally at no very distant date, and took his leave. He had no sooner left the box than Ferdy was moved to express himself unequivocally. "Shouldn't have invited him," he said. "He's a Bad Man."

Hero turned a wide, questioning gaze upon him. Sherry said: "Oh, fiddle! Nothing amiss with Monty! You don't know what you're talking about, Ferdy!"

"Bit of a commoner," said Mr. Ringwood dispassionately. "Always thought so."

"Nonsense!"

"Thinks he's at home to a peg," said Mr. Fakenham. "Well, he ain't. What's more, I don't like him. Gil don't like him either."

"Well, he can be devilish good company," retorted the Viscount.

"He don't keep devilish good company," Mr. Ringwood said stolidly.

"Good God, you may meet him everywhere!" exclaimed Sherry.

"Point is, we don't want to meet him everywhere," said Ferdy. "You know what Duke says?"

"Your brother Marmaduke is a bigger fool than you are," responded the Viscount.

"No, dash it, Sherry!" expostulated Mr. Ringwood. "That's coming it a trifle too strong! Nothing the matter with Duke! Very knowing fellow!"

"He says," pursued Ferdy inexorably, "that Monty's an ivory-turner. I don't say he's right, but that's what he says."

As this pronouncement could only be understood to mean that the Honourable Marmaduke Fakenham considered Sir Montagu to be employed in decoying hapless innocents into gaming-hells, it was not surprising that the Viscount should flush hotly, and refute such a slander with more vehemence than civility. Mr. Ringwood, seeing how anxiously Hero's puzzled eyes travelled from Ferdy's face to Sherry's, trod heavily upon Ferdy's foot, and refrained, with considerable self-restraint, from reminding Sherry that his own initiation into the disastrously deep play obtaining at such discreet establishments as Warkworth's, and Wooler's, had been made under the auspices of Sir Montagu. Luckily, the curtain rose just then on the second act, and although Ferdy and Sherry were both perfectly prepared to continue their acrimonious discussion, they were obliged, on account of the representations made to them by persons in the neighbouring boxes, to postpone it until the play had run its course. By that time they had naturally forgotten all about it; and as no further rift had occurred to mar the harmony of the evening the whole party went off happily to eat supper at the Piazza, Hero being conveyed there in a sedan chair and the three gentlemen walking along beside it.

This circumstance put Mr. Ringwood in mind of something which he had been meaning to say to Sherry all day; and as soon as the supper had been chosen, and the wine broached, he fixed him with a serious gaze, and said; "Been thinking, Sherry. Carriage for Lady Sherry. Can't keep driving her about in hacks. Not the thing."

"No, not the thing at all," Sherry agreed. "I'm glad you put me in mind of that. Come to think of it, we ought to decide just what she'll need."

"Must have a carriage," Mr. Ringwood said. "Landaulet."

Mr. Fakenham, who had been narrowly inspecting a dish of curried crab through his quizzing-glass, looked up at this, and said positively: "Barouche. All the crack nowadays! Can't have Sherry's wife driving about town in a landaulet like a dowd."

"Oh no!" agreed Hero. "I am going to be all the crack. I have quite made up my mind about that. Sherry said I might cut a dash, and I think I should like to very much."

"Spoken like a right one!" grinned Sherry. "Of course she can't have a landaulet! Dash it, that's what my mother uses! A barouche, with a pair of match-bays: slap up to the echo!"

"Best look in at Tatt's to-morrow," nodded Ferdy. "Nothing in your stables fit for a lady, dear old boy."

Mr. Ringwood, who had produced a visiting-card from his pocket, made a note on it. "Tatt's," he said. "Coachman and footman. Pageboy. Abigail."

"Chilhan is attenting to that," said the Viscount. "Says he knows just such a one as will suit."

"Riding horse," said Ferdy.

"She don't ride."

"Yes, I do!" Hero interrupted. "At least, I have often ridden the old pony, and you know you put me up on your hunter when I was only twelve, Sherry!"

"Well, you aren't going to sit there saying you rode him, are you?" demanded Sherry. "Never saw a horse get rid of anyone faster in my life!"

"You shouldn't have put her up on one of your wild horses, Sherry," said Mr. Ringwood disapprovingly. He made another note on his card. "She'd best have a nice little mare. Mare. Lady's saddle."

"Yes, and a riding-habit," said Hero. "And also I should like to have a carriage like that one we saw this morning, Gil, and drive it myself."

"Phaeton," said Mr. Ringwood, writing it down.

"And Sherry will teach me how to drive it," said Hero happily.

Sherry's friends spoke as one man. "No!"

"Why not?"

"Because he can't drive," replied Mr. Ringwood, not mincing matters.

"Sherry can drive! He drives better than *anyone!*"

Ferdy shook his head. "You're thinking of someone

else. Not Sherry. Wouldn't have him in the F.H.C. Wouldn't look at him. No precision. Gil's your man. Drives to an inch: regular nonpareil!"

Mr. Ringwood blushed at this tribute, and was understood to murmur that he would be happy to teach Lady Sherry anything that lay within his power. Hero thanked him, but it was evident that her faith in Sherry's skill was unshaken. Sherry, who had merely grinned at his friends' strictures, said with unwonted modesty that she had best let Gil take her in hand. His style of driving, although he would back himself to take the shine out of most of the men on the road, was not, he owned, quite suited to a lady. He engaged himself, however, to find her a really sweet-going horse, unless—with a challenging look at Mr. Ringwood—he was not thought to be a judge of horse-flesh?

Mr. Ringwood hastened to assure him that he had perfect confidence in his ability to choose proper high-bred 'uns; and since every provision for Hero's future well-being seemed now to have been made, put away his visiting-card and began to address himself to his supper.

CHAPTER 6

The Viscount's first action on the following morning was to sally forth to pay a call on his uncle, the Honourable Prosper Verelst. This gentleman occupied a set of chambers in Albany, and since it was one of his idiosyncrasies never to stir forth from his abode until after noon, his nephew was sure of finding him at home. He found him, in fact, partaking of a late breakfast, his valet being under orders to let no one in. The Viscount overcame this hindrance by putting the valet bodily out of his way, and walked in on his uncle without ceremony.

The Honourable Prosper was by far too corpulent a man to be anything but easy-going, and beyond fetching a groan at sight of his nephew, he evinced no sign of the annoyance he felt at being disturbed at such an hour. Merely he waved Sherry to a chair and went on with his breakfast.

"I wish you will tell that fool of a man of yours not to try to keep me out, sir," complained the Viscount, laying his hat and cane down.

"But I want him to keep you out," responded Prosper placidly. "I like you, Sherry, but I'm damned if I'll be fidgeted by your starts at this time of day."

"Well, he ain't going to keep me out," said Sherry. "Not but what I shan't want to see so much of you now. Come to tell you I was married yesterday."

If he had expected his uncle to betray surprise, he was destined to be disappointed. Prosper turned a lack-lustre blue eye upon him, and said: "Oh, you were, were you? Made a fool of yourself, I suppose?"

"No such thing! I've married Hero Wantage!" said Sherry indignantly.

"Never heard of her," said Prosper, pouring himself out some more coffee. "Not but what I'm glad. You can take charge of your own affairs now. They've been worrying me excessively."

"Worrying you excessively!" ejaculated Sherry. "Well, if that don't beat all! Much you've done to take care of 'em! You've left it all to that platter-faced sharp, my uncle Horace, and if he hasn't feathered his nest I know nothing of the matter!"

Prosper added a lavish amount of cream to his coffee. "Yes, I should think you're right, Sherry," he said. "I always did think so, and very worrying it was, I can tell you."

"Well, why the devil didn't you do something to stop it?" demanded Sherry, pardonably irritated.

"Because I'm too lazy," replied his uncle, with the utmost frankness. "If you were my size, you'd know better than to ask me a damned stupid question like that. What's more, I never could abide that fellow Paulett, and if I'm not to go off in an apoplexy there's only one thing for it, and that's to keep away from him."

Saving your presence, nevvy, I don't like any of your mother's relatives, while as for Valeria herself—well, that's neither here nor there! Why do you have to come pestering me at this hour just because you've got yourself tied-up, boy?"

"Because you've got to wind up the Trust," replied Sherry. He produced a document from his pocket and laid it on the table. "There's my marriage-lines, or whatever you call em. I'll write to my mother myself, but it's you who must deal with the lawyers."

Prosper sighed, but attempted no remonstrance. "Well, I don't mind seeing old Ditchling," he said. "What are you going to do, Sherry? Do you want your mother to retire to the Dower House? She won't like that."

"No," said Sherry, who had already given this matter a little thought. "Country life don't suit me, and I'd as soon she stayed at Sheringham Place to keep her eye on things as not. Mind you, I'd give something to kick Uncle Horace out, but I suppose it can't be done. Not without my mother having the vapours, and I don't want that. But I'm going to hold the purse-strings, and although I don't mind feeding him and housing him, I'm damned if I'll pay for his little pleasures any longer!"

"Well, it's not my affair," said Prosper, "but if I were in your shoes I'd be rid of him."

"You wouldn't. You're too lazy. Besides, I don't want to put my mother into one of her takings, and that's what would happen, if I kicked Uncle Horace out, as sure as check! Ten to one she'd come up to town to live, and that wouldn't suit me at all."

"No, my God!" agreed Prosper, impressed by this common-sense point of view.

"As for the town house, I haven't made up my mind about that," continued Sherry. "I'm bound to say it ain't much in my line, but I'm taking Hero to have a look at it to-day, and if she wants to live there she shall."

"She will," said Prosper cynically. "Trust any woman to jump at the chance of living in a draughty great mansion in the best part of town!"

He was wrong. When the Viscount took his bride to the shrouded house in Grosvenor Square, some of her vivacity left her. Whether it was the astonished disapproval of the retainer who led them from room to room, or whether it was the depressing effect of the Holland covers which draped most of the chairs and sofas, not even she knew; but a damper was certainly cast over her spirits. She clung tightly to Sherry's arm, and stole wide, scared glances about her at all the sombre oil-paintings in heavily gilded frames, at the huge mirrors, massive chandeliers, draped curtains, and formal furniture. She was conscious of feeling small and defenceless, and she was quite unable to picture herself as mistress of all this outmoded grandeur.

Sherry, naturally, was in no way oppressed by the house, but he knew from experience that an army of servants was needed to keep it up, and he had all a young man's horror of finding himself saddled with so much responsibility. Moreover, he thought the furniture outrageously dowdy, and he had a vague premonition that if he obeyed his instinct, and made a clean sweep of everything in the house, he would raise a storm of protest that would be very unpleasant, however unavailing. By the time he and Hero had inspected the saloons, the bedchambers, and were being inexorably led in the direction of the servants' quarters, he had made up his mind. "You know, Kitten," he said, "I don't think you'll like to live here."

"No," Hero replied thankfully. "But—but I will live here if you wish me to, Sherry."

"Well, I don't," he said. "Never could stand the place myself, and Ferdy's quite right about the furniture. What we need is a much smaller house, if you ask me. Later on, when you're older—more up to snuff, you know—I dare say we may decide to live here, but we needn't worry about that now. Damme, the place feels like a tomb! Come, let's go!"

Hero accompanied him readily out into the square again, but asked, as he handed her up into the phaeton, whether they were to continue living at Fenton's Hotel. Sherry, on whom the sobriety of this hostelry was already beginning to tell, said that not only would nothing prevail upon him to take up a permanent abode there, but that if he did not contrive to get clear soon he would not answer for the consequences.

"Well, I must say I am glad you don't wish to stay," said Hero, disposing her skirts elegantly, and unfurling her sunshade. "They stare at one so! It puts me quite out of countenance. How shall we set about finding an eligible house?"

"Lord, I don't know!" replied Sherry. "We'll tell Stoke to manage the whole for us. He's the family's man of business, you know. Come to think of it, I ought to inform him that he has me to deal with now, and not my uncles. Should you care to drive with me into the City? May as well be off to see the old fellow at once, and get the business settled."

As Hero was perfectly ready to drive with him to the City, or, in fact, to any other locality he might take a fancy to visit, it was not long before Mr. Philip Stoke was startled by the announcement, made to him by his clerk, that Lord and Lady Sheringham were in the outer office, and desired speech with him. Mr. Stoke was quite taken aback, for although he was aware that the Viscount was a harum-scarum young man who would be more than likely to come impetuously in search of him, instead of summoning him to his lodging, he could not conceive of any circumstance unusual enough to have induced his lordship's Mama to have accompanied him on his quest. He hurried out at once to beg his lordship to come into the private office, and was still more startled to find himself confronting a very youthful lady, whom his noble client carelessly announced to be his wife. Suppressing an involuntary gasp, he bowed deeply, and begged his lordship to come into the private office. Here he set a chair for Hero, at the same time assuring the Viscount that he would have been happy to have waited on him at his lodging had he but known that his services were required.

"No, there's no time to be wasted," replied Sherry.

"Besides," added Hero, "I have never been into the City before, and only fancy, I have now seen St. Paul's!"

Before the bewildered Mr. Stoke could think of a reply to this artless confidence, the Viscount had divulged the object of his visit. "The thing is, I want you to procure a house for us to live in," he said. "We're putting up at Fenton's, and I don't like it above half."

Mr. Stoke glanced from him to Hero. He was well-accustomed to his lordship's starts, but this one seemed uncommonly odd. He could not recall having seen any announcement of the Viscount's nuptials in the *Gazette,* and he was perfectly sure that when he had had occasion to wait on the Honourable Prosper Verelst, not ten days previously, nothing whatever had been said of a wedding.

Sherry, reading the puzzlement in his face, said: "We were married yesterday. Matter of fact, we made a runaway match of it, but all quite above board, you know. And that means that that damned Trust comes to an end. You won't have to deal with my uncles any longer."

Mr. Stoke met his eye. "May I say, my lord, that I shall be glad?"

"Mighty pretty of you," grinned Sherry.

Mr. Stoke regarded the tips of his fingers. "I believe I have repeatedly informed Mr. Verelst that the sums of money drawn by Mr. Paulett for the maintenance of Sheringham Place and Sheringham House have appeared to me to have been in excess of what could be considered necessary. I fancy your lordship is aware of this."

"Lord, yes, you told me of it an age since! But I shall leave all that business—the estate, you know—in your hands, Stoke," he promised.

Mr. Stoke permitted himself to smile primly. "I fancy I may assure your lordship that Mr. Paulett will not out-jockey me," he said.

"No, I'll wager he won't! But never mind that now! The first thing is to find a house."

"But has your lordship forgotten that there is already a house belonging to you in Grosvenor Square?"

"No, that's just it: we don't like it. Just been to take a look at the place, and of all the curst gloomy holes I ever was in—why, it's worse than Brooks's! What we want is a snug little house where we can be comfortable."

"Do I understand your lordship to be desirous of disposing of Sheringham House?" asked Mr. Stoke, very much shocked.

"No need to do that," replied Sherry, in a large-minded way. "Dare say we may take it into our heads to remove there one day, and in the meantime there's my mother to be thought of. Got to have somewhere to stay when she comes to town, after all."

Mr. Stoke, who was of the opinion that the dowager's handsome jointure was more than sufficient to enable her to buy a house of her own, looked as disapproving as he dared, and said: "Your lordship can scarcely have considered the expense of maintaining a fourth establishment."

"Dash it, I've only got two places! Oh, you're thinking of that little hunting-box you procured for me in Leicestershire, are you? I don't count that."

"Oh!" said Mr. Stoke rather faintly.

"I'm a rich man, aren't I?" demanded Sherry, stretching his long legs out before him.

"Your lordship is a very rich man, but—"

"Of course I am! And that reminds me, we must settle a few of my debts. Stupid sort of a business, but I may as well be beforehand with the world, at any rate to start with."

"That, my lord, was what I had in mind," said Mr. Stoke. "Your lordship was good enough to entrust me with the task of ascertaining the extent of your lordship's obligations, and I fear that the sum———"

"Badly dipped, am I? Oh, well, you'd best sell me out of the Funds, and be done with it! No need to pull a long face: it's my money, damn it all! But first I must have a house I can live in."

Mr. Stoke knew his lordship too well to argue with him when it was plain, from the obstinate look round his mouth, that he had made up his mind. The best he could hope for was to be able to persuade Sherry into hiring instead of buying a house, and with this end in view he began to discuss the size of the proposed establishment, its locality, and the most expeditious way of acquiring it. Hero soon lost interest in the conversation, and left her chair to go and look out of the window into the busy street. When the Viscount at last rose to go she was employed in drawing faces on the dusty window-panes.

"If ever I saw such a troublesome chit!" exclaimed Sherry. "Now look at your glove! What's more, I dare say Stoke don't like to have his windows looking like that."

Mr. Stoke, watching in some amusement her ladyship's conscience-stricken scrutiny of one dirty finger-tip, said that he thought her window sketches brightened the room, and earned a grateful smile. The Viscount then swept his bride off to make a preliminary tour of the best furniture-warehouses, and his man of business, having escorted them to their phaeton, returned to his office and sat for quite some time gazing at the faces on his window, and wondering what would be the end of his client's most extraordinary marriage.

The bridal couple spent the rest of the day in the delightful occupation of choosing furniture. They wandered about several warehouses, attended by solicitous salesmen; and after squabbling light-heartedly over the rival merits of Hepplewhite and Sheraton, and loudly condemning each other's taste in hangings, they laid the foundations of their future home by purchasing a set of gilded chairs covered with straw-coloured satin, a wine-cooler, a tambour-top writing-table, a crystal lustre, and a shaving-stand, which happened to be just what Sherry had been wanting for months past.

Such an exhausting day naturally put the writing of a letter to the Dowager Lady Sheringham out of count, and by way of whiling away the evening Sherry escorted his bride to Vauxhall Gardens. Here they danced, supped in one of the booths on wafer-thin slices of ham, and rack-punch, and watched a display of fireworks. Hero enjoyed every moment of it, and since she made no objection to Sherry's quizzing the prettiest women present, and was happy to dance or to stroll about with him, whichever he preferred, he was able to gratify her by declaring that he had always known they should deal famously together.

On the following day Mr. Stoke waited on them with a list of the houses at present available in the fashionable part of town. He had also drawn up an advertisement of the marriage for insertion in the *Morning Post*. The Viscount gave his gracious permission to have it forwarded immediately; and the entire party then set forth in a hackney to visit the first of the houses on Mr. Stoke's list. This was condemned at once on the score of being too large; a second, in Curzon Street, had a very ugly fireplace in the drawing-room, which gave Hero an ineradicable distaste for it; a third was discovered to be situated only two doors from the residence of a family of whom the Viscount spoke with concentrated loathing; and a fourth had such a mean staircase that it would have been superfluous to have penetrated farther than the narrow hall. By this time, the Viscount was becoming bored with such domestic matters, and he began to talk of leaving Hero and Mr. Stoke to finish the business between them. However, he consented to accompany them to one more house, which was situated in Half Moon Street; and by the greatest good fortune this proved to be exactly what he had had in mind all along. Hero was equally enthusiastic over it, and although Mr. Stoke, with his patron's dignity to consider, pointed out that the drawing-room was not handsome, and the bedchambers inadequate, his objections were over-ruled. Hero was settling with Sherry that he should have the back dining-room for his library and the front room on the second floor for his bedchamber; and allotting to herself the room behind the drawing-room for her own bedchamber. To Mr. Stoke's reminder that she would require a dressing-room, she replied innocently that she had never had one, and could not conceive what she should do with one. Naturally, neither she nor Sherry saw the smallest necessity for penetrating either to the attics or to the kitchen premises in the basement: they supposed them to be like any other attics or kitchens, and in any event that could all be safely left to Bootle to arrange. Of far more importance was the redecoration of the reception-rooms and the hall. Sherry did indeed bethink himself of the staff that would be necessary for the comfortable maintenance of the house, but beyond saying that he didn't want a butler like old Romsey, who would water the wine, and had no notion how many abigails were usually employed in an establishment of this size, he had no views to advance. He said that they would leave it to Stoke. Mr. Stoke, who had foreseen that this would be the end of it, then inaugurated a discussion of the matter, during the course of which, Sherry, who had not attended to a word, wandered off to take another look at the dining-room, for the helpful purpose of deciding where his wine-cooler should stand. Hero was left with Mr. Stoke, and at once shocked and enchanted him by confiding that she had no notion how many servants she ought to employ, but hoped he would not think it necessary for her to have too many. "For I dare say I shan't know how to go on at all. At least, just at first I shall not, though I expect I shall soon get into the way of it."

Finally, it was decided that a cook, a butler, two abigails, and a pageboy or footman should, in addition to his lordship's man, her ladyship's personal maid, a coachman, two grooms, and the Tiger, be sufficient to ensure the young couple a moderate degree of comfort. Mr. Stoke engaged himself to interview all menials applying for the various posts, and to hire those he considered the most desirable. He then took his leave of his patrons and went away in an extremely thoughtful mood.

Nothing now remained except to choose the requisite number of carpets, chests, beds, tables, and chairs for the house. The Viscount, who had had enough of warehouses, conceived the happy notion of enlisting the services of his cousin Ferdy, to whose charge he consigned Hero, while he himself went off to Tattersall's with Mr. Ringwood.

Ferdy, much gratified by the confidence reposed in his taste and judgment, professed himself to be very willing to place both at Hero's service, for not only was he always ready to gallant a personable female, but his knowledge of all matters of *ton* was extensive and extremely nice. He knew just what elegant knick-knacks a lady of fashion should have in her drawing-room, had no hesitation in deciding upon a wallpaper to set off the straw-coloured chairs, and was able unerringly to guide Hero's taste in the choice of carpets and hangings. As it occurred to neither of them to consider the Viscount's purse, Ferdy's genius was allowed full rein, and the proprietors of the several warehouses they visited showed a flattering, not to say obsequious, attention to such an open-handed pair.

The Viscount, meanwhile, having, under Mr. Ringwood's auspices, purchased a very pretty mare for his Hero to ride, two high-stepping bays to draw her barouche, and a light-mouthed grey to run between the shafts of her phaeton, lingered only to add a neatish bay, described by the auctioneer as "complete to a shade," to his own stables before dragging Mr. Ringwood off to a coach-builder's in St. Jame's Street. Here they had no difficulty in selecting a smart barouche with a yellow body; and a light phaeton. They were just about to leave the premises to go in search of a set of silver-mounted harness when an elegant travelling chariot caught the Viscount's eye, and he at once decided to buy that too, since not only would it be quite out of the question for Hero to travel post—his mother, he knew, never did so—but he himself liked nothing better than to tool a coach-and-four, and would no doubt derive no small degree of pleasure from possessing a coach of his own. As the purchasing of this vehicle made it necessary for him to return to Tattersall's to negotiate for a team to draw it, it was evident that the Viscount was spending money quite as lavishly as his bride.

When Hero learned that she was now the owner of no fewer than three carriages and eight horses, she

111

turned quite pink, and after struggling for a few moments to express herself suitably, stammered out: "Oh, Sherry, it is just like K-King Cophetua and the beggar-maid!"

"Who the devil was he?" demanded Sherry.

"Well, I don't precisely remember, but he married a beggar-maid, and gave her everything she wanted."

"Sounds to me like a hum," said her sceptical husband. "Besides, what's the fellow got to do with us?"

"Only that you made me think of him," said Hero, smiling mistily up at him.

"Nonsense!" said Sherry, revolted. "Never heard such a silly notion in my life! If you don't take care, Kitten, you'll have people saying you're bookish."

Hero promised to guard against earning this stigma; and after fortifying himself with some very tolerable burgundy from the hotel's cellars, Sherry sat down to write a somewhat belated letter to his parent.

After a second day's intensive shopping with Ferdy, there really seemed to be nothing left to buy for the house in Half Moon Street, except such dull necessities as kitchen furnishings and linen, and as Hero was getting tired of choosing furniture she greeted with acclaim Sherry's suggestion that the rest should be entrusted to Mr. Stoke to provide. "And I'll tell you what, Kitten," he added, "I've had a devilish good idea. We'll be off to Leicestershire until the house is ready for us to step into. I've got a snug little hunting-box there; just the very thing for us!"

"Leicestershire, dear old boy?" exclaimed Mr. Ringwood, who happened to be present. "What the deuce should take you there at this time of year?"

"Time I ran an eye over my young stock," said Sherry. He met his friend's eyes, and said: "Well, dash it, why shouldn't we go to Leicestershire? The house won't be ready for weeks, from what I can see of it, and I'll be damned if I'll kick my heels in this place much longer! What's more, I've got a strong notion we shall have my mother posting up to London. Seems to me a good moment to go into the country."

Hero turned pale at the thought of having to confront the Viscount's enraged parent, and faltered: "Anthony! Do you indeed think she will come to town?"

"There isn't a doubt of it," replied Sherry tersely.

Hero clasped her hands tightly together. "And do you think—Cousin Jane as well?"

"Shouldn't be at all surprised. It never rains but it pours. Dare say she'll bring my uncle Horace along with her too."

"Would it—would it be very poor-spirited of us to run away?" asked Hero anxiously.

"I don't care a fig for that," replied Sherry. "It'll be deuced unpleasant if we stay! Thing to do is to give 'em all time to get used to the notion of us being married. By the time we come back to town I dare say they won't be having the vapours any longer."

Mr. Ringwood, who had been sitting apparently lost in thought, suddenly said: "Brighton."

"Too late in the season: we should never find a tolerable lodging," replied Sherry. "Besides, I was down there in May, and it didn't agree with me."

"Lady Sherry would like it better than Leicestershire."

"No, she wouldn't. I'm going to teach her to ride."

"Oh, are you, Sherry? Then do let us go to Leicestershire!" cried Hero.

"Lady Sherry," said Mr. Ringwood obstinately, "would like the balls at the Castle Inn. Like to be presented to the Regent, too. Believe he's still down there."

"Yes, and a pretty time I should have of it, looking after her!" retorted Sherry scornfully. "You know very well she's no more fitted to keep the line amongst the set of fellows she'd meet there than a half-fledged chicken!"

"Very true," said Mr. Ringwood, nodding wisely. "Better go to Leicestershire. Tell you what; give it out you've gone on your honeymoon."

"That's a devilish good notion, Gil!" approved the Viscount. "You'd better come along with us!"

This suggestion took Mr. Ringwood aback, but as it was heartily endorsed by Hero, and as settling-day at Tattersall's had left him without any expectation of being able to meet the more pressing of his obligations in the immediate future, he gratefully accepted the invitation. The reflection that the Dowager Lady Sheringham, with whom he was only too well acquainted, might conceivably take it into her head to summon him to her presence to account for his having aided and abetted her son in his clandestine marriage, also weighed with him, but this circumstance he prudently kept to himself, trusting that his friend, Mr. Fakenham, when the inevitable summons came to him, would not put two and two together, and accuse him of ratting. Experience of Mr. Fakenham's processes of thought seemed to make it reasonably certain that this mathematical exercise lay rather beyond his powers.

CHAPTER 7

The Viscount had not been mistaken in thinking that the letter announcing his marriage to Hero Wantage would have the effect of bringing his Mama hotfoot to London. The news of Hero's mysterious disappearance had naturally reached her some days before the arrival of Sherry's missive: she had, in fact, sustained a morning-call from Mrs. Bagshot, who had enumerated all the kindnesses she had for years shown her ungrateful young relative, and had confided in the bored matron's ear the intelligence that she had always expected the wretched girl to disgrace her. It occurred to neither lady to connect Hero's flight with the recent visit of the Viscount to his home. Not unnaturally, it did not occur to Miss Milborne either. Miss Milborne said roundly that she was sure she did not blame poor little Hero, and only trusted that she had sought refuge with some member of her family who might treat her with more consideration than had ever been shown her in the Bagshot household.

When the Viscount's letter arrived, its effect was stunning. Unable at first to believe the evidence of her eyes, his mother had sat staring at it as one in a trance. As the dreadful tidings penetrated to her intelligence, she gave vent to a shriek which made her brother, who was in the act of mending a pen, cut his finger with his pocket knife. "Read that!" uttered the shattered lady, holding out the letter with a trembling hand. "Read that!"

To say that Mr. Paulett was put out by the news of his nephew's marriage would be grossly to understate his reactions. He had not believed that Sherry would tie himself up in the bonds of matrimony to any other than Miss Milborne, and was almost inclined to think the letter a hoax, designed merely to alarm him. A second perusal of the objectionable letter, however, put his hope to flight. There was, he did not pause to consider why, a ring of the authentic about St. George's, Hanover Square, and more than a ring of the authentic in the information that the family lawyer would shortly be communicating with himself. Mr. Paulett saw the end in sight, and gave a groan. A gleam of hope shot through his despondency; he said: "Hero Wantage? She is a minor—it may yet be put a stop to! She had not the consent of her guardian!"

The dowager rose tottering from her couch. "Desire them to send the carriage round to the door immediately!" she said. "Heaven knows I do not expect the least show of good feeling from Jane Bagshot, who I dare say contrived the whole miserable business, designing woman that she is! but I will leave no stone unturned to rescue my son from so ruinous an entanglement, and I will drive round to call upon her this instant!"

The same post which had brought the Viscount's letter to his mother had also brought one, a much briefer one, to Mrs. Bagshot. The Viscount had enjoyed writing it, and had read it aloud to Hero before fixing the wafer to it.

"Dear Madam," it ran,*"it is my duty to inform you that your cousin, Miss Wantage, has done me the honour to accept my hand in marriage. Should you be wishful of addressing your felicitations to her, a letter to The Viscountess Sheringham, care of Fenton's Hotel will find her. Believe me, etc., Sheringham."*

Mrs. Bagshot, reading with starting eyes this curt note, suffered all the rage and the chagrin the Viscount had desired her to feel when he gleefully penned it. She declared at once that the marriage was illegal, and should be instantly set aside; she said that she had always known Hero to be a minx and a baggage; she said and if Cassy had only made more regular use of the Denmark Lotion she had procured for her to eradicate the spots on her face this would never have happened. Cassy then fell into a fit of hysterics which brought her father into the room to enquire testily what the devil was amiss. Leaving Cassy to her sisters' ministrations, Mrs. Bagshot thrust the Viscount's note into her husband's hands, and commanded him to do something about it at once! Mr. Bagshot, having calmly affixed his spectacles over his ears, read the note with maddening deliberation, and then desired his wife to inform him what she expected him to do about it.

Mrs. Bagshot told him. He heard her out in patient silence, and, when she paused for breath, enunciated one word: "Rubbish!"

She glared at him, quite taken-aback. Perceiving that she was momentarily bereft of speech, Mr. Bagshot said: "Pray, why should you desire to have so advantageous a marriage set aside? I wish you will put yourself to the trouble of considering a little before flying into these odd humours, my dear. To be sure, I do not understand why young Sheringham must needs elope with Hero, for there can have been not the least reason for him to fear that you would not give your consent to the match."

"I?" gasped Mrs. Bagshot. "I consent to that penniless beggar's marrying Sheringham? I would die rather!"

Her husband looked her over coolly. "Indeed! Then no doubt Sheringham knew what he was about when he carried her off in this improper fashion."

"I shall have it put a stop to!"

"You will do no such thing," he replied. "Unless you wish to appear a greater fool than I take you for, you will accept this highly flattering alliance with the appearance at least of complaisance." He added dryly: "I imagine you are not desirous of giving the world cause to say that you are jealous because his lordship would not throw his handkerchief in Cassy's direction. For my part, I am happy to think that Hero, who I have always considered to be a nice little thing, has had the good fortune to become so creditably established."

These words of calm good sense did not fail of their effect. By the time the Dowager Lady Sheringham's landaulet was at the door, Mrs. Bagshot had had time to think the matter over. Nothing would serve to abate the strong sense of chagrin that possessed her, but she was intelligent enough to realize that to attempt to overset the marriage would only serve to make her look extremely foolish.

The dowager, therefore, found Mrs. Bagshot

118

unresponsive. Mrs. Bagshot was certainly much shocked, but although she was lavish in her expressions of sympathy for her dearest Lady Sheringham, she made it quite plain that she had no intention of interfering in the marriage. When Lady Sheringham said that she had quite counted on having that sweet Isabella for her daughter-in-law, the thought crossed her mind that however infuriating it might be to find one's despised poor relation suddenly a great way above one in the social scale, it would not have afforded her the smallest gratification to have seen the Viscount married to Miss Milborne.

As for the Incomparable Isabella herself, the news came to her as an undeniable and not very welcome shock. Sherry was the first of her suitors to have found consolation elsewhere, and she would have been more than human had she not experienced a strong sensation of pique. However, she had a good deal of pride, and was a good-natured girl, and she told Lady Sheringham that she had always known Sherry to be uncommonly fond of Hero, and she was sure she wished them both very happy.

This dignified way of receiving the news met with Mrs. Milborne's shrewd approval. "Very prettily done of you indeed, my love!" she said, as soon as the dowager had left them. "But it is a shocking thing, to be sure! To marry a wretched little nobody like Hero Wantage, without a penny to her name, when the whole town has known him to have been at your feet this age past!"

"You are forgetting, Mama, that he offered for me, and I refused him."

"To be sure you did. I wish you had not been so vehement in your refusal, I must own, my love. It cannot add to your consequence to have him running off straight away to wed another. I dare say he did it from mortification, and I only hope he may not live to rue the day. All things considered, my dear, I think he will return to London. And it will be a good scheme for you to send Hero your felicitations."

"I have the intention of doing so, Mama."

"Viscountess Sheringham!" said Mrs. Milborne, in a disgruntled tone. "Well, I am sure I did not think to see that chit married before you, my love, with all the splendid chances you have had!"

The dowager, meanwhile, had taken the momentous decision of travelling to London, with what purpose she would have been unable to state with any clarity. She said in a vague but impressive way that Anthony must at least listen to the words of his Mother, though upon what grounds she based this conviction no one could imagine. She commanded her brother to escort and support her on her pilgrimage, and set forth in an enormous travelling chariot, attended by her abigail, a coachman, a footman, and outriders, and preceded by a similar (but less magnificent) vehicle, containing her trunks, and as many servants as she considered necessary to ensure her comfort in the house in Grosvenor Square for a few days. This put her in mind of a fresh injury, and she told her brother that she had little doubt that her undutiful son would throw her into the street, and instal his wretched bride in the house his sainted Papa had brought her home to twenty-four years ago. Mr. Paulett, appreciating at least the spirit of this, forbore to remind her that the late Viscount had, in fact, brought her home to Sheringham Place.

But when the afflicted lady reached town, and dispatched a peremptory note to Fenton's Hotel, a civil message was conveyed to her that my Lord Sheringham had gone out of town with his lady. The clerk of Fenton's Hotel obligingly added the information that his lordship could be found at Melton Mowbray.

Herein the Viscount had made a grave mistake. Had he but remained in London, had he but shown a dutiful penitence, had his bride but placed herself in her mother-in-law's hands, craving forgiveness and instruction, that lady might have been brought to realize all the advantages of the marriage, and would have needed little persuasion to sponsor her son's wife into the Polite World. But nothing could have alienated her more than Sherry's craven retreat, which she had no hesitation in ascribing to Hero's influence. That her own conduct over the past ten years might have had something to do with it, she naturally did not consider. She sent first for Prosper Verelst, and upon learning from him that he had had nothing to do with the elopement, but that Gilbert Ringwood and young Ferdy Fakenham knew all about it, she sent for Mr. Ringwood. She parted on very cool terms with her brother-in-law, that gentleman having had the temerity to say that he thought Sherry's bride a pretty little creature, and—with a roll of his eye in the direction of Mr. Paulett—that he was devilish glad to see the boy assume the control of his affairs.

Upon learning that Mr. Ringwood too was out of town, the dowager lost no time in sending a summons to Mr. Ferdy Fakenham. But as she made the mistake of stating her reason for wishing to see him, she defeated her own ends, Mr. Fakeham, with rare presence of mind, instructing his servants to inform her that he was out of town, cancelling all his engagements, and retreating, like a hare startled from its form, to join the bridal couple (and his friend Mr. Ringwood) in Leicestershire.

Baulked of even such minor prey as Ferdy, the dowager lost what little common-sense she possessed, and proceeded to make known her wrongs. They lost nothing in the telling, nor was the injured Mr. Paulett slow to add his mite to the whole. The town began to hum with the story of Sherry's amazing marriage, and the most coldly correct of Almack's patronesses, Mrs. Drummond Burrell, remarked casually to one of her fellow-patronesses, Lady Jersey, that no voucher of admission to that most exclusive of clubs could, of course, be granted to young Lady Sheringham.

"Good gracious, why not?" asked Lady Jersey lightly.

"I have been in Grosvenor Square, visiting Valeria Sheringham."

"Oh, that *tedious* creature!"

Mrs. Burrell smiled slightly. "Very true, but in this instance I believe her to have been shamefully used. That wild young man, Sheringham, has made a shocking mesalliance. To make matters the more unsupportable, he seems actually to have eloped with the young female."

Lady Jersey, who was drinking morning chocolate with her friend, selected an angel-cake from the dish before her, and bit into it. "Yes, I believe he did elope with her," she admitted. Her mischievous smile dawned. "But Prosper Verelst assures me that Sherry otherwise behaved towards the girl with the greatest propriety! Only figure to yourself!—Sherry considering the proprieties!"

"I shall not allow Mr. Verelst to be a judge. Valeria

has told me the whole. The girl is the veriest Nobody—actually a governess, or some such thing!"

"No such thing! She is one of the Wantages, and I am sure nothing could be more respectable. It is by no means a brilliant match, but only such a goose as Valeria Sheringham would make so great a piece of work over it."

Her hostess turned a calm, cold gaze upon her. "Pray, my love, have you met the young person?"

"No, but I have been with Maria Sefton, and she has met her, and what is more, she says she is quite unexceptionable—very young, of course: hardly out of the schoolroom, but unquestionably a lady! You must know that she had been under the guardianship of Mrs. Bagshot—the same who is for ever thrusting her shockingly plain daughters into the arms of all our eligible bachelors!"

"I do not find it a recommendation. Where, pray, did Lady Sefton encounter her?"

"Oh, down at Melton Mowbray! You must know that the Seftons have been staying with Assheton Smith, at Quorndon House. Maria tells me that they were driving out there when they came upon Sherry and his bride. She tells me it was quite pretty to see Sherry—he was teaching her to ride, it seems—taking such pains over the child."

"I imagine he might, since he married her."

"Certainly, but I confess I am agog with curiosity to discover *why* he married her, since we know him to have been a pretender to Miss Milborne's hand not a fortnight ago!"

"It is very true. Lady Sheringham told me that he had actually offered for the Milborne girl, and had been rejected. He married the Nobody from pique.

123

There can be no other explanation."

"Did she tell you that? Upon my word, she is a great fool, then, to be spreading such a story about! I declare it gives me a feeling of strong compassion for the poor little bride, and I shall certainly give her vouchers for Almack's, if Maria Sefton has not already done so!"

"Of couse, if you are to take the girl up, there is no more to be said," shrugged Mrs. Burrell.

Lady Jersey gave a trill of laughter. "What, in granting her vouchers for the club? How absured!"

"I wish you may not be taken in."

"If I am, I shall be in Maria Sefton's company, and I am sure I do not desire to be in better."

"Both Lord and Lady Sefton's good-nature is too well-known to occasion remark. I believe it leads them to bestow their favours indiscriminately rather frequently. Valeria Sheringham assures me the girl is quite *farouche*, no *ton*, no accomplishments, her looks no more than passable, her fortune non-existent."

"It will be time enough to deny her the right to come to Almack's if we find that for once in her life Valeria Sheringham has been speaking the truth."

"Valeria does not advise us to relax our rules in her favour."

Lady Jersey's eyes sparkled. "What, did she say so? Of all the spiteful creatures! No, that is the outside of enough, my dear, and makes me perfectly determined to give the girl a chance to prove herself!"

Mrs. Burrell was silent for a moment. She said presently: "You are very right. We shall see how she conducts herself. It is plain, however, that Sheringham is ashamed to show her in town."

"Nonsense!" replied Lady Jersey. "Prosper Verelst says they have gone upon their honey-moon."

"Into Leicestershire?" said Mrs. Burrell, raising her brows.

"So it seems. The truth is, of course, that Sherry has gone off because he doesn't care to run the gauntlet of Valeria's vapours. He would have done better to have stayed, but it is all of a piece! He is a charming young man, I grant, but the most selfish and careless imaginable. I am sorry for his poor little wife."

CHAPTER 8

Hero would have been astonished, and, indeed, indignant, had she been aware that she was the object of
Lady Jersey's sympathy. For she had never been so
happy in her life. Sherry had been quite right in thinking that his hunting-box at Melton Mowbray would be
just the thing for her. She was delighted with it; and the
happy-go-lucky way of life pursued by Sherry when sojourning there could not but appeal to a young lady
who had been irked all her own short life by shib-
boleths and restrictions.

The hunting-box, which was not large, was kept by a
married couple who, from having had things very
much their own way under their casual master, at first
looked upon Hero with suspicious hostility. But as she
showed no disposition to interfere in the management
of the house, and never dreamed of levelling criticisms
where they would certainly be resented, it was not long
before Goring and his wife accepted her in much the
same spirit as they accepted Mr Ringwood, or any
other of the Viscount's cronies.

It might have been supposed that a very few days

spent at Melton Mowbray at the fag-end of the summer would have sufficed to have sent his lordship hotfoot back to town, but thanks to the amusement afforded him by teaching his wife to ride her mare creditably; taking her to Six Hills, and showing her the pick of the best coverts; initiating her into the mysteries of hazard, faro, deep basset, and several other games of chance; playing picquet with Mr. Ringwood; trying out his young stock; and attending a cock-fight held in the district, he contrived to while away the time very tolerably. Before these simple pursuits had palled upon him, a diversion was created by the arrival in the district of Lord Wrotham, who had come down on a visit to his encumbered estates. Since they were situated only a few miles from Melton, he naturally spent a good deal of his time with his friends, and was delighted to discover in Hero a sympathetic listener. It was not long before he had confided to her his hopeless passion for the Incomparable Isabella, and although an unthinking reference to the complaint which had necessitated the Beauty's withdrawal from the Polite World seriously endangered, for a few moments this promising new friendship, the rift was speedily healed by Hero's assurance that the rash had by no means disfigured Isabella. George rode with Hero to Wartnaby Stone-pits, and, being a very keen rider to hounds was able to forget his troubles in describing some classic runs to Hero, passing strictures on Assheton Smith, who hunted his own hounds, and often drew his coverts so quickly that he drew over his fox, besides failing sometimes to lift his hounds, which, if you wanted runs in Leicestershire, said George, you must do. Hero, fired with the spirit of emulation after listening to George's heroic tales, attempted to jump what George called a regular stitcher, and came to grief. Fortunately she was only bruised by her tumble, but the mare strained a tendon, and Sherry, who had been a helpless spectator of the enterprise, no sooner ascertained that his bride was unhurt than he soundly boxed her ears, and swore he would never bring her out with him again. His two friends, though deprecating this violence, endorsed his strictures, having by this time fallen very much into the way of treating Hero as though she had been one of their own young sisters.

When Mr Fakenham joined the party, his presence was felt to be an advantage, as he was able to make a fourth at whist. Some convivial evenings were spent at the hunting-box, under the auspices of a hostess who, however little she might know of the uses of Polite Society, was learning to admiration how to become excessively popular with a party of young bloods. Formality very soon went by the board; she became Kitten to them all; and so accustomed did they grow to her presence at their sessions that they often forgot that she was in the room at all. But they usually remembered her before the party became too convivial for propriety, and the Viscount would send her up to bed, informing her frankly that they were getting a trifle boosey. Upon one occasion, when he omitted to perform this ritual, she horrified Mr. Ringwood by casting a knowledgeable eye over Mr. Fakenham, and saying innocently: "Must I go now? I think Ferdy is quite disguised, don't you?"

The Viscount shouted with laughter, but Mr. Ringwood not only begged his hostess never to use such vulgar language, but later made representations to Sherry that they really must all of them be careful what they said in front of her.

A letter from Isabella, written from London, and conveying her felicitations to her dearest Hero, had the effect of breaking up the party. George was no sooner apprised of the Beauty's return to the haunts of men than he left the greater part of the business which had brought him into the country undone, and posted back to town with the fiercely expressed intention of thrusting a spoke in his Grace of Severn's wheel. Ferdy and Mr. Ringwood took their departure a few days later, and the hunting-box felt sadly empty. The young couple received a morning-call from kind Lord and Lady Sefton, during the course of which her ladyship promised Hero the entree to Almack's when she should take up her residence in London. Sherry informed his wife that this connaissance was the greatest piece of good luck that could have befallen her, since (although he himself might find such company a trifle flat) there was no doubt that the approval of Lady Sefton would be of the greatest value to a lady making her debut in fashionable circles.

"Ten to one," said Sherry carelessly, "she will have them all leaving their cards in Half Moon Street—Lady Jersey, Lady Cowper, Countess Lieven, Princess Esterhazey, and all their set, you know—and then you will be fixed all right and tight."

By the time Mr. Stoke wrote to apprise him that his new house stood ready to receive him, Sherry had had enough of the country, and not even the annoying intelligence, conveyed to him in a brief scrawl from his uncle Prosper, that his mother was still to be found in Grosvenor Square availed to keep him longer away from the metropolis. He was under the obligation, too, of returning his watch to the Honourable Ferdy, this young gentleman having written to him from London that since this handsome timepiece was missing from his effects he would be glad if his cousin would recover it from his damned Tiger. Why Ferdy's watch should exercise such a fascination over Jason no one knew. The Viscount was extremely incensed over his backsliding, and was not in the least mollified by Jason's tearful explanation that to have the watch within his reach for days together was more than flesh and blood could stand. Matters would have gone ill indeed for Jason had not Hero intervened on his behalf. She had the happy thought of promising to bestow a timepiece upon him as a Christmas gift if he would but refrain, in the interim, from stealing Ferdy's.

"Or anything else!" said Sherry sternly.

Jason sniffed, wiped his nose on his coat sleeve, and promised to behave impeccably. He further pronounced his guv'nor's lady to be bang-up, which piece of elegant language, Sherry assured her, masked a compliment of no mean order.

When the Sheringhams were set down at dusk one evening in Half Moon Street, they found that Mr. Stoke had done his work well. Nothing could have been more charming or more tasteful than the disposition of the furniture in the little house. Hero was enchanted and ran from room to room, exclaiming how well the writing-table looked, how pretty was the wall-paper in the drawing room, how glad she was she had chosen the blue brocade instead of the green, and did not Sherry think that Ferdy had selected precisely the right furniture for his library? Both Ferdy and Mr. Ringwood had called in Half Moon Street earlier in the day, Ferdy to leave a bouquet of flowers with the butler, and Mr. Ringwood a canary in a gilded cage. Hero was so touched by this piece of thoughtfulness that she sat down at the tambour-top writing-table before she had even removed her hat, and dashed off her first note, on the very elegant, gilt-edged paper provided by the competent Mr. Stoke, and had it carried round immediately to Stratton Street by the page-boy.

No such agreeable surprise awaited the master of the house. The imposing knee-hole desk in the room which his wife insisted on calling his library, bore a collection of staggering bills. The Viscount was a trifle startled, not so much by his own expenditure as by Hero's. He could not for the life of him see how she could have contrived to squander such sums merely upon furniture, but he handsomely made up his mind to level no reproach at her. Sundry accounts presented by milliners and mantua-makers made him whistle thoughtfully, but his previous experiences of such establishments precluded his feeling any extraordinary astonishment at the cost of a simple gown, or of a wisp of net and feathers fashioned into the semblance of a hat. He stuffed all the bills into a drawer, resolving to hand them over presently to his man of business for settlement. Anyone having an intimate knowledge of the Viscount's career would have recognized at once that the sobering influence of marriage was already making itself felt, since a month ago he would have consigned them to the fire.

The young couple dined *tete-a-tete* at the fashionable late hour of eight o'clock on their first evening in their new home, sitting opposite one another in their smart dining-room, and waited on by a butler whose spare frame and pallid countenance seemed to indicate that he was of a suitably abstemious character. The dinner, which consisted of a broiled fowl with mushrooms, preceded by a dressed lobster and a

132

delicacy of cockscombs served in a wine-sauce, and followed by a pupton of pears, in the old style, and a trifle, was excellently cooked, and earned the Viscount's praise. Hero, who had already been obliged to receive a stately visit from the superior being who presided over the kitchen, said in a very housewifely way that she was glad they had decided to take away the old fireplace from the kitchen, and to instal a closed stove in its place.

The Viscount rather spoiled the effect of this utterance by grinning across the table at her, and demanding what the devil she knew about kitchen stoves. Hero twinkled merrily back at him, and replied: "Well, not very much, but Mrs. Groombridge says that they are excellent contrivances, and there is a *great* saving of coal."

"Well, that's something, at all events." said Sherry, putting up his glass to inspect the bottle the butler was exhibiting at his elbow. "No, not that. Bring up a bottle of sparkling champagne. You'll like that, Kitten."

As the Viscount liked his wine to be very dry, Hero had to school her features to an expression of appreciation she was some way from feeling. That made his lordship laugh, but he told her that he could not permit her to be everlastingly maudling her inside with such stuff as ratafia, and bade her drink it up like a good girl. "A glass of wine with you, my lady!" he said, raising his glass. "Damme, we must drink to our first home, so we must!"

Under his instruction. Hero very correctly left him at the end of dinner, and withdrew to the drawing-room abovestairs, while he drank his port in solitary state. Since this was dull work, he soon joined her, dropping into one of the straw-coloured chairs, and stretching out his long legs towards the grate, where a small fire had been kindled, and saying, with a yawn, that there was a deal to be said for a fellow's getting married after all.

"At least," he added, "there would be, if you hadn't bought such an uncomfortable set of chairs! What the deuce was Ferdy about to countenance it?"

"Oh, don't you remember, Sherry? We bought these together, on that first day, when you went with me to choose our furniture."

"Good God, I must have been foxed!"

"Well, perhaps you are sitting in the wrong one," said Hero. "I wish you will try this one instead: indeed, it is very comfortable!"

The Viscount made no objection to changing places with her, and as he pronounced this second chair to be tolerably easy, she was perfectly satisfied.

Before the Viscount had had time to find an evening spent at his own fireside very flat, a knock sounded on the street door, and in a few minutes Sir Montagu Revesby's card was brought up to Sherry. He commanded Groombridge to beg this late caller to step upstairs, and himself went out on to the landing to welcome him.

Sir Montagu came in, full of graceful apologies for intruding upon her ladyship so soon after her arrival in town. He had been imperfectly informed: would have left his card at the house that morning; trusted she would forgive such informality: he had come only to discover if Sherry liked to accompany him to a little meeting of a few friends in a house near-by.

"Brockenhurst begged I would prevail upon you to join us, if you should have returned to London, my dear Sherry, but I fear"—with a bow, and one of his ironic smiles in Hero's direction—"I have come on a fruitless errand."

"Oh, lord, no, nothing of the sort!" Sherry said. "You won't mind my leaving you, will you, Kitten?"

Mindful of his warning that once they were settled in London they would not interfere with each other's pursuits, Hero swallowed her disappointment, and assured him that she was on the point of retiring to bed.

"That's right," said his lordship. "I knew you would be tired after the journey." He picked up one of her hands, dropped a kiss on her wrist, and took himself off with Sir Montagu.

Hero lifted her wrist to her cheek, and held it there for some moments after he had gone. She felt a strong inclination to cry, and concluded that she must indeed be tired, since she knew very well that she had nothing whatsoever to cry about, but, on the contrary, everything in the world to make her happy. On this elevating thought she retired to her bedchamber, and talked in a very cheerful way to her abigail while she was undressed and put to bed.

Sherry, who did not return to the house until the small hours put in no appearance at the breakfast-table. When he did emerge from his bedchamber, it was past eleven o'clock, and not only was he clad in a dressing-gown, but he still looked remarkably heavy eyed. He said simply that they had had a pretty batch of it at Brockenhurst's, and also that he was dipped a little at hazard. Altogether, Hero did not think that it would be wise to remind him that they had planned to wait upon his mother at noon. He retired again to his room, irritably demanding why the devil Bootle had not brought up the water for his shave; and Hero was just deciding that it would be pleasant to go for an airing in

Hyde Park in her barouche, when the first of her morning callers knocked on the door.

It was Mrs. Bagshot, bringing her two elder daughters in her train. She came sailing into the drawing-room almost before Groombridge had had time to announce her, paused in the middle of the floor, and, after throwing an appraising glance round, uttered the one word: "Well!"

Hero rose from her chair in some confusion, and came forward, blushing faintly, and stammering: "C-cousin J-Jane! C-Cassy! Eudora! How do you do?"

"I wonder you can look me in the face!" said Mrs. Bagshot. Her eyes ran over Hero's high-necked gown of worked French muslin, with its double flounce and rows of tucks. "Upon my word!" she said. "I dare say you have never worn such a dress in your life!"

This was an unfortunate observation, since it gave Hero the opportunity to retort: "You must know that I have not, cousin!"

"Whatever have you done to your hair?" demanded Cassandra. "You look so strange! I should scarcely have known you."

"It is the very latest fashion," replied Hero. "My maid did it."

Mrs. Bagshot gave a short laugh. "Fine feathers make fine birds! I see that you have set yourself up in the very latest mode. I suppose we shall have you setting up your carriage, and renting your box at the opera, in imitation of your betters. When I consider—However, I did not come to quarrel with you, and heaven knows I am thankful to see you creditably established, even though you may have had to accept an offer made to you in a fit of pique to do it. I am sure it would not surprise me to find that you are now too

136

grand to recognize the humble cousins who gave you a home when you were left destitute upon the world."

"No," said Hero seriously. "Indeed, I am not so ungrateful! And I would be glad to try to find husbands for my cousins, if I could, only Sherry says—" She broke off short, colouring to the roots of her hair, the most comical expression of dismay on her face.

"And pray what may your husband say?" demanded Mrs. Bagshot in menacing accents.

"I've forgotten!" said Hero desperately.

"I abhor prevarication," remarked Eudora. "I am sure you need not fear to repeat what he said, for it does not matter a fig to us what such a rackety young man may say!"

Stung by this criticism of her idol, Hero retorted without hesitation: "Well, he said he wouldn't have you in the house, because he doesn't like you!"

Mrs. Bagshot turned quite purple, and struggled in vain for words. Before she could find any at all adequate to the situation, Hero had said penitently; "Oh, I beg your pardon! But Eudora should not have said that about Sherry! Do, pray, sit down, Cousin Jane, and—and let me ring for Groombridge to bring some fruit, and a glass of wine!"

Mrs. Bagshot coldly refused this offer of refreshment, but she condescended to seat herself on the sofa, remarking as she did so that she was sorry to see that her exalted position had not led Hero to mend her manners. Her daughters wandered about the room, inspecting the furniture, criticizing the colour of the hangings, and wondering how Hero could bear to have a canary deafening her with its odious noise. Hero replied to their strictures and exclamations with what patience she could muster, and tried to counter Mrs. Bagshot's extremely searching questions with dignity and civility.

She was succeeding very well when the door opened to admit Sherry, who came in all unawares, saying: "Here's a damned thing, Kitten! That fool of a man of mine has lost my—"

What Bootle had lost they were not destined to learn, for Sherry, perceiving the morning-callers, broke off in mid-sentence, ejaculated: "My God!" in accents of horror, and retired precipitately.

Hero made a desperate attempt to keep her countenance, failed, and went into a peal of laughter. Her affronted relative rose majestically, and, addressing her daughters, said in a terrible voice: "Come, my loves! It is plain that we are not welcome in your cousin's house."

"Oh, pray do not take a pet, Cousin Jane!" begged Hero. "It—it is just that poor Sherry is not feeling quite the thing to-day! He will be sorry presently, I dare say."

Mrs. Bagshot, however, was adamant, and was in the act of delivering herself of a severe valedictory speech when a welcome diversion was caused by Groombridge's announcing Lord Wrotham.

George came in with his usual impetuosity, and with the inevitable lock of raven hair straying across his romantic brow. He grasped his hostess's hand warmly, saying: "I heard you was come up from the country! How do you do? You look to be in famous shape! What a capital little place you have here! It is just the thing, Kitten!"

"Oh, George, I am so glad to see you!" Hero said. "Oh, do you—are you acquainted with Lord Wrotham, Cousin Jane?"

Mrs. Bagshot bowed, but lost no time in shepherding her daughters out of the room. She was naturally unable to suppose that any man could look upon these damsels without experiencing a start of admiration, and although his lordship had the undoubted advantage of being a peer of the realm it was well known that his pockets were (in vulgar parlance) pretty well to let. She scolded Hero, who escorted her downstairs to the front door, on the impropriety of encouraging familiarity from so unstable a young man, and expressed the pious hope that the oddity of her manners would not be her ruin.

Having seen her relative off the premises, Hero sped upstairs again, and danced into the drawing-room, exclaiming; "Oh, George, I was never so glad to see anyone! She was scolding me dreadfully when you walked in upon us, and I thought she would never go! I don't know where Sherry has hidden himself: only fancy!—he came in here, not having the least notion my cousins were with me, and he cried out *My God!* and ran out of the room! It was the drollest thing! Did you come to find him?"

"No, no—though I shall be happy to see him, of course! I came to pay my respects and to leave my card, and to discover if you would care to watch a balloon ascension at three o'clock?"

Hero was naturally delighted with this proposal, and said there was nothing she would like better. "How kind it is in you to be thinking of me, George! Indeed, I thank you *very* much!"

"No such thing! I assure you——Well, I thought perhaps you might not have witnessed the spectacle. It is an odd circumstance that Miss Milborne has not either. She has a great fancy to see it, only, as it chances, Mrs. Milborne is engaged with some friends, and so the whole project must come to nothing,

139

unless——" a disarmingly ingenuous smile swept across his face—"Oh, hang it, Kitten, the long and the short of it is that if you would but offer to take her up in your carriage, I think Miss Milborne would like it excessively! If you could but persuade Sherry to make one of the party, nothing could be more snug!"

"George, you are the most complete hand!" Hero told him, borrowing from Sherry's vocabulary. "I have a good mind to bring my cousin Cassy instead of Miss Milborne. How confounded you would look!"

"I swear you are the best of good fellows!" George exclaimed. "Well, no! I don't mean that! What am I saying? I declare I am so up in the world to-day—or I shall be, if only you will send a note round to Green Street, to beg Miss Milborne to bear you company!"

"Well, I will," promised Hero, sitting down on the sofa, and patting the place beside her invitingly. "But what has occurred to put you in such spirits? Isabella has not—oh, George, she has not accepted you?"

"No," he said, the sparkle dying out of his expressive eyes. "No, not that, but——Look, Kitten!"

He thrust a hand into his pocket as he spoke, and drew out a small package. This he reverently unwrapped, disclosing a dejected pink rose, which was fast reaching the stage of decomposition.

Hero opened her eyes very wide as she stared at this relic, and then, glancing enquiringly up at George, said in an awed tone; "Did she give it to you, George?"

He nodded, his emotions for the moment making it impossible for him to speak. When he had cleared his throat, he said; "She was wearing a posy of them, pinned to her dress, last night. This one fell into her lap, and Severn——" he ground his teeth at the recollection—"Severn had the temerity to demand it of

140

her! As though he had but to ask, and she must submit to his wishes! I was within an ace of calling him to account, I can tell you! I must have done so, had not Miss Melborne given him such a set-down as—Kitten, she held it out to me, and said with the kindest smile, the most speaking expression in those glorious eyes, that I should have her rose, if I cared to take it! If I cared to! I slept with it beneath my pillow, and I shall carry it next my heart until I die!" He looked imploringly at Hero, and said with an effort: "She could not have done so had she not felt a preference—could she?"

"Oh no, indeed she could not!" Hero cried. "It must be certain! It is the most touching thing I ever heard! Oh, Sherry, is that you? Do, pray, come in, and see what Isabella has bestowed upon dear George!"

"Hallo, George!" said the Viscount, strolling across the room. "My God, Kitten, what a scrape you put me into just now!"

She gave an involuntary giggle. "I know. And if you could but have seen your own face! But never mind that now! Only look!"

The Viscount eyed the rose disparagingly. "Where's the sense in keeping that?" he asked. "It's dead. I see nothing at all wonderful in it."

"But, Sherry, you do not understand! Isabella gave it to George last night!"

"Did she, by God?" said Sherry incorrigibly. "Lord, what a flirt the girl is!"

Lord Wrotham sprang to his feet, quick rage kindling in his breast. Hero, well accustomed by this time to his starts, shrieked: "George, if you call Sherry out, I won't invite Isabella to go with us!"

His lordship paused, clenching his fists. "Sherry!" he

said menacingly, "unsay those words!"

"Damned if I will!" responded Sherry. "You can't call me out in my own house. Devilish bad *ton!* Besides, of course the Incomparable is a flirt! Nothing in that! I'd lay a monkey she did it to make Severn jealous. Don't tell me he wasn't there! You can't humbug me, my boy!"

"If I thought that———!" said George, thrusting back the lock of hair from his brow.

"She would not be so cruel!" said Hero indignantly. "Don't heed him, George!"

"If I thought it," George said, "if I believed that she was trifling with me so heartlessly, I would—I would grind the rose under my heel!"

"No need to make a damned mess on our new carpet," said Sherry. "Throw it out of the window!"

"Sherry, I don't know how you can be so unfeeling!" Hero said reproachfully.

"Well, dash it, what *is* he to do with it?" asked Sherry. "A fellow can't carry a lot of withered rose-leaves about in his pocket! Just look at the thing already!"

George appeared to be a little daunted by this point of view. "I suppose it will fall to pieces," he said disconsolately.

"No, no, there is not the least need!" Hero assured him. "You must press it between the leaves of a book, and then it will keep its shape. Sherry, George desires us to go with him to witness a balloon ascension! We are to take Isabella along with us, if she cares to come. You will like to go, will you not?"

"What, to watch a curst balloon go up?" exclaimed Sherry. "No, I wouldn't!"

"But Sherry, if you will not accompany us I do not

know how we are to contrive!"

"Well, I'll be damned if I'll make such a cake of myself! If George wants to look like a Johnny Raw he may do so, but he ain't going to drag me into it!"

Hero was about to argue the point when she suddenly recollected that Sherry too had been one of the Incomparable's suitors. She thought that perhaps he was trying to mask a natural disinclination to spend a whole afternoon in the company of the unattainable, and tactfully forbore to press him any farther. She suggested to George that they should invite Mr. Fakenham to make a fourth in their party. George agreed to this, but when he had had a moment in which to think it over he remembered that Ferdy also formed one of Miss Milborne's court, and he said that he fancied balloons were not much in Ferdy's line, and would instead bring his friend, Algernon Gumley, to share in the treat. The Viscount let out a most unseemly crack of laughter at this, but refused to explain why. George informed Hero, a trifle stiffly, that she would find Mr. Gumley a very good-humoured fellow, and took himself off, carefully carrying his rose with him.

Hero sat down at the writing-table to compose a suitable note to Isabella. Sherry said; "What a fellow George is! Dead roses and balloon ascensions! You wouldn't think it, but he used to be as game a man as you would meet in a twelve-months before he clapped eyes on Isabella. I'll swear she means to have Severn, too—if she can get him! They're laying bets against it at the clubs, you know."

"Oh, Sherry!" Hero said, turning round to look at him. "She could not be so heartless as to bestow a flower upon him if her affections were not seriously engaged!"

143

"Much you know about it!" he responded. "Why, she's the most heartless girl I ever met in my life! Look at the way she treated me!"

"Yes," Hero said, hanging down her head a little. "She was very unkind to you, of course. I am sorry I teased you to go with us this afternoon. I forgot that it must give you pain."

"Give me pain?" repeated Sherry. "Oh—ah! Exactly! Slipped my mind for the moment. Do you mean to be writing letters for ever, or are we to drive round to Grosvenor Square?"

Hero assured him that she would be ready to set forth with him in a quarter of an hour, so he went off to send a message to the stables, while she finished her note, and despatched it by the hand of her page.

The visit to the dowager was not a success. She was discovered reclining on a sofa, with the blinds half-lowered and Hervey's *Meditations Among the Tombs* significantly open on her knee. She greeted her daughter-in-law with a visible shudder, and embraced her son with all the tenderness of one conveying speechless sympathy for a victim of fate. A suggestion put forward by Sherry that she might present Hero at Court brought on all her most alarming symptoms. She held out no hope of her health's permitting her to visit the house in Half Moon Street; and a blunt request from Sherry for the family emeralds apparently brought up a series of the most affecting memories, which obliged her to have recourse to her vinaigrette, and to dab at the corners of her perfectly dry eyes.

"But you never wear 'em, ma'am!" Sherry protested. "Dash it, you were always used to say green was not your colour, and you teased my father into giving you the diamond set in their stead! Besides, you know very well they belong to me—have done, ever since my father died!"

"Alas, that you should have so little sensibility!" quavered his parent. "The jewels which your dear papa clasped about my throat when we were first married——"

"No, he didn't," interrupted Sherry. "My grandfather was alive then, and, what's more, my father had the devil of a work to induce my grandmother to give 'em up when the old man died! Yes, and you went into one of your miffs, ma'am, and said she had no right to 'em! Remember it as if it was yesterday."

Perceiving that the widow showed every sign of sinking into a swoon, Hero hastily said that indeed she did not wish to have the emeralds until her mama-in-law was dead. But this turned out to have been an unfortunate remark, as it gave the widow an opportunity of saying that she had no doubt her son and his wife were eagerly awaiting that day. She added that it could not be far distant, and this so much annoyed Sherry that he became quite obstinate about the emeralds, and said that if they were not delivered at his house within a week he should instruct old Ditchling to collect them.

"Perhaps," said the dowager, her colour much heightened, "you would also wish me to send your wife the pearl set and the diamond studs?"

"Yes, by Jupiter, I would!" declared Sherry. "I'm glad you put me in mind of them: they're just the things for Hero!"

"Oh, Sherry, don't please!" whispered Hero.

"Nonsense! The pearls are always handed over to the brides in my family: nothing new in that!" said Sherry briskly. "Come along! If you are to go on this expedition with George, it is time we took our leave!"

The dowager was so overcome by the reflection that she had tumbled into a pit of her own digging that she could barely master her voice sufficiently to bid her visitors farewell. Hero curtsied, as though she had still been a little girl in the schoolroom; the Viscount dropped a chaste salute upon the trembling hand held out to him; and they both withdrew with feelings of great relief at having, as Sherry put it, brushed through the ordeal tolerably well.

A civil note from Isabella, accepting Hero's obliging invitation, was reposing upon the spindle-legged table in the passage which served the house in Half Moon Street as a front hall, and at three o'clock George arrived, with his friend, Mr. Gumley. One glance at this gentleman sufficed to enlighten Hero as to the cause of Sherry's rude laughter: he had plainly been chosen for his lack of address, and palpable terror of the female sex. He was a plain young man, and although George assured Hero, in an under-voice, that when he overcame his shyness he could be perfectly conversable, he stammered so much that whenever he made a remark, which was not often, it was even more painful for his listeners than for himself. However, he appeared to derive deep, if silent, satisfaction from the spectacle he had been brought to witness, and managed to tell Hero, when they finally parted company, that he had enjoyed himself excessively.

Hero, although she was naturally interested in the first balloon she had ever seen, did not spend an afternoon of unmixed enjoyment. For this the behaviour of Miss Milborne was to blame. Nothing could have been more affectionate than Miss Milborne's manner towards her hostess, and nothing more wayward than her behaviour towards her maddened lover. Hero was

146

unable to acquit her of coquetry, and was indeed quite shocked to see how she would blow first hot and then cold upon the unfortunate Lord Wrotham. Whether she regretted having given him as much encouragement as lay in a rose dropped from her corsage, or whether she resented the introduction into the party of so unprepossessing a gentleman as Mr. Gumley, no one could tell, but although she relented towards him from time to time, even allowing her hand to rest in his for a moment longer than was necessary when he handed her down from the barouche, she was for the most part a little pettish in her manner, and made it plain that he could no nothing to please her. Hero, who had a warm affection for George, could not refrain once from looking at her in a very speaking way, but the Beauty seemed not to notice the reproach in her old friend's eyes. She launched into a sprightly description of a masquerade she had attended a week earlier, and although Hero might be extremely young and unversed in the ways of spoiled beauties, she could not but recognize that Miss Milborne's reason for introducing this topic lay in the circumstance of her having been gallanted to this party by his Grace of Severn.

It was no wonder, Hero thought, that George should look worn and stormy at the end of the expedition. She was impelled to clasp his hand between both of hers when he left her at the door, and to say shyly: "Don't mind her, dear George! I dare say she may have had the headache."

He flushed, muttered something inarticulate, and strode off down the street. Hero was left to reflect that perhaps her adored Sherry was not so much to be pitied as she had supposed.

CHAPTER 9

During the course of the next few weeks, a number of
persons left cards in Half Moon Street, the ubiquitous
Mr. Stoke having obtained the Viscount's leave to in-
sert into the society column of the *Morning Post* a
notice informing the Polite World that Lord and Lady
Sheringham were residing at this address. The more elderly of the callers came because they felt it to be their
duty to pay their respects to Sherry's wife. It was hardly
to be expected that matrons with hopeful young
families ranging from University to nursery ages would
concern themselves much over a bride of seventeen;
and as there was no matron of consequence whose
business it was to launch Hero into the most correct society, it was natural that such friendships as she made
were with ladies of a younger and, for the most part,
more dashing set.

One of her earliest visitors was Mrs. Hoby, a smart,
lively young woman who announced herself to be a distant cousin of Hero's, and almost overwhelmed her
with protestations and attentions. She was the wife of
an Irishman who, being heir to a respectable property,

was at present living precariously on eight hundred a year and the expectancy. She confessed that she had not known of Hero's existence until the announcement of her marriage had appeared in the press, but upon discovering that she had a cousin who was actually the daughter of dear Cousin Geoffrey she had lost no time in coming to visit her. One swift glance having informed her that her new-found relative was extremely young and inexperienced, she engaged herself to take her under her wing. That the protection of a flighty young woman, living upon the fringes of society, could not add to her consequence Hero was not in a position to know, and she had no hesitation in accepting an invitation to make one of an evening party at the Pantheon, once Mrs. Hoby had laughed indulgently at the notion that she could not go without Sherry to escort her.

"Oh, my dear Lady Sheringham, I assure you it is quite the establish mode! I do not scruple to tell you—for I perceive how strange you are to this frippery life we all lead in London!—that to be seen for ever with one's husband in one's train will not do at all! No, positively, it would be to conduct yourself like a dowd, and *that* I can see at a glance you are far from being!"

Since Sherry had told her very much the same thing, Hero was perfectly ready to accept this dictum, and to consider herself uncommonly fortunate when she learned that Sherry was willing to go with her to Almack's Assembly Rooms.

"I fancy I had best take you there myself," Sherry said, with the air of one having a nice regard to his obligations. "Mind you, it ain't in my line, but the patronesses are so deuced starchy I dare say it will be more comfortable for you if I go with you, at any rate the first time. Ten to one you won't care for it; devilish slow, I warn you!"

He raised no objection to her new friendship; he had not heard of Mrs. Hoby before, but if she was one of Hero's cousins he had no doubt of her being an acceptable acquaintance; in fact, he was glad to find that she was beginning to make friends of her own, since his own engagements prevented him from being with her as much as he had feared she might expect. These engagments seemed to take his lordship rather frequently to certain discreet establishments in Pall Mall and Pickering Place, generally in the company of Sir Montagu Revesby, whose chosen mission in life appeared to some older heads to be to introduce young men of fortune to such gaming-houses as could be expected to relieve them of their wealth in the least possible space of time. His address, his decided air of fashion, had gained him the entree into all but the most exclusive circles; and there was little doubt that he exercised a considerable degree of charm over his young friends. Monty, with his worldly wisdom, his caressing manner towards his favourites, was, they said, a regular top-sawyer, a nonpareil, a knowing 'un. The older generation of dandies who sat at Olympian aloofness in the Bow window at White's, refusing to acknowledge salutations from the street, might lift supercilious eyebrows at Sir Montagu, but their indolent disapproval was not likely to weigh with youthful bloods bent on kicking up what larks they could, and already beginning to think men like Worcester, and Alvanley, and "King" Allen old stagers. The ladies, too, were not impervious to Sir Montagu's charm, and there were few who were not secretly a little flattered if he appeared to pay them distinguishing attentions. For he was by no means one of those who dangled at the ladies' apron-strings. Always civil, there was a light, faintly amused note in his soft voice, even when he was paying a handsome compliment, and this could not but be provocative to the fair sex, not one of whom could as yet plume herself on having added him to her list of conquests. He had certainly shown himself to be an admirer of the famous Miss Milborne's beauty, but Miss Milborne was not quite sure that his manner towards her was entirely free from mockery. This circumstance naturally aroused the interest of one who was accustomed to receive whole-hearted homage, and whenever he presented himself before her, or appeared in a house where she was a fellow-guest, she found herself to be a great deal more conscious of his presence than she liked.

His charm failed to captivate one lady at least. Hero could not like him. She knew it to be her duty to find Sherry's friends all that was amiable, and she made every effort to overcome her repugnance. But it was too often Revesby, as on that first evening in Half Moon Street, who took Sherry from her side. Ferdy's strictures, too, lingered in her memory, and were reinforced by a tactful hint from her kind patroness, Lady Sefton, that it would be well to wean Sherry from the company of his *ame damnee*. She did not think that she could bring herself to explain to Lady Sefton that she and Sherry had agreed not to interfere in each other's lives, for some instinct warned her that her ladyship would not approve of this tolerance. Sir Montagu came once or twice to dine in Half Moon Street, and she was a kind and considerate hostess, concealing the scarcely recognized jealousy that rose in her heart when she saw the influence this assured, smiling man exercised over the volatile Viscount. But if Sir Montagu made one of the convivial little card-parties held in Sherry's library, Hero withdrew after dinner, in a very correct way, and did not reappear. It was only when the guests were Mr. Ringwood, Ferdy, and his brother Marmaduke, and Lord Wrotham, that conventionality went by the board and the hostess, as at Melton, curled herself up in a large chair and interestedly watched the play.

She herself was beginning to go to quite a number of card-parties. From a sedate pool of quadrille or one of commerce, it was no great step to the headier excitements of loo, faro, and whist. Mrs. Hoby was very fond of gaming, and Hero was perfectly ready to spend an evening in her smart little house off Park Lane, putting into rather inexpert practice all she had learned from Sherry. She lost more than she won, but the allowance which Sherry, under Mr. Stoke's advice, made her seemed so handsome that there could be little point in considering a few losses at cards.

Mr. Ringwood had been as good as his word in teaching her how to drive her phaeton, and as she discovered an aptitude in herself for handling the ribbons it was not long before she was to be seen driving in dashing style through Hyde Park at the fashionable hour of the promenade. This was quite unexceptionable, and was applauded by the Viscount, since it brought his Hero to the notice of the Polite World, and made her appear to advantage. She sometimes took Isabella up with her, but the Beauty was a trifle nervous of being perched up behind a very high-stepping horse, and had no great confidence in her friend's mastery over this animal. She perceived that the new Viscountess was bent on making a stir in the world and could not help envying her her position, and her freedom from the shackles that hampered a single lady. Sometimes she felt a little jealous of Hero's undoubted popularity with Sherry's friends, but she was generally able to comfort herself with the reflection that they treated her with a camaraderie which seemed to preclude the sort of devotion she herself inspired in male breasts. His Grace of Severn, who was slightly pompous, gave it as his opinion that Hero was inclined to be fast, and never accorded her more than a common bow in passing, a circumstance which Miss Milborne tried hard not be glad of.

The visit to Almack's was, as far as Hero was concerned, one of unmixed contentment. She thought that everyone was very kind, scarcely noticed the cold propriety of Mrs. Drummond Burrell's manners, or the critical stare of Princess Esterhazy. She could not but be happy with her hand in Sherry's arm, and if he found an evening spent where dancing and not cards was the order of the day somewhat flat, he was so well-pleased with the reception accorded his bride that he even forebore to comment unfavourably to her on the nature of the refreshments. He magnanimously stayed thoughout the proceedings, bore his part in several of the dances, presented Hero to all the most influential persons present, and generally behaved in an exemplary fashion. On their way home, however, he said that he would take her to something a little more amusing than one of these assemblies, and see how she liked it. She did not think that she could like anything as well, but she was ready to go anywhere with him, and set forth three or four days later to a masquerade at Covent Garden with every expectation of enjoyment.

And indeed it was, as he had promised, a most entertaining evening, though of a very different character from the sedate assembly at Almack's. They went masked, and found a vast rout of people of all sorts and conditions in the Opera House, making a good deal of noise, and apparently enjoying themselves hugely. Sherry had taken one of the lower boxes for the evening, and after he had danced once or twice with his wife, he led her to the box to partake of a varied supper there, washed down with iced champagne punch. While they sat over this, the Viscount, rather forgetful of his company, quizzed any woman who took his wandering fancy, levelled his eye-glass at any well-turned ankle, and laughed with his wife over several of the couples within their range of vision. Hero had no objection to any of this, even pointing out good ankles or particularly neat figures to Sherry, speculating on the identity of various persons, and interestedly learning from her incorrigible husband the signs by which she would in future be able to recognize what he gracefully termed "a bit of muslin."

One of these bits of muslin, who had been watching their box for some time, presently took occasion to stroll past it, with such a provocative glance over her shoulder, such an alluring swing of her hips that no gentlemen of the Viscount's mettle could withstand the challenge. "I fancy I know that little love-bird!" he exclaimed. "I must discover if she is not Flyaway Nancy, for I'll lay you a monkey she is, the saucy little piece!"

With this, he abruptly left Hero's side to pursue the alluring siren through the press of persons on the floor of the vast house. Hero thought this a very good joke, and sat watching his audacious advances to the suddenly coy damsel, her eyes dancing through the slits of her mask.

All at once she found that she was no longer alone in the box, a masked stranger having entered by the simple expedient of climbing over the low partition that railed it off from the floor. She turned in surprise as an arch male voice said in her ear: "All by yourself, my dear?"

"Yes. Who are you?" asked Hero innocently.

"Another lonely soul!" responded the visitor, seating himself unasked in Sherry's vacant chair and laying an arm along the back of hers. "Take pity on me, pretty stranger!"

Hero had at first imagined that the intruder must be someone with whom she was acquainted, but his voice was quite unknown to her, and she did not at all relish the familiarity of his manners. She said reasonably: "You cannot know whether I am pretty or not, sir, and I am perfectly certain that you have not been introduced to me. Please go away!"

He laughed at this. "Why, what a prudish little puss! Shall I make myself known to you in form? And if I do, will you tell me what name I may call you by?"

"No, I won't," said Hero bluntly. "And I don't in the least desire to know yours! Go away!"

"Naughty puss to show her claws!" chided her tormentor. "Now, why can't I please you, I wonder? I am sure I shall be pleased with you—when I see you!"

"You will not see me, and if you don't immediately leave my box I shall!" said Hero, sitting very straight in her chair and flushing under her mask.

He slid an arm round her shoulders. "No, no, I am persuaded you won't deny me a sight of your charms!" he said, fumbling with his free hand at the strings of her mask.

Hero gave an outraged little cry, and struggled to

thrust him off. The Viscount, who was attempting much the same thing as the intrusive stranger, chanced at that moment to glance in the direction of his box. An oath escaped him; the astonished lady who had been trying very half-heartedly to repulse him found herself suddenly free, and watched in some dudgeon his hasty and impetuous descent on his box. He vaulted lightly over the partition, plucked the enterprising city buck from his chair, and floored him with what he himself would have called a facer.

"Oh, thank you, Sherry!" gasped Hero. "I can't think who he is, but he is a most odious person, and he seems to fancy that I am a bit of muslin! I am so glad you came back!"

This slight fracas had naturally attracted a good deal of attention from the near-by loungers. "Damn!" said Sherry, perceiving this. "I'm sorry, Kitten: it was all my fault! Get out of my box, you, if you don't wish to be thrown out on your—on your ear!"

The city buck, having picked himself up, and had time to measure the size and style of his assailant, muttered something that might have been an apology, and slid out by way of the door, leaving a front tooth on the floor of the box. Sherry sat down in his chair again, rubbing his knuckles. "Broken my hand on his bone-box," he said cheerfully. "Don't pay any heed to those gaping gudgeons, Kitten! I oughtn't to have left you. Keep on forgetting I'm a married man! He didn't hurt you, did he?"

"Oh no!" responded Hero. "I think he was a trifle foxed. He only wanted to see my face but I didn't at all see why he should. Is that a trifle? Please, I would like some. And perhaps a little more of this nice cold drink. Was it Flyaway Nancy?"

"Kitten," said the Viscount warmly, "you're the best wife I ever thought to have, 'pon my soul you are! Here's to you, brat!"

"Well, I am sure you are quite the best husband, Sherry," said Hero, turning pink with pleasure.

"I'm not," said his lordship, with unwonted humility. "And nine women out of ten would be swooning all over the box after what happened, and reproaching me all the way home! I'll tell you what: I'm glad I married you. It wasn't what I set out to do, but it answers famously. I thought it would."

"Oh, Sherry!" sighed Hero, deeply moved.

He refilled her glass. "I couldn't have brought the Incomparable to a Covent Garden Masquerade, that's certain," he observed. "Come to think of it, I suppose I ought not to have brought you either."

"What, just because that stupid creature tried to take my mask off? What stuff, Sherry! I am enjoying myself excessively!"

"You're a good girl," he informed her. "Dashed if I don't rent a box at the opera for you after all!"

This generous concession cast Hero into gratified transports, but, as ill-fortune would have it, was the cause of a speedy fall from favour in her husband's eyes. The box acquired through the kind offices of Lady Sefton, Hero lost no time in putting in an appearance at the Italian Opera. She bought a new dress for the occasion, and, the dowager having reluctantly disgorged the family jewels, wore the pearl set, which included a very pretty tiara. Having persuaded Sherry to make one of the opera party, she invited Mr. Ringwood and Mrs. Hoby to join them.

Nothing could have been more auspicious than the start of the evening. The Viscount was pleased to see his bride in such looks; and Hero was always happy to have him at her side. In addition to this felicity, she had all the comfort of being able to bow and wave to acquaintances in other parts of the house, for thanks to several parties, assemblies, and morning calls, she was now in a fair way towards knowing a great many of the people who made up the world of fashion. This was certainly an advantage, and she could not help contrasting her appearance to-night with the one she had made on the first night of her marriage, when she had not been able to recognize one face in the whole of the audience. She was pleased to have Mr. Ringwood seated beside her, for she felt him to be quite one of her best friends; and judging from his frequent bursts of laughter, and a certain bright look in his angelic blue eyes, her cousin was contriving to keep Sherry well amused.

It was during the ballet that the unfortunate incident occurred. Absorbed in the first display of dancing she had seen, Hero sat leaning a little forward in the box, her eyes taking in every detail of what was going on behind the footlights. They did not fail to mark the pronounced attention being paid to her box by a neat little dancer with a roguish twinkle in her eyes, and a dimple that peeped beside her inviting mouth. Forgetting her surroundings, and Sherry's stern reminders to her to guard her unwary tongue, she turned impulsively towards him, and said in the most innocent way across Mr. Ringwood; "Oh, Sherry, is *that* your opera-dancer?"

The instant the words had left her lips she could have bitten her tongue out, for Sherry not only flushed scarlet, but shot her such a kindling look as made her

159

quake in her little satin sandals. A stifled giggle from Mrs. Hoby, who put up her fan to hide her face, made matters worse.

It was left to Mr. Ringwood to come to the rescue. He saw his friend's discomfiture, the bride's dismayed expression, and he rose nobly to the occasion. "No," he said, with beautiful simplicity. "Sherry, don't admire her dancing as much as the dark one's, on the right."

The Viscount was visibly lost in wonder at such ready address in one whom he had not been used to think quick-witted; Hero, still covered in confusion, slid a grateful hand into one of Mr. Ringwood's and clutched it eloquently, saying in a subdued tone: "Yes, that is what I meant, Gil!"

During the interval, when they repaired to the saloon for refreshments, the Viscount bore Mrs. Hoby off without so much as glancing at his wife. Mr. Ringwood procured her a glass of lemonade, and would have struggled to make polite conversation had she not interrupted him, saying with the devastating candour which characterized her: "Gill, I don't know how I came to say it! He is very angry with me, isn't he?"

"No need to refine too much upon it," said Mr. Ringwood kindly. "Dare say he'll have forgotten about it by the end of the evening. Never one to take a miff, Sherry!"

"I forgot that we were not alone," said Hero unhappily. "My wretched tongue! If only my cousin had not been present!"

"Yes, but, Kitten!" expostulated Mr. Ringwood, "you ought not to know anything about Sherry's well, what I mean is——"

"I know," Hero said. "Bit of muslin."

Mr. Ringwood choked over his lemonade. "No, I

don't! No, really, Kitten, you must not say such things!"

"Love-bird," Hero corrected herself docilely.

Mr. Ringwood regarded her in considerable perturbation. "You know what it is, Kitten: if you use expressions like that in company you'll set up the backs of people, and find yourself all to pieces. You will indeed! Sherry has no business to talk as he must in front of you!"

"It isn't Sherry's fault!" said Hero, firing up in defence of her free-spoken husband. "He is for ever telling me what I must not say! The thing is that I don't perfectly remember what I may say, and what I may not. I dare say I ought not to call that dancer a fancy-piece either?"

"Upon no account in the world!" Mr. Ringwood said emphatically.

"Well, I must say I think it is very hard. What may I call her, Gil?"

"Nothing at all! Ladies know nothing of such things."

"Yes, they do. Why, it was my cousin Cassy who first told me about Sherry's opera-dancer, so that just shows how mistaken you are!"

"Well, they pretend they do not, at all events!" said Mr. Ringwood desperately.

"Oh, do they? But Sherry told me himself that everyone has an opera-dancer, or something of the sort, and there is nothing in it. Gil, have you——"

"No!" said Mr. Ringwood, with more haste than civility.

"Oh!" said Hero, digesting this. She raised her eyes to his face and heaved a tiny sigh. "I am *not* a prude, Gil."

"No," agreed Mr. Ringwood feelingly.

"And I am not going to be missish, for my cousin says there is nothing gentlemen dislike more. But I cannot help wishing—a *very* little—that Sherry had not an open-dancer either."

Mr. Ringwood made an inarticulate sound in his throat and took his embarrassingly outspoken charge back to her box. Here they were joined in a few moments by the Viscount and Mrs. Hoby, and as the curtain went up almost immediately, there was no opportunity for any further confidences.

The whole party left the Opera House in the Sheringham's barouche, Mrs. Hoby maintaining a sprightly flow of small-talk until she was set down at her own door. Mr. Ringwood went on to Half Moon Street with the Sheringhams, and cravenly refusing an invitation to enter the house with them, parted from them on the doorstep and walked the remainder of the way to his lodging. It went to his heart to ignore the pleading tug Hero gave his sleeve, but he was of the decided opinion that he would make a very uncomfortable third in the quarrel that was obviously brewing.

The door being opened to the returning couple by the butler, Hero, after one surreptitious glance at his lordship's ominous face, said: "I am so tired! I think I will go straight up to my room."

"Send your abigail to bed!" returned his lordship. "I want a word with you in private."

The agitating prospect of a word alone with a husband who was looking like a thunder-cloud made Hero feel quite sick with apprehension. She would have liked to have kept the abigail at her side, but as it seemed more than probable that Sherry would order the woman out of the room if he found her there when he came up, she dared not do it.

He entered without ceremony not five minutes after the door had closed behind the abigail. Hero had just locked the pearl set away in her jewel-case, and without these gauds she looked much younger, in fact, so like the tiresome little girl the Viscount had bullied in his schooldays, that he straightway forgot the dignified speech he had been preparing all the way home from the Opera House, and strode across the room to her, seized her by the shoulders, and shook her unmercifully. "You abominable little wretch, how dared you?" he demanded wrathfully. "Didn't I tell you—didn't I warn you to guard that damned, indiscreet tongue of yours? '*Ah, Sherry, is* that *your opera-dancer?*' No, it was *not* my opera-dancer, and you may take *that* with my compliments!"

Tears started to Hero's eyes. Released, she pressed a hand to one tingling cheek, and quavered; "Oh, Sherry, don't! I didn't mean to say it! I forgot we were not alone!"

"If you had the smallest elegance of mind," said his lordship furiously, "it would not have entered your head to have said it!"

"Well, but, Sherry, she did so look at you, and smile, that I could not but wonder. . . . But I quite see that I should not have said a word about it, and I am very sorry, and I will never do so again."

"It will be better for you if you do not!" retorted her implacable spouse. "If I know anything of females, that cousin of yours will spread it all over town in a week—or she would if she moved in the first circles, which she don't! And that's another thing! I do not know how you come to have a cousin of such bad *ton*, but I can tell you that if you mean to be seen for ever in her company it will not do!"

Stung by the injustice of this, Hero retorted: "It was you who said that I was fortunate in having a relative in town! You said that there could not be the least objection to my visiting her!"

"I had not spent an evening in her company when I said that—*if* I said that!" replied Sherry grimly.

"It seemed to me that you were very well amused by her!" Hero flung at him. "I am sure you laughed enough at the things she was saying to you!"

"Well, I won't have you jauntering about with her any more!" said Sherry, in a very imperious style. "Mind that!"

"I shan't!" promptly replied Hero, losing her temper. "I shall make a friend of anyone I choose, and I shall go where I choose, and I shall do what I choose, and I shall——"

"Will you, by God!" interrupted his lordship, descending purposefully upon her.

Hero retired strategically begind a small table. "Yes, I shall, and it is of no use to say Will I, By God! because it was you who said we would not interfere with one another, you know it was!"

The Viscount halted and stared at her suspiciously. "I said that? I'll swear I never in my life said anything so damned silly!"

"Yes, you did! You said I should not find you the sort of husband for ever kicking up a dust over trifles! You said that as long as I was discreet——"

"Well, you ain't!" said his lordship, pouncing on this. "In fact, there was never anyone less discreet! And as for letting you do precisely as you choose, yes, a pretty piece of business you would make of that, my girl! With no more sense than that damned canary

Gil was fool enough to give you, and no more notion of how to behave in society than Jason has!"

"I don't *steal!*" hotly exclaimed his wife.

"I never said you did!"

"Yes, you did, because you said I was like Jason, and of all the *odious* things to say——"

"I did not say you were like Jason! All I said was that you had no more idea——"

"It is just the same, and it is just like you, Sherry, to say it is all my fault, when it was you who told me about bits of muslin and opera-dancers!"

"How the deuce was I to know that you would blurt it out like a regular hoyden?" demanded his lordship.

"Well, you ought to have known I might very likely do so," Hero said candidly. "You have been acquainted with me for a long time, and I have made you as m-mad as fire with me times out of m-mind, through s-saying things I ought not. And Gil says you have no business to talk as you do in front of me, so it is just as much your fault as mine!"

"Oh!" said his lordship awfully. "So that's it, is it? Not content with putting me to shame in public, you must needs discuss the matter with Gil! Upon my word, Hero, if that don't beat all! I might have guessed how it would be! No doubt you asked him if he had an opera-dancer too!"

"Yes, and he said——"

"What?" thundered the Viscount.

"He said he had not," ended Hero simply.

The Viscount appeared to have some difficulty in getting his breath. "Hero!" he uttered at last. "Have you *no* sense of propriety?"

"Yes, I have!" replied Hero, her bosom swelling. "I have much more than you have, Sherry, for *I* do not have opera-dancers, or get foxed, or——Oh, I wish you will go away! You are unkind, and unforgiving, and unreasonable, and I hate you!"

"I am obliged to you, ma'am!" said the Viscount, seeking refuge in sudden and awe-inspiring dignity."I have not the least notion of inflicting my presence on you another instant, and I will wish you a very goodnight!"

On this grand valediction he stalked from the room, closing the door with unnecessary violence, and leaving his over-wrought wife to the indulgence of a hearty bout of tears.

They met next morning at the breakfast-table, both very conscious of the previous night's quarrel. The Viscount bade Hero a punctilious good-morning, and busied himself in the newspaper. Hero poured out the coffee, and slowly consumed a roll. After a slight pause, she cleared her throat of an unaccountable lump, and said: "Sherry?"

The Viscount lowered the paper. "Well?"

"Will you have a little ham?" said Hero, quite dismayed by his forbidding aspect.

"No, I thank you, I will not."

"Or—or some more coffee?"

"No," said the Viscount, retiring once more into the paper.

Hero fortified herself with a few sips of her own coffee. She tried again. "Sherry?"

"Well, what is it now?"

"N-nothing!" said Hero, on a distinct sob.

"For heaven's sake," said his lordship, "don't start to cry!"

"Perhaps I had best g-go out of the room then,

because I c-can't help crying when you're so dreadfully unkind to me!" offered Hero.

"I'm not unkind to you."

"Oh, Sherry, it is so very like you to say that, when you know very well you have used me quite shockingly!" Hero said, a smile quivering on her lips. "You always did so! But you never called me ma'am in that horrid way before, and I would rather you boxed *both* my ears than did that, indeed I would!"

"Serve you right if I did!" said his lordship, stretching out a hand across the table. "No, really, Kitten, I'm devilish sorry I hurt you! But of all the things to have said———! However, you won't do it again!"

"No, truly I won't!" Hero assured him, tucking her hand in his.

A reluctant grin stole across the Viscount's face. "Lord, I'd have given a monkey to have seen Gil's phiz when you asked him if he had an opera-dancer!" he said.

"Do you think he may not have liked it?" Hero asked anxiously. "He is such a particular friend that I thought I might say what I pleased to him. And I did want to know, because you said that everyone had them, and———"

"Oh, my God, the things I say!" groaned Sherry. "I wish you will forget them, brat! and as for *my* operadancer, that is all over and done with now that I am a sober married man, so let us have no more talk of it!"

"I won't say another word," promised Hero, brightening perceptibly. "Can you not have them if you are married?"

The Viscount laughed and tossed a bill across the

167

table. "Not if you have a wife who spends as much money on a couple of trumpery hats as that!" he replied.

"Oh, dear!" Hero said, conscious-stricken. "Ought I not to have done so? Only, one is the hat I wore when we drove out to Richmond, and you particularly commended it, Sherry!"

"No, no, there's no harm done!" Sherry said, tweaking one of her ringlets. "Extravagant little puss! Wear it again to-day! I'll drive you round the Park, if you care to go with me. I want to try the paces of that pair of chestnuts I bought at Tatt's last week."

"Yes, indeed I do!" Hero said, every cloud vanishing from her horizon.

CHAPTER 10

It was not, of course, to be expected that this was the only tiff which disturbed the peace of the house in Half Moon Street. A young lady, reared in the heart of Kent and uninstructed in the niceties of social etiquette, was to be depended on to make mistakes, and to get into all the minor scrapes which lurked in the path of any high-spirited damsel bent on cutting a dash in the world. The Viscount had been aware when he married his Hero that she knew nothing of the ways of the Polite World, but partly through a misplaced confidence in his mother's willingness to take Hero under her wing and partly through an airy belief that Hero would soon learn the ropes, he had not anticipated that he would be required to play a large role in her debut. The fashionable ladies of his acquaintance were seldom dependent upon their husbands for their amusements, nor had they to be extricated from the consequences of ignorance. The Viscount had, in fact, plunged into matrimony with the light-hearted intention of squiring his wife to a few parties and assemblies, driving her out occasionally in the Park, and being pleasant to her over the breakfast-cups. Such concessions as these to convention would scarcely interfere with the pursuit of his usual amusements. As for Hero, the Viscount was not an ill-natured or an unreasonable young man, and he meant to make no objection to her forming her own court, with its attendant cicisbeos, and even (if discreetly conducted) its amorous intrigues. He supposed that she would hold her card-parties, and possibly fritter her pin-money away at silver-loo; buy herself her favourite number in the lotteries at Richardson's; air all her most expensive toilets in the Park; and generally conduct herself like any other female of birth and fortune. It had never occurred to him that he would return from a shooting-match at Epping to be met by the intelligence that her ladyship would not be at home to dine with him, as she had gone with a party of friends to Margate on the steam-boat; nor that he would stroll in the Royal Saloon, in Piccadilly, in search of such amusement as this Turkish kiosk of a building offered, only to be brought up short by the spectacle of his wife partaking of supper in one of the booths, in company with a very fast young widow, and two of the wildest blades of his acquaintance. The fact that it was just such a party as he himself was in the habit of frequenting in no way mitigated his shocked wrath. The widow, with whom he was well acquainted, hailed him with arch good-humour, and received for her pains a frosty glance, and the very stiffest of bows; the two young blades, recognizing from experience the unmistakable signs of an enraged spouse, suddenly became painstakingly discreet in their dealings with my Lady Sheringham; and only the erring wife herself remained unaffected by his lordship's joining the party. This he did, and those who were used to look upon him as a regular out-and-outer who might be depended on to become the life and soul of a gathering of this order would have been hard put to it to recognize him in the punctilious young gentleman who took his seat at the rustic table, and proceeded to cast a damper over the evening. He removed Hero at the earliest possible moment, and lectured her all the way home on the impropriety of her appearing at such places, and in such company. She was at once contrite, but said that Mrs. Chester, the smart widow, had claimed friendship with him, so that she had supposed that she must be unexceptionable. The Viscount was confounded by this, and ended the discussion by saying hastily that that was neither here nor there, and she was on no account to go to the Royal Saloon again. She promised that she would not, and the affair blew over. But a week later, the Viscount, having been made aware by the veriest accident of his wife's fell intent, was only just in time to prevent her visiting a haunt known as the Peerless Pool. She was perfectly docile as soon as she was assured that no lady of quality would visit the Pool, and made so little lament at having her projected party of pleasure spoilt, that his lordship was touched, and voluntarily sacrificed his own plans to take his unsophisticated bride to Astley's Amphitheatre, where they saw a spectacular piece entitled *Make Way for Liberty*, or *The Flight of the Saracens*. This was an unqualified success, and Sherry, who had thought himself above being pleased by such an airless entertainment, enjoyed himself amazingly, deriving even more amusement from Hero's naive wonder than from the marvels exhibited on the stage.

At her request, he made a list for Hero of the fashionable places it would not be consonant with her dignity for her to be seen at. She conned it carefully, but it proved to be incomplete. The Viscount walked into his house early one afternoon to find a twisted note from his wife awaiting him on the table in the hall. *"Dearest Sherry,"* ran this missive, *"only fancy! Gussie Yarford, Lady Appleby, I mean, came to visit me, and she has a famous scheme for such a frolic! We are to go in our plainest gowns to Bartholomew Fair, and she says there can be not the least objection, for Wilfred Yarford and Sir Matthew Brockenhurst are to go along with us, so I know you will not mind if I am not back in time for dinner."*

The Viscount let a strangled groan, and so far forgot himself as to clutch at his fair locks. His friend, Mr. Ringwood, who had accompanied him home, regarded him with anxious solicitude.

"She's gone off the Bartholomew Fair!" said Sherry, in despairing accents.

Mr. Ringwood thought this over and shook his head. "Can't do that, Sherry. Not the thing at all. Shouldn't allow it."

"How the deuce was I to guess such a motion would ever enter her head? Wild to a fault! Let me but get my hands on Gussie Yarford, that's all! Gussie Yarford! The maddest romp in town! Why, not all her connections can get her a voucher for Almack's, since she started to set the world by the ears! What I have ever done to deserve——However, it ain't her fault: she's no more notion of how to go on than—dash it, than a kitten!"

Mr. Ringwood unravelled this painstakingly, and asked if he was to understand that Hero had gone to Bartholomew Fair with the notorious Lady Appleby?

"Yes, I tell you!" said Sherry impatiently. "Dare say

she thinks it's all right and tight, for you must know that the Yarfords live down in Kent. She has known Gussie any time these nine years—more's the pity!"

Mr. Ringwood looked very serious. "Very bad *ton*, Lady Appleby, Sherry, Appleby, too. Hope he hasn't gone to the Fair with them. Can't be trusted to keep the line at all."

"Oh no!" said Sherry bitterly. "Not Appleby! Kitten knows I can have no objection to this expedition, because, if you please, they are taking Wilfred Yarford and Brockenhurst along with them!"

Mr. Ringwood's jaw dropped, for he had some acquaintance with Lady Appleby's enterprising brother Wilfred, and still more with Sir Matthew Brockenhurst. After a stunned moment, he said with great earnestness: "Sherry, dear old boy! No wish to put you in a pucker, but that fellow Yarford—no, really, Sherry, he's a devilish ugly customer!"

"Lord, don't I know it?" Sherry retorted. "And as for Brockenhurst——Dash it, I suppose I ought never to have had him to dine here! Ten to one Kitten thinks all's right because of it! Well, there's only one thing for it: I must go after them! I'm curst sorry, Gil, but you'll have to find someone to take my place in our little jaunt. Try Ferdy! You see how it is: can't help myself!"

"But, Sherry!" protested Mr. Ringwood. "Can't have considered! Won't find 'em! Not in that vast rout!"

"Well, I can make a devilish good attempt, can't I?" retorted Sherry. He added with some shrewdness: "If I know anything of Kitten, she'll be sitting in Richardson's Great Booth, watching some shocking bad play, or staring her eyes out at a Learned Pig, or some such stuff!"

Upon reflection, Mr. Ringwood was forced to own that this was very likely. Perceiving the frown on his friends's face, he gave a cough, and ventured to say; don't mean an ounce of harm! Only saying to George last night: dear little soul! Not up to snuff at all!"

"No, my God!" agreed the Viscount feelingly.

"Tell you what, Sherry; if I had a wife, which I'm deuced glad I haven't, I'd rather have one like your Kitten than all the Incomparables put together."

"You would?" said Sherry, staring at him.

"I would," said Mr. Ringwood firmly.

"Well, I don't know but what I wouldn't too," said Sherry, cheerfully unconscious of having, by these simple words, bereft his friend of all power of coherent speech.

They left the house together and parted in Piccadilly, Mr. Ringwood wending his steps back to his lodging, and trying all the way to puzzle out what kind of a marriage it was that he had assisted at; and the Viscount going off in a hackney to Smithfield.

The market, which was extremely large, was so crowded with people and booths that the task of discovering one small lady in the seething mob might have daunted a more dogged man than Sherry. He paid off the hackney, and was just wondering whether to repair immediately to the Great Booth or to make a tour of the tents advertising such attractions as a Living Skeleton, a Fireproof Lady, or Mr. Simon Paap, the Celebrated Dutch Dwarf, when, by the most astounding stroke of good fortune, he perceived his wife, making her way through the crowd in his direction, and escorted, not by Mr. Yarford or Sir Matthew Brockenhurst, but by a perfectly unknown citizen, dressed in his Sunday best, and having all the appearance of being a respectable tradesman. The Viscount stood transfixed in amazement, and while he was still staring at the unexpected and quite inexplicable vision of his wife of his bosom tripping along with her hand resting on the arm of an obvious Cit, Hero caught sight of him and gave a squeak of joy. She came hurrying up to him, dragging her cavalier with her, and almost cast herself on his chest, saying: "Oh, Sherry, I am so very glad to see you! Don't scold me! Indeed, I did not know how it would be! As soon as I saw what kind of a place it was, I told Gussie I was sure you would not like me to be here, but she said I was a little goose, and I should be safe with that *odious* Wilfred; and then she went off with Sir Matthew, and I tried—indeed I did, Sherry!—to make Wilfred take me home, but he was quite abominable, and I ran away from him, and he pursued me, and Mr. Tooting—oh, this is Mr. Tooting, Sherry, and he has been so very obliging!—Mr. Tooting knocked him down, and there was such a dreadful rout, you can't conceive!—but all passed off in the end, and Mr. Tooting said he would convey me home in a hackney, and then suddenly I saw you, so he need not be put to so much trouble after all!"

Sherry, detaching the grasp on his coat lapels, firmly tucked his wife's hand in his arm and turned to express the sense of his obligation to the crimson-faced Mr. Tooting. This young gentleman, recognizing at a glance regular top-sawyer in his protegee's husband, was quite overcome, and stuttered out a few disjointed sentences to the effect that he was happy to have been of service. Sherry, who was always very easy with his fellow-men, grasped his reluctant hand, and shook it, said that he was very much obliged to him, and that if he should ever be in a position to serve him in any way, he should be glad to do it. He then enquired after Mr. Yarford, and upon learning precisely how he had been floored, approved heartily of a blow which must, he opined, have been a wisty castor. He said that he himself was considered to be handy with his fives, and took lessons from Jackson, in New Bond Street. This naturally led to one or two boxing reminiscences, with a few reflections on the leading prize-fighters of the day, at the end of which both gentlemen were very well pleased with each other. They parted with mutual expressions of esteem, the Viscount bestowing his card on Mr. Tooting, and Mr. Tooting going off with his head in a whirl at the thought that he had rescued a real live peeress from annoyance, and chatted on the friendliest of terms with her young blood of a husband.

No sooner had he vanished into the crowd than the Viscount turned his attention to his troublesome wife. "First it's one thing, and then it's another!" he said austerely. "I'm damned if ever I met such a tiresome chit as you, Hero!"

"Don't scold me, Sherry! Indeed, I am very sorry to be in another scrape!" Hero said disarmingly. She raised her worshipful eyes to his face, and said, with a small sigh: "I quite see that it is not the style of thing you would approve of, and I haven't been into any of the booths, though I *did* watch the droll puppet show."

"I should think not indeed!" said his lordship severely. He then ruined his whole effect by abandoning his role of outraged spouse, and saying boyishly; "Well, since we *are* here we may as well take a look at the sights. Damme, if I choose to take my wife to Bartholomew Fair, who the devil's to stop me? Besides, we shan't see a soul we know!"

"Sherry!" gasped Hero, clinging ecstatically to his arm. "Do you mean it? May I see the Fireproof Woman washing her hands in boiling oil? And, oh, Sherry, there is a theatre here, and there is to be a piece acted called *The Hall of Death*, or *Who's the Murderer?* Sherry, *could* we——?"

Sherry gave a shout of laughter. "Of all the nonsensical brats! *The Hall of Death!* Come along, then, but I warn you, I won't have you clutching me every time you take fright at the mummery, as you did at Astley's!"

Hero promised to comport herself with the utmost propriety, and they went off together, bought themselves a two-shilling box for the forthcoming performance at the Great Booth, and filled in the time until the curtain should rise on this promising melodrama in wandering about the market, inspecting all the freaks, and buying one another several perfectly useless fairings. *The Hall of Death* was so bloodcurdling that Hero held Sherry's hand tightly from start to finish, responding to his enquiry as to whether she was enjoying it with an eloquent shudder which he correctly interpreted as signifying contentment of no mean order.

On their way home he warned her that on no account must she divulge where she had been, and most strictly forbade her to frequent Lady Appleby's company. Close questioning on the subject of Mr. Yarford's advances made him reject, not without regret, his first intention to send his cartel to this callow young gentleman. The Viscount finding for the first time in his life that he had to be wise for two people, realized that to call Mr. Yarford to account would be to plunge his Hero into the very scandal he wished to avoid.

177

Much as it went against the grain with him, he had sense enough to perceive that his best course would be to remain in official ignorance of his wife's escapade. Since Mr. Yarford had been made to appear ridiculous at the hands of a sturdy Cit, it was safe to assume that he would certainly preserve the most discreet silence concerning the day's doings.

"None of the Yarfords are at all the thing, Kitten," he said abruptly. "Brockenhurst ain't either. Yes, I know I'm pretty well-acquainted with him, but that don't signify. A fellow may know any number of bloods he don't choose to present to his wife." He suddenly recollected that this was precisely what he had done, and added: "Never ought to have invited him to dine with us. The thing is I keep forgetting I'm married."

"Well, to tell you the truth, Sherry, I did not care for him very much," confessed Hero. "And I was quite shocked by Gussie's headstrong manners. You know, she never used to behave in that odd way, when we were children. And although, of course, I know that a great many ladies have lovers I do *not* think that it is good *ton* to permit them to treat them with such familiarity as Sir Matthew uses towards her."

"Who told you that a great many ladies have lovers?" demanded the Viscount. "Don't say it was me, now! I never told you any such thing, I swear I didn't!"

"Oh no, but I have been about the world now, and I know hundreds of things I never had the least notion of before!" said Hero, not without pride. She glanced shyly at him. "And that was what you meant, wasn't it, Sherry, when you said that you would not mind what I did if only I were discreet?"

The Viscount met her eyes full. It was, in fact, exactly what he had meant. He wondered if there were any insanity in his family, and replied shortly: "No, it was not!"

"Oh!" said Hero. She suggested: "I dare say you think me too young for such things?"

"I do. Much too young!" replied his lordship emphatically.

"Oh!" said Hero again, and said no more.

A few nights later he took her to a Grand Gala at Vauxhall Gardens, making up an agreeable party for the expedition. Miss Milborne was amongst their guests, her parent having been persuaded, not without misgiving, to entrust her to Hero's chaperonage. Nothing could have been more decorous, however, than the party, or more correct than the Viscount's attentions to his guests; and the only thing that happened to mar the peace and propriety of the evening was the stormy quarrel which took place between Miss Milborne and Lord Wrotham, consequent upon the Duke of Severn's detaching himself from his own party, on first catching sight of the Incomparable, and joining the Viscount's for the greater part of the evening. This was of course regrettable, but as Miss Milborne was far too well-bred to permit her annoyance to appear, and everyone was quite accustomed to see Lord Wrotham in a fit of the sullens, the incident was not allowed to spoil the pleasure of the remainder of the guests.

with him to find money. He produced a letter was
for transfer to his family, and termed money... there
was not.

"Oh," said Hero. She suggested, "I dare say you
think he too young for such things."

"Too. Much too young," replied the teacher's emphatically.

"Yes," said Hero again, and said no more.

A few night later, he took her to a Grand Gala at
Vauxhall Gardens, making up an agreeable party for
the expedition. Miss Milborne was amongst their
guests, her party having been persuaded, not without
misgiving, to conduct her to Hero's entertainment.
Nothing could have been more devoted, however,
than the polite or more correct than the Viscount's
attention to his guests; and the only thing that had
vexed during the party and brought up the evening
was the worry quarrel which took place between
Miss Milborne and Lord Wrotham, consequent upon
the Earl of Severn's canciling himself from improper
party on that enchanting sight of the incomparable,
joining the Viscounts for the greater part of the evening. This was of course regrettable, but as Miss Milborne was too well bred to permit her annoyance to
appear, and everyone was quite determined to be
grid Wrotham in a fit of the sullens, the Viscount was
not allowed to spoil the pleasure of the remainder of
the guests.

CHAPTER 11

The quarrel which had sprung up at Vauxhall Gardens between Miss Milborne and Lord Wrotham flourished longer than was expected, Wrotham's temper having been worn thin, and Miss Milborne being so much incensed with him for choosing such a public spot for a quarrel that she refused to receive him when he called upon her next day to make his apologies. As the Duke of Severn ascended the steps of the Milborne's residence just as George came down them, and was instantly admitted into the house, it was not surprising that that fiery young man's patience should there and then have deserted him. Encouraged by his long-suffering friends, he determined to relinquish his pretensions to the hand of the most hardened flirt in London, and for some time made great efforts to abide by this resolve, even allowing himself to forget his broken heart for long enough to enable him to challenge Sherry to a grand driving contest, in praiseworthy emulation of a feat once accomplished by Sir John Lade, who had driven his curricle twenty-two times in succession through a gateway only just wide enough to admit the vehicle. Neither young gentleman succeeded in bettering this performance, Sherry coming to grief at the fifth lap and George at the seventh. Sherry was quite unhurt, but George wrenched his shoulder, and went about for several days with his arm in a sling, looking even more romantic than usual, and causing ill-informed persons to spread the rumour that he had called someone out, and had himself sustained a wound. This story reached Isabella's ears in due course, and she naturally supposed that she must have been the cause of the duel. She strongly disapproved of duelling, but she could not help feeling a little touched, as well as anxious; and as George did not come to see her she made an excuse to pay a morning call in Half Moon Street to discover what she could learn from Hero.

Hero, who had just come in from a ride in the park, and was wearing a saucy little hat, with a most provocative plume curling over its brim, which quite wrung Miss Milborne's heart with envy, received her guest with her usual sunny good-humour, accepted with thanks the marble-covered novel, straight from the Minerva Press, which was Miss Milborne's excuse for the call, and begged her guest to be seated. Miss Milborne complimented her on the saucy hat, and confessed that if only she herself rode better, and were not so nervous of horses, she should be tempted to ride in the park too.

"Well, I don't ride very well, you know," said Hero frankly. "Sherry says I'm cow-handed. It isn't true, because I drive my phaeton *most* creditably. Gil taught me, and he, you know, is quite a nonpareil. The thing is, my mare bolted with me yesterday, and there was such a commotion!" She gave a little gurgle. "Sherry was as mad as fire, but of couse he could not scold me on account of that nonsensical match of his. And I was not thrown, and so there was nothing to be in a pucker over. In fact, George said I kept my seat admirably."

This gave Miss Milborne her opportunity. She lowered her fine eyes to her lap and said gravely: "I hope Lord Wrotham has sustained no lasting injury?"

"Oh no, not the least in the world!"

"I was very much grieved when I heard—I hold such practice in abhorrence, as I am sure everyone must. Who—who was the other man?"

"Why, Sherry, to be sure!" replied Hero. "Are you indeed shocked, Isabella? I did not think you would be so stuffy!"

"Sherry?" gasped Miss Milborne, looking up quickly. "Impossible! Oh, I would not have had such a thing happen for the world!"

"I declare you are as bad as Lady Sheringham!" Hero cried. "She actually came to call on me, only to tell me that if I were not such a wretched wife I should put an end to such pranks!"

"Hero, what happened?" asked Miss Milborne, a crease beginning to appear between her brows. "I collect that George's injury was *not* sustained in a duel?"

"A duel? Good heavens, no!" cried Hero, laughing. "It was the most absurd start! Merely, George challenged Sherry to drive his curricle through a narrow gate, and backed himself to beat him—which, indeed, he did, though he only contrived to scrape through seven times to Sherry's five!"

A tide of colour rose to the very roots of Miss Milborne's admirably cut and dressed copper locks. She said in a strictly controlled voice: "I had heard nothing of this. How—how absurd! Really, it is beyond everything! I do not wonder at Lady Sheringham's displeasure." She encountered a sparkling look from her hostess, and gave a little laugh. "Oh! do not eat me, my dear! I am sure it is no concern of mine. Shall you be at Almack's to-morrow evening?"

Since Sherry, when tentatively approached on the subject, had said (with a groan) that he was willing to do his duty, Hero was able to say that she would certainly be there; and the remainder of the morning visit passed in the discussion of the ladies' respective toilets.

Unfortunately, it transpired, when Hero burst upon her husband on the following evening in all the glory of a new dress of Italian crape, lavishly trimmed with lace and floss-silk, that he had forgotten all about the engagement, and had made an assignation with a party of his intimates at Cribb's Parlour. He looked extremely discontented, not to say sulky, supposed she would expect him to send a message round to Gil's lodging, and wondered what she could possibly find to amuse her at Almack's.

"Should you prefer not to go, Sherry?" Hero asked, trying very hard not to let a wistful note creep into her voice.

"Oh! I suppose you have set your heart on it, and there is nothing for it!" he responded. "Only I shall be obliged to change my clothes, and I must say I think it is a great bore. However, it don't signify."

She could not agree to this. It would be a shocking thing if he had to forgo his pleasure on her account, and the knowledge that he had done so would most effectively destroy her own pleasure. She instantly said: "But I do not at all care to go, Sherry. Indeed, I have the headache a little, and if you are engaged with your friends I should be quite glad to stay at home!"

His face cleared at once. "Should you indeed?" he asked eagerly. "You know, I am prepared to take you if you really wish to go, only I dare say you would find it pretty flat."

"Oh, yes!"

"And if you are dull, why, you may send a note round to invite your cousin to spend the evening with you!" suggested Sherry, forgetting that he had censured her intimacy with Mrs. Hoby. "Besides, I do not go until after I have dined. I dashed off a billet to ask George to go along with us all, and he will be calling here to join me."

But when Lord Wrotham presented himself, towards the end of dinner, he was seen to be in knee-breeches, a circumstance which made Sherry exclaim; "Good God, we're not going to a ball, old fellow! What the deuce are you about? Knee-breeches for Cribb's Parlour!"

"Cribb's Parlour?" repeated George, shaking hands with Hero. "But I thought we were to go to Almack's!"

"Oh!" Hero cried, in a little confusion. "I had quite forgot that you said you would go with us! Indeed, I am very sorry, George, but I cannot think how I came to be so stupid!"

"Well, it's of no account," said Sherry, pouring a glass of wine for his friend. "Hero don't care to go to the Assembly, and I have made up a snug little party to meet at Cribb's Parlour."

Lord Wrotham looked enquiringly at Hero. The significance of her ball-dress was not lost on him; he said: "Is this so indeed? Are you sure you do not care to go?"

"No. truly I had as lief stay at home," she assured him. "I have the headache, you know, and Sherry thinks I should very likely find it quite flat."

"Oh!" said Wrotham, frowning over it. He glanced from one to the other, and said that he supposed he had best return home to change into raiment more suited to Cribb's Parlour. This, however, Sherry would not permit him to do, saying that they were late already, and must be on their way. He gave Hero a careless pat on the shoulder, recommended her to go early to bed, and swept his friend off with him to Mr. Ringwood's lodging. Here they took up Mr. Ringwood into their hackney, and all drove off to the tavern owned by the ex-champion of the Ring. Lord Wrotham's doubts were still troubling him, and when Mr. Ringwood expressed surprise at Sherry's having selected one of the Assembly nights for this meeting, he said abruptly; "She did not look to me as though she had the headache."

"Lord, how do you know?" responded Sherry. "She did not wish to go to Almack's, I tell you! She said so herself. I told her I would go if she had set her heart on it, and she replied at once that she would be glad not to be obliged to go." He added naively: "I must say I was deuced happy to hear it, for it is not in my line at all."

The hackney stopping in Jermyn Street at this moment, to take up Sir Montagu Revesby, the subject was allowed to drop, and the rest of the journey was beguiled in discussing the rival merits of two promising young heavyweights, now in training for an early encounter. Lord Wrotham bore little part in this, but sat lost in a fit of brooding which outlasted his first glass of daffy at the Parlour. He was just about to embark on a second glass when he came to a sudden decision, and startled his friends by saying in accents of strong conviction: "She *did* want to go!"

Mr. Ringwood eyed him with some misgiving. "Go where?" he asked.

"Almack's, of course!" Wrotham said impatiently.

"Who did?"

"Kitten—Lady Sherry!"

"Nonsense!" said Sherry. "What a fellow you are, George! Once put a notion into your head, and, damme, there's no getting it out again! Fill up his glass, Monty!"

"No!" said George. "I tell you she was dressed for it. I'd lay a monkey it was all your doing, Sherry! I shall return to Half Moon Street and offer to be her escort!"

"But I keep on telling you she did not wish to go!" Sherry said, quite tired of the subject.

"Well, I think she did. And, damme, I never wanted to come here, now I think of it! I'm going back."

The Viscount shrugged, casting an expressive glance at Mr. Ringwood, and Lord Wrotham took his impetuous departure. He had not appeared to be in a convivial mood, but his going threw an unaccountable damper over the party. The Viscount's countenance wore something very like a scowl, and he drank off his second glass of daffy rather defiantly. Upon some acquaintances coming up to exchange salutations and bets, he roused himself from his abstraction and entered pretty readily into the transactions. But when these friends moved away, he sat down again at his table, looking moody, and drinking his third glass in unbroken silence. An attempt by Mr. Ringwood to rouse him failed; and a rallying jest from Revesby only drew a perfunctory smile from him. The third glass seemed to help him to come to a decision. He set it down empty upon the bare table and suddenly demanded: "What *right* has George Wrotham to take my wife to Almack's?"

Mr. Ringwood considered this carefully. "Don't see any harm in it," he pronounced at last. "Quite the thing."

"Well, I won't have it!" said his lordship belligerently.

"My dear Sherry, let me call for another glass!" smiled Revesby.

His lordship ignored this. "He comes here, don't say a word, hardly blows a cloud, and then what does he do? Without so much as a by your leave, too!"

"Don't see that," objected Mr. Ringwood, shaking his head. "Told you what he was going to do, didn't he? If you didn't like it, ought to have told him so. Too late now. Call for another glass!"

"I don't want another glass, and I won't have George taking my wife off under my very nose!"

"Sherry, Sherry!" Sir Montagu remonstrated, laying a hand on the Viscount's arm.

It was shaken off. "Don't keep saying Sherry at me!" said his lordship irritably. "If she wanted to go to the damned Assembly why the devil did she say she didn't? Tell me that!"

"I am sure she did not wish to go, and she will send Wrotham about his business," Revesby said soothingly.

Mr. Ringwood, rendered percipient by a judicious guantity of gin, said wisely: "Wouldn't say she wished to go if you didn't, Sherry. Noticed it often. Always does what you wish. Mistake, if you ask me." He recruited himself with another pull at his glass. "Selfish!" he produced.

"Who is?" demanded his lordship.

"You are," said Mr. Ringwood simply.

"I am no such thing!" Sherry retorted, stung. "How the devil was I to know she wanted to go when she said she didn't?"

"My dear Sherry, poor Ringwood is a trifle disguised! Why put youself in a pucker?" Revesby said.

"No, I ain't!" Mr. Ringwood contradicted, eyeing the elegant Sir Montagu with dislike. "Sherry's a fool. Always was. George knew she wanted to go. George ain't a fool." He thought this over. "At least, not as big a fool as Sherry," he amended.

"You're as full as you can hold!" said Sherry furiously. "And George had no right to walk off like that! What's more, he shan't take my wife to Almack's, because I'll take her myself!"

· Revesby caught his sleeve as he sprang up. "No, no, my dear fellow, you're too late now! Consider! George has been gone these twenty minutes, and more!"

"I shall go straight to Almack's and give him a set-down!" promised Sherry, a martial light in his eye.

Mr. Ringwood sat up. "You're not going to call George out, Sherry! Mind, now!"

"Who said anything about calling him out? Merely, if my wife goes to Almack's, I'm going to Almack's too!"

"Really Sherry, you are making a great to-do about nothing," said Revesby gently. "There is no impropriety in Wrotham's escorting Lady Sheringham, I assure you!"

"Are you accusing my wife of impropriety?" said Sherry, whose pugnacity was fast reaching alarming proportions.

"Certainly not!" replied Revesby. "Such a notion never entered my head, my dear boy! I wish you will sit down and forget these crotchets."

"Well, I won't!" Sherry returned. "I'm going to Almack's."

Mr. Ringwood groped for his quizzing-glass, and through it scrutinized his friend's person. He let if fall again and lay back in his chair. "Not in pantaloons," he said. "Can't be done, Sherry."

The Viscount looked very much put out for a moment, but having taken a resolve he was not one easily to relinquish it. He said, with immense dignity, that he was going off home to change his dress, and stalked out of the Parlour before either Revesby or Ringwood could think of an answer.

When he reached Half Moon Street it was to hear from his butler that her ladyship had gone out with Lord Wrotham. Sherry said grandly that he knew all about that, and demanded his valet. This gentleman was not immediately to be found, and by the time he had been fetched by a breathless page from the select tavern which he patronized in his leisure moments, the Viscount was in a worse temper than ever, and had ruined no fewer than five neck-cloths in some fumbling attempts to achieve a Waterfall style. It was more than half an hour later when he was at last correctly attired for the Assembly, and five minutes after eleven when he arrived at Almack's. Nothing could have been more unfortunate, for the rules laid down by Almack's despotic patronesses were not even relaxed for the Duke of Wellington himself; and although the civility of Willis, who presided over the club, could scarcely have been exceeded, not all the Viscount's stormings or blandishments availed to get him beyond the portals.

He was obliged to return home, since he had no longer any desire to spend the night at Cribb's Parlour, and to while away the time in flicking over the pages of a library book, casting the dice, right hand against left, and brooding over his injuries. Whatever he might do when amongst his cronies, he was not one who took pleasure in drinking alone, so that when Lord Wrotham brought his fair charge back to the house, shortly before two o'clock, the door was opened to them by a sober but awe-inspiringly stiff young man, who bowed to his friend, thanked him in frigid terms for his kind offices, and expressed the hope—bleakly—that he and my lady had been tolerably well amused.

George, somewhat astonished by his reception, said that he had passed a charming evening. Hero, on whom the Viscount's punctilious manner was thrown away, said vivaciously: "Was it not kind of George to take me after all, Sherry? It was so pleasant, too! I wish you had been with us. Everyone was there to-night! Your uncle Prosper came with the Cowpers, and only fancy, Sherry! he complimented me on my gown, and he said I had an air of decided fashion! Oh, and Cousin Jane was there, with Cassy and Eudora, and Cousin Jane was most civil, because I had that instant been dancing the waltz—dear Lady Sefton said I might do so now that I have been approved, so do not be thinking that I am in a scrape!—dancing the waltz with Duke Fakenham, and she most particularly desired to have him presented to her. Oh, Sherry, only to think of *my* being able to oblige Cousin Jane! And I wish it might have answered, but it did not, I am afraid, for Duke only bowed and talked the merest commonplace for a few minutes, and never asked Cassy to dance at all." She turned and held out her hand to Lord Wrotham. "Thank you, George! It was so comfortable, and very pretty in you to have gallanted me to the party."

He took her hand and pressed it, assuring her warmly that the obligation was on his side, that he had done delightfully, never wished to spend a more pleasant evening. Then, as the Viscount offered him no encouragement to linger, he said good-night and departed.

"I did not expect to find you at home so soon, Sherry," Hero said innocently."Was it flat, after all, your party?"

"If I had known—though to be sure I do not know how I could have done so!—that you had a desire to go to the Assembly, I would have taken you myself," said his lordship stiffly. "I do not know why you should tell me that you had the headache, and then, when you had fobbed me off, have gone to it with Wrotham!"

"Fobbed you off?" exclaimed Hero, quite dismayed. "Oh, Sherry, no! I thought you did not wish to go! Oh, don't say you did wish to go! I would so much, much rather have had you with me than George!"

"I am flattered!" said his lordship. "I had thought you dealt delightfully with George!"

"Yes, indeed I did, but I had rather be with you than with anyone. Sherry, why did you not join us? It would have been beyond anything!"

"Well, as a matter of fact, I did think I might do so," said Sherry, thawing. "Only it was after eleven when I reached the curst place, and nothing would prevail upon Willis to let me enter."

"Oh, Sherry!" Hero cried, flushing in distress. "Had

I known that, all my pleasure would have been destroyed! Oh, how vexatious! how sorry I am! It is all my fault for having been so stupid as to fancy you did not wish to go!"

"I must own that considering I was perfectly ready to escort you," began his lordship in an injured tone, "I do not know why——" He stopped, meeting her anxious, uncritical gaze. "No, it wasn't your fault, and you know it wasn't!" he said "I didn't wish to go, but you are not to be giving up your amusements for any such cause as that. Dash it, Gil was right!"

"Gil? Why, what has he to do with it, pray?"

"Oh, nothing! Only he would have it I was a fool, and curst selfish, and I dare say I may be, but I tell you this, Kitten——"

"How dared Gil say such a thing?" interrupted Hero hotly. "It is the wickedest untruth! You are no such thing! I should think he must have been quite foxed to have said it!"

"No, no, only slightly disguised!" the Viscount assured her. "Anyway, it don't signify, only I wish I had taken you, and I'm sorry, Kitten. There!"

She took his outstretched hand and carried it to her cheek. "Oh, Sherry, how silly! I think *you* must be slightly disguised, to be offering me an apology for such an absurdity!"

"Sober as a judge!" the Viscount asserted. "I don't say I wasn't a trifle bosky when I left Cribb's, but that's long since. Damme, I've been waiting for you to come home these three hours, with nothing to do but read some dashed book or other!"

Hero found the thought of his spending an evening at home with a book so droll that she broke into a peal of laughter, which was so infectious that his lordship was obliged to join in. They went upstairs together in excellent accord, and when they parted outside Hero's door, Sherry did her the honour of informing her that she was a good little puss, and that he had always had a fondness for her.

CHAPTER 12

Hero might have enjoyed the evening spent at Almack's Assembly Rooms, but it had not been one of unmixed pleasure for her escort, while for one other person it had been an evening of almost unleavened annoyance. Miss Milborne, seeing the most ardent of her admirers enter the rooms with Hero on his arm, had suffered something in the nature of a shock. Never before had she seen George in attendance on any other lady than herself! When he came to Almack's it was to form one of her court; and when she did not dance with him he had a gratifying habit of leaning against the wall and watching her, instead of soliciting some other damsel to dance with him. Now, on the heels of the most obdurate quarrel they had had, here he was, looking perfectly cheerful, actually laughing at something Hero had said to him, his handsome head bent a little to catch her words. Hero, too, was in very good looks: in fact, Miss Milborne had not known that her little friend could appear to such advantage. She could never, of course, aspire to such beauty as belonged to the Incomparable, but Miss Milborne was no fool, and she was obliged to own that there was something particularly taking in the bride's smile and mischievous twinkle. Watching George, she came to the reluctant conclusion that he was fully sensible of his partner's charm. He had given his adored Isabella nothing more than a common bow upon catching sight of her, and it was plain that he meant to devote his evening to Hero. Miss Milborne could think of a dozen reasons to account for his gallanting Hero to the ball, but none of them satisfied her; nor could the distinguishing attention paid to her by her ducal admirer quite restore her spirits. She was even a trifle pettish with Severn, a circumstance which later drew down upon her the slightly tart reproaches of her Mama, who had no notion of her daughter's playing fast and loose with such a dazzling suitor.

The truth was that Miss Milborne was in the uncomfortable situation of a young lady who had had her head turned as much by the ambition of her parent as by the admiration which had been hers ever since she had first appeared in Polite circles. She had been educated with a view to making a brilliant match, and until Lord Wrotham had swept stormily into her orbit no other idea than that of obliging her Mama had so much as crossed her head. But Lord Wrotham's was a disturbing presence, and it was not long before the Beauty's docile and well-ordered ambition was in direct conflict with the scarcely recognized promptings of her heart. For no one could seriously consider Wrotham would provide any girl with a brilliant match. His birth was certainly unexceptionable, but it was common knowledge that his estates were grossly encumbered; and instead of being, like his ducal rival, a dignified young man of notable steadiness of character, he was wild to a fault. He had quite as many libertine tendencies as Miss Milborne had complained of in Sherry; he was a gamester; he mixed with low persons, such as prize-fighters and jockeys; and his hot temper led his anxious friends to prophesy that one day he would kill his man, and be obliged to fly the country. Miss Milborne knew that the very thought of allying herself to him was an absurdity, and she made many praiseworthy attempts to put him out of her mind. After all, he was not the only one of her suitors to attract her. She had been by no means impervious to Sherry's careless charm, for instance; and she found one Sir Barnabas Crawley very much to her taste, not to mention the elusive Sir Montagu Revesby. In her more honest moments, she was bound to own to herself that nothing but his high degree appealed to her in the Duke of Severn; but when George had been more than usually tiresome she could convince herself that she would be very comfortable if wedded to a nobleman who would certainly never give her a moment's anxiety, and who would treat her with unfailing, if slightly tedious, civility and consideration. He was, in addition, extremely wealthy, but since she was herself a considerable heiress she was able to banish such a mercenary consideration as this from her mind. Nothing, in fact, was farther from Miss Milborne's admirably trained mind than to marry to disoblige her family, as the saying was, yet when she saw Wrotham enter the ballroom at Almack's with Hero on his arm, a pang of something so like jealousy shot through her that she was shocked at her own meanness of spirit, and felt all her pleasure in the evening to have been destroyed. Nor was she able to think well of Hero for purloining George in this shameless way, and—as though that were not injury enough!—contriving to keep him in apparently sunny spirits all the evening.

The reflection that he was the second of her suitors to be filched from her by Hero could not but cross her mind. It was all very well to say that Sherry had married poor little Hero in a fit of pique: possibly he had done so, but anyone who believed that Sherry was eating his heart out for his first love would have had to have had less than common sense or a greater degree of conceit than Miss Milborne. The dreadful suspicion that the passion her admirers declared themselves to feel for her was nothing more than an evancescent emotion, soon recovered from, could not be stifled, and made Miss Milborne wretched indeed. She waited for George to come across the room to her side, which he would surely do as soon as another man relieved him of the charge of Hero. Hero was led on to the floor by Marmaduke Fakenham to dance the waltz: George strolled away to exchange greetings with a group of his friends. Miss Milborne, too mortified to remember that she had refused to receive him when he had called to pay her a morning visit, could only suppose that his passion for her had burnt itself out, and immediately began to flirt with the dashing Sir Barnabas. Later in the evening she found herself partaking of lemonade in the refreshment saloon beside Hero, and she was excessively affectionate to Hero, even, with the utmost nobility of character, telling her that her dress was the prettiest in the room, and the new way she had of doing her hair quite ravishing.

"I observe," said Mrs. Milborne on the way home, "that our little friend has lost no time in acquiring a cicisbeo! Well! I wish her joy of young Wrotham! He seemed to me to be quite epris in that direction. It is all of a piece; I dare say if I have said once that he is incurably volatile I have said it a dozen times. But I did not quite like to see you dancing twice with Sir Barnabas Crawley, my love. I am sure a most elegant creature, but *not* a man of substance. To flirt a little—but always in a ladylike way, remember!—can do no harm, but I fancy Severn did not quite like to see Crawley make you the object of such persistent gallantry. I just mention the matter, my dear, and no more, for I am sure I need have no fear for your good sense."

"None, Mama," said Miss Milborne in a colourless tone.

She was seated in her Mama's barouche next day outside a shop in Bond Street, waiting for Mrs. Milborne to accomplish the purchase of a bottle of Distilled Water of Pineapples (to discourage wrinkles), when Sherry came sauntering down the street, looking rather rakish, with his curly-brimmed beaver set at an angle on his fair head, and the drab Benjamin he wore (for the autumn morning was chilly), hanging negligently open to allow the interested a glimpse of a tightly fitting coat of superfine, a very sporting waistcoat, and a natty pair of yellow buckskins. He stopped beside the barouche, and stayed chatting to Miss Milborne with his usual good humour, and a complete absence of the sort of constraint that might have been expected in a young gentleman finding himself vis-a-vis the lady who had so lately rejected his proffered suit. He had been at Jackson's Saloon, attempting like every other young blood of the Fancy to pop in a hit over the ex-champion's guard, and was now on his way to White's, where he had an assignation with Mr. Ringwood. He paid Miss Milborne an extravagant compliment or two, but as he followed these up by saying that now he came to think of it he had not seen her very lately, she was in no danger of taking his gallantry seriously.

"You were not at Almacks's last night, or you might have seen me," she remarked.

His brow darkened, for although he bore his wife no grudge for the events of the previous evening, he still felt unaccountably aggrieved whenever he thought of George's share in them. "No," he said shortly.

Miss Milborne, quick to catch the note of dissatisfaction in his voice, would have been less than human had she forborne to probe farther. She cast down her eyes to the lavender kid gloves she wore and said, smoothing them over her wrists: "I was glad to see Lady Sheringham, however, and in such spirits."

The Viscount's blue gaze became fixed on her face. "Oh!" he said. "In spirits, was she? Ha!"

"She was much admired," said Miss Milborne calmly. "Indeed, I wish you had been there, for she looked delightfully!"

"I'll take precious good care I'm there the next time she goes to that dam—dashed place!" promised his lordship.

"I am sure Lord Wrotham took excellent care of her."

"Well, I'll thank him to take care of someone else's wife!" said his lordship irascibly.

Miss Milborne began to feel alarmed. She abandoned her formal manners and asked directly; "Sherry, you are not jealous of George, are you?"

"Who said anything about being jealous of George?" retorted the Viscount. "I suppose I need not care to have him walking off with my wife, without so much as a by your leave, or——However, that's neither here nor there! But what the devil he wants with my Kitten when he's been making a cake of himself over you for the past six months is more than I can fathom!"

Miss Milborne passed over this unflattering description of Lord Wrotham's devotion, and said: "I am persuaded you have not the least cause to feel uneasy. There was nothing in his manner last night to warrant any jealousy on your part, upon my honour!"

"There had better not be, by Jove!" said his lordship, his eye kindling.

There was no opportunity for further discussion. A widow's lozenge-coach had drawn up alongside the Milborne's barouche, and the Dowager Lady Sheringham was already leaning out of the window to bestow a greeting upon her dear Isabella. She acknowledged her son with a sigh and a sad smile, but appeared to derive some comfort from the spectacle of him conversing with Miss Milborne. Her manner, if not her actual words, held so strong a flavour of the might-have-been that Miss Milborne felt her colour rising, and the Viscount, recalling his engagements, sheered off in a hurry.

"Ah, my love!" murmured Lady Sheringham. "If only things had been otherwise! I live in dread of his bitterly regretting his rash marriage. When I saw him beside your carriage, I could not suppress the thought that——"

"I am persuaded, ma'am, that you need harbour no fears for his happiness!" Miss Milborne said quickly, conscious of the ears on the box of her carriage.

"I wish I might believe you are right," sighed the dowager, who had a sublime disregard for servants. "I

201

own I was dismayed to learn from Mrs. Burrell that my daughter-in-law, as I suppose I must call her, elected to appear at Almack's last night with that dreadful young Wrotham as her cavalier. But I knew how it would be from the outset! I believe he is for ever in her company."

Miss Milborne was spared the necessity of answering by the somewhat acid and over-loud comments of a hackney-carriage driver whose progress was being impeded by the lozenge-coach. Lady Sheringham was obliged to desire her coachman to drive on, leaving her young friend to digest at her leisure her sinister remarks.

Lord Wrotham, meanwhile, by a superhuman effort of will, continued to hold aloof from the Beauty, not, indeed, as his well-wishers hoped, from a resolve to be done with her, but in the hope that this change of treatment might induce her to look more kindly upon his suit. One of his married sisters, who desired nothing so much as to see him married to an heiress, had given him a great deal of worldly advice, and however poor an opinion he might hold of his sisters' advice in general, he thought that Augusta very likely knew what she was talking about when the subject under discussion was the capriciousness of the female sex. So far, events seemed to have borne out Augusta's dictum: Wrotham had not failed to perceive the effect his escorting Hero to Almack's had had upon Miss Milborne. It had gone to his heart to respond only with a bow to the most welcoming smile he had received from the Beauty for many weeks, but he had done it; and if it gave him a good deal of pain to see her subsequent passages with Sir Barnabas Crawley, at least he was shrewd enough to suspect that these were designed to make him jealous. He determined to make no sign for several days, and spent a happy hour in devising a romantic gesture which must melt a heart already thawing towards him. Miss Milborne had told him once that violets were her favourite flowers. The fact that she had chosen to present him with this information at a moment when he had laid an enormous bouquet of roses at her feet was a little daunting, but he had treasured up the knowledge against a future occasion, and he now perceived how to put it to excellent account. It was not perhaps the easiest task in the world to obtain violets at this season of the year, but to a forceful young man in love all things were possible. Miss Milborne should receive a posy of violets in an elegant holder upon the evening of Lady Fakenham's ball. She would surely know who must have sent them, but just in case there should be any mistake he would enclose his card with the flowers, with a brief message written upon it. He was unable to decide between *Wear these for my sake*, and *If you wear these to-night I shall know what to think*, and he ended by carrying this problem to Hero.

Hero naturally thought the whole notion very pretty, and could not conceive how any female could resist wearing flowers which had cost so much time and trouble to procure. But as she had a very practical mind she felt herself obliged to point out to George that Isabella could hardly wear a posy of violets in a filigree holder. George saw the force of this argument, but when he had written out another card, with the words *Carry these for my sake*, he could not like the alteration.

"Well, I know what I should write if I were you, George,"said Hero. "I should just write *With my love*."

"With my homage!" corrected George reverently.

203

"Yes, if you choose, but for my part, I think it would be more touching to put *love*."

"How if I wrote, *Carry these and you carry my heart?*" said George, attacked by sudden inspiration.

Hero gave a gasp, and said in a shaken tone: "I don't at all know why it should be so, dear George, but—but *I* think that would make me want to laugh, if I were Isabella."

"It would?" he exclaimed, shocked.

She nodded.

"Well, I do not understand how it could possibly do so. However, I dare say you may be right. I should like to mention my heart, though. Would it make you laugh if I wrote, *Hold these to-night, my heart is in them*—or *with them*, or perhaps *goes with them?*"

"Yes, it would," replied Hero frankly.

"I should not like to run such a risk," he said looking very much put out. "I think I will write *Wear these for my sake*, after all. Dash it, she will know what I mean!"

Having settled this to his moderate satisfaction, he soon took his leave of Hero, and went off in tolerably good spirits. He met Sherry on the doorstep, but he was too intent on pursuing his quest for violets to do more than exchange a brief greeting with him. Sherry regarded his retreating figure with dark suspicion, and went straight upstairs to the drawing-room to demand of his wife if George lived in Half Moon Street?

She said innocently: "I thought he lived in Ryder Street? Has he removed from there, Sherry? He said nothing of it to me, and he was with me not five minutes ago."

"I'm well aware of that!" said his lordship tartly. "And I should like to know what he was doing here! I suppose you will say he called to me!"

"Oh no, I don't think he wanted to see you, Sherry! He came to ask my advice about something. You won't mention it, will you? He is going to send a bouquet of violets to Isabella for the Fakenhams' ball. He says they are her favourite flowers."

"Oh!" said his lordhsip. "Well, I don't see what he wants with your advice!"

"He did want my advice, but I think I ought not to tell you what it was about, because I dare say he would not like it known," confided Hero.

"It seems to me," said Sherry severely, "that Bella Milborne ain't the only female George has an eye to!"

"Oh no, Sherry!" Hero said earnestly. "Indeed, you are quite wrong! Why, you cannot mean that you suspect George of having an eye to me? Oh, Sherry, how nonsensical! I assure you, he does nothing but talk of Isabella!"

"Well, I don't know," said Sherry, looking her over critically. "The fact of the matter is you seem to have grown so devilish pretty since I married you that there's no knowing what will happen next."

She blushed rosily. "Have I, Sherry? Have I really? I expect it is just the new way I have of dressing my hair, and all my grand gowns."

"Yes, very likely," he agreed. "I must say, I never thought you above the ordinary myself, but if you go on like this the lord only knows where it will end!"

"But, Sherry, you do not mind my growing to be pretty, do you?"

"Oh, I don't *mind* it!" replied his lordship. "The thing is, I didn't bargain for it, that's all, and if you are to have fellows like George for ever haunting the house, I can see it will be a dashed nuisance. And now I come to think of it, George ain't the only one! There's Gil! Hardest case I ever met in my life, and what must he do but take you out driving to Salt Hill, just as though he were in the habit of driving females, which he ain't. Yes, and who was that curst rum touch I found with you last week?"

"Mr. Kilby, do you mean, Sherry?"

"I dare say. Not that it signifies, for I fancy he won't come here to make sheep's eyes at you again!"

She gave a little giggle. "I must say, I think you were very uncivil and disobliging to him, Sherry. I don't know what he can have thought!"

"Oh, don't you?" retorted Sherry grimly. "Well, he knew dashed well what to think, let me tell you!" He returned unexpectedly to the original bone of contention. "But that's neither here nor there. Whoever heard of a fellow's wanting the advice of a chit like you, I should like to know? Rather too brown, Kitten! In fact, a dashed sight too brown!"

"But indeed he did, Sherry! The case is that he had great hopes that Isabella may relent towards him, and he wished to know my opinion of a—well, a little billet that he means to send her, with the flowers for Lady Fakenham's ball. But you must not mention the matter, for indeed I think he would not wish me to have spoken of it!"

As he really knew very well that he had not the least cause to regard Lord Wrotham with suspicion, Sherry consented to be satisfied with this explanation, and the matter was allowed to drop. An interview with his man of business, a few days later, provided his lordship with other, and more serious, affairs for thought. Mr. Stoke felt it to be his duty to bring certain disagreeable facts to his lordship's notice. Since this interview followed on a more than ordinarily Black Monday at Tattersall's, the Viscount escorted his wife to the Fakenhams' ball in a mood of considerable dissatisfaction. His friend, Revesby, in whom he had confided, had done his best to raise his spirits by asserting his conviction that the luck would shortly turn, and had even introduced him to the newest gaming-hell, which was located in Pickering Place, and conducted on such discreet lines that the Viscount would not have been surprised to have been asked to give a password before being admitted by the individual who conversed with him through an iron grille in the door. He had played macao into the small hours of the morning, but with indifferent success; and although Sir Montagu was of the opinion that initial losses were to be regarded as auspicious, it was an undeniable fact that his lordship was not in his usual sunny spirits when he arrived at the Fakenham mansion in Cavendish Square.

"Scorched, dear old boy?" asked Mr. Fakenham, who had also visited Tattersall's on settling day.

Sherry grimaced at him.

"You'll come about," said Ferdy encouragingly. "Thought I was aground myself, until Brock gave me the office to back Sweeter When Clothed last Wednesday."

"I laid my blunt on First Time of Asking," said his lordship gloomily.

Ferdy shook his head. "Mistake," he said "Ought to have listened to Brock. Very knowing one, Brock. come and have a glass!"

This advice seemed good to Sherry, and he went off with his cousin to try whether champagne punch would recruit his spirits. They would have taken Lord Wrotham along with them, but his lordship, whose expressive dark eyes were glowing with mingled anticipation and excitement, declined to leave the ballroom.

But the evening was not destined to come up to Wrotham's expectations. Miss Milborne, receiving the bouquet of violets by the hand of her Mama's black page, was torn by conflicting emotions. She could not but be touched by Wrotham's having taken such pains to obtain for her flowers which he believed to be her favourites. She recalled, with a twinge of her conscience, having bestowed this mendacious piece of information on him, and her more compassionate feelings prompted her to carry his offering to the ball, instead of the yellow roses left at the door earlier in the day with his Gace of Severn's compliments. But several circumstances militated against this impulse. In the first place, Wrotham had been inspired at the eleventh hour to send the flowers with the second of his messages in place of the first. *Wear these, and I shall know what to think,* ran the inscription on his lordship's card. This was going too fast for Miss Milborne, who felt that until she herself knew what to think it would be better for his lordship to remain in his present uninformed state. She was ready to indulge herself and her numerous suitors with a little harmless flirtation, but she was a good-hearted girl, and unless she was prepared to accept Wrotham's hand in marriage she did not feel that she should carry to the ball flowers which came to her with so pointed a message attached to them. As she thought the matter over, a slight indignation mingled with her compassion for one so stricken. Really, it was the outside of enough, she thought, that George should neglect her for nearly a fortnight, and then toss a posy of violets to her with an ultimatum attached to it! There was yet another consideration—and not the least of them—that led to George's violets being rejected. Miss Milborne, whose striking beauty could well support the trying colour, was wearing a new gown of pale puce satin and net to the ball, and with this George's violets could not be said to agree. Miss Milborne laid the violets aside, and pinned a spray of Severn's roses to her corsage, determining, as she did so, to soften the blow to George by treating him with more than ordinary kindness.

Alas for such good intentions! No sooner did George, on the watch for her arrival, clap eyes on those yellow roses than he turned pale, and abruptly left the ballroom. In his disordered state he would undoubtedly have rushed from the house had he not encountered his hostess in the ante-chamber. Lady Fakenham, who had known him from his cradle, asked him severely where he was going, and without giving him time to reply bore him inexorably back into the ballroom, and presented him to a young lady who gratefully accepted his reluctant hand for the quadrille which was forming. By the time he had performed his part in this, all the impropriety of fleeing from the house had been recollected, and he retired to prop the wall by the door, his arms folded, and his stormy gaze following Miss Milborne's progress down a country-dance. Since Severn was her partner, he was unable to support this spectacle for long, and soon sought refuge in a small chamber adjoining the ballroom. This had been designed to accommodate any persons who preferred a quiet rubber of whist to the more fatiguing exercise of dancing, but George's aspect was so forbidding that a timid-looking man, who peeped into the room, withdrew in haste to inform his companions that he rather thought they had better find another room for their projected game.

Hero, who had not failed to notice Miss Milborne's roses, and George's haggard appearance, took the earliest opportunity that offered of following him to his retreat. Her tender heart ached for the pain she knew him to be suffering. It was a pain she was not quite a stranger to, and her own susceptibility made it seem the more imperative to offer such comfort as she could to George.

She found him sitting moodily on a small sofa, a glass of brandy in his hand. He looked up, with a challenging expression in his eyes, but when he saw who had come in his brow cleared, and he rose, setting down his glass, and managing to conjure up the travesty of a smile.

Hero clasped his hand between both hers, saying: "Dear George, do not heed it! Indeed, she could not have carried violets with that gown!"

"She is wearing Severn's roses," he replied.

"Oh, no! You cannot know that!"

"Mrs. Milborne told Lady Cowper so within my hearing."

Hero looked dismayed, but rallied. "It can only be because they were more suited to that gown. Sit down, George! I am persuaded you refine too much upon it."

He allowed himself to be pulled down on to the sofa beside her, but gave a groan. "I told her that if she wore my violets I should know what to think. I have had my answer, and may as well go and blow my brains out without more ado."

"Oh, do not say so! You know, George, I think you
210

should have not have sent that message. Perhaps she may not have quite liked it. Have you spoken with her?"

He shook his head. "I could not trust myself. Besides, if I came within reach of that curst fellow, Severn, I should very likely find a means of picking a quarrel with him."

"No, no, don't do that! Should you like it if I were to try if I can discover Isabella's feelings upon this occasion?"

"Thank you! I have observed her to be in excellent spirits!" he said bitterly. "That one so fair should be so heartless!"

"Indeed, I am sure she is no such thing! She has a little reserve, perhaps, and she does not confide in one, but I feel quite certain Severn has not engaged her affections."

He was silent for a moment, pleating and repleating the handkerchief he held, his attention apparently absorbed in this foolish task. His lip quivered; he said in a hard voice: "She will marry him for his possessions, and his rank. It is plain enough."

"Oh, no! You are unjust, George! She has more heart than you believe."

"Once I believed——" He stopped, and dropped his head in his hands, with a groan. "It don't signify! I beg your pardon! I should not be boring on about my affairs. But you cannot know the anguish of having one's love scorned, indeed, I dare say hardly regarded!"

"Dear George, do not say so!" Hero besought him, putting up her hand to smooth his unruly locks. "I know—oh, I know! But do not allow yourself to think there is no hope of her affections animating towards

211

you! It cannot be but that if one truly loves——" Her voice became suspended; she was obliged to wipe a tear from her cheek.

He put his arm round her, in a brotherly way, and gave her a slight hug. "Yes, yes, where there is a heart to be won, of course you are right, Kitten! But in *my* case——! There, do not let us dwell upon it any longer! I am the greatest brute alive: I have made you cry, and I would not do so for the world!"

She gave a shaky laugh. "Only for your sake, dear George! Indeed, I am the happiest creature imaginable, in—in general!"

He turned her face up. "Are you! I hope you may be, for you deserve to be."

She smiled mistily, and because it seemed a natural thing to do under the circumstances, he bent his head, and kissed her.

There was nothing at all passionate in this embrace, and Hero had no hesitation in receiving it in the spirit in which it was clearly meant. Unfortunately, Sherry chose this precise moment to walk into the room with Ferdy and Mr. Ringwood. Having imbibed enough champagne punch to restore him to his usual buoyancy, he had recollected his duty, and was looking for his wife, to do her the honour of dancing with her. He was indebted to Mr. Ringwood for the knowledge of her whereabouts, but it is doubtful if either Mr. Ringwood or Ferdy would have accompanied him on his quest had they known in what a situation he was to find his bride. He arrived in excellent time to see Lord Wrotham, one hand under Hero's chin, plant his kiss on her pretty lips. One moment he stood transfixed, the next he uttered a crashing oath, and took a hasty stride forward. Mr. Ringwood, recovering from his own stupefaction, closed with him, just as George, flushing vividly, sprang to his feet.

"*Sherry!*" Mr. Ringwood said warningly. "For God's sake, dear boy, remember where you are! You can't choke George to death here!"

George folded his arms, and curled his lip sardonically, looking extremely noble and romantic, and awaiting events with a sparkle in his eye. Hero, faintly surprised by her careless husband's extraordinary behaviour, said without the least trace of guilt, or discomposure: "Why, Sherry, what is the matter? Were you looking for me?"

"Yes, by God, I was!" replied Sherry, wrenching free from Mr. Ringwood's grasp. "Damn you, Gil, let go!"

Ferdy, who had been standing with his mouth open, staring, suddenly rose superbly to the occasion, and offered his arm to Hero with a graceful bow. "Let me escort you back to the ballroom!" he said.

"Yes, but—Sherry, you must not mind George's kissing me!" said Hero, looking from one to the other in a little dismay. "Indeed, there was not the least harm in it, was there, George?"

"Dear Kitten," promptly replied George, bowing with even more grace than Ferdy, "there was much pleasure!"

Horrified at such provocative behaviour, Ferdy exchanged one startled glance with Mr. Ringwood, and bore Hero out of the room.

"Of course there wasn't any harm in it!" said Mr. Ringwood. "All the same, you oughtn't to kiss Sherry's wife, George, and as for you, Sherry, if you hadn't drunk so much champagne punch you'd have more sense than to kick up a dust over—dash it, you

213

know what I mean! She's as innocent as a new-born lamb!"

"*She!*" the Viscount ejaculated. He ground his teeth in a very alarming manner, and rolled a fiery eye at Wrotham. "I don't need you to tell me my wife's innocent, I thank you, Gil! But as for that—that rake, that wolf in sheep's clothing, that—that commoner——"

"No, dash it, Sherry, you can't call George a commoner!" protested Mr. Ringwood. "All a mistake! George wouldn't— I wish to God you will stop standing there looking like a hero, George, and beg Sherry's pardon!"

"Never," said Wrotham, flicking an imaginary speck of dust from his sleeve with a flourish of his handkerchief, "in my life, have I begged any man's pardon!"

"Nothing in that, George!" said Ferdy, who had just come back into the room. "Never know what you may come to! Why, look at me! Always swore I'd never bet on a horse with three white stockings, but I did it, and look what came of it! Won in a canter! All goes to show!"

The Viscount ignored this helpful intervention, and, heedless of an anguished plea from Mr. Ringwood, cast to the winds the guiding principle which had carried him scatheless through several years of intimacy with Lord Wrotham. "Name your friends, my lord!" he said fiercely.

"Sherry!" almost wailed Mr. Fakenham. "Consider, dear boy! Not yourself! Can't be in your senses! Put. it down to the champagne! Pay no heed to him, George."

Lord Wrotham, however, replied promptly; "With the greatest pleasure on earth! Gil, will you serve me?"

"You can't have Gil! exclaimed the Viscount hotly.

"I'm going to have him myself!"

"Oh, no, you ain't!" retorted George, abandoning his heroics. "You can have Ferdy."

"I shall name both Ferdy *and* Gil," said the Viscount loftily.

"Well, you won't, because I've bespoke Gil already."

"Dash it, you must have other friends besides Gil!" said Sherry.

"I have, but if you haven't enough sense to keep this affair between the four of us, I have!" said George.

"Something in that, Sherry, dear old boy," said Ferdy wisely. "Won't do to spread it about George kissing your wife. If you must call him out—but, mind you, I'm not in favour of it, because you know what he is, and ten to one the whole thing is a hum!—I'll act for you, and between us Gil and I will fix it up all right and tight. But mind this, George! if you choose pistols you're not the man I thought you!"

"Well, I shall," said George instantly.

"Let him choose what he likes: it makes no odds to me!" said Sherry grandly. "I shall send Mr. Fakenham to wait on your second, my lord, and let me tell you that I consider it a curst mean trick of you to name Gil before I had a chance to do so myself!"

CHAPTER 13

It was laid down in the Code of Honour that the first duty of the seconds in an encounter was to do all that lay in their power to bring about a reconciliation between their principals, and never did seconds use greater endeavours in this direction than Mr. Ringwood and the Honourable Ferdy Fakenham. Indeed, neither of these gentlemen confined his powers of persuasion to his own principal; severally, and together, they exhorted and cajoled both would-be combatants. Their efforts met with no success, the Viscount stating bluntly that however innocent George's intentions might have been he was not going to draw back from an engagement; and George taking up the attitude that since he was not the challenger it was useless to address any representations to him whatsoever.

"Dash it, George!" said the exasperated Mr. Fakenham. "You can't expect Sherry to take it back!"

"I don't," said George.

"No getting away from it," said Mr. Ringwood. "You're in the wrong. Ought to own it. No business to kiss Sherry's wife."

"Sherry's a dog in the manger!" said George, his eye kindling. "Why don't he kiss her himself? Tell me that!"

"Nothing to do with the case," replied Mr. Ringwood. What's more, not your affair, George, I don't say you're wrong, but it don't alter facts; *you* ought not to kiss her!"

"Very well! Let Sherry blow a hole in me—if he can!"

"I'm surprised at you, George!" Mr. Ringwood said severely. "You know very well poor Sherry's no match for you!"

"Yes, and there's another thing!" interposed Ferdy. "it's devilish shabby of you, so it is, George, to stand out for twenty-five yards!"

"George!" said Mr. Ringwood, with all the earnestness at his command. "I tell you it won't do! He may not choose to own it, but Sherry knows as well as I do there was nothing in it! Whole affair can be settled as easy as winking! Need only explain the circumstances to Sherry—feel persuaded he would meet you half-way!"

"Do you expect *me* to draw back from an engagement?" demanded George.

"He's in his airs again!" said Ferdy despairingly. "I never knew such a fellow, never!"

"I see no reason why you should not, George," said Mr. Ringwood. "If anyone ever knew anything about it, which they won't, they wouldn't think you was afraid to meet Sherry. The idea's absurd!"

"That's it; absurd!" corroborated Ferdy. "What's more, if they did think it, they wouldn't dare say so," he added, naively. "If you ask me, it's a pity no one does dare say a word you don't like to you: do you good! It would really, old fellow! However, it's no use worrying over that now!"

"Unless you can prevail upon Sherry to withdraw his cartel, I shall meet him at Westbourn Green to-morrow morning," said George inexorably. "And if you think you can so prevail upon him, you don't know Sherry!"

Upon this intransigent note he parted from his friends, leaving them in great perplexity. The trouble was, Ferdy said, that you never could tell, with George. Mr. Ringwood agreed that when Geroge was in his high ropes there was no knowing at all what mad act he would take it into his head to commit. Both gentlemen sat in gloomy silence for some minutes, meditating on all the grim possibilities of the approaching duel. Mr. Ringwood could not but feel that the Honourable Ferdy had touched the very kernel of the matter when he raised his head and said that the devil of it was that George couldn't miss. He drew a breath, and said; "Got to be stopped. Dash it, can't let George kill poor Sherry! Tell you what, Ferdy; nothing for it but to talk to Lady Sherry."

Mr. Fakenham, always very nice in all matters of etiquette, looked shocked, but his scruples were overborne.

"I know it ain't usual," said Mr. Ringwood, "but Kitten is mighty friendly with Miss Milborne, and if there's anyone alive can stop George when he has the bit between the teeth it's she!"

Mr. Fakenham was moved to seize his friend by the hand, and to shake it fervently. "Gil, dear old boy, you're right!" he said. "Always knew you had a head on your shoulders! Not but what it's dashed irregular, you know! Ought never to mention such things to females!"

"Never mind that!" said Mr. Ringwood impatiently. "Go round to Half Moon Street now, while Sherry's safely out of the way!"

The two gentlemen accordingly set forth together, and were fortunate enough to find Hero at home, and alone. They were ushered upstairs into the drawing-room, and here Mr. Ringwood bluntly informed his hostess of the nature of his errand.

Having already a very fair idea of what was toward, Hero did not, as Mr. Fakenham had a horrid fear she might, faint, or go into strong hysterics. Her husband's strictures on her conduct, delivered on their way home on the previous evening, had been so forceful that she had quailed under them, and barely found enough voice to enable her to explain to him that she had been attempting merely to comfort poor George, who was in such despair over Isabella's cruelty. His wrath had cooled by that time, and he had no difficulty in believing her account of the affair; but the stern lecture of which he delivered himself on the impropriety of offering that particular kind of comfort to young bachelors would have done credit to the strictest duenna, and made his wife weep with penitence. The Viscount then unbent, dried her tears, told her that it was not her fault—at least, not entirely her fault—and that he should have known better than to have introduced such a hardened reprobate as George Wrotham to her. This she could by no means allow, and she explained, sniffing dolefully between sentences, that it was indeed her fault, and that George had kissed her in the most brotherly fashion, and without really considering what he was doing. The Viscount replied with some asperity that since she had no brothers she knew nothing of the matter; but being a gentleman of varied experience he was perfectly well able to appreciate the situation, and even—though this he kept to himself— to wish that he had not allowed his temper to get the better of him. But when Hero timidly expressed the hope that he had not quarrelled with George, the only answer she could get from him was an unconvincing assurance that there was no need for her to worry her head over him.

She was therefore in no way surprised by Mr. Ringwood's disclosure. She nodded her head, turning a little pale; and fixing anxious eyes on his face, said: "But George will not hurt Sherry! He could not!"

"Yes, he could," said Ferdy. "Devil of a fellow with the pistols, George! Never misses!"

Her eyes widened. "He *would* not! Not Sherry!"

"Wouldn't put it beyond him at all," said Ferdy, shaking his head. "Tried to call him out a dozen times. Sherry always said he wasn't fool enough to stand up for George to put a bullet through him. Pity he changed his mind."

"But he must not!" Hero cried, starting up. "He *shall* not! Oh, but you are wronging him! I know he would not do so!"

"Queer fellow, George," said Mr. Ringwood heavily. "I don't say he ain't a right one: he is: as game a man as any I know! The thing is, he's got the devil of a temper, and once he's in one of his fits there's no saying what he may do. Do you remember pulling him off that stupid fellow's throat, Ferdy? Can't recall his name, but you'll know! The quiz that married his sister Emily. What I mean is, that shows you, Kitten! His own brother-in-law!"

221

"Mind you, I never blamed him for that!" Ferdy said. "Didn't like the fellow myself. What the deuce *was* his name?"

"Oh, never mind!" Hero exclaimed. "What can it signify? How are we to prevent Sherry's meeting George?"

"That's just it; you can't," said Mr. Ringwood. "Couldn't expect Sherry to hedge off. Why, if I were ever fool enough to call George out, *I* wouldn't hedge off!"

"George ought to beg Sherry's pardon. Trouble is, he won't," said Ferdy. "Come to think of it, he's been spoiling for a fight for a long time. Never can find anyone to go out with him in the general way. If it weren't for Sherry, I'd say it was a shame to ruin the only bit of pleasure the poor fellow has had in months."

"But it is Sherry!" Hero cried.

"Yes," agreed Ferdy mournfully. "Pity!"

"Never mind that!" interposed Mr. Ringwood. "It's got to be stopped. Don't pay any heed to Ferdy, Kitten! You listen to me! And mind! not a word of this to Sherry, for he'd be as mad as Bedlam if he knew I'd breathed a syllable to you, and very likely call me out, and Ferdy too!"

"No, no, I promise I will not say a word to Sherry!"

"*I* can't move George; Ferdy can't move George. Tried our best already. Only one person he'll listen to."

"Isabella!" exclaimed Hero.

"That's it. The thing is for you to see her. Friend of yours. Won't refuse to help you. Persuade her to send for George. Tell her not to spread it about the town, though! Get her to coax George out of the sullens, and send him along to see Sherry. I know Sherry: let

George but hold out his hand, and the whole thing will blow over in a trice!"

"I will go to Isabella at once!" Hero said, the peril in which Sherry stood ousting every other consideration from her mind.

She set forth immediately, arriving at the Milborne residence just as Isabella mounted the steps, with her abigail. Isabella greeted her affectionately, and would have shown her some interesting purchases she had been making, had it not been plain to a much meaner intelligence than hers that Hero had come to visit her on more urgent affairs than frills and furbelows, She at once took her friend up to her dressing-room, and begged to be allowed to know in what way she could serve her.

Until that moment it had not occurred to Hero that there could be the least difficulty in disclosing the whole of her story to Miss Milborne, but under the steady gaze of those lovely eyes she found herself faltering in her recital, blushing a little, stumbling over what before had seemed so simple and so natural.

Miss Milborne heard her out, in slowly gathering wrath. It was just as she had suspected: Hero had indeed stolen another of her suitors, and Wrotham was as volatile as her Mama had so often assured her he was! If she needed any confirmation of the gravity of the episode, she had it in Sherry's challenge to George. Miss Milborne was well aware that no sane man would call George out, except under the most extreme provocation, and since Sherry had shown no signs of inebriety at the ball she failed to allow for the exhilarating properties of champagne punch as mixed by the Honourable Ferdy Fakenham. Her bosom swelled, and she was conscious of a humiliating desire to burst into tears. As for Hero's explanation that George had kissed her because *she* had rejected his violets, she had never heard anything so lame in her life. She said in a trembling voice: "I am sure I do not wonder that Sherry should have called him out! But you, Hero!—how could you do so? I had not thought you so fast, so lacking in principle!"

"I am not so fast or lacking in principle!" said Hero indignantly. "I was so sorry for poor George that if he wanted to kiss me—just for comfort, you know!—it would have been quite horrid of me to have repulsed him!"

"My dear Lady Sheringham, I wish you will not put yourself to the trouble of telling me nonsensical stories!" said Miss Milborne, in what she meant to be a stately manner but which, even to her own ears, sounded merely pettish.

"Isabella Milborne, I think you are the cruellest creature alive!" said Hero, her eyes flashing. "I would not credit it when George said you had no heart, but I think you have none indeed! How can you have looked at poor George last night and not pitied him?"

Miss Milborne averted her face, replying stiffly: "What pity I may have felt for Lord Wrotham—and you are not to be a judge of that, if you please!—was plainly thrown away, since he contrived very speedily to console himself."

"Fudge!" retorted Hero. "He wanted to kiss you, but since he could not, and I was there, he kissed me instead; but as for consoling himself—why, how can you be so stupid? Do you not know how it is with gentlemen? They kiss so easily, and it does not mean anything at all!"

"No, I am happy to say I do not," replied Miss Milborne.

"Good gracious. I quite thought you knew much more than I did, for you have been out for so much longer!" exclaimed Hero ingenuously.

Miss Milborne flushed, and answered in a voice with an edge to it: "Do you mean to suggest, ma'am, that you consider me to be in danger of becoming an old maid?"

"No, I do not—though perhaps you will be one, if you do not learn to be a little kinder, Isabella!"

"Indeed! Perhaps you would advocate my bestowing my kisses with that generosity you youself show?" said Miss Milborne, her colour now much heightened.

Perceiving that she had thoroughly enraged the Beauty, Hero made haste to say contritely: "No, indeed! I beg your pardon: I had no business to say that. It is only that I have a particular kindness for George, and I cannot bear to see him made unhappy."

"I do not presume to advise you, ma'am, but I must hope that your *particular kindness* for Lord Wrotham may not lead you into a worse scrape than this unsavoury affair. Forgive me if I speak too boldly! You have done me the signal honour of confiding in me—with what object I am at a loss to understand——"

"Oh, Isabella, pray do not talk in that missish way!" Hero besought her. "Can you not guess why I have come to beg you to help me?"

"I have not the remotest conjecture."

"Oh, dear, and I was used to think you so clever! The thing is, you must know what George is, Bella!

They say he never misses, and, oh, he must not kill Sherry, he *shall* not kill him!"

Miss Milborne shrugged her shoulders. "I imagine there can be little fear of either killing the other."

"So I thought, but Gil and Ferdy have been with George all the morning, and they say there is no moving him! He *likes* fighting duels—isn't it odd? They say that when he is in one of these tiresome moods there is no doing anything with him! Isabella, I must stop this dreadful meeting!"

"I am sure I do not know how you will contrive to do so."

"That is why I have come to you. Isabella, though he will not listen to Gil or Ferdy, George will listen to you! Oh, will you be so very obliging as to send for him, and make him promise he won't fight Sherry? *Please*, Isabella, will you do that for me?"

Miss Milborne rose to her feet somewhat suddenly. "*I* send for George?" She repeated, in stupefied tones. "Have you taken leave of your senses?"

"No, of course I have not! You must know that there can be nothing he would not do for your sake! You have only to beg him——"

"I would sooner die an old maid!"

Startled by the suppressed passion in the Beauty's voice, Hero could only blink at her in surprise. Miss Milborne pressed her hands to her hot cheeks. "Upon my word, I had not thought it possible! So I am to send for George, and to supplicate him not to engage in a duel! After he has been making shameless love to you! Nothing—*nothing* could prevail upon me to do it! I am astonished you should ask it of me! Pray tell me why you, who are on such intimate terms with him, do not supplicate George yourself! I am persuaded your words must carry quite as much weight with him as mine. More, I dare say!"

Hero sprang up, her hands tightly locked together within her ermine muff, quite as angry a flush as Isabella's in her cheeks. "You are right! I *will* go to George! He does not make shameless love to me; no, for he has no love for me! but he is fond of me, a little, and he did say he would not wish to make me unhappy! I do not know how I can have been so foolish as to think that you would help me, for there is nothing behind your beauty but vanity and spite, Isabella!"

With these words she fairly ran from the room, and down the stairs, letting herself out of the front door, and shutting it behind her with a slam. She entered her barouche, and told the surprised footman to direct the coachman to drive to Lord Wrotham's lodging.

His lordship was at home, and had barely time to straighten his neck-cloth, and run a hand over his tumbled locks before his visitor came tempestuously into the room.

"George!" Hero said, casting her muff on to a chair, and advancing upon him with both hands stretched out.

"My dear Lady Sheringham!" George said, bowing formally, one eye on the wooden countenance of his servant.

This individual reluctantly withdrew from the room, just as Hero cried sharply: "Oh, don't, George! I am in such distress!"

He caught her hands, and held them warmly. "No, no, but Kitten, you *must* think what my man would imagine! You should not have come here!"

"No, I know I should not, but what else could I do? for I know very well you would not come to Half Moon Street."

"Hardly!"

"Then you see that I was obliged to come!"

He glanced quickly out of the window, perceived the crest on the panel of her barouche, and exclaimed: "In your own carriage! Kitten, you are incorrigible! Good God, if Sherry gets wind of this there'll be the devil to pay, and no pitch hot!"

"How can it signify? Nothing could be worse than it is at this moment! George, you must not meet Sherry!"

"I shall certainly do so, however."

She clasped the lapels of his coat, giving him a little shake. "No, I say you shall not! George, you know it was very wrong of us, although we meant no harm. *Please*, George, beg Sherry's pardon, and let us all be comfortable again!"

He shook his head obstinately. "I have never drawn back yet from an engagment, and by God, I will not do so now!"

"Yes, but, George, this time——"

"Besides, I'm dashed if I'll apologize for kissing you! I liked it excessively!" said George brazenly. "If Sherry had a grain of sense, he'd know it didn't mean a thing, too!"

"George, you said you would not wish to make me unhappy!" Hero said desperately.

"No, by Jove, not for the world!"

"But don't you see, you stupid creature, that if you kill Sherry I shall be so unhappy I shall die?" Hero cried.

"Oh, I'm not going to kill Sherry!" said his lordship carelessly. "What put that into your head?"

She released his coat, and stood staring at him. "But they told me—Gil and Ferdy——"

"You don't mean that that brace of gudgeons blabbed the whole thing to you?" George ejaculated.

"But what else could they do, when they thought you meant to kill Sherry?"

"Pooh! nonsense! Who said anything about killing anyone? Good God, Sherry's a friend of mine!"

"Yes, but—but if you do not mean to beg his pardon, I am much afraid he will insist on fighting you," said Hero.

"Oh, lord, yes! He's a regular good 'un, Sherry!" said George, with the utmost cordiality.

Hero regarded him blankly. "George, if you mean to wound Sherry, I would much, much rather you did not!"

"No, no, I won't hurt a hair of his head!" he assured her. "I shall delope."

"What is that, please?"

"Oh!—fire into the air!"

"Well, George, indeed I am very much obliged to you, but would it not be better not to meet Sherry at all?"

"Hang it, no! We must meet! He challenged me!"

"Yes, I know, but—George, if you mean to fire into the air, it seems to me that Sherry may very likely kill you!"

"Sherry? At twenty-five yards?" said George. "Wouldn't hit a haystack at that range! That's why I chose it. Not but what I don't care if he does put a bullet through me," he added, his brow clouding suddenly.

"Well, I care!" said Hero tartly. "He would have to fly the country, and what would become of me then?"

George's gloom vanished in a grin. "Oh, Kitten, you horrid little wretch! Don't tease yourself! He won't hit me."

"You don't feel that I had better warn him you mean to fire in the air?" she asked anxiously.

He took her by the shoulders, and gave her a shake. "You dare tell Sherry one word about this!" he said. "If he knew what you'd done he'd be fit to murder the pair of us! Besides, you've no business to be mixed up in it! You must go home. And not a word to a soul, mind!"

"But I must tell Gil——"

"No, you must not! I'll settle Gil! Deserves to be called out himself for frightening you like this!"

"Oh, no, pray don't do that, George!" she said hastily.

"Wouldn't be any use if I did: there's no getting Gil out at all. But you know, Kitten, I do think you should have known I wouldn't hurt Sherry!"

"To tell you the truth," she confided, "I did not think so, until Gil and Ferdy came to see me. But how odious it was of you to lead them to think you meant to kill him! You are quite abominable, George, you know you are!"

He admitted it, but pleaded that Gil and Ferdy had been in such a pucker that he could not help himself. Hero laughed at this; he escorted her out to her barouche, and they parted on the best of terms. Hero drove back to Half Moon Street, and George sent round a note to Mr. Ringwood's lodging, desiring him to stop making a cake of himself. Mr. Ringwood showed this cryptic missive to Mr. Fakenham, and both gentlemen came to the conclusion that whatever had been the outcome of Miss Milborne's intervention

George had no intention of killing Sherry on the morrow.

Sherry, meanwhile, had been spending a singularly depressing morning with his lawyer. He had been making his Will, a task that engendered in him such a mood of melancholy that he despatched a note to Sir Montagu Revesby, excusing himself from making one of a card party that evening, and would have spent the evening by his own fireside had it not occurred to him that such tame behaviour might be thought to augur a disinclination (to put .it no higher) to meet Lord Wrotham upon the morrow. So instead of indulging his gloomy reflections in his wife's drawing-room he took her to the theatre, and, since the piece was a lively one, contrived to be tolerably amused. Hero enjoyed herself hugely, a circumstance which led his lordship to suppose that she could not be aware of his assignation at Westbourn Green. He naturally would not have dreamed of mentioning such a matter to her, but he could not help thinking that it might come as a severe shock to her if his lifeless corpse were to be borne into the house just as she was sitting down to breakfast, so he tried to drop her a hint.

"You know, Kitten," he said, outside her chamber door, "if anything were to happen to me any time—mind you, I don't say anything will, but you never know!—well, what I mean is, I've made all the proper provisions and—and no strings tied to 'em, so that you'll be able to marry again, if you choose."

"I never, never should!" Hero said, holding his hand very tightly.

"No reason why you shouldn't. Only don't have George, brat! He wouldn't suit you at all!"

231

"Sherry, don't!" she begged. "Nothing will happen to you!"

"No, I dare say not, but I thought I might just mention the matter," he said carelessly. "And if it *did*, I wouldn't wish you to fret about it, you know."

"No, no, I won't!" she promised. "Only don't talk in that way, Sherry, for even though I know nothing will happen to you I do not like it!"

"Silly little puss!" he said, pinching her nose. "Did you enjoy the play?"

"Oh, I *did*!"

"Well, I'm glad of that, at all events," he said, and on this altruistic thought took himself upstairs to bed.

His cousin Ferdy called at the house for him at a chill, slightly misty hour on the following morning. The Viscount was quite ready for him, and except that he looked a trifle more serious than was customary, he seemed to be in good spirits. He jumped up into the tilbury beside Ferdy, his many-caped greatcoat buttoned up to his throat, and asked briskly; "Got the pistols?"

"Gil has," replied Ferdy. He added: "Thought we had best engage a surgeon too, just in case. . . . Still, I dare say he won't be needed."

"You never know," said the Viscount. "Mist's lifting nicely. Couldn't have had a better morning for it!"

They arrived at the appointed meeting-place to find George and Mr. Ringwood already upon the ground. The two principals exchanged formal bows. The seconds, inspecting the deadly weapons, held a short, whispered colloquy.

"George said anything to you?" asked Ferdy.

"No. Putting on airs to be interesting," replied Mr. Ringwood, with brutal candour.

"Dash it, he *can't* mean to blow a hole through Sherry!"

"Just what I think myself. Queer I didn't hear from Lady Sherry, though."

While this dialogue was in progress, Sherry had cast off his drab driving-coat, and buttoned the plain, dark coat he wore under it up to his chin, so that it completely hid his white shirt. He had been careful to choose a coat with small, dark buttons, so that he should afford his adversary no unnecessary mark; and he noticed, with some annoyance, that Lord Wrotham, as though in open contempt of his marksmanship, was wearing the blue and yellow-striped waistcoat of the Four Horse Club, and a coat with gleaming silver buttons.

The paces were measured; the principals took up their positions, the duelling pistols, with their ten-inch barrels and hair-triggers set at half-cock, pointing earthwards; the seconds retreated eight paces; the doctor turned his back upon the proceedings; and Mr. Ringwood took out a handkerchief, and held it up. As it fell, George jerked up his right hand, and deloped. A second later the Viscount's bullet buried itself in a tree-trunk quite three feet to the left of his opponent. The next instant he had lowered his pistol, and said furiously: "Damn you, George, will you *stop* being noble?"

"Good God, Sherry!" George said, disgustedly surveying the wounded tree, "you can do better than that, dash it, man!"

"Better than that? I meant to hit it!" retorted Sherry much incensed.

"Who's being noble now?" demanded George,

strolling across the ground to give his pistol up to Mr. Ringwood. "You must have been practising. Here you are, Gil!"

Mr. Ringwood, too relieved for speech, took the weapon, held out his hand for Sherry's, and restored both to their case. The late antagonists looked at one another measuringly.

"What I've a dashed mind to do," said Sherry, "is to take my coat off to you, George, and see if I can't draw your claret! It's what I ought to have done in the first place!"

"No, my God, not before we've had breakfast!" replied George. His reluctant grin dawned, he thrust out his hand. "I'm sorry, Sherry! Never meant to do it, you know, and really there wasn't a mite of harm in it!"

"Oh, go to the devil!" responded Sherry, gripping his hand. "If ever I met such a fellow! Here, did you think to order breakfast, Ferdy?"

CHAPTER 14

The last shreds of animosity vanished over the substantial breakfast provided by the landlord of an adjacent inn; and so mellowing was the effect of the ale with which the four young gentlemen washed down vast quantities of beef, ham, and pigeon-pie, that Sherry had no hesitation in allowing his friends to share the jest of his having actually gone to the lengths of drawing up his Will on the previous day. George shouted with laughter when he heard about this, and said that if he had known that Sherry could hit a tree when he aimed at it he would very likely have drawn up his own Will. This naturally put Sherry on his mettle, and he at once challenged George to a shooting contest, to be held at Manton's Gallery. Mr. Ringwood, and Mr. Fakenham, always ready for a side-bet, objected that unless George were to be suitably handicapped no one in his senses would bet against him, and the rest of the meal passed in arguing over all the more impossible forms of handicap which suggested themselves to four gentlemen in the sort of high spirits into which sudden relief from twenty-four hours of anxiety had plunged them. When they finally left the inn, Ferdy and Mr. Ringwood went off together in Ferdy's tilbury, and George took up Sherry in his phaeton, promising to set him down in Half Moon Street.

"Kitten will be wanting to be assured of your safety," he grinned.

"Oh, she don't know anything about it!" replied Sherry.

George made no remark upon this for a moment or two, but when he had thought the matter over he decided to be open with Sherry. He said frankly: "Yes, she does. Wasn't going to tell you, but now I come to think of it your coachman knows, and ten to one if you heard of it through him you'd be wanting to cut my liver out again. It was Gil's fault. Ferdy's too. The silly gudgeons thought I meant to kill you. They must think I'm a rum 'un! What must they do but go off to tell Kitten the whole! The lord knows what they thought she could do, for even Ferdy can't have supposed you'd rat, and they can't either of them have meant that she should come to see me—which is what she did do."

"What?" gasped Sherry.

George nodded. "Yesterday morning. You know, Sherry, you ought to keep an eye on your Kitten. Not my business, but she's such a baby there's no knowing what she'll do next. Came to beg me not to meet you."

"If that isn't like Kitten!" exclaimed Sherry. "You know, George, there's no keeping pace with her at all! How was I to guess I ought to have warned her to take a hackney, if she meant to call at a man's lodgings?"

George looked a trifle startled, and said: "The point is she ought not to call at a fellow's lodgings, old boy."

"No, by Jove, she ought not!" agreed Sherry. "Devil of a business being married, George! You've no notion! Never thought I should be kept so busy, but what with the Royal Saloon, the Peerless Pool—yes, I was only in the very nick of time to stop her going off there!—Bartholomew Fair, and now this, not to mention a few other starts—dash it, I don't have a quiet moment!"

"She don't mean a bit of harm, Sherry," said George awkwardly.

"Oh, lord, no! The thing is she ain't up to snuff yet, and that cousin of hers never put her in the way of things."

George feather-edged a corner before saying: "I dare say she wouldn't do anything she thought you might not like. Devilish fond of you, Sherry."

"Yes, I've known her since she was eight years old, you see," responded Sherry, with an unconcern that effectually silenced his friend.

While these events had been taking place, Hero had received an early morning visit from Miss Milborne, who was ushered into the dining-room before the breakfast dishes had been removed from the table. She was looking rather pale, and she bore herself with something less than her usual poise. Without pausing to apologize for calling at so unreasonable an hour, she said impetuously: "You were right! I have not been able to sleep for thinking of it! Indeed I did not mean to be so disobliging! I will do what I may to dissuade Wrotham from engaging in this affair!"

There was not a particle of malice in Hero's nature, and she responded at once with the sunniest of smiles, and a warm hand-clasp, "Oh, I knew I could not be mistaken in you, Isabella! I am very much obliged to you, only it is too late, for they went off some hours ago to Westbourn Green. I cannot imagine what can be detaining them so long!"

Miss Milborne stared at her in horror. "They have gone? And you can sit here, eating your breakfast, as

237

though—— And you called *me* heartless!"

Hero gave a little chuckle. "Oh, but there is nothing to be worried about! George promised me he would not hurt a hair on Sherry's head. He said he would fire in the air, so I can be quite comfortable, you see!"

"And what," asked Miss Milborne, in a strangled voice, "if it is Sherry who kills George?"

"Well, I thought of that, too," admitted Hero. "But George assured me Sherry could not hit him at twenty-five yards, and I expect he must know. Do let me give you some coffee, Isabella!"

"Thank you, no. I collect that you actually called on Wrotham at his lodging?"

"Yes, for what else could I do, when you would not help me? And, indeed, I am very sorry that I troubled you, Isabella, for there was not the least need: George told me instantly that I need have no fear for Sherry. And Gil said I must particularly request you not to mention the matter to a soul, and I forgot to do so."

"Make youself easy on that score: I should not think of prattling upon such a subject!" Miss Milborne said, in a colourless tone. "I must not stay. I am happy to know that my intervention was not needed."

Hero perceived that she had in some way erred, and said nervously: "No, but—but I do hope you do not think—George said that he had not the least notion of killing Sherry, you see, so perhaps my intervention was not needed either."

"Very likely," said Miss Milborne. "It is a case of all's well that ends well, in fact."

"Yes, only—Isabella, pray do not be thinking that George cares a button for me, for nothing could be more nonsensical!"

Miss Milborne gave a tinkling little laugh. "My dear,
238

if I trust that he does not it is quite for your own sake, I assure you! It is nothing to me whom he cares for. Now, indeed, I must go, for I have to drive out presently with Mama! We shall meet at Almack's I dare say. Do you go to the Cowpers' party? I need not ask, however! all the world and his wife will be there, I collect!"

Hero was so much quelled by this bright manner that she could summon up no more courage than sufficed to allow her to escort her friend to the front door, and bid her a somewhat faltering farewell. She began to be much afraid that she had done poor George a very ill-turn; and until the sound of Sherry's step in the hall banished any but the most cheerful thoughts she sat wondering how she could best set matters to rights for that ill-starred lover.

Sherry came cheerfully in, and, as she jumped up, took her by the shoulders and shook her, not very hard, saying; "Kitten, you little wretch, how dared you ask George not to blow a hole through me?"

"But I did not wish him to blow a hole through you, Sherry!" she replied reasonably. "What else could I do? Only I am afraid I have made Isabella very angry, and I don't know what to do!"

"What the deuce has Isabella to say to anything?" he demanded.

"Well, you see, I asked her if she would speak to George, but she—she did not seem to understand any more than you did how George came to kiss me, and she would not do it, and now she is——"

"You asked Isabella to intercede with George for me?" gasped Sherry, the indulgent grin wiped suddenly from his face.

She raised a pair of dismayed eyes. "Oh, perhaps I

239

should not have mentioned that! Please do not mind it, Sherry!"

"Not mind it! Do you know that you have done your best to make me the laughing-stock of town?"

"Oh, no, Sherry, truly not! Isabella was not in the least amused, I assure you!"

He looked very hard at her. "Did Gil and Ferdy set you on to do it?"

"No, no!" she said hastily. "It was quite my own idea!"

"You deserve I should box your ears!"

"No, pray do not!" she said earnestly. "Isabella will not speak of the matter: she said she should not! But, Sherry, I fear she believes that he has been flirting with me! Would you be so very obliging as to tell her that it was no such thing?"

"No, by Jove, I will not!" he declared. "Upon my word, what next will you ask me to do?"

"But if she knew that you do not mind George's having kissed me——"

"But I do mind!" said Sherry, incensed.

"Do you, Sherry?" she asked wistfully.

"Well, of course I do! A pretty sort of a fellow I should be if I did not!"

"I won't do it again," she promised.

"You had better not, by Jupiter! And while I think of it, brat, you are not to visit men's lodgings again either!"

"I do know *that*, Sherry, but it was so very awkward, on account of George's not liking to come to this house, that I did not see what else I could do."

"That's all very well," responded Sherry severely, "but you shouldn't have gone there in your own carriage. Don't you know enough to take a hackney upon such an occasion?"

"I never thought of that!" she said innocently. "How stupid of me it was! I shall know better another time. I am so glad I have you to tell me these things Sherry, for Cousin Jane never told me anything to the point."

It occurred to his lordship that the piece of worldly wisdom he had imparted to his bride was not in the least what he had meant to say, but after all the excitements of the morning he did not feel capable of entering more fully into the ethical and moral aspects of what he knew to have been a perfectly harmless visit to George's lodging. He said that she was on no account to do it again, and abandoned the whole topic.

The relief he had felt when George had deloped on the ground had been considerable, and not even a visit from his man of business availed to subdue a mood of somewhat riotous optimism. His lordship was strongly of the opinion that he would shortly come about, since it was absurd to suppose that a run of ill-luck could last for ever. Mr. Stoke, unable to share his employer's sanguine belief, was obliging enough to cite a depressing number of cases in refutation of it; but the Viscount, having listened with a good deal of impatience to the horrid tale of the gentleman of fortune who, having lost even the coat upon his back at play, hanged himself from a street lamp, while his late opponent waited to collect his coat when he should have done with it, triumphantly produced in defence of his theory the evidence of his having only three days since backed the winner in a race between a turkey and a goose. He was, indeed, slightly taken aback when he read the sum of his obligations, and agreed that to be continually selling out his holding in the Funds would be a dashed bad thing.

"And the next step, as, I am persuaded, I need hardly point out to your lordship," said Mr. Stoke gently, "will be the sale of your lands."

The Viscount had upon more than one occasion stated his dislike of Sheringham Place, and he had not, so far, betrayed the smallest sign of taking more than a perfunctory interest in the management of his considerable estates, but at these words a sudden flash came into his blue eyes, and he exclaimed involuntarily; "Sell my land? You must be mad to think of it! I will never do so!"

Mr. Stoke looked thoughtfully at him, his expression of close interest at odd variance with the meekness of his tone as he said: "After all, your lordship does not care for Sheringham Place."

The Viscount stared at him. "Dash it, what's that to say to anything?" he demanded. "It's my home, ain't it? Good God, there's been a Verelst at Sheringham Place since I don't know when, and not even my grandfather sold a foot of land, and if ever there was a loose-screw it was he! Because I don't happen to like the place——" He stopped suddenly, remembering his boyhood, before the descent of his Uncle Paulett upon his home, recalling companionable rides about the estate with his father, stolen days with an old fowling-piece, a hundred pleasant memories. He flushed. "Besides, I do care for the place!" he said shortly.

Mr. Stoke cast down eyes that all at once held a good deal of satisfaction. "Your lordship finds life in the country a trifle slow," he said.

"Yes, well—well, that ain't to say that I don't mean to settle down presently! In any event, I won't sell my

242

land, so let me hear no more of that!"

"It is my duty to warn your lordship that if your present rate of expenditure is maintained, your lordship will have no choice in the matter," said Mr. Stoke.

"Nonsense! I don't deny I am a trifle scorched this year, but I shall come about!" Sherry said, in a tone that forbade further discussion.

But the shocking thought put into his mind by his man of business refused to be quite banished, and actually cost his lordship an hour's sleep. A heavy plunge on an outsider, backed on the advice of the ubiquitous Jason, did much to raise his spirits, and he told that very safe man at the corner, Jerry Cloves, as he collected his winnings at Tattersall's, that he had best look out for himself now, as the luck had turned. Jerry grinned, and wished his noble patron the best of good fortune, but fortune still appeared to be a little fickle, for his lordship lost a large sum at Watier's that very evening, and was so much exasperated that he threatened to forswear macao altogether.

He had barely recovered from the gloomy reflections provoked by this unsuccessful evening when he received a visit from the Honourable Prosper Verelst, who caught him on the steps of his house, just as he was preparing to saunter down to White's, and bore him inexorably back into the house.

"For you need not suppose, my boy, that I've put myself to the trouble of coming to see you only to have you slip off like that!" said Prosper.

"What the deuce brings you to see me?" asked his undutiful nephew, ushering him into the library behind the dining-room.

"Fond of you, Sherry: always was!" replied Prosper lowering himself into a deep arm-chair. "If you have some of that madeira left which I gave you, I'll take a glass."

His lordship tugged at the bell-pull. "That's all very well, but you don't have to come to see me just when I was about to join a party of friends!" he objected.

"Yes, I do, because you're never at home," said Prosper. "How badly were you dipped at Watier's last night, Sherry?"

Sherry swung round to face him. "What the devil has it to do with you if I was, Prosper?" he demanded dangerously.

"Don't get into a miff now! Damme, I was one of your trustees up till a month or so ago!"

"And a devilish bad one too!" retorted Sherry.

"Well, never mind that! Been hearing tales of your doings, my boy. Too deep! Much too deep!"

"That comes mighty well from you, sir!"

"Nothing to do with the case. I'm a single man, for one thing, and for another I'm a gamester. Fact is, you ain't, Sherry."

"What?" gasped his lordship, touched on the raw.

Prosper shook his head. "Never met a worse one," he said. "Your heart's not in it. Queer thing, when you consider the way my father——However, I'm bound to say your own father was no hand at play. Dare say you take after him. You're a young fool, boy, because it's my belief you only go to those rubbishing hells of yours out of——" He broke off as Jason came into the room, and exclaimed in accents of horror: "Don't tell me you have that fellow in the house! Damme, you might have warned me Sherry! I've left my drab Benjamin in the hall, and there's my snuff-box in one pocket, and——"

244

"Give it to me!" said Sherry briefly, holding out his hand.

Jason sniffed, and reminded his master that he was keeping his fambles clean until Christmas, when the missus had promised him a tattler as good as Mr. Fakenham's.

"Yes, that's true enough," said Sherry. "No need to worry your head about Jason until after Christmas, sir. What the deuce are you doing here, Jason? Where's Groombridge?"

"In his altitudes," responded the Tiger promptly. "A-snoring fit to bring the plaster down, he is."

"Drunk?" ejaculated his lordship. "The devil! I thought he never touched liquor! Where's Bootle?"

"Gorn out. What do you expect, guv-nor, when you said you was going yourself? They'll look as queer as Dick's hatband, they will, the silly chubs, when I tells 'em you was at home all the time. What was you a-ringing for?"

"A pretty state of affairs!" said his lordship wrathfully. "Fetch me the madeira out of the dining-room, and a couple of glasses, Jason! And don't tell me you don't know it when you see it, because I'll lay my life you do!"

"Well, I do, then," said the henchman, with dignity. "I knows all the rum-bumbs, but mind, now, guv'nor! I ain't no bingo-boy, so don't you go a-setting it about you ever seen me with the malt above the water, because you ain't!" With this admonition, he left the room, returning in a few minutes with a decanter in one hand, and two wine glasses in the other. These he planted on the table without ceremony. He then withdrew, turning back in the doorway to inform the Honourable Prosper that his greatcoat pockets contained various other items besides his snuff-box, and that if he did not desire to be bled by a bite he would do well to hide the Ready-and-Rhino more securely.

"If I were you, Sherry, I'd send that rogue packing!" said Prosper.

"He doesn't worry me," responded Sherry, handing him a glass of wine.

"No! He don't steal your property!" retorted Prosper. "When I think of the things of mine that rascal has walked off with—— However, that's not what I came to talk to you about! If you're not mighty careful, my boy, you'll find yourself under the hatches! What the devil takes you to 12 Park Place? Young fool! Frittering a fortune away at French hazard, eh?"

"Fudge!" said Sherry, colouring.

"Fudge, is it? They tell me you're seen about with that fellow Revesby. He take you to Park Place?"

"What if he did?"

"Thought as much," said Prosper, nodding. He sipped his wine, adding matter-of-factly: "Got a strong notion they load the dice there."

Sherry stared at him. "It's a hum! You know nothing of the matter!"

Prosper gave an indulgent chuckle. "If any man in town is to be trusted to know when he's playing with downhills it's I!" he said. "Think you're up to all the tricks, don't you, Sherry? Well, you ain't!" He finished what remained in his glass, and heaved his bulk out of the chair. "Said all I want to," he grunted. "Know why Revesby ain't a member of Watier's? They blackballed him."

This interview annoyed Sherry very much; and as Hero came in not ten minutes after he had seen his uncle off the premises, he naturally told her about it, expatiating at length on the folly of persons who held it possible for a fellow's luck to continue bad indefinitely, and expressing some startling views on the correct measures to pursue when the dice were falling against one. Hero drank all this in, never doubting that every word he spoke was not only infallible, but represented his considered opinion; but she was a little alarmed by a glancing reference to Mr. Stoke's visit earlier in the week. No sooner had she been favoured with a scathing description of this gentleman's errand than she conceived the notion of returning to the modiste who had created them, two ball-dresses, one opera-cloak, and a delicious promenade dress, with gathered sleeves and a high-arched collar, which was designed to be worn with a Spanish lapelled coat of fine orange merino adorned with epaulets and a border of raised white velvet. Sherry, however, when she suggested this sacrifice, was horrified, and forbade her either to do any such thing or to bother her head over such matters. He then passed a few strictures on the household bills, wondered that she should not contrive better, and said that he had no doubt that Groombridge was drinking all the best champagne.

So Hero nerved herself to remonstrate with the ruler of her kitchen. Such was her trepidation that Mrs. Groombridge eyed her with overt contempt, and answered her in a very insolent manner. This was a mistake, for her mistress had a temper. The interview then proceeded on wholly unpremeditated lines, and ended with the abrupt departure of the Groombridges from Half Moon Street. As the master of the house was holding a bachelor dinner-party there that evening, it was small wonder that Bootle, Jason, and the fat page-boy should have looked with as much dismay as respect upon their mistress. But however little Cousin Jane might have taught Hero of the ways of the world, she had unquestionably attended to the domestic side of her education. The page-boy was sent off with a note from my Lady Sheringham to my Lady Kilby, excusing herself, on the score of the headache, from attending a soiree that evening; the superior abigail above-stairs was staggered to learn that she was to assist my lady in the kitchen; Bootle bowed politely to a decree that he was to act as butler; and Hero penetrated the fastnesses of the basement regions, thereby frightening the kitchen-maid so much that she dropped a dish on the stone floor, and was very little use for the rest of the evening. However, this was not felt to signify, since Jason, recommending her to stop napping her bib, offered his services to Hero in her stead, stipulating only that his livery should be protected by a belly-cheat. As soon as the assembled company had grasped that this elegant phrase was a euphemism for an apron, the desired article of clothing was produced; and the Tiger proved himself to be extremely expert amongst the cooking-pots.

It was not until dinner was nearly over that the Viscount noticed that he was being waited on by his valet. Since the party consisted of Lord Wrotham, the Honourable Ferdy Fakenham, and Mr. Ringwood, he had no hesitation in demanding the reason for this departure from the normal, freely hazarding the guess that Groombridge was lying incapable on the pantry floor. Bootle, who disapproved of such unceremonious behaviour, returned a non-committal answer; but Jason, who was waiting to deliver the next course into his hands, put his head into the room and announced that both Groombridges having piked on the bean the

Missus was cooking the dinner, and in bang-up style.

Upon receipt of this amazing information the whole party repaired at once to the kitchen, Sherry having the forethought to take the wine-decanter along with him, and Ferdy pausing only to secrete his watch-and-chain in one of the vases on the dining-room mantelpiece. Hero, delightfully unconscious of dishevelled tresses, flushed cheeks, and a smut on her nose, made them welcome. They drank her health, ate up all the apricot tartlets she had prepared, sampled the contents of the jars on the big dresser, and wondered that they should never before have had the happy thought of invading a kitchen. After that they swept Hero off with them upstairs, leaving the servants to wash up the dishes. Bootle and the superior abigail exchanged speaking glances, the kitchen-maid retired to indulge a mild fit of hysterics in the scullery, and Jason, seating himself at his ease at the table, requested the pageboy to flick him some panam and cash. This intelligent lad, who had for months been enriching an already varied vocabulary from Jason's store, at once complied with the request by cutting the Tiger a large slice of bread and cheese.

On the following day, Bootle, whose sense of what was due to himself would not allow of a repetition of the previous night's performance, volunteered to find and instal a respectable couple to fill the Groombridges' places. He magically produced a cousin of his own, who, with his wife, almost immediately took possession of the kitchen. There was no noticeable diminution in the household bills, but since Mrs. Bradgate grilled kidneys just as Sherry liked them, and always agreed smilingly with everything Hero said; and as Bradgate's depredations on the cellar were too discreet to attract attention, the young couple were able to congratulate themselves on having made a change for the better.

Sherry's more personal affairs seemed to be on the mend too, his friends Revesby and Brockenhurst having counselled him to alter his habits a little. So instead of pursuing his ill-fortune at Watier's, where they played hazard and macao for stakes varying from ten shillings to two hundred pounds, he began to patronize a snug little establishment in Pall Mall, which was presided over by a charming female of considerable address, and where rouge et noir and roulette were extensively played. Sherry passed several successful evenings in this house, and began to nourish the hope that he would soon find himself up in the stirrups again. His uncle, hearing of this new departure, cast up his eyes, and said he washed his hands of the boy.

Others besides Prosper Verelst and Mr. Stoke regarded Sherry's gaming excesses with disfavour. Ferdy Fakenham, dining at Limmer's Hotel with his brother and Mr. Ringwood, actually said that something ought to be done about it, adding hopefully that he thought it might answer tolerably well if Gil spoke to Sherry. Mr. Ringwood declined this office with great firmness, saying that *he* was not Sherry's cousin.

"George might drop him a hint," said Ferdy dubiously. "I wouldn't set any store by what George said myself, but Sherry might."

"Where is George?" asked the Honourable Marmaduke. "Thought he was dining with us to-night?"

Ferdy sighed. "No. He's gone off to the Cowpers' ball. Poor fellow! Don't like to tell him, but the odds are shortening at the clubs: the time was when you could get tens anywhere against Severn's coming up to scratch, but no one's offering better than evens now, and I shouldn't be at all surprised if before long it's odds on."

"Ah!" said Marmaduke profoundly. "What are the odds against the Milborne's accepting him, though?"

Ferdy stared at him. "Wouldn't find a taker, Duke."

"Wouldn't I, my tulip?" retorted his sapient brother. "Let me tell you that that fellow, Revesby, is a good deal fancied by the knowing ones. They say he's been making the running these last few weeks."

"You don't mean it!" said Ferdy, thunderstruck.

"I never liked the Incomparable above half myself," said Mr. Ringwood, "but I never heard there was any harm in the girl, and I don't believe it. She wouldn't have him."

"Just the sort of rum customer females take fancies to," said Marmaduke.

Mr. Ringwood considered this, and was obliged to agree that there was much in what his friend said. "Not that I give a button whom she marries," he said, refilling his glass. "All I say is, it's a pity Sherry has a fancy for the fellow. Got my reasons for thinking he's badly dipped. Bad enough when he's full of frisk; devilish dangerous when he's aground. Wonder if that's why he's throwing his handkerchief towards the Incomparable?"

"You know Mrs. Capel's place in Pall Mall?" asked Ferdy.

"Heard of it," replied Mr. Ringwood. "Sharps and flats."

"Well, Sherry's taken to going there."

"He has?" Mr. Ringwood said, shocked.

Ferdy nodded gloomily. "Plays rouge et noir there."

"Bad, very bad!" Mr. Ringwood said. "What the

251

deuce does he do it for? Don't mind a fellow's gaming a trifle: do it myself! but it's getting to be a curst habit with Sherry! What's come over him?"

"Revesby," replied Marmaduke shortly. He pressed his thumb down on the table. "Got Sherry there. Only has to crook his finger: Sherry's off. Same with Tallerton. Saw it happen."

"Tallerton!" exclaimed Mr. Ringwood, staring.

The elder Mr. Fakenham bowed his head portentously. "You know what happened to Tallerton, Gil?"

"He had an accident when he was out shooting," replied Mr. Ringwood slowly.

"Blew his brains out," said Marmaduke.

"Perfectly true," corroborated Ferdy. "All to pieces, he was. Hushed it up, of course, but there it is. Plain as a pike-staff. Duke had it from Nat Tallerton. The thing is, can't have Sherry doing the same. Dash it, cousin of ours! Besides—— Sherry, y'know!"

"Sherry wouldn't!" Mr. Ringwood said positively.

"No, because Revesby's claws ain't firm enough in him yet," said Marmaduke.

Mr. Ringwood sat up. "What are we going to do?" he demanded.

"Can't do anything," replied Marmaduke. "If you don't know Sherry, I do. Never would listen to reason, and the only time I tried to use my influence on him he went straight off and did the very thing we didn't want him to do."

"That's Sherry all over," agreed Ferdy. "Obstinate! Like it from a child. No managing him at all."

"Lady Sheringham might contrive to check him," suggested Marmaduke.

Mr. Ringwood shook his head.

"She's his wife," insisted Marmaduke. "Dare say he'd listen to her."

"Well, he wouldn't," said Mr. Ringwood, frowning at his glass.

"I don't see that. Taking little thing—still a bride! Stands to reason!"

"No, it don't!" Mr. Ringwood said curtly. "Got to think of something else."

"That's it," agreed Ferdy. "Open his eyes! Might tell him about Tallerton."

"He wouldn't believe you. Tell you what, Ferdy: we shall have to think about it."

They were still—in their leisure moments—considering the problem, when fate took an unexpected hand in the affair.

CHAPTER 15

Ever since the evening when Lord Wrotham had escorted Hero to Almack's Assembly Rooms in his stead, Sherry had been careful to afford no other altruistic gentleman an opportunity for displaying his chivalry. If Hero were invited to attend the Assembly under some matron's wing, he hailed this as a reprieve, and took himself blithely off on his own amusements; but if no matron came forward he offered himself up on the altar of duty with a very good grace, even going so far as to check any attempt on Hero's part to convince him that she would be pleased to stay at home. Heedless his lordship might be, but however little, during the twenty-four years of his existence, he had been in the habit of considering any other desires than his own, he was not deliberately selfish, and he would have thought it a shocking thing to have condemned his wife to forgo a pleasure she obviously enjoyed merely because he himself would have preferred to have been disporting himself in quite another fashion. It was true that when he had so lightheartedly embarked on matrimony he had not bargained for the obligations attached to it; it was equally true that he had warned Hero that he had no intention of altering his habits to suit her convenience. He had moulded his ideas on the conduct of various sportive young matrons of his acquaintance, who certainly felt no overmastering desire to keep their husbands at their sides, but contrived—perfectly discreetly, to be sure—to amuse themselves without these complaisant gentlemen. But Sherry had realized early in his married career that Hero differed essentially from such worldly-wise ladies. Having neither the training that would have fitted her for fashionable life, nor relatives to whom she could turn, she was dependent her husband to a degree that would have alarmed him very much had he known at the outset how it would be. Within a month of their taking up their residence in Half Moon Street, it had been borne in upon his lordship that his wife was no more fit to carve her way through life than the kitten he called her. His lordship, who had never known responsibility, or shown the least ability to regulate his own career on respectable lines, found himself sole lord and master of a confiding little creature who placed implicit faith in his judgment, and relied upon him not only to guide her footsteps, but to rescue her from the consequences of her own ignorance. A man with a colder heart than Sherry's would have shrugged and turned a blind eye to his wife's difficulties. But the Viscount's heart was not cold, and just as his protective instinct had once made him search all night through the woods at Sheringham Place for a favourite dog which had dug deep into a rabbit burrow and had been trapped there, so it compelled him to take such care of his Hero as occurred to him. She had always looked up to him and adored him, and while he took this for granted he was by no means oblivious to it, and did his best to be kind to her. He was amused, but a little touched, to discover that no deeper felicity was known to her than to go about in his company; she would grow out of that soon enough, he supposed, quite forgetting that when she had shown a willingness to go out with Lord Wrotham the instinct of possessiveness in him had led him to discourage such practices in no uncertain manner.

So the Viscount gratified his wife and all his well-wishers by appearing with staggering regularity at the Assemblies, causing even leading optimists, like Lady Sefton, to prophesy that his marriage would be the making of him.

Another gentleman who had taken to patronizing Almack's more than was usual was that ladies' favourite, Sir Montagu Revesby. Blackballed he might have been by his fellow men at Watier's, but for all their exclusiveness the patronesses of Almack's were not proof against air, manner, and the easy address which characterized Sir Montagu. Had he been of plebeian birth, of course, no amount of air or manner would have availed him in those august eyes, but happily for himself his lineage was irreproachable. Such censorious remarks as were made by Mr. Fakenham, and others of his kidney, were generally ascribed to jealousy and not much heeded and it was only the older and soberer members amongst the ladies who viewed with disapproval Sir Montagu's increasing attentions towards Miss Milborne.

For there could be no doubt that Sir Montagu's sudden predilection for dancing had its root in his admiration of the Incomparable. Until his entry into the lists, the knowledgeable had considered Lord Wrotham to be his Grace of Severn's most serious rival. But Wrotham had never succeeded in walking away with Miss Milborne from under his grace's nose, and this was what Sir Montagu in the easiest manner possible contrived to do. It may have been that the Beauty did not altogether relish the certainty with which Severn claimed her hand for the German waltz; it may have been that she found Sir Montagu's light touch a relief after the passionate earnestness of her younger admirers; certain it was that she bestowed her hand on him for the waltz, and left his grace discomfited. His self-consequence was too great to allow of his following George's example of folding his arms and gloweringly watching Miss Milborne's progress round the room. He led another lady out to dance, but his manoeuvres on the floor to keep Miss Milborne under observation were extremely diverting to several persons who had been watching the little comedy, notably my Lord Sheringham, who gave a spurt of laughter and bade his wife, with whom he was dancing, watch Monty cutting Severn out with the Incomparable! His grace was too pompous to be popular with the greater number of his contemporaries, and the notion of cutting him out himself occurred to Sherry. He entered into a wager with his cousin Ferdy that he would do it, backing himself for a handsome sum, and engaging not to make the attempt until the Duke was again soliciting Miss Milborne's hand. He surrendered Hero to Mr. Ringwood, who had come with them to the Assembly Rooms, and bore down upon Miss Milborne just as the Duke made her a formal bow, and began to say; "May I hope, ma'am——?"

" 'Evening, Severn!" interrupted his lordship cheerfully. "My dance, Bella, I think!"

The Duke eyed him frostily. "I was about to beg Miss Milborne to do me the honour of bestowing her hand upon me," he said. "Ma'am——"

His most mischievous smile danced in Sherry's eyes,

258

drawing an answering gleam from Miss Milborne. "Oh, I was before you in the lists!" he said outrageously. "For old times' sake, Bella, my sweet life!"

"Sherry, how can you?" she said, a tremor of laughter in her voice But she gave him her hand and let him lead her on to the floor. "You are quite shameless!" she told him, as they began to circle round the room. "I had not thought what a long time it is since I danced the waltz with you!"

"Too long, by Jove!" responded his lordship promptly. "Ah, Bella, you should have never refused me! What a couple we must have made!"

She laughed up at him. "I never liked you as well until you gave up wanting me to marry you, Sherry!"

"I? Good God, don't I carry a broken heart in my breast?"

"You hide it admirably! Wretch! You did not wear the willow for my sake for as much as one day!"

His arm tightened round her waist; he smiled down into her eyes. "If there weren't so many people watching, do you know what I would do, Bella? I'd kiss you! Dashed if I ever saw you look more beautiful!"

"For shame, Sherry! Remember, you are a sober married man now!"

"Lord, yes, so I am!" He glanced round the room. "What has become of Kitten? I left her with Gil, and I'd give a pony to see the old fellow waltzing! No, by Jupiter, he's ratted! She's dancing with George."

"Yes," said Miss Milborne, losing her sparkle. "How well they suit, to be sure! I am happy to see George in better spirits."

"Kitten always can contrive to cheer the poor fellow

up," said his lordship unconcernedly.

The poor fellow was saying at that moment; "I should like to know what the deuce Sherry means by making Isabella laugh like that! Yes, and he made her blush a moment ago! I saw her!"

"Do not look at them!" said Hero. "If I were you, I would not let Isabella see that I cared whom she danced with, George!"

"Well, I do care," he replied unnecessarily. "Besides, I don't see what should get into Sherry to make him flirt with her when he is married to you! For that is what he is doing, Kitten! There's no getting away from it!"

"Well, if I do not mind it I am sure you need not."

His brilliant, dark eyes glanced down into hers. "Do you not mind it?" he asked forthrightly.

She sighed faintly. "Only a very little, George. If we went into the other room we need not see them, and you could bring me a glass of orgeat, and we should be comfortable, don't you think?"

He led her off the floor. "No. There is no comfort for either of us!" he said, with suppressed passion.

However, a certain measure of comfort was found in the refreshment saloon, for they discovered Mr. Ringwood and Ferdy there, and Ferdy at once disclosed the nature of the wager which he had lost. Hero was a good deal amused, and George's brow lightened for a moment. But it soon clouded again when he recalled that when he had made just such an attempt as Sherry's earlier in the evening, it had not met with a like degree of success. When Sherry presently brought Miss Milborne into the saloon in search of iced lemonade, he bore down upon them instantly, and, ignoring Sherry, earnestly besought the Beauty to dance the next waltz with him. She excused herself, and would have joined the group round Hero had he not barred the way.

"You shall not fob me off so!" he said in a vibrant tone. "Why will you not so much as dance one waltz with me? What have I done to offend you? Answer me, Isabella!"

"Good gracious, nothing in the world!" she replied. "It is merely that I am engaged to dance——"

"With Severn! It will not do! You will scarcely dance every waltz with him! You use me as though——"

"For God's sake, do not make a scene, my lord! Remember where you are, I beg of you! We are attracting attention!"

"I care nothing for that! Will you dance with me?"

"The next country dance, then, if you will but conduct yourself towards me with more propriety!"

He was obliged to be satisfied, but nothing could have been more disastrous than the dance so grudgingly granted to him. He attempted every time the movement of the dance brought them together to continue a conversation which soon developed into a lively quarrel; and as Miss Milborne disliked being made to look ridiculous, and was well aware of the amused eyes upon them, she came near to losing her temper, and said some cutting things, which she did not mean, but which George took in very bad part.

"Dashed if I ever thought I should be so diverted at one of Almack's Assemblies!" said Sherry frankly. "All the same, Kitten, I think we'll be off before George comes off the floor, or I shall have you kissing him again as like as not, for he'll certainly need comfort from the looks of it. Are you coming, Gil?"

Mr. Ringwood expressed his readiness to leave the rooms, and as Ferdy wandered up at that moment, the Viscount invited them both to return with him to Half Moon Street for some more invigorating refreshment than was to be found at Almack's. The Sheringhams' carriage was called for, and the entire party withdrew, falling in with Sir Montagu Revesby in the vestibule downstairs, and leaving the building in his company. Sherry naturally begged him also to repair to Half Moon Street, but before Sir Montagu had time to reply to this invitation an interruption of an entirely unexpected nature occurred. A figure which had been standing motionless alongside the house started forward, and was seen in the light of a street lantern to be a young woman, clasping in her arms a bundle wrapped in a shawl. If she had not been so haggard, she would have been remarkably pretty, but her face was deathly pale, and there was such a distraught look in her eyes that they seemed scarcely sane. She paid no heed to Hero, descending the steps of the house on Sherry's arm, but put herself in Sir Montague's way, and said in a low, imploring voice; "They told me at your lodging that you would not see me, that you was come here, but I must, I must speak with you! For God's sake, do not cast me off! Again and again I have been to your lodging, but it is always the same answer which I get! I am desperate, Montagu, desperate!"

There was a moment's appalled silence. Everyone stood still, Ferdy goggling at the stranger, and Revesby holding himself tense, his hand clenched on his walking-cane. He looked suddenly pale, but it might have been the uncertain lamplight which made him appear so. His voice broke the silence. "My good young woman, you are making a mistake," he said languidly.

"I fancy I have not the pleasure of your acquaintance."

A moan burst from the girl. "Cruel! Cruel!" she uttered. "Acquaintance! Oh, my God! You shall not cast me off so, you dare not! I will follow you wherever you go! Have you no pity, no compassion? Will you disown your own child? Look! Can you see this innocent, and be unmoved by the ruin you have brought on me?" She opened the shawl as she spoke and disclosed a sleeping infant.

"Good God!" said Mr. Ringwood.

"I never saw you before in my life," said Revesby, still smiling. "You are certainly mad, and I must suppose you to have escaped from bedlam."

"Mad! No! Yet if I am not it is small thanks to you!" she cried wildly. "You said it should be well with me, you promised me—you swore to me——"

"For the lord's sake, Sherry, get your wife out of this!" said Mr. Ringwood, in an urgent under-voice. "We shall have a crowd about us in a trice!"

Sherry, who had been standing transfixed by amazement, pulled himself together. "Yes, my God!" he said. "Here, Kitten, into the carriage! Can't be dawdling here all night!"

But Hero had withdrawn her hand from his arm. "Oh, the poor creature!" she exclaimed pitifully, and ran down the remainder of the steps to the distracted girl.

"Now we are in the basket!" muttered Sherry. "Good God, Gil, what's to be done? What a damned thing!"

"Think I'll be going home, Sherry, dear old boy," said Ferdy in a very cowardly manner. "Won't be needing me!"

"No, Ferdy!" said Mr. Ringwood firmly. "Can't rat

on Sherry. Devilish awkward situation!"

"You know what, Gil?" Ferdy confided in his ear. "Always said the fellow was a commoner! Proves it!"

"Well, I don't like him: never did: but dash it, I'm deuced sorry for any fellow in a fix like this!" responded Mr. Ringwood frankly.

"Yes, by God!" agreed Ferdy, struck most forcibly by this point-of-view.

Hero, meanwhile, had put her arm round the stranger. "Oh, pray do not——! There, let me cover up the dear little baby! Don't cry! Only tell me what it is, and indeed I will help you!"

"Kitten! No, really, Kitten! Dash it, you can't—— Not our affair!" expostulated Sherry.

For once she paid no heed to him; the girl was speaking in a panting voice. "Ask him if he dare deny his own child! Ask him if he did not promise me marriage! Ask him if I was not an honest maid when he saw me first! O God, what is to become of me?"

"No, Kitten, for heaven's sake——!" said Sherry quickly, as Hero turned towards Revesby. "You can't ask Monty—— Why the devil don't you do something Monty, instead of standing there?"

"I beg Lady Sheringham will not allow herself to be imposed upon," Revesby said, his voice a little strained. "The unfortunate female appears to be out of her senses. I recommend she should be escorted to the nearest Roundhouse."

A moan from the girl made Hero clasp her more securely in her arms, and say indignantly: "How dare you? Have you no compassion for this poor soul? Is this dear little baby indeed yours?"

"His! his!" cried the girl. "Look, is she not like him?"

Ferdy, peering at the unconscious infant, said

dubiously: "Queer thing, the way females can see a likeness in a baby. Well, what I mean is they don't look like anything much. Remember thinking so when my sister Fairford's eldest was born. She and my mother would have it it was the image of poor Fairford. Mind you, I'm not saying he isn't a plain-looking fellow, Fairford, but——"

"Oh, be quiet, Ferdy!" interrupted Sherry, quite exasperated. "Yes, I thought as much! Now we are beginning to attract a crowd! Ten to one, someone will be leaving Almack's at any moment, too, and a pretty set of gudgeons we must look——For God's sake, Monty, take the girl away!"

"My dear Sherry, I have already stated that I never set eyes on her before in my life. I must decline any responsibility in this affair. If you are wise, you will summon the Watch and have the wench removed."

All this time the Sheringhams' footman had been standing holding open the door of the barouche, apparently deaf and blind to what was going on. A couple of sedan chair bearers, who had lounged over from the opposite side of the street, now showed an inclination to take up the cudgels in defence of the deserted girl; the door of the Assembly Rooms opened and voices sounded. Revesby turned abruptly on his heel and strode off down the street. A despairing cry from the girl made Mr. Ringwood shudder, and goaded Sherry into desperate action.

"Here, for the lords' sake ·get into the carriage!" he said, pushing both women towards it.

"Yes, do pray come with me!" Hero said to her protegee. "The baby will take cold in this horrid, draughty street, and I promise we will look after you, won't we, Sherry?"

"Yes. I mean—well, never mind that now!" replied her harassed husband. "Drive home, John!"

The coachman acknowledged this command with great stateliness; the door was shut on the two women; the footman jumped up behind; and the barouche moved forward, just as a party of ladies, with their attendant squires, began to descend the steps of Almack's.

Ferdy was still staring at the spot where he had last seen Revesby. Mr. Ringwood thrust a hand in his arm and drew him to walk with himself and the Viscount towards Half Moon Street.

"Never seen anything to beat it!" Ferdy said. "Fellow just walked off! Not a word to anyone! Ratted, by God! Bad, very bad!"

"You wanted to rat yourself," Mr. Ringwood reminded him. "Devilish awkward start! Don't know that I blame him."

"No right to leave Sherry with the baby," said Ferdy severely. "Not Sherry's baby, dash it!"

"The girl's mad!" Sherry said.

"No, she ain't," contradicted Mr. Ringwood. "Dare say it is Revesby's baby: wouldn't be the first."

"Well, damn it, man, what of it? Deuced unfortunate she should have run Monty to earth outside Almack's, but no one ever supposed he was a saint!"

"Ferdy's right," said Mr. Ringwood. "Fellow *is* a commoner! No business to leave the baby to starve. Easy enough to provide for it if it is his baby."

"Girl seemed very certain of it," offered Ferdy. "Said it was like him. Tell you what, Gil: take another look at the baby!"

"No use doing that. Fellow disowned it. Can't force him to provide for it."

"Dash it!" Sherry exclaimed. "If every bit of muslin——"

"Didn't look to me like a bit of muslin, Sherry."

"I don't believe Monty——"

"No, very likely you don't," said Mr. Ringwood ruthlessly. "Fellow's a damned rake, if you ask me."

"Lord, who cares for that? Anyone would think——"

"No one cares. Point is——"

"Fellow has a perfect right to be a rake," agreed Ferdy. "No harm in that. No right to leave the baby in the gutter. Bad *ton*."

"That's what I was going to say," nodded Mr. Ringwood. "Devilish bad *ton*!"

"It's a damned coil!" Sherry said, frowning. "I wouldn't have thought it of Monty! Dash it, there must be a mistake! Monty wouldn't walk off like that if the wench had been one of his fancy pieces!"

"Looked devilish sick," said Mr. Ringwood dispassionately.

"Sick as a horse," corroborated Ferdy. He added, after a moment's reflection: "Would have myself. Dash it, middle of King Street! Everyone coming away from Almack's! But I'll tell you what, Gil: I wouldn't have left Sherry with the baby. Not Sherry!" Struck by a sudden thought, he looked at his cousin. "What are you going to do with the baby, Sherry?"

"Damme, I'm not going to do anything with the baby!" replied Sherry indignantly. "It ain't my affair!"

Mr. Ringwood coughed discreetly. "Dear old fellow——Lady Sherry! What does *she* mean to do with it?"

"That's it," nodded Ferdy. "Seemed very taken with it."

"She'll do what I tell her," answered Sherry shortly.

"Well, what are you going to tell her?" asked Mr. Ringwood.

"I shall think of something," said Sherry, with cold dignity.

Mr. Ringwood began to think that there was more in Mr. Fakenham's desire to disassociate himself from these proceedings than he had at first perceived. He said tentatively: "Dare say you'd like us to leave you, dear boy. Delicate situation: won't want guests!"

"Oh no, you don't!" retorted his lordship.

"Just as you please, Sherry!" said Mr. Ringwood. "Only thought you might prefer to be alone with Lady Sherry!"

"Well, I wouldn't!" said his lordship bluntly.

They had arrived by this time at his house. They were admitted by Bradgate, who informed them that my lady had taken the young person upstairs to her bedchamber. His manner indicated that he accepted no responsibility for this, and washed his hands of whatever consequences might ensue. The Viscount told him to fetch the brandy to the drawingroom, and escorted his two friends up the one pair of stairs which led to this apartment. A fire burned in the grate, but the candles had not been lit. The Viscount thrust a taper into the fire and went round the room kindling the wicks, a heavy scowl marring his countenance. The canary hanging in the wndow-embrasure awoke, apparently in some confusion of mind, and began to sing its morning hymn. The Viscount, with a few bitter animadversions on birds in general, and misguided friends in particular, cast a cloth over the cage and the song ceased abruptly. The butler shortly appeared with a tray, and said in accents of extreme repulsion that he understood that the young person would be spending the night in the spare bedroom. He then withdrew, and the Viscount exclaimed: "Well, that's a nice thing! If it isn't just like Kitten! Now what am I to do? I'm dashed if I'll have Monty's *chere-amie* in my spare bedroom!"

"Baby, too," said Ferdy, shaking his head. "Bound to squall. They do. Very awkward, Sherry. Don't know what you *can* do."

"Well, for God's sake let us have a little brandy!" said his lordship, striding over to the table and seizing the decanter.

It was some time before Hero came downstairs, but after about half an hour she put in an appearance, still wearing her silk and gauze ball-dress, but with her jewels discarded and her curls a little ruffled. She came quickly into the room, a look of great distress in her face, and went towards Sherry with her hands held out, and saying impetuously: "Oh, Sherry, it is so shocking! She has told me the whole, and I never thought anyone could be so wicked! It is all too true! That dear little baby is indeed Sir Montagu's own child, but he will not give poor Ruth a penny for its maintenance, no, nor even see Ruth! Oh, Sherry, how can such things be?"

"Yes, I know, Kitten. It's devilish bad, but—but you have only the girl's word for it, and I dare say, if we only knew——"

"Might be a mistake," explained Ferdy, anxious to be helpful.

She turned her large eyes towards him. "Oh no, Ferdy, there can be none indeed! You see, she told me everything! She is not a wicked girl—I am sure she is not! She is quite simple, and she did not know what she was doing!"

"They all say that," said Mr. Ringwood gloomily.

"How can you, Gil? I had not thought *you* would be so unjust!" Hero cried. "She is nothing but a country maid, and I can tell that her father is a very good sort of a man—respectable, I mean, for no sooner did he discover the dreadful truth than he cast her out of his home, and will not have anything to say to her, which always seems to me shockingly cruel, though Cousin Jane says it is to be expected, because of the wages of sin, which comes in the Bible! Indeed, she is quite an innocent girl, for how could it be otherwise when she believed in Sir Montagu's promise to marry her? Why, even I know better than that!"

Ferdy, who had been listening intently, said at this point: "Now, that's a thing I wouldn't do, Gil! One thing to seduce a girl—though, mind you, I think it's a mistake, myself! Only leads to trouble, and the lord knows there are plenty of lady-birds on the town!—quite another to tell her you mean to marry her. Dash it, too smoky by half!"

Disregarding this interruption, Hero hurried on: "Sherry, she is in such distress! I do not know how she has survived, and if it had not been for a good-natured woman who took pity on her, she must have died of starvation! But it seems that this woman is one of the fruitwomen at the Opera-house, and perhaps Ruth ought not to stay with her, for I recall that you told me, Sherry, that those women——"

"Yes, well, never mind that!" said Sherry hastily.

"Oh no! I remember you said I must not mention it! But the thing is that she took Ruth in, for Ruth came to London to find Sir Montagu, never dreaming that he would refuse even to see her! But he is the most heartless—— Sherry, indeed I am sorry to speak so of a friend of yours, but it is beyond anything! To seduce this poor, ignorant girl—for that is what he did!——"

"Yes, but wait a moment, Kitten!" protested Sherry. "Where? I mean, if she is a simple country maid, as you say she is, I don't see——"

"It was when he was staying in Hertfordshire last winter. I did not know of it, but I dare say you will, Sherry: Ruth says he has an uncle who lives near Hitchin. And it seems he had gone down to stay with him for Christmas, and that is how he met Ruth."

Mr. Ringwood nodded. "That's true enough, Sherry. Old Fortescue Revesby. Expectations," he added darkly.

"I know all that!" Sherry said impatiently. "But what on earth should take him to seduce this wretched girl——"

"Oh, I don't know, Sherry!" interposed Ferdy fairmindedly. "Pass the time away—devilish dull, I dare say!"

"Yes, that is what I think," Hero agreed. "But how wicked, Ferdy! How heartless! How *could* he do so? He has ruined her for mere sport, for I don't believe he ever cared for her in the least degree!"

"You know what?" suddenly said Ferdy, addressing himself to Mr. Ringwood. "Couldn't make out why it all sounds so dashed familiar! Got it now! Saw a piece at the Lyceum Theatre just like it. Father threw the girl out into the snow. Ruth's father throw her into the snow, Kitten?"

"No, no—at least, I don't know! But this is true, Ferdy!"

"Never heed Ferdy!" commanded the Viscount. "The thing is, Kitten, it ain't our affair, and we can't—"

271

Under the wide, shocked gaze from Hero's eyes he faltered, and cast a wild look towards Mr. Ringwood for support.

Mr. Ringwood did his best. "Sherry don't care to have Revesby's baby in his spare bedroom, Kitten. Can't blame him: might keep him awake."

"Oh no, but just for to-night—— Sherry, you would not be so unkind as to turn the poor soul away at this hour of night! You could not!"

"No, I don't say I'll do that, but the thing is, Kitten—— Dash it, what the devil does Monty mean by saddling me with his by-blow?" exclaimed Sherry, in accents of strong indignation.

"Now I come to think of it," abruptly remarked Mr. Fakenham, "it wasn't the Lyceum. It was the Non-Pareil. I'll think of the name of the piece in a minute."

"I thought such things only happened in the theatre," Hero said sorrowfully. "I did not know men could be so wicked!"

"Well, but, Kitten, you don't quite understand!" Sherry said desperately. "It sounds bad, but ten to one there's another side to the story. These little affairs, you know—it don't do to be talking of them, but—dash it, it's the sort of thing that might happen to anyone!"

"Oh *no!*" Hero cried in a breaking voice, her eyes swimming in tears. "Not you, Sherry! Not *you!*"

"No, no—— My God, I hope not!" said his lordship, with a sudden hair-raising vision of the scene which had taken place in King Street. He discovered that his cousin and Mr. Ringwood, both much moved by Hero's cry and look of anguish, were gazing at him reproachfully, and demanded in a voice of wrath: "What the devil are you looking like that for, the pair of you? I never seduced anyone in my life, I'll have you know! What's more, I'm not the sort of fellow to leave his bastards to starve in the gutter. I mean, I wouldn't if I had any, but I haven't—at least, if I have I never heard of them! Oh, the devil!"

His friends, greatly discomposed, at once begged pardon, Ferdy explaining that he had been momentarily carried away. The Viscount was seriously ruffled, but Mr. Ringwood had the presence of mind to refill his glass, and Hero, holding one of his hands between both of hers, said: "Oh no, Sherry, I know you would not! And you will let me help this poor girl, will you not?"

"I suppose something will have to be done about her," said his lordship. "Though I'm damned if I know what! I shall have to speak to Monty, but I can tell you I don't like to do it, for it's as plain as a pikestaff he don't mean to own the child."

"No, no, do not speak to him!" Hero said. "He has done harm enough, and he shall not come near poor Ruth again! I have thought of a scheme that will answer delightfully! She shall go to Melton, and you will let her live in the little empty cottage by the west gate, Sherry, won't you? And she will help Mrs. Goring at the hunting-box, because you know how Mrs. Goring told me when we were there that she could not come by a respectable girl to assist her—oh no, perhaps you do not, but it was so indeed!"

"Hang it, Kitten, she isn't a respectable girl!" expostulated Sherry. "And if I know Mrs. Goring——"

"No, but only consider!" begged Hero. "You may buy her a wedding ring, and we will say that her husband is dead, and no one need know the truth, and she can be comfortable! He was killed at Waterloo. No one could wonder at that!"

"Killed at Waterloo?" interpolated Mr. Ringwood.

"Very good notion," approved Ferdy. A doubt shook him. "At least, I'm not very sure, now I come to think of it."

It was apparent that both he and Mr. Ringwood were bending their minds to mathematical calculation. Mr. Ringwood was the first to reach a conclusion. "No," he said. "June of last year, wasn't it? That's eighteen months ago."

"I make it that, too," said Ferdy, pleased to find himself in agreement with his friend. "Have to think of something else. Very happy to assist you. Dare say I shall hit upon a good notion."

"Oh, we will say he died of some illness!" Hero decided. "There can be no difficulty! And Ruth was used to be a chambermaid in an inn, so she will know how to go on, Sherry. And if you should not object, I think we should give her what we give to Maria. I know it is a little expensive, but we must consider the baby, you know."

Sherry was so much relieved to find that Hero had no wish to keep her unfortunate protegee permanently in the spare bedroom that he agreed to this plan, even going so far as to hand over, upon demand, a bill to defray the cost of suitable baby-clothes for the destitute infant. Hero thanked him warmly and went away to set Ruth's mind at rest, leaving Sherry to congratulate himself on having brushed through the business better than had at one time seemed possible, Mr. Ringwood to wrap himself in apparently profound thought, and Ferdy to devise an artistic death for the hypothetical husband.

CHAPTER 16

Since he was not a young gentleman who was much given to reflection, it did not occur to the Viscount that his next meeting with his friend Revesby need necessarily be attended by constraint. He had been a good deal shaken by the disagreeable light cast on Revesby's character, and by the time he had had a slightly difficult interview with Ruth Wimborne (which was thrust upon him by his wife on the following morning) he had no doubt that her story was true in all its essential features. But he was ready to believe that there might be another side to the story, and had Sir Montagu offered him an alternative version he might have accepted it. But he did not see Sir Montagu for several days, and when they did encounter one another again, Sir Montagu made no reference to the affair. He was at his most urbane; the fracas might never have taken place. Sherry was nettled. He was a generous young man, and he had raised no demur at being called upon to provide for another man's mistress and child, but when he found Revesby apparently forgetful of the whole episode the notion, first put into his head by his cousin Ferdy, that it was not right of the fellow to leave the baby on his hands, began to take strong possession of him.

It began to dawn upon him, too—not quite at once, but very soon—that whatever Revesby's attitude had been, there must be considerable awkwardness in continued intimacy with a man whom one could not, under the circumstances, permit to approach one's wife. Hero had asked him shyly not to invite Sir Montagu to Half Moon Street when she was expected to be present at the party; he had replied that she need have no fears on that score.

"And if he should ask me to stand up with him at Almack's, Sherry, you won't be offended with me if I excuse myself? For, indeed——"

"Make yourself easy: he will not do so! You need do no more than bow to him, should you meet him at any time. It will be better you should do so, you know, for it would cause a deal of talk if you were to cut him. And mind this, Kitten! Not a word of this business to a soul!"

"No, I will not mention it," she promised. "That is—he is paying particular attentions to Isabella, Sherry. Do you not think that I ought to warn her that he is not a proper person for her to know?"

"On no account in the world!" he said emphatically. "Isabella has her mother to keep an eye on her, and you may depend upon it Mrs. Milborne has a very good notion of what Monty is! I wish to God you had a mother too!"

"Oh, but you keep an eye on me, Sherry, so it is of no consequence!" she assured him.

"Yes, it is," he said. "I'm not a female, so how the deuce should I guess what you will be up to next? It is a thousand pities my own mother don't take a fancy to you!"

So far from taking a fancy to her daughter-in-law, the dowager had been solacing herself for the past two months with the task of collecting and brooding over all the indiscretions committed by Hero which were known to the world at large. By some mysterious means she had contrived to discover her son's predilection for deep play at unsavoury gaming-hells, and had actually put herself to the trouble of visiting Hero for the purpose of impressing upon her that such excesses had been unknown to poor Anthony before his marriage had wrecked his life. Hero was quite overpowered, but the dowager arose from the session much refreshed and went away to tell her sympathetic brother that if the worst came to the worst, at least she had told Hero what she thought of her behaviour. After that, and finding that her friends were disinclined to listen to a repetition of her troubles, she withdrew again to Sheringham Place, and the house in Grosvenor Square was once more swathed in holland covers.

Hero, meanwhile, having spent an enjoyable morning buying clothes for Ruth's baby, greatly exasperated her husband by electing to escort this unfortunate young female down to Melton for the purpose of installing her in her new home, and making her known to the Gorings. So the Viscount, returning to his house in good time to accompany his wife to a dinner-party, was met by the pleasing intelligence that her ladyship had gone into the country with Mrs. Wimborne, and would not be back until the following evening. It was apparent, from the hurried note Hero had left for him, that she had forgotten all about the dinner-party; so the Viscount was obliged to create on the spot an aged relative on the distaff side of Hero's family, to endow this mythical person with the feeblest of health, to lay her low upon her death-bed, and thus to account for his wife's precipitate departure from town.

It was more than a week later before he met Sir Montagu under circumstances which permitted of private conversation, and Sir Montagu did not avail himself of the opportunity to take his young friend into his confidence. He had, instead, an amusing history to recount, and a successful day at the races to describe. Sherry, for once impervious to his charm, heard him with rising impatience, and presently broke in on his talk to say bluntly: "Yes, I dare say, but about that affair the other night, Monty——!"

Sir Montagu's brows rose. "What affair, my dear boy?"

"Outside Almack's, of course! You know——"

"Good heavens, Sherry, I had forgotten all about it!" said Sir Montagu, amused. "If the poor young female was not mad, which I am persuaded she must be, it is one of the oldest tricks in the world, my dear fellow! Only she made a bad choice in her victim; I am a little too experienced to be caught by such an imposture, believe me!"

"Doing it rather too brown, Monty!" said Sherry, with quite unaccustomed dryness.

Sir Montagu's smile seemed to harden on his lips. After a moment's pause, he said lightly: "My poor boy, you are very innocent, are you not? Come! let us banish such unsavoury matters! Do you care to join me this evening at a little party in my lodging? I have

Brock coming, and one or two others whom you are acquainted with."

"Mighty good of you, but I'm engaged with a party of my own!" returned Sherry, and swung round on his heel, leaving Sir Montagu to some disagreeable reflections on the unwisdom of mishandling young gentlemen of such uncomfortable mettle.

Unfortunately for his own schemes, it was not given to Sir Montagu to appreciate the fundamental honesty in Sherry which made him shy off in disgust from a disingenuity blatant enough to amount to actual falsity. Sir Montagu, whose pecuniary embarrassments made him all the more disinclined to acknowledge even so trifling an obligation as a bastard child, had decided on the spur of a most unnerving moment to deny all knowledge of a wench whose existence he had indeed almost forgotten, and it would have been quite impossible for one of his character to have recanted, even to Sherry. He consoled himself with the reflection that Sherry's miffs were never long-lived; but when, some days later, he ran into Sherry in St. James's Street, and detected a good deal of reserve in his manner, he felt a considerable degree of chagrin, and had little hesitation in ascribing this coldness to Lady Sheringham, who had bestowed the smallest of unsmiling bows upon him at the theatre a couple of evenings previously.

It was not to be expected, of course, that his estrangement from Sir Montagu would have the immediate effect of weaning Sherry from his gaming habits. But it did keep him away from certain establishments in Pall Mall and Pickering Place where he would be bound to meet Revesby, and send him back to Watier's and White's. And this, as Mr. Ringwood confided to Ferdy Fakenham, was an advantage, for although the play was deeper at Watier's than anywhere else in town, at least that holy of holies was not patronized by sharps or ivory-turners.

It was not long, in the nature of things, before the knowledge of Ruth Wimborne's present whereabouts came to Sir Montagu's ears, for Ferdy told the story to his brother, and Mr. Ringwood let it out to Lord Wrotham over the second bottle of port at a snug little dinner at his lodgings. It was rather too good a joke to be kept from such gentlemen as could be counted on to appreciate it, and the whisper began to circulate in strictly male circles. Sir Matthew Brockenhurst slyly twitted Sir Montagu upon it, and while Sir Montagu laughed at the notion that he could be implicated in the affair, under his mirth he seethed with rage. Correctly assuming that left to his own devices Sherry would never have thought of befriending Ruth Wimborne, Sir Montagu chalked up a fresh score on his tally with Sherry's wife, promising himself the satisfaction of paying it off in full measure. He had a good deal of effrontery, but the situation evoked by the knowledge that his discarded mistress had found an asylum for herself and her infant on one of Sherry's estates was not one he felt himself able to carry off with any degree of grace. He was obliged to face the fact that one of the most richly feathered pigeons to come in his way had flown out of his reach, and showed no disposition to flutter back to him.

It was while Sherry was away at Newmarket that Hero made a new acquaintance. She was one of a party invited by her cousin, Mrs. Hoby, to visit the Pantheon Assembly Rooms on the night of a Grand Masquerade, and it was during the course of the evening that a fashionably dressed woman, with quiet manners, and a great air of elegance, came to Mrs. Hoby's box, and begged to know if she was not right in believing that she was addressing Lady Sheringham.

Hero acknowledged it, and the lady sat down beside her, introducing herself as Mrs. Gillingham, and adding that Lord Sheringham had perhaps mentioned her name to his bride? Upon Hero's replying that he had not, she laughed, and said that it was so very like Sherry to have forgotten all about her.

"I have not been in good health these past few months, or I should have done myself the honour of calling upon you, Lady Sheringham, be sure! I have known Sherry any time these past five years, and I have had the greatest desire to meet his wife. I feel we must be friends: I pride myself on knowing at first glance when I wish for a better acquaintance with anyone!"

Hero blushed, and thanked her, and begged leave to present her cousin. Mrs. Gillingham, who was a good many years senior to any of Mrs. Hoby's party, was extremely gracious and amiable, remained for a short while, chatting easily, and departed only when she had obtained Hero's promise to waive the formality of the morning call, and to make one of a little card party she was giving on the following evening.

"Do you think I should go, Theresa?" Hero asked doubtfully, when Mrs. Gillingham had withdrawn.

"Oh, unquestionably, my dear cousin! Such a distinguished air, and her gown in the first style of elegance! The address too; Curzon Street: it is unexceptionable! She is acquainted with your husband, moreover, and *that* must make her acceptable to you, I have no doubt!"

"Y-es," said Hero. "But Sherry told me once that he knows many people he does not wish to present to me."

Mrs. Hoby gave a little shriek of laughter. "Oh, my dear, what will you say next, I wonder? Depend upon it, Mrs. Gillingham does not come under *that* category! Why, she must be thirty-five, if she is a day, and very likely more!"

So upon the following evening Hero was set down at a slip of a house in Curzon Street, and made a somewhat shy entrance into a saloon already full of guests. Her hostess came forward at once, and made her welcome in the kindest way, introducing her to one or two complete strangers, and pressing a glass of champagne upon her. Hero was a little surprised to find that she knew no one in the room, and after looking about her for a while she began to feel uneasy, and to fear that perhaps Sherry would not have wished her to have come. When Sir Matthew Brockenhurst arrived, with the Honourable Wilfred Yarford, she wished it more than ever, and had she known how to excuse herself without giving offense to her hostess, or drawing upon herself the particular notice she wished to avoid, she would certainly have done so. She did not know, however, and when the company adjourned to a much larger apartment on the first floor, where card tables were set out, she meekly allowed herself to be shepherded up the stairs with the rest of the guests.

She liked playing cards, and since she had been initiated into the mysteries of faro, rouge et noir, macao, and a number of other games of chance by Sherry himself, she naturally considered that she was well able to hold her own in any company. This proved, however, not to be the case. The stakes, too, were much higher than any she had yet played for, and she was soon put into a little confusion by finding herself without any more money to stake. Mrs. Gillingham was kindness itself, smiling at her innocence, and explaining to her how everyone punted on tick until the luck turned for them, and showing her how to write a vowel. Hero remembered hearing Sherry talk of having given vowels, so she knew that this must be the accepted custom, and settled down to win back her losses. She became so absorbed in the game that she scarcely noticed anything beyond the turn of a card; and what with the excitement of the play, the heat of the room, and the champagne which was continually poured into a glass, she began to plunge more and more heavily, arising in the small hours a much greater loser than she had had any very clear idea of. Her vowels appeared, incredibly, to run into four figures, and how she was ever to pay such a sum until her next quarters allowance should be paid to her account she had not the least idea. But here again Mrs. Gillingham was most understanding, assuring her that Jack Cranbourne, who had held the bank, would not dream of pressing for payment, and expressing her conviction that another evening's play would see all the vowels redeemed, and a stream of guineas pouring into her young friends lap. Hero, effectually sobered by her losses, had no desire to spend another evening in this house, but she knew that what Mrs. Gillingham said was true, because Sherry had said the same. One had only to have courage, to ignore one's losses, and to continue playing, for the luck to change, and set all to rights.

But the second night's play was even more disastrous than the first; and some warning instinct in Hero told

283

her that a third would be no more successful. Thoroughly frightened, shivering at the thought of the vast sums she had lost, and not knowing which way to turn in her extremity, she spent what was left of the night in tossing about in her bed, and racking her brains to find a way out of her difficulties. To present Sherry with the sum of her obligations seemed to her unthinkable, for poor Sherry had his own obligations, and had said only a week earlier that they must really try to practise economy. Hero wept into her pillow with grief to think that she should have added to Sherry's embarrassments; and thought that her mother-in-law had spoken no less than the truth when she had accused her of having wrecked his life.

He came home from Newmarket that day, to find a heavy-eyed wife, who explained nervously that she had the headache. He said that he had one himself, and had no hesitation in ascribing it to the malignant behaviour of four out of five of the horses he had backed. Hero turned pale, and faltered: "Was your luck so very bad, Sherry?"

"Devilish!" he replied. "If it goes on like this I shall find myself in the hands of some curst cent-per-cent, I can tell you!" He broke the wafer of one of the letters which had been awaiting him, and ejaculated: "Bills! nothing but bills! There's no end to it! What a damned homecoming for a man!"

"What—what is a cent-per-cent, Sherry?" asked his wife in a small voice.

"Moneylender," he replied, consigning another bill to the fire, and breaking open a more promising-looking billet.

"Do people lend one money?" she asked anxiously.

"Usurers do—at a devilish rate of interest, too! I

know 'em all too well! Used to be for ever at Howard and Gibbs before the Trust was wound up."

"Howard and Gibbs, did you say, Sherry?"

"Yes, they're about the best of the blood-suckers, and that ain't saying much." He looked up from his letter. "What the deuce do you want to know about moneylenders for, Kitten?"

"I—only that I did not perfectly understand what a cent-per-cent is!" she said quickly.

"Well, don't go talking of 'em!" he warned her. "It ain't a genteel expression!"

That highly successful firm of philanthropists, Messrs. Howard and Gibbs, received upon the following morning a visit from a closely-veiled lady, who drove up in a hackney, and was plainly ignorant of the principles which governed the particular form of finance practised by the firm. The respectable gentleman who interviewed this lady seemed at first strangely disinclined to accommodate her. He bewildered her by talking suavely of securities and credentials, but when she disclosed to him her identity his manner underwent a gratifying change, and he not only explained the terms on which the firm would be ready to advance a loan, but expressed his willingness to serve her in any way possible. He seemed to have no difficulty in understanding how it came about that she had lost such a sum in only two nights' play, and showed himself in general to be so sympathetic that his client presently left the building with a high opinion of the whole race of moneylenders.

But while his wife was happily redeeming vowels with the money so generously advanced to her by Messrs. Howard and Gibbs, Sherry had received a billet on gilt-edged, scented notepaper from a lady with whom he had had no dealings since his marriage. He frowned over this missive, for he was not in the mood to embark on the kind of intrigue its mysterious wording seemed to promise. The writer said that she did not like to ask him to visit her, but she had something to say to him which was of vast importance, and which he would regret not hearing. Sherry read this through twice, decided that Nancy had never been one to play tricks on a fellow, and took himself off to the street in which she had her lodging.

He found her at home, and was received by her with her merriest smile and most welcoming manner. "Sherry, I hoped you would come!" she said. "I oughtn't to ask it of you, I dare say, but give me a kiss for old times' sake!"

He obeyed this behest willingly enough, for if she was growing to be a little faded she was still a cosy armful, and he had a fondness for her quite apart from his amorous dealings with her. "Yes, this is all very well, Nancy, but I'm a married man now! Turned over a new leaf!" he said, giving her plump shoulders a hug.

"Lord bless you, Sherry, don't I know that? And you need not be thinking that I've sent for you to make trouble, for that's what I would never do, and so you should know! It's because we had some delightful times together, and I always liked you, that I asked you to come. Yes, and I like the look of that little wife of yours, Sherry—and that's the root of the matter!"

"What the deuce has my wife to do with it?" he demanded.

"Sit down, my dear, and take that ugly frown off your face, do! You've been at Newmarket, haven't you?"

"Yes, but——"

"Well, now, Sherry, if I'm telling you something you don't care to hear from me, just you rememberer that I wouldn't breathe a word if I weren't fond of you, and if I didn't happen to have heard—never mind where!—that that little wife of yours is only a baby who ain't up to snuff like half the fine ladies that hold their noses so high in the air!"

The Viscount's blue eyes were fixed intently on her face. "Go on!" he said briefly.

She smiled at him. "Well, my dearie, I saw your wife where she'd no business to be, and how she came there is what I can't tell you, for try as I will I can't discover who put her in the way of meeting Charlotte Gillingham."

"*What?*" exclaimed his lordship incredulously.

"Yes, my dear, that's where I saw her, and mighty ill-at-ease she looked, poor little creature, not knowing a soul, and wishing she had not come, if I know anything of the matter! And the long and the short of it is, Sherry, that there were some deep doings, and your wife was badly dipped. Now, maybe I wouldn't have said anything about it to you if I hadn't discovered that she went again, the very next night, but she did, and you know as well as I do that if she gets into the hands of that set she will be ruined in more ways than one."

"My God!" Sherry said. "Oh, my God, what next will she do?"

Nancy patted his hand. "Now, don't put yourself in a pucker, for there's very little harm done yet! And don't fly into one of your tantrums with the poor child, for she looked frightened to death when I saw her, and I don't doubt she's had her lesson without your scaring her worse than ever."

"No," he said. "No, I won't. Charlotte Gillingham!

Who in the devil's name——" He broke off, and got up abruptly. "By God, if I thought—Nancy, I'm off! You're a deuced good friend, my girl, and I'm devilish grateful to you!"

"Well, give me another kiss, then!" she said, laughing.

The Viscount reached home again to find that his wife had gone out driving in the Park. It said much for his new-found sense of responsibility that, after a glance at the ormolu clock on the drawing-room mantelpiece, he sent round a note to Stratton Street, briefly excusing himself from accompanying Mr. Ringwood on an expedition to Richmond.

When Hero presently returned to the house, she ran lightly upstairs, and the Viscount heard her moving about in the room behind the drawing-room. She did not sound to be in dejected spirits, which surprised him a little, and when she at last entered the drawing-room the start she gave upon seeing him there was one of unadulterated gladness. "Sherry! I had not thought you were at home! Do you not go with Gil, after all?"

"No. I'm dining at home. Come over here, Kitten: I want to talk to you."

She blushed rosily. "Do you, Sherry? How comfortable that sounds!"

"That's just what it ain't in the least likely to be!" muttered his lordship.

She came to the fire. "What did you say, Sherry'?'

"Nothing. Sit down! Oh, the devil take that bird!" He strode over to the canary, and covered its cage, and turned back to Hero. "Now, brat, out with it! How badly were you dipped at Charlotte Gillingham's house while I was away?"

The colour fled from her cheeks, and the look of

trustful expectancy from her eyes. "Oh, Sherry, who told you?" she said, in a frightened voice.

"Never mind that! How much, Kitten?"

She shuddered. "Oh, don't ask me! It was so shocking!"

"Not ask you!" he exclaimed. "How the deuce am I to settle your debts if I don't know what they are? Don't be nonsensical!"

"Oh, Sherry, Sherry, I am so very sorry! Indeed, I never meant to be such a bad wife! And you are not to settle for me at all, because I am going to pay it myself, and I shall do so, Sherry, because you give me such a big allowance for my pin-money, and I won't purchase any more new gowns, or anything! I promise!"

"That's fudge, brat. Besides, you must pay your gaming-debts at once, you know. Can't expect people to wait for what you owe 'em. Shocking bad *ton*, my girl!"

"Yes, yes, I know that, and indeed I have redeemed all my vowels, though at first I did not know how in the world I could do so, and I felt as though I would rather die than——"

"Just a moment!" Sherry said, catching her unquiet hands, and holding them in a hard grasp. "How did you contrive to come by the money to redeem your vowels? I'll swear you'd little enough left of this quarter's allowance! Kitten, you haven't sold the emeralds?"

"Oh, *no*, Sherry! Of course I have not done such a wicked thing! Why, they are not mine to sell! How could you think I would dream of doing so?"

"Then how the devil did you raise the wind?"

"I borrowed the money!" she replied triumphantly.

"*Borrowed* it? Good God, I had rather you had sold

the emeralds! Who—Kitten, don't tell me you came down on poor old Gil to lend you money!"

"No, no! I knew *that* would not do! I went to those people you told me about, and they were very obliging, and——"

"What people?" he interrupted, turning a little pale.

"I do not recall their names, but you will know, Sherry! you called them cents-per-cent, and they live——"

"Howard and Gibbs!" he ejaculated, in a stunned tone.

"Yes, those are their names," she nodded. "And as soon as I told them I was your wife they—at least, it was just one man—he was most civil, and he said he was perfectly willing to lend me the money, and I need not fear that he would press me for an early settlement."

"I'll warrant he did!" Sherry said. He released her hands. "Howard and Gibbs! Kitten, how *could* you?"

"You are angry!" she faltered. "Was it wrong of me? I did not know. You said you had had dealings with them, and I thought——"

He groaned. "The devil! I said! *I* said! For God's sake, girl, did I ever say that you were to have dealings with them?"

"No, Sherry," she replied, in a small voice. "But you did not tell me I must not, and what else could I do, when I owed all that money?"

He said sharply: "In the devil's name, why could you not have told me? Hang it, I may have boxed your ears once or twice, and I dare say I might have done so again, but you can't have been afraid of me!"

She got up quickly, colour surging into her cheeks. "Afraid of you, Sherry! Oh, never, never! But I felt so dreadfully! You do not understand! You have had such a shocking run of luck and then those horrid horses behaved so badly at Newmarket—I would have done *anything* rather than ask you to pay my gaming-debts!"

He stared at her. "Hero, you could not suppose that I would permit you to fall into the hands of those blood-suckers?"

"But, Sherry, I am persuaded they are no such things! I am to pay back the principal out of my allowance, and——"

"You little fool, they know very well you will do no such thing! They hope you will become more deeply dipped than ever, and fall more securely into their talons, until—— Oh, the devil, where's the use? Listen, brat!—*Never*, whatever happens, have anything to do with moneylenders! It's the surest road to ruin of them all! Yes, yes, I know I've been in their hands myself, but that's another thing altogether—at least, it isn't! I can tell you this: I'll take precious good care I don't fall into 'em again. Promise me, now!"

"I promise. I am very sorry! If I had known you would not like it——"

"I fancy you did know, Kitten," he said shrewdly. "It ain't like you not to tell me what tricks you've been playing."

She hung her head. "Well, I—well, I did not feel *quite* comfortable," she confessed. "But that was mostly because I feared you would be cross with me for going to that house, and gaming for such high stakes."

"So I am," he said. "What were the stakes?"

"F-fifty pounds, Sherry," she whispered.

He gave a whistle. "Were they, by God! What's the figure?" He glanced down at the bowed head. "Come along, brat! I won't eat you!"

"Oh, Sherry, I lost over five thousand pounds!" Hero blurted out.

His lordship preserved his control over himself with a strong effort. After a moment of inward struggle, he said: "Drawing the bustle with a vengeance, weren't you? No, don't cry! It might have been worse. But what possessed you, you little simpleton, to throw good money after bad? For I know very well you went a second night to that curst hell! Had you no more sense than to allow yourself to be plucked again? Good God! is gaming in your blood?"

"Oh, no, no, I am sure it is not, for I was never more uncomfortable in my life! Indeed, I wish I had not gone back, but I did it for the best, Sherry, and truly I thought you would have told me to if I could but have asked you!"

"Thought I—thought I——?" gasped his lordship. "Have you gone mad, Hero?"

"But, Sherry, you told me yourself, when your uncle Prosper had been teasing you, that the only thing to be done was to continue playing, because a run of bad luck could not last for ever, and——" She broke off, alarmed by the expression on his face. "Oh, what have I said?" she cried.

"It's what *I* have said!" replied Sherry. "No, no, don't look like that, Kitten! It's all my curst fault! Only I never dreamed you'd pay the least heed—Lord, I might have known, though! Kitten, don't listen to me when I talk such nonsense!"

Her eyes were fixed on his face enquiringly. "But is it not true, after all, Sherry?" she asked. "I must say, it did not seem to be true, for I lost more heavily than ever, but I thought perhaps I had not persevered for long enough. Only I disliked it so very much that I gave it up in despair."

"Well, thank God for that!" he said. "No, it's not true—at least—dash it, I mean———"

"I see!" she said helpfully, clasping his hand, and giving it a squeeze. "You mean it is the same as going to the Royal Saloon: you may do so, but I must not, on account of being a female."

"Yes, that's it. No, it ain't, though!" said Sherry, his natural honesty asserting itself. "It ain't true for either of us, brat, and if we don't take care we shall find ourselves in the basket. Lord, I couldn't tell you the fortunes which have changed hands over the gaming-table! It's what finished Brummell, and poor Tallerton, and that fellow Stoke prosed on about—fellow who hanged himself from a lamp-post, or some such flummery!" He laughed, as Hero instinctively clutched his arm. "No, I don't mean to follow his example, never fear! I'll see Stoke to-morrow, and settle with Howard and Gibbs, and you need not think any more about it."

"Yes, but I know it will mean that you must sell out those things Mr. Stoke does not like you to sell, and———"

"That's my affair."

"It isn't, Sherry: it is mine! I must own, it would be a great relief not to be owing money to strangers, but if you are to pay for me I will pay it back to you out of my pin-money."

He gave her cheek a rub. "Silly little puss! No, we shall be all right and tight, you'll see! But there's another thing I want to know! Who introduced Mrs. Gillingham to you, brat?"

"Well, no one, Sherry. She introduced herself. She

said she was a friend of yours."

"Are you telling me that that harpy had the effrontery to call upon you?" he demanded.

"No, for she told me she had been in poor health, and so could not do so."

"Ha!" ejaculated his lordship. "Very pretty, by Jove! She would not dare!"

"Oh, dear, I was afraid she could not be quite the thing when I saw the kind of company she kept!" Hero said remorsefully. "For when I went to her house there was no one there whom I was acquainted with, except Sir Matthew Brockenhurst, and Wilfred Yarford, and I know you do not like me to be upon terms with them."

"They saw you there? Damnation!" muttered his lordship.

"They—they did not pay much heed to me, Sherry, and I only bowed very slightly, I assure you!"

"It's not that. If Yarford saw you, it will be all over town! Nothing could be more unfortunate! We shall have all the old tabbies—yes, and not only the old ones!—spreading it about that you're fast. I dare say Brock may keep his mouth shut: dash it, he calls himself a friend of mine! Though, by God, if he were half the friend he'd like me to think him he'd have had you out of that den, and escorted you home! Why, Gil or George, or even Ferdy, wouldn't have hesitated! However, it's too late to worry ourselves over that now! Where *did* you meet the Gillingham?"

"At the Pantheon Assembly Rooms, Sherry. There was a masquerade."

"Whom were you with?"

"With my cousin, Theresa Hoby, and a party of her choosing."

"I might have known! It was her doing, then?"

"No, indeed it was not! Mrs. Gillingham is unknown to Theresa, though she did say that she thought her quite unexceptionable—as I did myself, Sherry, for she seemed so, you know!"

"Yes, I know!" he said grimly. "Tell me the whole!"

She obediently recounted all the circumstances of her meeting with Mrs. Gillingham, and while he listened his brow grew darker and darker. By the time he had been made aware of the manner in which the lady had insinuated herself into his wife's company, of the arts she had employed to inspire Hero with confidence, and of her readiness to permit her to punt on tick, he was looking so much like a thundercloud that Hero faltered in her recital, and could only gaze imploringly at him. She saw then that there was more than anger in his face, an intent expression in his eyes, which seemed to be frowning not so much at her as at something beyond her. She ventured to say; "I have done very wrong, but I did not mean to, Sherry."

He paid no heed; he was looking at the clock. "I am going out," he said abruptly. "I shall be back to dine with you, however."

"Going where, Sherry?" she asked uneasily.

"Never mind that! There is something I have to do—and I'm not dining until I've done it!"

"Don't go! So angry with me——!"

"I'm not angry with you." He put his arm round her, and hugged her. "There! You are the most troublesome brat alive, but you don't mean to be! I ought never—— However, it's done now!" He turned her face up, and kissed her cheek. "Now, don't cry while I'm away, for there is not the least occasion for it! Besides, it don't suit you to have red eyes, and I don't like it. Promise?"

She nodded, rather mistily smiling, and he left the room, ran down the stairs, shrugged himself into his greatcoat, caught up his hat and cane, and let himself out of the house, striding off in a southerly direction down the street.

He had not far to go to reach his goal, and he was fortunate enough to find that the quarry had not yet left the house, although a chair had been called for to carry him to an evening-party, his valet informed the Viscount.

"You need not trouble to announce me," Sherry said, mounting the stairs to the first floor. "I'll announce myself!"

The valet, perceiving nothing unusual in this, bowed, and retired again to the nether regions. Sherry continued on his way to the front parlour, and entered without ceremony.

Sir Montagu, who was dressed for a ball, was adjusting the folds of his cravat in the mirror, and it was in this mirror that his eyes met Sherry's. For an instant he did not move, then he turned, smiling urbanely, and stretching out his hand. "Why, Sherry!" he said caressingly. "You young rascal, you gave me quite a start!"

"Did I?" said Sherry, ignoring the outstretched hand.

"Indeed you did! But you are always a welcome visitor, as I hope you know! What fortune did you have at the races?"

"I've not come to talk to you about the races."

Sir Montagu's brows rose. He said in a chiding tone: "You sound out of reason cross, my dear boy! Now, what has happened to put you in one of your miffs?"

"This has happened!" Sherry said, a very ugly look in his eye. "I find that someone—someone,

296

Revesby!—has been trying to do my wife a mischief while I've been away from home!"

"Well, that is certainly very shocking, Sherry, but what has it to do with me?"

"Spare yourself the trouble of playing off your tricks on me!" Sherry flung at him. "I'm not the fool you take me for! I know what ladybirds you fly with, and Charlotte Gillingham is one of them!"

"Sherry, what in the world——"

"Who set the Gillingham on to lure my wife into her house? She never did so for her own ends! Very clever, Revesby! But not clever enough! My wife was present when you disowned your bastard brat! It was she who took the girl under her protection, and you knew it! Yes, and all the town knows it, but it was not she who split on you, my buck! It was some others whom you would not dare to be revenged on, I fancy! By God, I should have known with what a fellow I had to deal! But I know now, and you shall answer for it!"

Sir Montagu was looking a trifle pale, but he replied with perfect composure: "You are out of your senses, my dear boy. I suspect that you are even a little foxed. I do not know what you are talking of."

"Oh, yes, you do!" Sherry said fiercely. "*I'm* not a country wench to be fobbed off so easily! I knew whom I had to thank for this start as soon as I heard the Gillingham's name mentioned! You fool, did you believe I should not? Why, what a flat you must think me!"

"I think you a hot-headed young man, my dear Sherry. Go and ask Mrs. Gillingham if I had anything to do with Lady Sheringham's visit to her house, if you do not believe me!"

"Where did you raise the money to pay for her playing your game?" Sherry asked insultingly. "Or does she do it for love of you?"

"Go home, Sherry: you are certainly a trifle bosky! I shall not allow you to pick a quarrel with me, you know."

"Won't you, by God!" Sherry said, and struck him across the face with the gloves he held clenched in his hand.

Sir Montagu's pale cheek flamed under the blow, and he stepped back quickly, breathing rather hard, and glaring at his antagonist.

"Well?" Sherry said. "Well? What's your choice? Will you have swords or pistols?"

"I repeat; I shall not permit you to pick a quarrel with me. You are drunk! If you say that I set Mrs. Gillingham on to ruin Lady Sheringham, you will be made to look a fool. I deny it utterly, and she will do so also!"

Sherry stood looking at him for a moment with narrowed, contemptuous eyes. Then he turned away, and set his hand on the door-knot. "My cousin Ferdy told me you were a commoner, Revesby," he said. His words were like the flick of a whip-lash, and Revesby stiffened under them. "He don't know the half of it!" Sherry said. "You're cowhearted—and I never guessed it!"

He waited for a minute, but Sir Montagu neither spoke nor moved. Sherry gave a scornful laugh, and passed out of the room.

CHAPTER 17

When it was gradually borne in upon the Viscount's two best friends that his annoyance with Sir Montagu, instead of blowing over, as they had gloomily supposed it would, had developed into what bore all the appearance of implacable hostility, they were so overjoyed that it was some time before they troubled to enquire into the cause of so complete a break in a most undesirable friendship. It presently occurred to Mr. Ringwood, however, that the Viscount was not in quite such volatile spirits as of yore; and at a convenient moment, as he sat in his friend's library, sampling some burgundy which Sherry had just acquired, he asked simply: "Anything amiss, dear old boy?"

Sherry looked up, surprised. "No, what should be?"

"That's what I wondered. No wish to pry into your affairs. Just thought you wasn't in your usual spirits. Very tolerable wine, this."

"What do you mean, not in my usual spirits? Never better in my life, Gil!"

"Well, I don't know, now I come to think of it, what I mean. Took a notion into my head. I do sometimes.

299

Dare say it was because you left Watier's early last night. Not like you. You ain't at a standstill, Sherry?"

"O, lord, no! Fact of the matter is, I don't mean to be. I've been talking to my man of business, and the long and the short of it is I've been having some over-deep doings, and it don't answer. No harm done, but I don't mean to go Tallerton's way, I can tell you."

"I'm deuced glad of it, Sherry!" Mr. Ringwood said. "Never liked to see you going off with Revesby to those hells of his. Sharps and flats, my boy! Sharps and flats!"

"Well, you won't see me going off with him again to a hell, or anywhere else, for that matter!" Sherry said, an edge to his voice.

Mr. Ringwood met those smouldering blue eyes with a gaze of steady enquiry. "Quarrelled with the fellow, Sherry?"

Sherry gave a short laugh. "I tried to call him out. Called him all the names I could lay my tongue to! Jupiter! I even hit him in the face! He's cow-hearted. Told him so—and he took that along with all the rest!"

"He would," said Mr. Ringwood. "But what made you try to call him out, old boy? Not the baby?"

"The baby? Oh, that! Lord, no!"

Mr. Ringwood maintained a tactful but not unhopeful silence. Sherry refilled the glasses, and wandered over to the fire, and stirred the log on it with his booted foot. He glanced down at his friend. "This ain't to go any farther, Gil."

"Can rely on me, dear boy."

"Yes, I know. I wouldn't tell you if I couldn't. Concerns my wife."

Mr. Ringwood sat up, a look of horror on his countenance. "You ain't going to tell me that ugly customer———"

"No, no, it ain't as bad as that!" Sherry said quickly. He sat down on the opposite side of the fireplace, and told his friend, in a few well chosen words just what had occurred while he was at Newmarket.

Mr. Ringwood listened attentively, uttering sounds, at intervals, indicative of his amazement. He had no hesitation in endorsing the construction the Viscount had put upon the episode. He said that it was as plain as the nose on his face; and when he heard of Sir Montagu's denial he made a derisive noise. By this time the glasses needed to be refilled once more, and when the Viscount had attended to this, both gentlemen spent an agreeable half-hour in recalling various incidents in Sir Montagu's career which did him no credit; and in freely exchanging views on his character and morals which grew steadily more slanderous as the wine sank in the bottle. Their spirits derived much benefit from this exercise, and Mr. Ringwood went so far as to state that he had not felt in such a capital way since first Revesby appeared on his horizon. "All for the best, Sherry, you mark my words! As long as he don't try to play off any more of his tricks on your wife, and he's such a chicken-hearted fellow I don't suppose he would dare to, now that he knows you've smoked him. All the same, you'd best keep your eye on him, dear old boy."

"I mean to," Sherry replied. "Yes, and on Kitten too, my God! You know, Gil, it's the devil of a business! Beginning to keep me awake, I can tell you! It ain't that she means to get into these curst scrapes. But—oh, well!"

Mr. Ringwood studied the wine in his glass. "Wouldn't do anything she thought you might not like, Sherry," he said tentatively.

"I know that, but the devil of it is she thinks I shall
301

like the most shocking things!" Sherry said. "What with her taking every word I say to be Gospel-truth, and fancying that whatever I do must be the correct thing—well, it's enough to turn a fellow's hair white, it is really, Gil! She would never have thought to go to those bloodsuckers, for instance, if I had not been fool enough to say I'd had dealings with them. and I am dashed if she didn't plunge deeper the more she lost at that damned house, all because that's the gudgeon's trick I've been playing myself! Fairly made my blood run cold when I found that out!"

Mr. Ringwood agreed that this was certainly enough to shake any man's nerve; but said after a short pause: "You know what I think, Sherry?"

"Yes: that she don't mean any harm," replied Sherry. "You've said it before—in fact, you're always saying it!—and I know it without your telling me."

"I wasn't going to say that," said Mr. Ringwood. "Going to say, she don't make the same mistake twice. Noticed it."

"Well, I don't see anything in that," replied his lordship impatiently.

"No. There's a deal you don't see, Sherry. Thought so several times," said Mr. Ringwood, and relapsed into meditative silence.

The Viscount was not one to waste his time speculating on the significance of cryptic utterances, and he therefore paid no heed to his friend's words. He had by this time wound up the Gillingham affair, as he called it; and although this process had entailed one or two disagreeable economies, such as the sale of several of his horses, he was inclined to think that he had come out of it better than might have been expected. The truth was that he had been taken aback by the figures laid before him by his man of business. He had not thought that he could have spent so much money. It had been clearly demonstrated to him that his losses over the gaming-table had been excessive, and since he was not so much addicted to gaming as the past year's exploits would have appeared to indicate he was able to resolve, with tolerable equanimity, drastically to regulate this pastime. At any other time of the year boredom might have driven him back to the tables, but the Viscount was a bruising rider to hounds, and the hunting-season was in full swing. He spent a considerable part of his time in Leicestershire, and the only thing that could have been said to have in any way clouded his enjoyment was the growing tendency in himself to wonder what Hero might be doing during his absence.

But Hero was making great efforts to keep out of scrapes, and except for driving down St. James's Street in her phaeton, she committed no very serious social solecisms. She accompanied Sherry to Melton for one week, entertaining Ferdy and Mr. Ringwood at the hunting-box, but as she insisted on riding to hounds and followed Sherry's line with touching if misplaced confidence in his wisdom, he refused point-blank to repeat the experiment. In this he was supported by his two friends, both of whom had had their day's sport ruined by the bride's intrepid behaviour. Since she followed Sherry, she had not committed the crime of riding over hounds, but even Mr. Ringwood admitted that no one could place the slightest dependence on her conducting herself with propriety or discretion in the field.

Lord Wrotham was spending much of his time in Leicestershire too, his last quarrel with Miss Milborne having led to an estrangement between them which was rather skilfully fostered by the Beauty's hard-headed parent. This lady's hopes were running very high, Severn's attentions having become marked enough to have reached his mother's ears. The Duchess arrived unexpectedly in London, bringing with her a formidable entourage which included her chaplain, housekeeper, steward, and a depressed female of uncertain years and crushed demeanour who appeared to fulfill the functions of a lady-in-waiting. The odds being offered at the clubs against his grace's coming up to scratch immediately lengthened; but when it was known that the Duchess had called in state in Green Street, those with handsome sums at stake fairly held their breaths. No one, of course, knew what passed during this morning call, but those who were best acquainted with the Duchess described her demeanour towards the Milbornes at the next Assembly night as extremely gracious. George, who was not well-acquainted with her, could detect no trace of affability in her Roman countenance, and considered her bearing to denote nothing beyond pride and self-consequence. His spirits soared, accordingly, but were soon cast down by the incredible news that her grace had invited Mrs. Milborne and her daughter to spend Christmas at Severn Towers.

It was too true. The Duchess, finding her usually tractable son displaying an obstinacy which reminded her forcibly of the deceased gentleman to whom she was in the habit of referring as "your poor father," was preparing to make the best of matters. She had indeed been agreeably surprised in Isabella. The most searching of enquiries having failed to bring to light any discreditable circumstance in the Milborne lineage, she permitted herself to describe Isabella as a pretty-behaved young female, an encomium which caused her son to become wreathed in smiles, and to exclaim gratefully: "I was certain you would be vastly taken with her, ma'am!"

When George heard of the projected visit to Severn Towers, he lost no time in presenting himself in Green Street. He was fortunate enough to choose a moment when Mrs. Milborne was out, and thus gained access to the Beauty. Without preamble, he demanded to be told if the news were true, and, upon Miss Milborne's admitting that her grace had indeed issued the invitation, conducted himself with so little restraint that Isabella, who had been wavering between a natural desire to make one of a ducal house-party and a maidenly disinclination to give Severn the encouragement which an acceptance of the invitation must imply, quite lost her temper, and not only declared her intention of doing precisely as she pleased, but added the rider that her actions were no concern of Lord Wrotham. His lordship then so far forgot himself as to seize her in his arms, enfolding her in a crushing embrace and covering her face with kisses. How Miss Milborne might have reacted to this treatment had her Mama's butler not chanced at that moment to open the door and to announce the Misses Bagshot no one, least of all herself, could have guessed. In the event, she was furious, and had she not been a very well-brought-up girl she would have slapped George's face. The violence of his ardour had disarranged her hair, she knew herself to be blushing hotly, realized from the butler's expression that he had been a witness of George's passion, and saw that Cassy and Eudora, though they might not have been in time to surprise her in George's arms, had a tolerably exact notion of what had been going forward. She could have screamed with vexation; and when Mrs. Milborne came home she was pleasantly surprised to find that the daughter whom she had left recalcitrant had suddenly become as malleable as the most exacting parent could wish. In fact, Miss Milborne was ready to oblige her Mama by spending Christmas at Severn Towers after all.

Lord Wrotham, dissuaded by his friends from putting a pistol to his head, sought a modicum of relief by quarrelling with the utmost violence with any gentleman obliging or foolhardy enough to join issue with him. He found three. One was Sherry, who succeeded in drawing the distracted lover's cork during the course of several spirited rounds; another was the Honourable Marmaduke Fakenham, who capped every insult flung at him with zest and aplomb, and then very meanly refused to give poor George the satisfaction he craved; and the third was a total stranger who had the ill-fortune to jostle George in a doorway, and who showed himself so ready to take umbrage at George's subsequent behaviour that it was manifest he had no notion with whom he had to deal. However, Ferdy and the inarticulate Mr. Gumley, who happened to be present, hastily drew him aside, and divulged George's identity before he had had time actually to commit himself.

Baulked of his prey, George retired to his ancestral acres, the general decay of which was exactly suited to his mood. Here he divided his time between being very disagreeable to his Mama and his young sisters, and riding to hounds in a reckless fashion, which led his friends to prophesy that he would end by breaking his neck.

The Sheringhams spent Christmas in Buckinghamshire, at the country seat of the Fakenhams, where they made two of a large and cheerful party of young persons, chaperoned not too strictly by Lady Fakenham, who was of an easy-going disposition that made her immensely popular with the younger set. The visit, which lasted for over a week, was only slightly marred by the ravages committed by Jason upon the moveable properties of his master's fellow-guests. These depredations took place immediately upon receipt of the timepiece bestowed on the Tiger by Hero, and were tearfully explained by him to be due to the strain placed on him by the past few months of abstinence. His wrathful master refused to accept this explanation, and a painful session in the stableyard seemed inevitable when Ferdy, whose watch no longer held any lure for Jason, intervened on his behalf, pointing out (to the indignation of several gentlemen whose fobs, seals, and purses had been stolen from them) that the circumstance of his being still in possession of his watch showed that the Tiger was morally much improved. An earnest entreaty from Hero settled the matter. The Viscount consented to pardon his shivering henchman, on condition that all the stolen property was restored. This was done, and upon his lordship's having the happy idea of threatening to send the Tiger back to London if he again allowed his instincts to get the better of him, Jason hurriedly and voluntarily restored to the Honourable Marmaduke a snuff-box which its owner had until that moment believed himself to have mislaid in town.

This affair having been settled to the satisfaction of everyone, nothing else of a like nature occurred to disturb the harmony of the visit. The Festive Season was whiled away in the pursuit of various sports and pastimes, including some pheasant-shooting, a ball, and a grand phaeton-race between Hero and Ferdy's sister, Lady Fairford, who was accounted a notable whip, and who gaily challenged the bride to a trial of skill. The gentlemen threw themselves into this with great zest, arguing over the conditions of the race, deciding upon a suitable course, and freely exchanging bets. Lady Fairford was naturally the favourite, but Mr. Ringwood, feeling his honour to be at stake, backed his own pupil heavily, and gave her some very sage advice. Lady Fakenham said they were a party of sad romps, but raised no real objection to the encounter. It took place within the extensive grounds of Fakenham Manor, and Hero, obeying Mr. Ringwood's instructions to the letter, won it by several lengths. The Viscount was delighted. He said his Kitten was a regular nonpareil, and could drive to an inch; and when she was toasted in extravagant terms at dinner that evening he looked so proud of her that her heart swelled in her bosom, and she could only blush, and shake her head, and look entreatingly at him. So he laughed, and rose to his feet to reply for her. Lady Fairford, who affected a very mannish diction, said that the shine had been taken out of her indeed: Lord Fakenham gave it as his opinion that Letty Lade in her heyday could not have beaten his young friend's performance; and Mr. Ringwood said simply that his pupil had shown herself at home to a peg.

But the race, so innocent and pleasurable in itself, was to lead to disastrous results. It was naturally talked of, and the news that a new and dangerous female whip had arrived in town reached the ears of Lady Royston, the wife of a sporting baronet, and herself no mean handler of the ribbons. She had not until then paid much heed to Sherry's bride, for she was some years her senior, and had, in any event, little time to waste on her own sex. But, meeting Hero at the house of a mutual acquaintance, she did her the honour of singling her out, making much of her, teasing her a little, and wondering what would be the outcome if Hero were to race against her. The notion took extremely amongst the gallants gathered about the two ladies. Lady Royston's admirers swore that no one could beat her ladyship, but a gentleman who had been present at Fakenham Manor at Christmas loyally stated his willingness to sport his blunt on Lady Sherry. In a very short space of time what had begun as the merest pleasantry became sober earnest. Lady Royston challenged Hero to race her over a given course, Hero accepted the challenge, judges and timekeepers were elected, rules agreed upon, a date fixed and bets recorded.

Epsom was to be the rendezvous; and the projected encounter soon became the most talked-of event in society. Hero, dreaming of a victory that would bring that warm look of pride into Sherry's eyes, and place her amongst the most dashing of the Upper Ten Thousand, was blind to the signs that should have warned her that this exploit was a great deal too dashing to recommend her to the more austere leaders of society. Lady Sefton was out of town; Sherry was hunting in Leicestershire with Mr. Ringwood and Lord Wrotham; even Miss Milborne was still at Severn Towers. The only person of experience to draw on the curb-rein was Mrs. Bagshot, and since Sherry had freely stigmatized this lady and all her daughters as a parcel of dowds it was not surprising that Hero should not have attended

to the severe lecture Cousin Jane read her. Mr. Ringwood, returning to London a day later, with a heavy
cold in his head, took to his bed, and therefore heard
nothing of the Ladies' Race; but Lord Wrotham, who
had accompanied him to town, did hear of it, and although he was not one to set much store by convention,
he felt uneasily that it was perhaps not quite the thing
for Sherry's wife to compete publicly in a chariot ract.
He consulted the Honourable Ferdy on the propriety of
it, and Ferdy, who had backed Hero to win without the
least misgiving, was immediately struck by the obvious
impropriety of the whole affair, and said by Jove, he
wondered he should not have thought of it before, and
what the deuce was to be done, now that bets had been
laid, a date fixed, and every arrangement made? Lord
Wrotham agreed that it was very hard to know what
ought to be done, but after he had slept on the problem
he conceived the notion of consulting Mr. Ringwood,
in whose solid judgment he had great faith. Mr. Ringwood, discovered with his feet in hot mustard-and-
water and a bowl of steaming rum-punch at his elbow,
had no doubt at all of what ought to be done. Lady
Sherry must, he said, be instantly warned that such a
start would never do.

"Yes, but who's to tell her?" demanded George
suspiciously.

"You," replied Mr. Ringwood, with great firmness.

"No, damme, I won't! Dash it, Gil, I can't tell
Sherry's wife how she should conduct herself!"

"Must tell her," said Mr. Ringwood. "I'd tell her
myself, if I hadn't this damned cold. Mustn't let this
come to Sherry's ears. Wouldn't like it at all."

Lord Wrotham, eyeing him grimly, favoured him
with a pithy and unsolicited opinion of his cold, his

morals, and his entire lack of bottom. Mr. Ringwood recruited his strength with a liberal allowance of punch, and said briefly: "Tell you what, George: Ferdy must do it."

"Yes, by God!" exclaimed George. "He's Sherry's cousin, and he *shall* do it!"

But Ferdy, hectored into calling on Hero the very next day, did not prove to be a successful envoy. He employed so much tact that he quite failed to impress Hero with a sense of her wrong-headedness. She laughed at him, assured him that he was as stuffy as Cousin Jane, and went off to change her library book at Richardson's before he had said a quarter of the things he had rehearsed on his way to Half Moon Street.

Mr. Ringwood, learning what had befallen, animadverted bitterly on the folly of one friend and the moral cowardice of the other, and announced his intention of calling on Lady Sherry himself upon the following morning.

It was too late. Mrs. Bagshot, coming away from her interview with Hero in high dudgeon, had lost no time in sending off an express to Sherry at Melton, informing him in good round terms of his wife's latest escapade, drawing a horrid picture of its inevitable results, graphically describing the evils of a lady's name being bandied about the clubs in connection with Horse-racing and Betting, and comprehensively washing her hands of the whole business.

This missive reached Sherry on the eve of what promised to be one of the best runs of the season, and it drew from him such an explosion of wrath that Mrs. Goring, who happened to be passing through the hall with a pile of clean linen, dropped six shirts and

311

eight handkerchiefs on to a floor made muddy by his lordship's boots, and promptly succumbed to a fit of hysterics.

Sherry arrived in London at dusk on the day of Ferdy's ill-starred visit to Half Moon Street, having driven himself in his curricle all the way. He was tired, chilled, and he had missed a capital day's sport. Informed by his startled butler that my lady was dressing for a party, he mounted the stairs two at a time, entered his wife's room without ceremony, and, ignoring the presence of her abigail, demanded furiously: "What the devil is this I'm hearing about you?"

The abigail shrank back in alarm; Hero, seated before her mirror, gazed at him in blank dismay, and faltered: "Sherry! *Sherry!* I didn't expect— I don't——"

"No, by God, I'll wager you didn't expect me!" he said. He pulled Mrs. Bagshot's letter from his pocket and thrust it into Hero's hand. "Read that!" He became aware of the abigail, and rounded on her promptly. "What the deuce are you doing here? Outside!"

The abigail then momentarily surprised her young mistress by asserting in a very noble way her fixed resolve to support and protect her ladyship, even though she should be assailed by wild horses. Hero was much affected by this wholly unexpected championship, but begged her to leave the room. Maria cast the Viscount a look of loathing which embraced the entire race of men, and retired to regale Mrs. Bradgate and the kitchenmaid with a recital of all the circumstances in her own career which had led her to look upon the male sex as being in all essentials lower than Beasts in the Field.

Hero, meanwhile, was perusing in a dazed manner

her cousin Jane's letter. She gave a little exclamation and looked up, stammering: "But, Sherry, why? *Why?* I made sure you would not have the least objection!"

"No objection?" he thundered. "No objection to your making such a show of yourself? Bets laid on you in all the clubs! Every goggling fool in town sniggering at you, and believing you to be as bad as Letty Lade!"

"But L-Lady Royston——"

"Sally Royston!" he interrupted. "*Sally Royston!* It needed only that, by God! The vulgarest hoyden—the most shameless baggage——"

"Sherry, no! Oh no, no, how can this be so? I have met her at the most exclusive houses, indeed, I have!"

"So have you met Lady Maria Berwick at the most exclusive houses, and a score of others! Do you desire to model your conduct upon theirs? Good God, will *nothing* teach you?"

She was trembling. "Sherry, if I have done wrong I am very sorry, but how could I guess? Lady Fakenham saw no harm——"

"*What?* She knows of this, and did nothing to put a stop to it?"

"No, oh no! She is in the country still. But at Fakenham Manor, when I beat Lady Fairford——Sherry, you were pleased! You said you were proud of me!"

He stared at her. "That! A private sport, amongst friends, under my aunt's eye! What has that to say to anything? How could you suppose it comparable to a public race at Epsom, of all places, with the whole world free to bet on it, and every Tom, Dick, and Harry to watch it? I think you must be mad indeed!"

She pressed her hands to her cheeks. "I didn't think—— I didn't know——Oh, Sherry, don't be angry with me!"

313

"Not angry with you! When you fall from one scrape into another, disgracing yourself, and me, and——You say you did not know! Did not your cousin tell you? Did she not come here expressly to warn you that you must on no account do such a thing?"

"Yes," Hero gasped, "But I did not heed her, for she said such stupid things, and you told me she was nothing but a dowd! I thought she was just——"

He broke in on this, his expression so alarming that she almost cowered in her chair. "So I told you not to heed her, did I? I might have supposed it would come to that, might I not? *I* said it! *I* encouraged you to race! Of course! It was I who told you to throw good money after bad at faro, was it not, my girl? To borrow from usurers, too, and——"

"Oh, Sherry, don't, don't! Oh, if only I had listened to Cousin Jane, and to Ferdy!"

"Ferdy?" he exclaimed. "Did he warn you, then?"

She nodded miserably. "Yes, but I didn't heed him because he is just as silly as Cousin Jane, and I thought—I thought you would be pleased if I beat Lady Royston!"

An unearthly cry broke from the Viscount, and he clutched his locks with all the appearance of a man driven to the verge of distraction. Hero covered her face with her hands and wept.

The Viscount, regaining control over himself, took a hasty turn about the room, a heavy frown on his brow. He cast a brooding glance at his wife, and said shortly: "It's of no use to cry. That won't mend matters. The odds are you have ruined yourself already with the only people who signify."

Hero could find nothing in this pronouncement to
314

encourage her to stop crying, but she tried hard to do so, blowing her little nose and resolutely swallowing her sobs while his lordship continued to pace about the room. After watching him timidly for a few moments, she got up and ventured to approach him, saying in an imploring tone: "Oh, Sherry, pray forgive me! I will not race—indeed, indeed, I would never have engaged myself to do so had I known you would dislike it so excessively! Sherry, I did not mean to do wrong! Oh, if I were not so ignorant!"

He paused, looking at her. "No, you did not mean any harm. I know that well enough. Are you trying to tell me it is my fault? Well, I know that too, but it don't make matters any easier."

She caught one of his hands and held it in a warm clasp. "No, no, it is not your fault!" she said. "It is I who am so stupid and so tiresome, and I am so *sorry!*"

"Well, it is my fault," he replied. "I should never have married you as I did. If I had not been such a rattle-pated fool I should have known——Well, there's no sense in going over that now, for the mischief's done. The thing is you were never fit to be cast upon the town with no one but me to tell you how to go on."

She dropped his hand, her cheeks whitening, her eyes fixed on his face. "Sherry!" she whispered.

He resumed his pacing. He was no longer scowling so heavily, but he looked suddenly much older and a little careworn. Suddenly he stopped and said crisply: "There's only one thing for it. You have no mother to advise you, so it must be for mine to teach you what you should know. I should have put you in her hands at the outset! However, it is not too late: I shall take you down to Sheringham Place tomorrow. Tell your maid to pack your trunks in good time. I'll give it out that

315

you're indisposed, and are gone into the country to recover your strength."

"Sherry, *no!*" she panted. "You cannot be so cruel! I will not go! Your mother hates me——"

"Stuff and nonsense!" he interrupted. "I tell you there's nothing else to be done! I don't say my mother ain't a deuced silly woman, but she knows the way of the world, and she can——"

She clutched at the lapels of his coat. "No, no, Sherry, don't send me to her! To go home in disgrace——"

"No one need know why you go. Why the devil should anyone wonder at your visiting your mother-in-law?"

"Cousin Jane will know, and all my friends there, and Lady Sheringham would tell everyone how wicked I have been!"

"Fudge! Who said you had been wicked, pray?"

"She will say so! She has said from the start that I had ruined your life, and now she will know it is true! Sherry, I had rather you killed me than send me back like that!"

He removed her hands from his coat-lapels, saying sternly: "Stop talking in that nonsensical fashion! I never heard such fustian in my life! Can you not see that I am doing what I ought to have done at the outset?"

"No! no! no!"

"Well, I am!" said his lordship, a mulish look about his mouth. "No, say no more, Hero! My mind is made up. You'll go to Sheringham Place to-morrow, and I shall take you there."

"Sherry, no! Sherry, listen to me! Only listen to me!" she cried frantically.

"I tell you it is of no use to put yourself in this passion! Good God, can you not understand how impossible it is that we should continue in this manner? I can't put you in the right way of doing things! But my mother can, and she shall!"

He put her resolutely out of his way as he spoke and strode to the door.

"Sherry!" she cried despairingly.

"*No!*" said his lordship, with awful finality, and shut the door upon her.

CHAPTER 18

That evening, his cold having yielded in some measure to judicious treatment, Mr. Ringwood felt so much better that the prospect of spending a solitary evening by his own fireside filled him with repugnance. His man having reported that there was a nasty wind blowing, with a suggestion of sleet in the air, he thought it might be foolhardy to sally forth to one of his clubs, and sent round a note instead to Cavendish Square, begging the honour of Mr. Fakenham's company to dinner and a rubber or two of piquet. Ferdy, moved by his friend's plight, good-naturedly cancelled an engagement he had made to meet some other of his cronies at Long's Hotel, and repaired in due course to Stratton Street, where he was received by a slightly pink-nosed host, clad in the purple brocade dressing-gown he had himself once worn, and with a Belcher handkerchief knotted incongruously round his throat. This ill-assorted attire naturally struck one who was a tulip of fashion to the heart, and Ferdy frankly informed Mr. Ringwood that he looked devlish.

"I feel devilish," said Mr. Ringwood morosely. He added with a flicker of spirit: "At all events I have let my man shave me!"

"Yes," admitted Ferdy, recalling with a shudder Mr. Ringwood's appearance earlier in the day. "If you had not, Gil, dear old fellow, I couldn't have dined with you. Couldn't have fancied a morsel!" He regarded the Belcher handkerchief with misgiving. "And, dash it, I'm not sure I shall be able to fancy anything as it is!"

However, he was presently able to do full justice to a very handsome dinner, consisting of buttered crab, a dish of mutton fry with parsnips, a pheasant pie, with several side-dishes, including some potted sturgeon, and a cold boiled knuckle of veal, and pig's face. Having washed down this repast with some excellent Chambertin, Mr. Ringwood felt much restored, and was even inclined to think that if he imbibed a sufficient quantity of port during the evening, with perhaps a little brandy to top off the whole, the morrow might find him a new man. The Honourable Ferdy having no fault to find with this programme, the covers were removed, the decanters set on the table and the two friends settled down to their game of piquet. In this they were presently interrupted by Lord Wrotham, who had looked in on Mr. Ringwood to discover what, since Ferdy had so lamentably failed in his morning's mission, was next to be done to prevent Lady Sherry's ruining herself in the eyes of the Polite World. Mr. Ringwood explained that he himself had resolved to call in Half Moon Street on the following morning; and the three gentlemen were just lamenting the absence of a fourth who could have made up a table of whist when another knock was heard on the door. The hope that this might herald the arrival of some convivial soul in search of entertainment was shattered a minute later by the entrance into the room of Hero, a bird-cage in one hand and an ormolu clock clutched under her other arm. A cloak was tied round her neck, its hood slipping from her head; she looked alarmingly pale, and there were tear-stains on her cheeks.

"Gil!" she uttered, in a breaking voice. "Help me! Oh, will you please help me?"

The three gentlemen had sprung instinctively to their feet upon her entering the room, and now stood rooted to the floor, gazing at her in the blankest amazement. Mr. Ringwood, horribly conscious of his unconventional attire, showed a craven desire to shrink into the background. It was Ferdy who first recovered his manners, and stepped forward, saying earnestly: "Anything in our power, Kitten! Gil not quite himself—shocking cold in his head! took a toss into a dyke, you know. Allow me to take your clock!"

She relinquished it, gave up the bird-cage to George, saying agitatedly: "Oh, thank you, Ferdy! I did not know you were here! And George! I am so very sorry you are not well, Gil, but what am I to do if you cannot help me, for I have nowhere to go, and no one to advise me, and I am quite desperate!"

"Good God!" exclaimed George, standing with the bird-cage in his hand and staring at Hero. "How can this be? What——"

Mr. Ringwood pulled himself together, assured Hero that his cold was a thing of the past, and drew her towards the fire. "Do, pray, sit down, Kitten, and be calm! Of course I will help you!"

"All help you!" Ferdy interpolated. "Greatest pleasure on earth! No need to worry—not the least in the world!"

"She is chilled to the bone!" said Mr. Ringwood, holding her small hands in his. "For God's sake, George, put down that bird-cage and pour her a drop of brandy!"

Hero allowed herself to be pressed into a seat by the fire, choked over the brandy, and said: "Oh, thank you, no more, if you please! It is only my hands that are cold, and there is such a wind outside!"

"You have not walked here?" exclaimed Ferdy, as though Half Moon Street were situated in the most remote quarter of the town.

"Yes, for what else could I do? Oh, Gil, promise me, promise me—all of you!—that you won't give me up to Sherry!"

Three pairs of eyes were riveted to her face. "Not—not give you up—— Kitten, have you gone mad?" stammered Mr. Ringwood.

"No," she replied, wringing her hands. "Indeed, I am not mad, Gil, though I shall be, or die, perhaps, if he finds me!"

Ferdy's jaw dropped. He swallowed once or twice and then said in a soothing tone: "Thinking of someone else, Kitten! Not Sherry! Very good sort of a fellow, my cousin Sherry. Thought you liked him!"

George, who had been standing gripping the back of a chair, demanded in a voice which boded ill for the absent Viscount: "What has Sherry done to you?"

"He has not done anything yet. That is why I had to run away, to prevent him! I could not bear it, I *could* not!"

"By God!" George swore, his brilliant eyes beginning to smoulder "Only tell me!"

Mr. Ringwood emerged from his stupefaction at this point. He poured himself out some brandy, tossed it off, and set down the glass with the air of a man who was now competent to deal with any emergency. "Hold your tongue, George!" he commanded tersely. "So Sherry's home, is he, Kitten?"

She nodded, two large tears rolling down her cheeks.

"I take it it's this curst race of yours?"

"Yes. How could I have been so wicked and stupid as to—— Oh, Ferdy, if I had but listened to you this morning!"

He shook his head sadly. "Pity," he agreed. "Thought so at the time."

"But even then it would have been too late, for Sherry says they are betting on me in the clubs, and my reputation is quite ruined! Everyone is talking of me, b-bandying my name about——"

"Let anyone bandy your name about in my presence!" said Geroge, grinding his teeth. "Only let them mention your name, that's all I ask! *I* shall know what to do if Sherry don't!"

"How did Sherry get wind of it?" interrupted Mr. Ringwood.

"My cousin Jane wrote him an odious letter and he came home at once, in such anger with me——" She broke off, her voice becoming totally suspended by tears.

Mr. Ringwood exchanged a glance with his friends. "Yes, well, you know, Kitten, can't be surprised at that. Couldn't expect Sherry not to be a trifle put out by this business, for it was not at all the thing. Going to tell you so myself, if Sherry had not come home."

"Oh, Gil, it is far, far more than being put out! You do not know!"

Ferdy cleared his throat. "Got a quick temper, Sherry. It don't mean anything: give you my word it don't! Dare say he's forgotten all about it by now."

She dried her eyes. "He is not in a temper now. I could bear that! But he says it is all his fault for having married me, and we cannot go on in this manner, and his mind is made up that I must go to Sheringham Place so that his mother may teach me—may teach me——But I would sooner die!"

"Sheringham Place at this season?" said Ferdy, horrified. "I wouldn't do that, Kitten! Wouldn't care for it at all! Can't think how Sherry came to take such a notion into his head. Absurd, that's what it is! Absurd! Tell you what: I'll go and have a word with Sherry. Agitation of the moment, you know: probably never thought what the place is like in winter."

"It would be of no avail. I implored him not to send me there in disgrace, but he would not heed me. He said his mind was made up, and he should take me there to-morrow. He means to do so. But he shan't, he shan't! Lady Sheringham hates me, and she will tell everyone what I have done, and how I have ruined Sherry's life, and when I saw his face to-night I knew that it was true! Oh, Gil, oh, Gil!"

"Did Sherry say that?" demanded George fiercely.

"No, no, but you do not know the whole! all the stupid things I have done, and now this! I can see that he is quite tired of it all, and wishes he had never run off with me. And I think he means to try to make the best of it, and he believes his mother will help him, but she will not! So I made up my mind to go away, but then I did not know where to go to, and so I came to you, Gil, because I thought you would advise me."

"But, Kitten, you can't leave Sherry like that!" protested Ferdy. "I mean to say—married to him—better or worse! Not the thing at all!"

"I know, but perhaps he will divorce me, and then he can be comfortable again," explained Hero, on a forlorn sob.

"Good God, no!" cried Ferdy, shocked. "Never had anything like that in our family, Kitten! Besides—well, what I mean is, no reason to divorce you!"

George released the chair-back and strode purposefully to the door. "Where's the sense in talking? I'm going to find Sherry, and when I *do* find him——"

"Oh no, George! Pray, pray do not! George, I implore you do not!" shrieked Hero, turning very pale.

"Don't put yourself about, Kitten! I give you my word, I won't do more than mill him down. I'll bring him here, and by God, I'll make him grovel to you, so I will!"

Ferdy considered this proposition on its merits. "Shouldn't think you would, George," he said judicially. "Very handy with his fives, my cousin Sherry. Drew your cork the other day. Very likely to do it again. No wish to cast a rub in your way, dear boy, but there it is. What's more, I've never known him to grovel to anyone. Mind you, I don't say he wouldn't, but I haven't seen it. Wonderfully stiff-necked, all the Verelsts."

"When Sherry hears what I have to say to him he's not the man I take him for if he don't come straight back with me to tell poor little Kitten he didn't mean a word of it!" declared George.

"You don't understand, George," Hero said sadly. "Perhaps he would listen to you, and perhaps he might relent towards me, because he is very kind to me, but you see—you see, it was all a dreadful mistake, and I ought not to have married him." She bent her head, looking down at her tightly clasped hands. "Sherry—Sherry doesn't love me, you see. He—he never did love me. If I had not been such a silly g-goose, I should not have—— For he never pretended that he loved me, you know."

George's face twisted. He came quickly back into the room and laid his hand over both Hero's and gripped them. "I know," he said, in a moved voice.

She nodded. "Yes, I—I thought you did, George. So, you see . . ."

There was an uncomfortable silence. George broke it, addressing himself with some asperity to Mr. Ringwood. "Why the devil can't you say something, Gil, instead of standing there like a dashed waxworks?"

"Thinking," said Mr. Ringwood curtly.

"Well, you'd best think quickly!" George said. "It only needs for Sherry to find she's here for the fat to be in the fire!"

"Sherry likely to miss you?" Mr. Ringwood enquired of Hero.

"Oh no! He has gone out, and he will think I am in bed when he comes in. No one knows that I am not in the house."

"Did you come here alone, Kitten?"

"No, Maria is with me. She is my maid, and oh, I never knew how much she liked me until to-day, for she never seemed to like me at all! But—but she came to me when Sherry had gone away, and she said a piece out of the Bible, about Ruth and Naomi, in the most touching way, and she is in the hall now, with my baggage, for I could not carry anything besides my clock and the canary, and those I had to bring!"

Ferdy surveyed these two necessary adjuncts to a lady's baggage rather doubtfully. "Dare say you're right," he said. "Very handsome timepiece."

"Gil gave it to me for a wedding present," Hero explained, her tears beginning to flow again. "I have your bracelet too, and how could I bear to leave Gil's dear little canary? It is named after him! And Sherry—Sherry does not love it as I do, and perhaps he might give it away."

"Quite right to bring it," said Ferdy firmly. "Company for you. All the same, Kitten, what beats me is where you mean to go. Can't stay with Gil, you know. Sherry wouldn't like it above half."

"Yes, she can," said Mr. Ringwood unexpectedly. "At least, not for long, but no reason why she shouldn't stay here to-night. In fact, she must."

"Good God, Gil, you must have taken leave of your senses!" said George explosively. "No reason why she shouldn't, indeed! If that's all your precious thinking leads to——"

"No reason at all," said Mr. Ringwood. "Got her abigail. Have a truckle bed put up in my room. I'll spend the night in your lodging."

"I suppose she could do that," George admitted grudgingly. "But it don't solve anything! Dash it, it's the damnedest coil! She has no relatives she may go to, or I'd say she was right to leave Sherry. But she can't live by herself! You know that! If her mother-in-law weren't such a curst disagreeable woman—— You are certain you could not bear to go to Sheringham Place, Kitten? I mean, Sherry's a brute to have put it to you like that, but I can't but see what's in his head. It *is* the dowager's business to have an eye to you, only——"

"No, no, George, pray do not ask me to go there!" Hero begged him. "I have made up my mind that I will become a governess, just as Cousin Jane always said I should be. But I do not know how to set about it, and

327

that is why I came to Gil, because he taught me to drive my phaeton, and I thought he might know."

"Do you know, Gil?" enquired Ferdy, looking at Mr. Ringwood with dawning respect.

"No," replied Mr. Ringwood.

"Didn't think you would," said Ferdy. "Tell you what: ask my mother! Bound to know!"

"She ain't going to be a governess," said Mr. Ringwood shortly. "Told you I'd been thinking. Well, I've got a notion."

George, who had been turning the matter over in his mind, said suddenly: "It's all very well, but she can't leave Sherry like this! Dash it, it's impossible!"

"No, it ain't," replied Mr. Ringwood, his stolidity unshaken. "Best thing she could do. Going to take her to stay with my grandmother."

"By Jove!" exclaimed Ferdy, much struck. "Devilish good notion of yours, Gil! As long as she ain't dead."

"Of course she ain't dead!" said Mr. Ringwood, with a touch of impatience. "How could I take Kitten to stay with her if she was?"

"That's what I was wondering," confessed Ferdy. "Thought she *was* dead. Thought you went to the funeral, what's more."

"If you weren't so cork-brained you'd know that was my other grandmother!" said Mr. Ringwood, quite exasperated. "I'm talking of my maternal grandmother, Lady Saltash."

Ferdy regarded him fixedly. "Forgot she was your grandmother too. You know what I think, Gil?"

"No, and I don't want to."

"No need to get into a miff, dear old boy! Only going to say, couldn't have had a better notion myself. Very sporting old lady, your grandmother. Dare say she and Kitten may deal extremely."

"Oh, do you think she would be so obliging as to teach me how to behave like a lady of fashion?" Hero asked anxiously.

"Shouldn't be at all surprised," responded Mr. Ringwood. "Never met any old lady so much up to snuff as my grandmother."

A qualm smote Hero; she said: "But perhaps she may not like to have me to stay with her, Gil?"

"Yes, she will. Like it above all things. Dare say you may be very useful to her. Got a pug-dog. Nasty, smelly little brute. Took a piece out of my leg once. You could take it for walks. Wants exercising. At least, it did when last I saw it. Of course, it may be dead by now. Good thing if it is."

Ferdy, who had been listening attentively, interposed at this point to object: "Don't see that, Gil, old boy; don't see that at all! Stands to reason Kitten can't take the pug for walks if it's dead. No point in her going to Bath."

"Bath! Does she live in Bath?" cried Hero, before the incensed Mr. Ringwood could wither Ferdy. "Oh, nothing could be better: for it was to Bath I was to have gone to be a governess, and Sherry does not like the place, and he will never look for me there! Oh, Gil, how kind and clever you re!"

Mr. Ringwood blushed and disclaimed. Ferdy agreed that Gil had always been a knowing one, and only George remained unconvinced. But he reserved his criticisms until Hero and her abigail had presently been escorted upstairs by Mr. Ringwood's impassive valet. He then spoke his mind in no uncertain fashion, the gist of his argument being that whatever the state of affairs might be between Sherry and his wife, they were legally married, and it was the height of impropriety for Gil or anyone else to aid and abet Hero in deserting her husband.

"I don't care a fig for that," responded Mr. Ringwood. He had by this time changed his dressing-gown for a blue coat and a waistcoat, and was engaged in stuffing into a cloak-bag such items as he might be supposed to need for a night's sojourn away from home.

"I dare say you don't," retorted Lord Wrotham, "but you're not the only one of us who can think, let me tell you! I don't mean Ferdy: I know he can't; but I can, and what's more, I have thought! I'm devilish fond of Kitten, but dash it, Sherry's a friend of mine!"

"Friend of mine too," said Mr. Ringwood, finding a snug resting-place for his hair-brushes inside a pair of bedroom slippers.

"Well, if he's a friend of yours, you've no business to hide his wife from him!"

"Yes, I have. Been thinking of it for a long time."

"Thinking of hiding Kitten for a long time?" demanded Lord Wrotham incredulously.

"You're a fool, George. Big a fool as Ferdy. Been thinking about Sherry and Kitten. Fond of 'em both."

"I'm fond of them both too," said Ferdy. "What's more, Sherry's my cousin. But he's got no right to behave like a curst brute to Kitten. Cousin or no cousin. Dear little soul! Dash it, Gil, almost an angel!"

"No," said Mr. Ringwood, after thinking this over. "*Not* an angel, Ferdy. Dear little soul, yes. Angel, no!"

"It don't matter what she is!" struck in George. "All that signifies is that she's Sherry's wife!"

Mr. Ringwood looked at him under his brows, but refrained from comment. After a slight pause, George said: "Not our affair, whatever we may think. The fact of the matter is, she does need some older female to school her."

"She'll have one," replied Mr. Ringwood.

"Yes, that's all very well, but though I don't say he set about it the right way, Sherry ain't so far wrong when he takes it into his head to send Kitten down to the dowager."

"Do you *know* my aunt Valeria, George?" asked Ferdy, astonished.

"Oh, lord, yes, I know her! But——"

"Well, I wouldn't have thought it."

"That ain't the point," interrupted Mr. Ringwood. "Point is what Kitten said just now: Sherry don't love her."

"I wouldn't say that, Gil," protested Ferdy. "Never told me he didn't love her!"

Mr. Ringwood closed his cloak-bag and strapped it. "I know Sherry," he said. "But I *don't* know if he loves Kitten or not. Going to find out. If you ask me, he don't know either. If he don't, it ain't a particle of use sending Kitten to the dowager. Come to think of it, it ain't much use sending her there if he does, because that ain't the way he'd find it out. But if he does love her, he ain't going to like not knowing what's become of her. Might miss her like the devil. Make him start to think a trifle."

George regarded him frowningly. "Are you going to tell Sherry you don't know where his wife is?"

"Not going to tell him anything," said Mr. Ringwood. "He won't think I had anything to do with it. Thought it all out. You're going to tell Sherry I've gone off to Herefordshire, because that uncle of mine looks like dying at last."

"I'll tell him, if George don't like to," offered Ferdy.

"No, you won't," answered Mr. Ringwood. "You're coming to Bath with me."

"No, dash it, Gil!" feebly protested Ferdy.

George, whose brow had cleared, said: "By God, I believe you've hit it, Gil! Damme, I've thought for a long time Sherry needed a lesson! I will tell him you've gone to Herefordshire! Yes, by Jove, and I'll take precious good care he don't ask me if *I* know what's become of his Kitten!"

"Yes, but I don't want to go to Bath!" said Ferdy.

"Nonsense! Of course you'll go!" George said briskly. "You can't leave poor old Gil to bear the brunt of it! Besides, it'll look better if you both escort Kitten. You know what Sherry is! Why, he even called me out, only for kissing her! If he got to hear of Gil's jauntering about the country with her he'd very likely cut his liver out and fry it. Can't take exception to the pair of you going with her."

When the matter was put to him like that, all Ferdy's chivalrous instincts rose to the surface, and he at once begged pardon, and said that he would stand by Gil to the death. Upon reflection, he admitted that he would as lief not meet his cousin Sherry on the following day. George then wished to be assured that Mr. Ringwood's man, Chilham, was to be trusted to keep his mouth shut, and upon being told that he was the most discreet fellow alive, said that there seemed to be nothing more to do in the matter until the following day. All three gentlemen thereupon left the house, Ferdy going off to Cavendish Square and Mr. Ringwood, his cold forgotten, accompanying George to his lodgings in Ryder Street.

CHAPTER 19

When Hero put in no appearance at the breakfast-table next morning, the Viscount was not much surprised, and he made no comment. He himself had passed an indifferent night. His visit to White's, on the previous evening, had confirmed his worst fears. One tactless gentleman had actually had the effrontery to mention Hero's projected race to him, and instead of landing this person a facer he had been obliged to treat the matter lightly, saying that it was all a hum, and that he wondered that anyone could have been green enough to have supposed that it could be anything else. After that he had gone home, and had written a stiff note to Lady Royston, cancelling the meeting. That had taken him an hour to compose, and he had wasted a great many sheets of paper on it, and had not even the satisfaction of feeling that the final copy conveyed his sentiments to the lady. Unquiet dreams had disturbed his sleep, and he arose in the morning not in the least refreshed, but more determined than ever to remove Hero from London until such time as the Polite World had forgotten her lapse from grace. His lordship was not going to run the risk of his wife's being refused a voucher for Almack's; and, to do him justice, this caution was more on her behalf than on his own. He made up his mind to explain it all carefully to Hero on the way down to Kent, for although he had been extremely angry with her on the previous evening, he was not one to nurse rancour, and he was already sorry that he had left her room so precipitately, and without comforting her distress, or making any real attempt to alleviate her alarms. He did not like to think of his Hero in tears, and he was much afraid that she had cried herself to sleep. When she did not come down to breakfast, he was sure of it. So as soon as he had finished his own repast he went up to her room and knocked politely on the door. There was no answer, and, after waiting for a moment, he turned the handle and walked in. The room was in darkness. Surprised, he hesitated for an instant before speaking his wife's name. There was again no answer. All at once the Viscount felt, without quite knowing why, that there was no one but himself in the room. He strode over to the window, and flung back the curtains, and turned. No erring wife lay sleeping in the silk-hung bedstead. The quilt had not even been removed from it, but on one pillow lay a sealed billet.

The Viscount picked it up with a hand that was not entirely steady. It was addressed to himself. He broke the seal and spread open the sheet of paper.

"*Sherry, I have run away, because I will never go to your Mama, and I see now that it would be to no avail, even if I did, for you were right when you said you should not have married me, though I did not know it*

334

then, when I was so ignorant and stupid. It was all my fault, for I always knew that you did not love me, and you have been so patient with me, and so very kind, and I know I have been very troublesome, and quite spoilt your life, besides getting into debt, and obliging you to sell those horses, and not knowing how to contrive so that Mrs. Bradgate should not order such expensive things, like that dreadful bill for candles, and a dozen others. So please, Sherry, will you divorce me, and forget all about me, and pray do not tease yourself with wondering what has become of me, because I shall do very well, and there is not the least occasion for you to do so. And also, Sherry, I hope you will not mind that I have taken the drawing-room clock, and my canary, for they were truly mine, like the ear-rings you gave me on my wedding-day, and Ferdy's bracelet.—Your loving Kitten"

The Viscount's lip quivered; he looked up from the letter, and stared about him at surroundings which seemed suddenly desolate. He found that he was not able to think very clearly, for when he tried to concentrate on the problem of Hero's present whereabouts his brain seemed not to move at all, and the only thought which reiterated rather stupidly in his head was that she had gone.

He had left the door open when he had entered the room, and after a few minutes he became aware that someone was standing in the aperture. He looked round quickly, and saw his valet gravely regarding him. They looked at one another in silence, the Viscount trying to think of something to say in explanation of his wife's disappearance, and Bootle just waiting. Nothing occurred to the Viscount, and suddenly he knew that it would be useless to attempt any explanation. He said abruptly: "Bootle, when did her ladyship leave this house?"

The valet came in and closed the door. "I do not know, my lord, but I think last night." He stepped over to the window, and methodically straightened the curtains which his master had pulled back so hastily. In a colourless voice, he added; "I fancy her ladyship took her abigail with her, my lord, for the chambermaid reports that Maria's bed has not been slept in."

He noticed with satisfaction that there was a perceptible lightening of the expression on his master's face. He said, even more disinterestedly than before: "I have taken the liberty of informing the staff, my lord, that her ladyship was called away hurriedly, one of her ladyship's relatives having been taken ill."

The Viscount flushed. "Yes, very well! Thank you." He folded the letter in his hand, and put it into his pocket. "They won't believe it, I dare say."

"Oh, yes, my lord!" replied Bootle tranquilly. "Your lordship may rely upon me. And, if I may be permitted to take the liberty, my lord, there is no occasion for your lordship to concern yourself over the Bradgates, them being related to me, and not ones to chatter about their betters."

"I'm obliged to you," the Viscount said, with an effort. "You do not know if her ladyship summoned a hackney, or—or a chair?"

"No, my lord. But if your lordship desires me so to do I could make discreet enquiries."

"Do so, if you please."

"Very good, my lord. Will your lordship receive my

Lord Wrotham, or shall I inform his lordship that you have stepped out?"

"Lord Wrotham!"

"Downstairs, in your lordship's library," said Bootle.

"I'll see him," the Viscount said, and went swiftly out of the room.

Lord Wrotham, arrayed in the much-coveted insignia of that most exclusive of driving clubs, the F.H.C., with a drab greatcoat sporting no fewer than sixteen capes over all, was standing by the fireplace in the library, one top-booted foot resting on the fender. One glance at his host's face, as he entered the room, his blue eyes bright and hard with something between hope and suspicion, made him speak before Sherry had had time to do more than utter his name. "Hallo, Sherry!" he said. "When did you get back to town? Thought you was at Melton still."

"No," said Sherry. "No. George———"

Lord Wrotham adjusted the monstrous nosegay he wore as a buttonhole. "Lady Sherry ready to drive out with me?" he asked. "Going to tool my curricle down to Richmond. Trying out my new pair. Prime bits of blood! Heard about Gil?"

"Gil . . ." said Sherry. "What about Gil?"

George laughed. "Why only that that old uncle of his looks like obliging him at last! Seems to be in a pretty bad way. Gil's posted down to Herefordshire to be in at the death. By God, I wish I had an uncle to leave me a handsome fortune!"

Sherry stared at him, a frown in his eyes. "George, are you sure of that?" he demanded.

"Saw him off not two hours ago. Why?" responded George.

"Nothing," Sherry said, passing a hand across his brow. "I only wondered—— No reason at all."

Lord Wrotham, who was finding it increasingly difficult to meet his friend's gaze, fell to contemplating the polish on one topboot. He had not expected to enjoy this interview, and he was not enjoying it. Sherry looked positively haggard, he thought; and if he had not promised Hero not to divulge her whereabouts to Sherry he would have felt extremely tempted to have told him the truth. But when he had seen the little party off from Stratton Street earlier in the morning he had given his word to Hero, and he was not the man to go back on that. He hoped that his confidence in Mr. Ringwood's judgment would not prove to have been misplaced, and said as casually as he could: "Does Kitten mean to come with me, Sherry?"

The Viscount pulled himself together. "No. The fact is, she's not feeling quite the thing. Asked me to make her apologies."

"Good God, I trust nothing serious, Sherry?"

"No, no!—At least, I can hardly say yet. Dare say she has been doing rather too much. Not accustomed to town life, you know. I am—I shall be taking her into the country in a day or so. Needs rest and a change of air."

"I am excessively sorry to hear it! You'll be wishing me at the devil, no doubt: I'll be off at once!"

Sherry, usually the most hospitable of hosts, made no effort to detain him, but accompanied him to the street door. As George descended the steps, he asked suddenly: "George, where's my cousin Ferdy?"

"Lord, how should I know?" replied George, drawing on his gloves. "Said he was going to dine at Long's last night, so he may be nursing his head in bed. You know what he is!"

"He did dine at Long's? You're sure of that?"

"He was certainly engaged to do so," George said, with perfect truth.

"Oh! Then—— No, he wouldn't——" Sherry broke off, flushing. "Fact of the matter is I've the devil of a head myself this morning, George!"

Lord Wrotham replied sympathetically, and left him. Sherry went back into his library, and sat down to think very hard indeed.

The result of this concentrated thought was to plunge him into quite the most horrid week of his life. His friends, daily expecting to see him at one of his usual haunts, looked for him in vain. His lordship was out of town, travelling first into Buckinghamshire, to Fakenham Manor, and thence all the way north to Lancashire, to Croxteth Hall, the Earl of Sefton's country seat. He drew blank at both these establishments, but both his aunt and Lady Sefton inexorably dragged his story out of him, and then favoured him with their separate, but curiously similar, readings of his character. Lady Fakenham was a good deal more outspoken than Lady Sefton, told him that he had come by his deserts, and sped him on his way to Lancashire with the depressing reminder that he had only his abominable selfishness to thank for whatever disaster might befall his wife, adrift in a harsh world. When he had gone (and it had cost him all his resolution to take leave of his aunt with common civility), her ladyship said thoughtfully to her husband that this affair might well prove to be the making of Anthony.

"Yes, but what the deuce can have become of that

poor little creature?" said Lord Fakenham, not particularly interested in Sherry's possible redemption.

"Indeed I wish I knew! I wish too that she had come to me, but no doubt she would not think to cast herself upon Anthony's relations."

Lady Sefton, having reduced the unfortunate Viscount to the condition of speechless endurance to which she could, upon rare occasions, reduce her eldest-born, my Lord Molyneux, relented towards him sufficiently to permit him a glimpse of two rays of sunlight. She thought it probable that Hero would presently return to Half Moon Street; and she engaged herself to smooth over any unpleasantness that might have arisen in influential quarters from the projected race.

The Viscount posted back to London. The house in Half Moon Street seemed desolate, almost as though someone had died there, he thought. He would have liked to have left it; but when he had made all his plans for shutting it up, and returning to his old lodgings, he changed his mind, and determined to stay there. To shut the house would give rise to much gossip and speculation; and if Hero came back to him it would be a shocking thing, he thought, for her to find the shutters up, and the knocker off the door.

Mr. Ringwood was back in town again, saying, with perfect truth, that he saw no reason why his rich uncle should not survive for another ten years. Mr. Ringwood said also that he was devilish sorry to hear from George that Lady Sherry was so indisposed as to have been obliged to retire into the country for a space.

Sherry, who had schooled himself to answer such remarks with mechanical civility, found a certain measure of relief in being able to throw off his mask before the friend whom he most trusted. He said abruptly: "It's not true. Only the tale I've put about. She's left me."

"I beg your pardon?" said Ringwood.

Sherry gave a short laugh. "You heard me, Gil! She ran away, because I said she was to go down to my mother, at Sheringham Place. She took some absurd notion into her head—all nonsense, of course!—and she was gone before I'd time to explain why I—— For naturally I meant to make all clear to her, and there was no question of——But that's a female all over!"

Mr. Ringwood, helping himself, with extreme deliberation, to a pinch of snuff, said; "Don't play off your tricks on me, Sherry! The truth is, I take it, that you quarrelled with her over that race?"

"Quarrelled! Gil, do you know what she meant to do? If it had been your wife——! I *was* very angry! dash it, any man would have been! But there was not the least occasion for her to have run away from me, as though I had been some deuced brute, or—or—I know it was as much my fault as hers, and, what's more, I said so! *That* was not why she ran away! I said she should go to my mother and she did not choose to. Talked some fustian about my mother's thinking she had ruined my life—fiddle!"

"No wish to say a word against your mother, Sherry, dear boy, but that's what she has been saying."

Sherry stared at him. "It's not possible! I never heard a word of this!"

"Not likely you would," said Mr. Ringwood. "True, for all you may not have heard it. Often thought you don't pay enough heed to what's dashed well under your nose, Sherry. Not surprised Kitten wouldn't go to Sheringham Place. Don't think her ladyship would have wanted her, either. If you don't mind my saying so, my dear fellow, the odds are she'd have tried to bully Kitten."

The Viscount's eyes sparkled. "Oh, no, she would not!" he said. "She'd have had me to reckon with! And if I'd seen her, or anyone else, bullying my Kitten——"

"Point is, you wouldn't have been there to have seen it," said Mr. Ringwood dryly. "Don't suppose *you* meant to stay at Sheringham Place, did you?"

"No, but—— Well, naturally I should have gone down there from time to time, and——" He stopped, looking sulky, and rather defensive. "So you think I was wrong to decide to take Kitten there, do you? Much you know about it!"

Mr. Ringwood disregarded this rider, and answered frankly: "Yes, I do."

"But, good God, man, what else could I have done?" Sherry burst out. "We could not have continued as we were! Dash it, we have not been married much above four months, and if you knew the half of the crazy things Kitten would have done had I not been at hand to prevent her——"

"Ah!" interrupted Mr. Ringwood. "Put your finger on it, Sherry, haven't you? Didn't do crazy things when you were at hand."

"In the devil's name, how could I always be at hand? Did you expect me to change my whole way of living, simply because I was married?"

"Expected you to settle down a trifle, dear boy. Never fancied the notion of it for myself, which is why I've stayed single. Seems to me a fellow can't continue in the same way once he ties himself up. What do you mean to do now?"

"Find her, of course! I made sure she would have gone to my aunt Fakenham, or even to Lady Sefton, but she did not. I tell you I'm at my wits' end, Gil! What with setting it about she's indisposed, and fobbing people off, and trying to undo the harm that infernal race caused, and not knowing where to look for her—yes, and being obliged to continue living in this damned house—well, there are moments when I'd like to wring Kitten's neck! I haven't had a day's hunting since she left home; I've had to career all over England in search of her; and I'm so worried I can't sleep at night! Dash it, she's no more fit to be fending for herself than that canary you gave her! And I don't need you to tell me I'm responsible for her! I should never have been mad enough to have married a chit out of the schoolroom, and that's the truth of it!"

Mr. Ringwood looked at him under his brows. "Wishing you hadn't, Sherry?"

"I wish I hadn't married anyone!" Sherry said petulantly. "Don't you, Gil! There's nothing but trouble, and anxiety; and the devil of it is that you can't alter it, and—no, you don't even want to! The thing is, I suppose a fellow grows used to having a wife, for all he may not think it, and then—— Damnation, I miss her like the devil, Gil!"

"Dare say she'll come back to you," said Mr. Ringwood, at his most phlegmatic.

"Yes, that's what I tell myself, and sometimes I believe it. It's possible she's playing a trick on me, for she was always the naughtiest chit imaginable! And then I think she ain't, and when I start wondering what kind of a scrape she may have got herself into by now—well, it ain't surprising I can't sleep! If only I had the least notion where to look for her!" He ran a hand

343

through his fair locks. "Isabella is back in town, or so they tell me. She may be able to help me, for she's known Kitten since they were children. I've sent round a note, asking her if she will see me privately. I don't know if I can trust her not to spread the truth round town, but if Kitten don't come back soon it will be bound to leak out, so I dare say it makes no odds."

Mr. Ringwood, retiring from this interview in due course, was not ill-satisfied with what he had heard. He told Lord Wrotham that he fancied the business would work out tolerably well, and strongly vetoed his lordship's suggestion that it was time they told Sherry the truth.

"Damn it, Gil, I don't like it!" George said. "You don't know what a man can suffer when the woman he loves——"

"No reason to think Sherry does love Kitten."

"I believe he does. He looks dashed ill, and he don't hunt, or go to the races, or even look in at Watier's!"

"Won't do him any harm," said Mr. Ringwood, unmoved by this pathetic picture. "Matter of fact, I think you're right, and he does love her. But he don't know it yet, and he'd best find out. Talked of wringing her neck to-day. Got to go a long way beyond that, George."

George was so indignant at the thought of anyone's wanting to wring Hero's neck that he made no further attempt to persuade Mr. Ringwood to relent towards Sherry. The only circumstance which still worried him, he said, was the unhappiness Hero must be suffering. Mr. Ringwood agreed to it, but said that it would be better for the poor little soul to be unhappy for a short space now than to grow estranged from Sherry, which was what he feared might have happened had the strange marriage continued along its unsatisfactory course. Moreover, he was able to assure George that Lady Saltash had taken an instant liking to Hero, and, having heard the whole story of the marriage, had accorded her grandson's intervention her unqualified approval.

What her ladyship had actually said was: "You're not such a fool as I had thought, Gilbert. Don't tell me what Anthony said and did! I've known that boy since before he was breeched. An engaging scamp, that's what he is! Go back to London, and take that silly creature, Ferdy Fakenham, with you, for if ever anyone gave me the fidgets it's he!"

When Sherry visited Miss Milborne, he found her not in quite her usual looks or spirits, but as his mind was wholly occupied by his own troubles, and he was not, in any event, an observant young gentleman, he noticed nothing amiss, but plunged immediately into the object of his visit.

She was very much shocked. Unlike his aunt, and Lady Sefton, and Mr. Ringwood, she neither said nor believed that Sherry was to blame for Hero's flight. Never having felt the smallest desire to depart from the strictly conventional herself, the story of the racing engagement quite dismayed her. She could not imagine how any female with the least pretension to elegance of mind, or propriety of taste, could have even listened to such a proposal without a blush of mortification. She could not find it in herself to blame Sherry for having been very much provoked; and she would have extended her warmest sympathy towards him would he but have accepted it. But such was his perversity that no sooner did he find himself in the company of a partisan than he spared no pains to assure her that the fault had been his from start to finish, and that if his

Hero had erred in judgment it was through innocence and his own neglect. Miss Milborne thought that such sentiments did him honour, and said so, to which his lordship replied shortly: "Fudge!"

She would have lent him any aid that lay in her power, but with the best will in the world there was nothing she could do, since she had no more idea than he where Hero might have hidden herself. For several years they had not been intimate. Only one idea, and that a painful one, occurred to her. She asked, with a little difficulty, if Sherry had spoken to Lord Wrotham.

"He don't know anything," Sherry replied impatiently. "Thinks she's in the country, indisposed."

Miss Milborne rather carefully smoothed out her handkerchief. "I only thought. . . . It has sometimes seemed to me that—that George displays a marked partiality for Hero, Sherry."

"Oh, there's nothing in that!" he said. "Good God, you should know George don't give a button for any female but yourself!"

Miss Milborne coloured faintly, and looked up as though she would have liked to have said more. But Sherry, having no interest outside his own pressing problem, was already on his feet, and wishing to take his leave. She did not detain him; upon consideration, she did not even know what it was that she wanted to say to him. As she shook hands, she informed him, a little consciously, that she was going into Kent for a time. He accepted this without surprise or interest, and so they parted. Miss Milborne did her best not to feel ill-used, but could not help reflecting that his lordship was a singularly impercipient young man.

For Miss Milborne, for the first time in her life, had behaved in a manner contrary to her own interests, thus disobliging her Mama, and leading that redoubtable dame to prophesy a single existence for her, attended by all the ills that were commonly supposed to wait on spinsters. Miss Milborne, travelling to Severn Towers with the dutiful intention of fulfilling her Mama's expectations, had been received by the Duchess with every mark of distinguishing attention. There had been a number of other, and certainly more exalted guests, but she had known herself to be the guest of honour, and had had no difficulty in interpreting her hostess's benign manner to signify approval of Severn's suit. She had been shown all over the vast pile, even down to the linen and stillrooms; obviously interested family retainers had bobbed curtsies to her; the housekeeper had initiated her into the mysteries of domestic management; and the Duchess had talked in a casual way of her own plans when her son should bring home a bride. Nothing could have been more gratifying, and why Miss Milborne should suddenly have taken fright was a matter passing the comprehension of her parent. Miss Milborne found herself unable to advance any reasonable explanation for her behaviour. All she would say was that she did not love the Duke, and this was too frivolous an utterance to be accepted by her Mama.

Miss Milborne, losing herself in the enormous mansion, being driven about the prosperous estate, dining off gold plate, and being waited on by armies of liveried servants, saw herself mistress of all this grandeur, and, since she was but human, was not unattracted by the vision. But at her side was the unromantic figure of her ducal suitor, a model of punctilious civility, treating her with pompous respect, bestowing his admiration on her rather as though it had been an accolade. His grace was as correct in his advances to the lady whom he designed to make his wife as in every other detail of his well-ordered life, the greatest display of ardour he permitted himself to indulge in being the fervent pressing of his lips to her hand. Miss Milborne doubted whether it would ever enter his head to seize her in a rough embrace, and to devour her with kisses as Lord Wrotham had shown lamentably little hesitation in doing. She knew that he would never rave and storm at her, make extravagant gestures, threaten to blow his brains out, or spend all his energy in procuring for her flowers that were out of season. She thought his notions of propriety would preclude his even quarrelling mildly with her, since whenever she displeased him a more than ordinarily stolid expression would descend upon his countenance, and he would withdraw from her vicinity, reappearing after a judicious lapse of time as though nothing whatever had happened to disturb the harmony of their intercourse. He disapproved of gaming, took no more than a fashionable interest in racing, chose his friends from amongst the more sedate of his contemporaries, and was prone to moralize upon such dismal subjects as the decay of modern manners, the frivolity of the younger set, and the lack of modest restraint observable in the damsels at present gracing Society.

And all at once, just as everything was in train for a brilliant betrothal, Miss Milborne knew that she could not marry Severn. Aghast at her own conduct in having encouraged his advances, wishing she had never allowed George to goad her into accepting the Duchess's invitation to Severn Towers, she did what she could to prevent his grace's coming to the point. Her manner towards him was retiring to the point of coldness. The Duchess, observing it, reiterated her opinion that she was a very pretty-behaved girl, for such formal reserve exactly suited her own ideas of well-bred behaviour. George might have been cast into despair by a tenth of such repulsive chilliness as was being shown to the Duke, but Severn, knowing himself to be the biggest matrimonial prize in the market, read it as admirable female modesty, and was not in the least discouraged. Miss Milborne felt hunted, and if Lord Wrotham had appeared at the Towers he might have ridden off with her across his saddle-bow with her very good will. But although his lordship would no doubt have obliged her had he had the least idea of her desire, he had no such idea, and the respectability of the Duke's ancestral home was undisturbed by his romantic presence. The Duke declared himself; Miss Milborne declined his flattering offer; the Duchess was both staggered and affronted; and Mrs. Milborne expressed her unshakable belief that her wretched daughter was out of her senses.

She brought her back to London, and it was in London that the full evils consequent upon the rejection of his grace's hand were borne in upon Mrs. Milborne. No one believed that his grace had come up to scratch. She read the truth in the discreetly veiled smiles which met any reference to the affair, and was mortified indeed. The Polite World had no doubt at all that his grace's Mama had triumphed by subtle means, and that the return of the Milbornes to town betokened defeat.

Miss Milborne was quite as conscious as her parent of this disagreeable circumstance. She had forseen it, and it had taken a considerable degree of resolution to make her refuse the Duke's offer. What she had not foreseen was that Lord Wrotham should fall into vulgar error.

But this was precisely what that impetuous young man had done, and it apparently led him to suffer a revulsion of feeling. Instead of being relieved and gratified at the Beauty's return, unbetrothed, to London, he laughed in a harsh and bitter way, and uttered some comments so caustic as to be almost insulting. These were naturally repeated, and came in due course to Miss Milborne's ears. She experienced a strong desire to box George's ears, but as he did not come near her she was unable to gratify it. A period of calm reflection made her acknowledge to herself that she might have been in some degree to blame for George's abominable lack of faith in her, and instead of wishing any longer to box his ears she would have given much to have had the opportunity of explaining herself to him. Such signs of encouragment as might be bestowed on a gentleman by a modest female she bestowed on George, and he received them with a curling lip, and an eye sparkling with contempt. Miss Milborne, who had fallen into the way of thinking that he might be treated with impunity like a stray mongrel, suffered a severe shock, and was torn by indignation and a curious satisfaction that he could not, after all, be whistled back to heel at her pleasure.

But to have lost in far too rapid succession three such notable suitors as my Lord Sheringham, his Grace of Severn, and my Lord Wrotham was a disaster hard indeed to bear. The most serious pretender to her hand was now a mere baronet, for she knew very well that such admirers as the Honourable Ferdy Fakenham paid court to her as a matter of fashion, and had no real intentions towards her. Sir Montagu Revesby's increasingly assiduous attentions came as a slight balm to a wounded spirit, but when Mrs. Milborne said that since all her undutiful child saw fit to do in London was to throw her future prosperity to the winds she would be better off in the country, she raised no demur. This retirement might savour of a retreat, but nothing could be more mortifying than to be obliged to face the sympathy or the amusement of the Polite World.

So Miss Milborne departed to recruit her spirits in Kent; and Lord Wrotham flung himself into the dogged pursuit of pleasure, behaving in a very reckless style; losing a great deal of money a the gaming-tables; all but breaking his neck on the hunting-field; accepting any and every wager offered him without the smallest hesitation; indulging in orgies of drinking at Long's, Limmer's, the Daffy Club, and other such haunts; flaunting a succession of Cyprians before the scandalized eyes of the world; being very short-tempered and aggressive towards his fellowmen; and causing thoughtful gentlemen to remove themselves from his vicinity by culping wafer after wafer at Manton's Shooting Gallery.

Sherry, meanwhile, was no nearer to discovering his vanished wife's whereabouts than he had been at the outset; and he was not finding that custom was making him grow any more reconciled to her absence. As day succeeded day he missed her increasingly, and the house they had chosen together became ever more unfriendly to him. He even missed the canary's shrill song, which had so often exasperated him. He had chafed at the bonds which matrimony had imposed on him; he had groaned at the necessity of escorting Hero to balls and routs; he had fancied his comfort to have been ruined by her habit of getting into scrapes from which he was obliged to rescue her; he had even remembered nostalgically the days of his untrammelled bachelordom, and had thought that he would like to have them back again. Well, Hero had given them back to him, and they proved to be Dead Sea fruit. While she remained lost to him, he had no zest even for hunting; and when one of his associates challenged him to paint all the turnpikes from London to Barnet a beautiful scarlet he stunned this enterprising gentleman by replying curtly: "Folly!" and utterly refused to accept the challenge.

The news of Hero's disappearance had of course reached the Dowager Lady Sheringham, and as she had the best of reasons for knowing that her daughter-in-law was not, as the world believed, recuperating at Sheringham Place, she wrote to demand an explanation of Sherry. After turning her letter over once or twice, Sherry drove down to Kent, and gave her the explanation in person. Mr. Paulett, who was present, started to bemoan a marriage which he had always foreseen would end in just such a way, and was startled to find himself confronting a nephew he did not recognize. Sherry was neither boyishly sulky, nor violently threatening. He was icily and implacably civil, and he showed his uncle out of the room, holding the door open for him, and bowing with a cold formality Mr. Paulett found singularly unnerving.

The Dowager, observing these signs of maturity in her son, then shed tears, and would have held his hand and condoled with him had he permitted it. She said that he must not mind her saying that she had never considered Hero Wantage to have been good enough for him. Unfortunately for the rest of the speech which

352

she had been about to make, the Viscount replied that he minded it very much; that there was no truth in the statement; and that he must request his mother never to repeat it. He then took from her all power of saying anything at all by informing her that he proposed to make certain changes in his way of life, which would necessitate her removal—at her convenience, he added, with this new and quelling politeness—from Sheringham Place to the Dower House. He further announced his intention of taking up his residence in the house in Grosvenor Square as soon as he should be reunited with his wife, and begged her ladyship to remove from it any such articles of furniture as belonged to her, or for which she had a partiality. He had formed the immediate intention of redecorating the house, and he was going to put this in hand without loss of time.

When the dowager had recovered her breath she attempted, though feebly, to expostulate. The Viscount cut her short. "My mind is made up, ma'am. It is time I was thinking of settling down. I should have done all this at the outset. It may be too late: I don't know that. But if—when—my wife returns to me we will contrive better, I hope."

"I am sure I am the last person alive to wish to keep you out of your own house," quavered Lady Sheringham. "But I do not know why you should suppose your wife will return to you, for ten to one she has run off with another man!"

"No," said his lordship, turning his back upon her, and staring out of the window at the bleak gardens. "That is something else I desire you will not repeat, ma'am. It is untrue."

"You cannot know that, Anthony, my poor boy! She

never cared for you! It was all vanity, and the wish of becoming a person of consequence!"

He shook his head. "She never thought of that. I didn't know it—never stopped to think, or—or consider it, but she did care for me. Much more than I cared for her—then. But if I could only find her—I've racked my brains, and I can't think where she can have gone, or to whom! She *must* have sought shelter with someone! Good God, ma'am, it keeps me awake at night, the fear that she may be alone, without money, or friends, or——No, no, she must be with some friend I know nothing of!"

"Very likely she went to that vulgar cousin of hers," said his mother waspishly.

He wheeled round, rather pale. "Mrs. Hoby!" he ejaculated. "How did I come to forget her? Good God, what a fool I have been! I am obliged to you, ma'am "

He set off for town again that very day, and repaired to the Hobys' house. A rather slatternly servant opened the door to him, when he had knocked on it for the third time, and informed him that her master and mistress were away from London. A few enquiries elicited the further information that the Hobys had left for a visit to Ireland the day following Hero's departure from Half Moon Street. With a darkening brow, the Viscount asked if this had been a long-standing engagement. The servant thought not; they had packed up and gone in a hurry; she thought a letter had arrived which made them take this course. But when he asked if they had gone alone, or had taken a friend with them, she shook her head and replied that she couldn't say, not having witnessed the actual departure, but she believed they had been alone.

The Viscount went home to think this over. The

more he thought, the more convinced he became that Hero had indeed flown to her cousin, and was now being concealed by this lady. He had never liked Theresa Hoby; her husband he barely knew but had little hesitation in condemning as bad *ton*; and gradually there grew up in this breast a feeling of indignation that Hero should have fled to the very people above all others whom he most disliked. He remembered that he had forbidden her to hold any close intercourse with Mrs. Hoby; remembered also that she had largely ignored this prohibition; and conveniently forgot that it had been uttered in the heat of the moment, and never seriously repeated. He began to be angry, and from picturing Hero in all manner of appalling plights passed to imagining her amusing herself amongst a set of people of whom her husband disapproved. A cynical remark let fall by his Uncle Prosper, that no doubt the minx was bent on giving him the fright of his life, took root in Sherry's mind, and drove him to throw himself, without the slightest enjoyment, into much the same kind of excesses which were being indulged in by Lord Wrotham. There was a good deal of bravado about this, a suggestion of gritted teeth, and more than a suggestion of obstinacy; but it made Mr. Ringwood pull down the corners of his mouth and shake a despondent head.

Six weeks after Hero's disappearance, the Hobys came back to London. Sherry heard of their arrival, and grimly awaited the return of his wife. She did not come; but her cousin did—to call upon her. The Viscount received her, and ten minutes in her company were enough to convince him that she knew nothing of Hero's whereabouts, had not the smallest notion of her being away from home, and had journeyed into Ireland

355

for the purpose of attending her mother-in-law's sick-bed.

The Viscount's brain reeled under the shock. Remorse, anxiety, and despair played havoc with him; and he seriously disquieted Bootle by spending the entire night in the back room, called his library, alternately striding up and down the floor and sitting with his head in his hands over the fire. He consumed a considerable quantity of liquor during this session, but he was not drunk when Bootle ventured to enter the room early the following morning; and this, the valet said darkly to Bradgate, was a very bad sign.

The Viscount looked at him unseeingly for a moment, and then passed a hand through his tumbled locks, and said curtly: "Send round to Stoke, and tell him I desire to see him immediately!"

Mr. Stoke, when he arrived, was shocked by his patron's haggard appearance. He listened in silence to the blunt story the Viscount related, and received, without visible discomposure, a command to set every possible means in motion to discover Lady Sheringham's whereabouts. He asked the Viscount one or two searching questions, did his best to hide his own absence of hope, and went away promising to strain every nerve to find her ladyship.

The Viscount was still waiting for his man of business to justify his existence when the dowager arrived in London, and summoned him to visit her at Grillon's Hotel, where she was putting up. He found her with Miss Milborne in her train, and learned from her that the unusually damp winter had so aggravated her numerous rheumatic disorders that nothing short of a visit to Bath was likely to be of benefit to her. Miss

Milborne, too, she said, had been sickly for some weeks. So she had had the idea of inviting the sweet girl to accompany her to Bath, to try what the waters would do for her, and to fill the place of Mr. Paulett, who was employed in making the Dower House habitable. She desired the Viscount to perform the filial duty of escorting them on their perilous journey.

The Viscount refused with wholly unfilial promptness. He said that nothing would prevail upon him to leave London; and that if his Mama thought herself in danger of being held up by highwaymen, she would find a couple of outriders of more practical use than himself. The dowager smiled wanly, rose up from her chair, saying that perhaps Someone Else would have the power to make him change his mind, and drifted out of the room, leaving him alone with Miss Milborne.

The Viscount stared at the shut door, and then at the Beauty, incredulity struggling with wrath in his countenance. "What the *deuce*——?" he demanded explosively.

Miss Milborne got up and took his hand, saying with a good deal of feeling: "My poor Sherry, you look so wretchedly! Have you had no word from Hero?"

He shook his head. "Not one. I've set my man of business on to it. Told him to call in the Runners if need be, though God knows I don't want——But what else can I do? And then my mother comes here teasing me to take her to Bath, of all places! And let me tell you, Bella, that while I have no wish to offend you, if her ladyship meant that you have the power to persuade me into going, she was never more mistaken in her life!"

She smiled. "Indeed, I know it! You never cared a

button for me, Sherry. I believe it must always have been Hero, though perhaps you did not know it until you lost her."

He stood looking down at her. "You said something of the sort the day I offered for you, and I told you Severn would never come up to scratch. We're an unlucky pair, ain't we?"

She withdrew her hand, flushing. "Sherry, you have known me since we were children, and if you are to believe that I am wearing the willow for Severn, I cannot bear it! Oh, I don't deny I was flattered by his making me the object of his attentions! and, yes, perhaps I did a little like the notion of being a duchess! But when I thought how it would be to be married to him, to be obliged to live with him for the rest of my life—oh, I *could* not!"

"What, you don't mean that he really did come up to scratch, and you refused him?" he exclaimed.

She nodded. "Yes, I could not prevent him. My going to Severn Towers at Christmas was fatal! But do not speak of this, Sherry, if you please! It would be so unbecoming in me to boast of having made such a conquest, and Severn would very much dislike to have it known!"

"Well, by God!" said Sherry, quite thunderstruck.

She tried to smile. "How odious you are! You may imagine how deeply I am in disgrace with Mama. The only person, except poor Papa, who has been kind is your mother, and that is in part why I am going with her to Bath. To be open with you, Sherry, I believe she has taken a foolish notion into her head that you may divorce poor little Hero, and end by marrying me after all."

"Well, I shan't," said his lordship, with an entire absence of gallantry.

"Don't flatter yourself I would accept you!" retorted Miss Milborne. "I care no more for you than I cared for Severn! Well, yes, perhaps a little more, but not very much!"

"I wish I knew who it is you do care for!" said Sherry.

She turned her face away. "I had thought you did know. If you do not, I am glad."

"George?" Then, as she made no answer, he said: "Of all the stupid coils! George took such a pet over you that there's no doing a thing with him these days. Riding as hard as he can to the devil. You'd best stay in London, Bella!"

"No," she replied. "I should not dream of doing so. George may think me what he wills: I shall go to Bath with Lady Sheringham."

"Don't you! It's a rubbishing place: can't stand it myself!" He stopped abruptly, his brows snapping together, his eyes holding an arrested expression. "Bath! When was I talking of the place last? Said I should be obliged to go there if—— Great God, why did I never think of that before? Bath—school —governess! That's what she's done, the little fool, the littre wretch! My Kitten! Some damned Queen's Square seminary, you may lay your life, and very likely turned into a drudge for a parcel of——Tell my mother I'll escort her to Bath with the greatest pleasure on earth, but she must be ready to start tomorrow!"

"Sherry!" she gasped. "You think Hero may be there?"

"Think! I'm sure of it! If I weren't a rattlepated gudgeon I should have thought of it weeks ago! Tell you what, Bella, if we mean to keep my mother in a good humour, we'd best say nothing about this. Let her suppose you persuaded me: it don't make a ha'porth of odds to me, but she can be deuced unpleasant if things don't go the way she wants, and if you're to be cooped up in a coach with her for two days—for she'll never consent to do the journey in one!—you'll get a trifle tired of the vapours!"

And with this piece of sound, if undutiful, advice, his lordship caught up his coat and hat and strode off to make his arrangements for an instant departure from town.

CHAPTER 20

While these events were in progress, Hero was residing in Upper Camden Place, Bath, the guest of Lady Saltash. At first a little frightened of an old lady who was generally held to be both formidable and sharp-tongued, she had soon settled down, and quite lost her shyness. The pug, not being as yet gathered to its fathers, was her particular charge; in addition to brushing this stertorous animal, and taking it for walks on the end of a leash, she played cribbage with her hostess, read to her from the newspapers, and accompanied her to the Grand Pump Room, or to the Assembly Rooms, where her ladyship was a subscriber to the Card and Reading Rooms. She had removed her wedding-ring and reverted to the use of her maiden name, two proceedings which drew an approving nod from Lady Saltash. It was at first difficult to remember that she was again Miss Wantage, and when Lady Saltage took her to one of the Dress Balls at the New Assembly Rooms she drew shocked eyes upon herself by moving unconsciously towards the benches set aside for the use of peeresses. But this little slip was easily glossed over, and as soon as the Master of Ceremonies had been presented to her, and had signified his approval of Lady Saltash's young protegee, her social comfort was assured. In the nature of things, she cared little for this, and would have been glad to have lived the life of a recluse would Lady Saltash but have permitted it. But Lady Saltash had no opinion of recluses, and she gave Hero some very good advice about never being led into the error of wearing one's heart upon one's sleeve.

"Depend upon it, my love, nothing is more tiresome than the person who is for ever bemoaning her fate. Recollect that no one has the smallest interest in the troubles of another! To be shutting yourself up because you fancy your heart is broken will not do at all. Do not wear a long face! As well heave sighs, than which nothing could be more vulgar!"

Hero promised to do her best to be cheerful, but said that it was sometimes hard to smile when she was so very miserable.

"Fiddle-de-dee!" replied Lady Saltash. "When you have had as much cause as I to talk of being made miserable you may do so, but believe me, my love, you know nothing of the matter as yet, and very likely never will. From what you have told me, you have not the least need to put yourself into a taking. I have known Anthony any time these twenty years, and you have gone the right way to work with him. I dare say he may be tearing out his hair by the roots by this time!"

"But I never, never meant him to be made unhappy or anxious!" Hero exclaimed, looking quite oppressed.

"Very likely you did not. You are a silly little puss, my love. My grandson has more sense, it appears, for he certainly means Anthony to be excessively anxious."

"Oh, he must not! That would be worse than all the rest!" Hero cried distressfully.

"Nonsense! It is high time that boy was made to think, which I'll be bound he has never done in his life. I do not scruple to tell you, my love, that I have been agreeably surprised by what you have told me. It appears that Anthony has behaved towards you with more consideration than I should have expected in one reared to consider nothing but his own convenience. I dare swear he has been in love with you all this while without having the least notion of it. It will do him a great deal of good to miss you."

Hero regarded her hopefully. "Do you think so indeed, dear ma'am? But perhaps you do not perfectly understand that he only married me because Isabella Milborne refused to accept his hand?"

"Do not talk to me about this Miss Milborne! She sounds to me just the insipid sort of a girl who passes for a beauty in these days! Now, when I was young ——However, that's neither here nor there! I shall be surprised if we find that Anthony cares a fig for her. Soon or late, mark my words! we shall have him posting down here to find you, and I will tell you now, my child, that if you mean to let him discover you half-way to a decline, I shall wash my hands of you! That is no way to handle a man. A little jealousy will work wonders with that boy: he has been too sure of you! I must tell you, my love, that these Verelsts are all the same! Like Pug there! Let no one seem to wish to touch his bone, and ten to one he will not look at it. Lay but a finger on it, and all at once he knows that there is nothing he wants more in the world, and he will snarl, and show his teeth, and stand guard over it with all his bristles on end! I am determined that if Anthony comes to look for you, he shall find you living in tolerable comfort without him."

Hero looked doubtful, but the idea of Sherry's coming to look for her was so precious to her that she raised no further demur at the programme outlined for her by her worldly-wise hostess.

Mr. Ringwood, though not generally held to be a good correspondent, wrote with painstaking regularity, reporting on Sherry's progress. Hero shed tears in secret over these letters, and had she not made up her mind to allow Sherry time to forget her, if he should wish to do so, she would have written to set his mind at rest at least a dozen times. When she heard that he had plunged into an orgy of gaiety, she really did feel as though her heart must break, and believed that he had ceased to grieve over her disappearance. When she could command her voice, she sought out Lady Saltash, and tried, for the third or fourth time, to broach the question of her applying for a post in a Young Ladies' Seminary. Her ladyship cut her short. "Don't put on those missish airs with me, Hero! What has happened to make you start on that nonsense again, pray?"

"Only that I have had a letter from Gil, ma'am, which—which——"

Her ladyship held out an imperative hand, a little twisted by gout. After a moment's hesitation, Hero gave up the letter. Lady Saltash read it with an unmoved countenance. "Going to the devil, is he?" she commented. "Very likely. Just as I expected! Pray, what is there in this billet, beyond the lamentable spelling, to make you pull that long face?"

"Don't you think Sherry is forgetting all about me, ma'am?" Hero asked wistfully.

"What, because he is behaving like a sulky boy? No such thing! He is determined no one, least of all yourself, my love, shall guess how much he cares. Really, I begin to have hopes of that tiresome boy! Put the letter up, my dear, and think no more of it! I apprehend we might find the piece they are playing at the Theatre Royal tolerably amusing. Have the goodness to sit down at my desk, and write two little notes, inviting Sir Carlton Frome and Mr. Jasper Tarleton to do me the honour of accompanying me there to-morrow evening. We will send one of the servants round to procure a box for us."

Hero obeyed her. She paused in the middle of her task to look up, and to say: "After all, if Sherry may amuse himself, I do not know why I should not too!"

"Excellent!" said her ladyship, laughing. "Do you mean to break Mr. Tarleton's heart? I wish you may do it!"

Hero gave a chuckle. "Why, he is quite old, ma'am!"

"Quite old! If he is a day more than thirty-five I will never wear my new wig again!"

"Well, too old to break his heart," amended Hero. "I like him extremely, for he is always so very kind and civil, and he makes me laugh."

Lady Saltash, who was deriving considerable entertainment from watching her old friend, Jasper Tarleton, succumb to her protegee's innocent charm, cast her a thoughtful look, but refrained from saying anything more. She had a certain fondness for Mr. Tarleton, but having attempted a great many times to interest him in some eligible damsel and having seen her efforts on his behalf quite wasted, she acknowledged that it would afford her a certain degree of satisfaction to know that he had lost his heart to a lady as unattainable as she was uninterested. Mr. Tarleton, thought her ladyship, was a great deal too sure of himself, and a little tumble would do him no harm at all.

Mr. Jasper Tarleton was a bachelor, the owner of a comfortable little property situated a few miles outside Bath. He was known to be bookish, a circumstance which possibly accounted for his not having felt the lure of London; and it was generally supposed that he had suffered a disappointment in youth, which had given him a distaste for matrimony. However that might have been, without betraying any of the signs of the confirmed misogynist, he had certainly contrived to remain single, and was held to be a hard case indeed. Numerous females had set their caps for him, for besides being possessed of a handsome competence, he was good-looking, his air distinguished, and his manners very pleasing. But while he was happy to oblige any lady by flirting with her in an elegant and quite unexceptionable fashion, he never left the favoured fair in any doubt of his total lack of serious intention.

He first met Hero at a whist-party at Lady Saltash's house. Something in her which made her different from the carefully drilled young ladies of his acquaintance instantly caught his attention, but he remained largely impervious to her charm until one evening at the theatre, when he walked with her between the acts in the foyer, and she delighted him by asking in the most innocent way if this was where the bits of muslin promenaded, just as they did at Covent Garden? He was enchanted, answered her without betraying the smallest sign of surprise, and only permitted himself to laugh when she exclaimed in dismay: "Oh, dear, I should not have said that! I am in a scrape again!"

He assured her she might say what she chose to him, and they had a very interesting conversation, which would certainly have horrified even Lady Saltash, who was known to be broad-minded to a fault. Mr. Tarleton supposed that Hero must have culled her knowledge from a brother, but when he tried tactfully to discover what her antecedents were, she flushed and returned such evasive answers that good-breeding forbade him to press his enquiries. But from that day onward it was noticeable that Mr. Tarleton was spending more of his time in Bath than ever before; and when he actually appeared at the Lower Assembly Rooms, and stood up with Hero for the minuet as well as for one of the country dances, his numerous friends and acquaintances could scarcely believe their eyes, and told one another that poor dear Jasper was in a fair way to being caught at last.

As might have been expected, no such idea crossed Hero's mind. She thought her new acquaintance past the age of falling in love, and treated him very much as she had been in the habit of treating Sherry's bachelor friends. From having associated largely with them during the past months, she found herself at home in male company; and from having, since the first moment of her appearance in society, enjoyed all the license of a married woman, she was not at all missish, and neither put on airs to be interesting, nor affected the maidenly shrinking in vogue amongst certain of her contemporaries.

Mr. Tarleton found this delightful, and when Hero caught herself up guiltily on a cant expression culled from Sherry's vocabulary, or committed some other

367

small solecism of a like nature, he begged her not to correct herself, but to continue as she was, without attempting to school either her speech or her actions.

"For you must permit me to tell you, Miss Wantage," he said, his gravity belied by the twinkle in his eye, "that you are the most refreshing young female who has yet come in my path! Tell me more about the Brixham Pet!"

She said seriously: "I am sure I ought not, for now I come to think of it, the—the person who told me about him said it was not at all the sort of thing I should talk about. He is a Black, you know, and a great many people fancy that he will perhaps become Champion. Have you been to a prize-fight, Mr. Tarleton?"

"Do you know, I fear I have not? Have you, Miss Wantage?"

She laughed. "Now you are smoking me!——Oh, I don't mean that! Making jest of me! Of course I have not! Females do not!"

"But you are so unlike any other female I have met that that is no guide!"

"No, indeed I am not! At least, if I am, I do not wish to be, I assure you! It is very uncomfortable to behave as other people do not: you can have no notion!"

"I should not care a button for that. If I had any say in the matter, I should insist on your behaving just as you chose."

She shook her head. "No, not when you saw what scrapes I fell into. You would be quite shocked, I dare say. I am myself."

"You wrong me: *I* have never been shocked in my life."

"Not even by a lady's going to the Peerless Pool?"

asked Hero, regarding him as though he had been a rare specimen.

"Certainly not! What is the Peerless Pool?"

"Well, I never went there, for it—it was not liked. But I did go to Bartholomew Fair, and the Royal Saloon, and to tell you the truth, I was excessively amused. But it was very bad *ton*, you know, and I should not have done it."

He threw back his head and laughed. "I perceive, Miss Wantage, that you are what is commonly known as a handful! Let me be very impertinent, and beseech you earnestly, when you come to marry, to choose a man, like myself, who cannot be shocked!"

She coloured and looked down at her fan. "Yes, well—well, I shall not come to marry."

"Why, how is this?" he rallied her. "I prophesy that the day is not far distant when you will be surrounded by your bridesmaids, and going to Church in a cloud of lace veil and orange-blossom, with all your rejected admirers gnashing their teeth in the background, and every female relative you possess weeping in the way female relatives have, and——"

"Oh no, indeed, you are wrong!" she interrupted. "Good gracious, how extremely I should dislike it, to be sure!"

He raised his brows in mock astonishment. "Dislike a wedding? No, no, you cannot be as different from the rest of your sex as *that*!"

"I am *not* different from the rest of my sex! I only meant that I should not at all care for such a wedding as you describe. I went to one once, in London, and oh, dear! it was so shockingly unromantic!"

He smiled. "I collect that you would prefer a

runaway match, with a fast team of post-horses, the Scottish border for your goal, and an angry Papa in hot pursuit?"

She replied seriously: "Well, I scarcely remember my Papa, for he died when I was a child, but I think runaway weddings are the best, for to elope suddenly with someone you—you have a decided partiality for, and to become his wife without the least contrivance, or ceremony, or preparation, is—would be—the most beautiful adventure imaginable! Like finding yourself all at once in heaven, or fairyland, at least, when you had never thought but that you would continue in the same humdrum fashion all your life."

His eyes wrinkled a little at the corners, but he said solemnly: "Miss Wantage, do you read novels?"

"Why yes!" she answered, looking enquiringly at him.

"From the Minerva Press, perhaps?"

Her enquiring look turned to one of suspicion. "Mr. Tarleton, you are bam-laughing at me again!"

"No, no!" he said. "I am merely taking a great delight in the refreshment of your company! Plainly, only the most dashing of bridegrooms will do for you!"

The tenderest little smile hovered on her lips. "Yes," she acknowledged.

"A Blood, a Tulip of Fashion, a Nonpareil——"

"Oh no, he need not be that! I know a nonpareil— quite a nonesuch, I assure you! Drives to an inch!—but I should not care to elope with him. Of course, I think a man should know how to stick to his leaders, do not you?"

"Unquestionably," he said gravely.

"And as for the tulips, I know several, and they would not do for me at all. Besides, they are not romantic, because they have to think so much about their cravats and their coats and the size of their buttons that they have no time for anything besides. The most truly romantic man I know does not give a fig for what he may look like. It would not do for everyone to be so careless, of course, but he is so extremely handsome that it don't signify a scrap."

"Ah, I begin to fear that this dangerous blade is the man destined to carry you off!"

She laughed. "No, indeed you are quite mistaken! He is madly in love with someone else! And in any event, I think he would make a very uncomfortable husband, for whenever he is out of humour he wants to fight a duel."

"That would certainly be a drawback," he agreed. "It is to be hoped he is not frequently out of humour!"

"Oh yes! He takes a pet for the least little thing!" said Hero cheerfully. "And the mischief is that he is such a fine shot that no one will oblige him by going out with him. It puts him out of all patience sometimes, and indeed one cannot wonder at it. But only conceive how tiresome it would be to be married to such a man!"

"You can have no notion how glad I am to discover that you favour a milder-tempered bridegroom, Miss Wantage," said Mr. Tarleton, keeping his face prim. "Er—must your future husband be a very *young* gentleman?"

She had forgotten herself in talking of Sherry's friends; Mr. Tarleton's last words recalled her to a sense of her surroundings. She started, almost afraid that she might have betrayed herself, and blushed vividly, saying in a hurried way: "It is all nonsense! I do not know how we come to be talking of such absurdities. Tell me about the chestnuts General Crawley

371

says you are meaning to buy from him! Do you mean to drive them in your curricle? Are they sweet-goers? I was used to drive a high-stepping grey, in a phaeton, you know—very free and fast, and with the lightest of mouths! I won a race once—a private race, I mean," she added, a stricken expression entering her eyes for an instant at the memory this conjured up.

"So you are a whip!" Mr. Tarleton exclaimed. "I might have guessed it indeed! But, come, this is famous! The chestnuts you speak of are a match pair—beautiful steppers! If I purchase them from the General, may I hope that you will honour them, and me, by driving them?"

The stricken look vanished. Hero turned impulsively towards him. "Oh, would you teach me to handle a pair? Gil—the particular friend who taught me to drive my phaeton—would not let me drive his curricle, but I have a great desire to! That is, if Lady Saltash will permit me to."

Mr. Tarleton assured her that her ladyship would have no objection to such a harmless pastime, and so indeed it proved. Lady Saltash chuckled and gave permission; and very soon it became quite an accepted thing for Mr. Tarleton to drive up to the house in Camden Place any fine morning and to take up his eager pupil. They drove about the country in the immediate vicinity of the town, and Hero had such a real aptitude that it was not long before she was acquitting herself creditably enough for her to wish that Mr. Ringwood could see her progress. While she held the reins in her hands she could almost forget the trouble that lay in her heart. She was often merry, always entirely natural, never dreamed that anyone so elderly as her companion could be falling in love with her, thought him one of the kindest men she had encountered, and so treated him in a confiding way that completed his downfall. Mr. Tarleton felt himself to be growing daily younger in her presence, began to think seriously of matrimony, and racked his brains to think how best to make his suit attractive to so youthful, so unconventional, and so romantic a lady. A still, small voice within him, whispering that he would regret this madness, he resolutely ignored. It occurred to him that he had hitherto led the most humdrum of lives, and that to indulge in a little madness would be a welcome relief.

CHAPTER 21

Upon leaving Grillon's Hotel, Sherry betook himself home to Half Moon Street, meeting on the way Lord Wrotham, who was driving his sulky down Piccadilly towards St. James's Street. The Viscount hailed him, and he drew up. His restless, handsome countenance betrayed no pleasure in the encounter, however; and he greeted his friend with a scowl and a curt: "Well, what?"

"Oh, the devil! are you in the sullens again?" retorted Sherry. "What a fellow you are, George! I've a deuced good mind not to tell you something you'd give a deal to hear!"

George shrugged his shoulders. "Do as you please! I don't know what should have happened to put you in spirits. When last I saw you——"

"Never mind that!" interrupted Sherry. "If you wanted to pick a quarrel with me, you should have done it then, for by God, I was in the humour to quarrel with anyone who offered! Change my mind now. Thought you'd like to know the Beauty is back in town."

George made as if to give his horse the office to start.

"If you have come smash up to me merely to tell me that, you have wasted your time! She might be in Jericho for aught I care!"

"Point is she ain't in Jericho. She's on her way to Bath with my mother. I am escorting the pair of them there to-morrow."

The rigid look was wiped suddenly from Lord Wrotham's face. "What?" he ejaculated.

"True as I stand here! But that ain't what I wanted to tell you. Severn did come up to scratch."

George's brilliant eyes were now fixed on his face, in an expression of painful eagerness. "Do you tell me she refused him?"

"That's it. Said she had liked the notion of being a duchess, but when she thought of having to live with Severn all her life, she couldn't stomach it. Can't say I blame her."

"I don't believe it!"

"Well, you may do so. I've known Bella Milborne all my life. Very truthful girl—a dashed sight too truthful, I used to think, when we were youngsters! Besides, she told me not to repeat it. Thinks Severn wouldn't wish to have it known he'd been rejected. Deuce take it, I never thought I should live to feel sorry for the Incomparable, but there's no getting away from it: she's looking downright peaky! Told me she was in disgrace with Mrs. Milborne, and her father and my mother were the only people to have been kind to her. Told me something else, too, and I'll swear she meant it!"

"What else did she tell you?" demanded George.

Sherry grinned up at him. "Wouldn't you like to know? Think I'm going to betray a lady's confidence? I'm not!"

George drew a deep breath and sat staring straight

between his horse's ears, After a moment he recollected the first of Sherry's disclosures, and transferred his intent gaze to his face again. "You said she was on her way to Bath with your mother!"

"Well, why the devil shouldn't she be?"

"But you said you was going there too!"

"So I am. My mother's afraid of highwaymen, or some such flummery."

George frowned at him. "She can hire outriders!"

"That's what I told her, but nothing will do for her but to have me to go with her."

George's eyes were beginning to kindle. "Oh, indeed? It's something new, by God it is! for you to be dancing attendance on your mother, Sherry! And let me tell you now that if you are meaning to have a touch at Isabella again——"

"Go and take a damper, you fool!" retorted Sherry. "I'm a married man! What's more, if I did mean to have a touch at her, I wouldn't tell you she was on her way to Bath!"

Mollified, George begged pardon, explaining that he was so worn down that he hardly knew what he was saying. Sherry accepted this, and would have taken his leave had not George detained him to say: "I wouldn't go to Bath, if I was you, Sherry. You don't like the place. If Lady Sheringham would allow me to take your——"

"Well, she wouldn't," interrupted Sherry. "Besides, I've got a fancy to go there."

"Why?" demanded George suspiciously.

"What the deuce has it to do with you? Tired of London. Not been feeling quite the thing. Need a change."

"Yes! You will drink the waters, no doubt!" said George sardonically.

"I might," agreed Sherry. "No saying what I may not do—except one thing! Make yourself easy: I don't mean to make love to the Incomparable!"

And with this, he strode on down Piccadilly, leaving George in a good deal of consternation.

George drove slowly on, turned down into St. James's Street, and had almost reached Ryder Street, where he lodged, when he bethought himself of Mr. Ringwood. After all, it was Gil who had taken Kitten down to Bath, and it must be for Gil to decide what was now to be done. He turned his sulky and drove back in the direction of Stratton Street. Sherry had rounded the corner of Half Moon Street by this time, and was out of sight. George drove up to Mr. Ringwood's lodging, called a loafer to hold his horse, and sprang down from the sulky.

The door of Mr. Ringwood's lodging was opened to him by the retired gentleman's gentleman who owned the house, who conveyed to him the intelligence that Mr. Ringwood was out of town.

"Out of town!" exclaimed George indignantly. "What the devil ails him to be out of town, I should like to know?"

The owner of the house, being accustomed to the vagaries of the Quality, and knowing this particular member of the Quality of old, showed no surprise at this unreasonable explosion, but said civilly that Mr. Ringwood had gone into Leicestershire for a day's hunting, and was not expected to return until the morrow.

"Confound him!" muttered George. "Taken his man with him, I suppose?"

"Yes, my lord."

"He would!" said George savagely. "Now what am I to do?"

Mr. Ford, not deeming that any answer was expected of him, discreetly held his peace. George stood glowering for a few minutes, and then said, with all the air of a man who has taken a momentous decision: "I'll leave a note for him!"

Mr. Ford bowed, and at once ushered him into Mr. Ringwood's parlour. George sat down at the desk in the window, cast Cocker, the *Racing Chronicle,* and several copies of the *Weekly Dispatch* on to the floor, drew forward the ink-well, found, after considerable search amongst a litter of bills and invitations, a sheet of notepaper, and dashed off a hurried letter.

"Dear Gil," he wrote. *"The devil's in it now, and no mistake, for Sherry's off to Bath to-morrow with his mother and Miss Milborne. I see nothing for it but to post down there ahead of him, to warn Lady Sherry, in case she does not desire to see him. I shall leave town tonight. Yours, etc., Wrotham."*

His lordship then folded this missive, affixed a wafer to it, wrote Mr. Ringwood's name on it in arresting characters, propped it up against the clock on the mantelpiece, and departed. He felt that in going to apprise Hero of her husband's approaching visit to Bath, he would be acting with extreme propriety; and the circumstance of this particular deed of friendship's happening to coincide with his own paramount desire to repair to Bath was nothing more (he told himself) than a happy chance.

While George was making these arrangements,

Sherry had astonished his man, Bootle, by commanding him to have everything in readiness for a journey to Bath by an early hour on the following morning. He was rather vague about the probable length of his stay in this watering-place, and from never having been obliged to pack for himself, he could not conceive why Bootle should think this a matter of even trifling interest. He decided to drive himself down in his curricle, since this would frustrate at the outset any attempt on his parent's part to force him into sitting with her in the family travelling coach. So Jason and his groom had immediately to be warned, and by the time this had been done, and the groom given his orders to arrange for suitable changes of horses at the various stages, it was going on for eight o'clock, and the Viscount began to think of his dinner. Since Hero's disappearance it had become increasingly rare for him to dine at home. On this evening, so firmly persuaded was he that he at last had the clue to Hero's whereabouts, he felt cheerful enough to have eaten his dinner in Half Moon Street, had Mrs. Bradgate made any preparation to meet so unexpected an eventuality. As she had not, he was obliged to go out again. He walked down to White's and ordered the most sustaining meal he had been able to fancy for many weeks. He was finishing it when his cousin Ferdy strolled into the coffee-room. Ferdy was engaged with a party of friends, but as they had not yet put in an appearance, he sat down beside Sherry and joined him in a glass of burgundy.

"Care to see a little cocking to-morrow night, Sherry, dear old boy?" he asked, sipping his wine.

"Can't," responded Sherry briefly. "I'm off to Bath."

Ferdy choked. It took a great deal of back-slapping to restore him, and when he was at last able to catch his breath again, his eyes were watering, and his countenance was alarmingly flushed.

"Well, what the deuce!" exclaimed Sherry, eyeing him in surprise.

"Crumb!" gasped Ferdy.

"Crumb? You weren't eating anything!"

"Must have been," said Ferdy feebly. "What takes you to Bath, Sherry?"

"My mother. She's putting up at Grillon's with the Incomparable. Both going to Bath to drink the waters. I'm to escort 'em."

Ferdy gazed at him in dismay. "I wouldn't do it, Sherry," he said. "You won't like it there!"

"Well, if I don't like it, I can come back, can't I?"

"Much better not go at all," said Ferdy. "Very dull sort of a place these days. Don't even waltz there. Won't like the waters either."

"Good God, I ain't going to drink 'em!"

"Pity to miss the cocking! Very good match!" Ferdy said, faint but pursuing.

"I tell you I'm going to escort my mother to Bath!" Sherry said impatiently. "What the deuce ails you, Ferdy? Why shouldn't I go to Bath?"

"Just thought you might not care for it, dear boy! No offence! Did you say the Incomparable was going too?"

"Going to bear my mother company."

"Oh!" said Ferdy, thinking this over painstakingly. "Well, that settles it: much better not go, Sherry! If the Incomparable goes, Revesby will, and you won't like that."

"I suppose Bath is big enough to hold us both. In fact, if he means to hang about Bella's apron-strings, it's as well I should go!"

381

Ferdy gave it up. He withdrew a few minutes later to join his friends, and Sherry went home. But Ferdy's friends found him preoccupied that evening. He sat in a brown study over dinner, followed the party in a trance-like fashion to the card-room, and there paid so little attention to the game that his brother accused him of being cast-away. Their host, considering the question dispassionately, shook his head. "Not cast-away, Duke. Very affectionate as soon as he's a trifle disguised. Not affectionate to-night. You quite well, Ferdy, old fellow?"

"Had a shock," Ferdy said. "Saw Sherry to-night."

"Sherry?" said the Honourable Marmaduke.

"My cousin Sherry," explained Ferdy.

"Dash it, he's my cousin too, ain't he?" said Marmaduke. "You're as dead as a house, Ferdy!"

"He may be your cousin too," said Ferdy, not prepared to dispute this, "but it wouldn't have given you a shock. No reason why it should. Sherry's going to Bath."

Marmaduke stared at him. "Why?" he asked.

"Just what I've been wondering all the evening, Duke. You know what I think? Fate! That's what it is: fate! There's a thing that comes after a fellow: got a name, but I forget what it is. Creeps up behind him, and puts him in the basket when he ain't expecting it."

"What sort of a thing?" enquired his host uneasily.

"I don't know," replied Ferdy. "It ain't a thing you can see."

"If it's a ghost, I don't believe in 'em!" said his host, recovering his composure.

Ferdy shook his head. "Worse than that, Jack, dear boy! I'll think of its name in a minute. Met it at Eton."

"Dash it, Ferdy, I was at Eton the same time as you

were, and you never said a word about anything creeping up behind you!"

"I may not have said anything, but it did. Crept up behind me when I broke that window in chapel."

"Old Horley?" Mr. Westgate said. "You don't mean to tell me he's come up to London? What's he creeping up behind you for?"

"No, no!" replied Ferdy, irritated by his friend's poverty of intellect. "Not old Horley! Thing that made him suspect me when I thought my tracks were covered. Not sure it ain't a Greek thing. Might have been Latin, though, now I come to think of it."

"I know what he means!" said Marmaduke. "What's more, it proves he's cast-away, or he wouldn't be thinking of such things. Nemesis! That's it, ain't it, Ferdy?"

"Nemesis!" repeated Ferdy, pleased to find himself understood at last. "That's it! Dash it, it all goes to show, don't it? Never thought the stuff they used to teach us at school would come in useful, but if I hadn't had to learn a lot of Greek and Latin I shouldn't have known about that thingummy. Forgotten its name again, but it don't signify now."

He seemed inclined to brood over the advantages of a classical education, but his brother brought him back to the point. "What the deuce has Nemesis to do with Sherry's going to Bath?" he demanded.

"You wouldn't understand," said Ferdy. "Think I'll go and see Gil."

"Dash it, Ferdy, you can't go off like that!" expostulated Mr. Westgate.

"Yes, I can," replied Ferdy. "Got a fancy to see Gil. Very knowing fellow. Come back again later."

"You know what, Duke?" said Mr. Westgate, watching Ferdy wend his way to the door. "I've never seen poor Ferdy so bosky in all my life! He'll be taken up by the Watch, that's what'll happen to him!"

This ignominious fate did not, however, overtake Ferdy. He reached Stratton Street unmolested, to be met by the same intelligence which had greeted Lord Wrotham earlier in the day. He was even more dashed than his lordship had been, but he reached the same decision. For the second time that day Mr. Ford ushered one of Mr. Ringwood's cronies into his parlour for the purpose of writing a note to him.

It cost Ferdy time and profound thought to achieve a letter that should explain the whole situation to Mr. Ringwood; but when he presently read the elegantly phrased document over to himself he was not ill-pleased with it. To his mind it contrived both to impress Mr. Ringwood with a sense of the urgency of the situation and to reassure him on the question of the writer's selfless loyalty to the cause at stake. It stated clearly that Ferdy would accompany his cousin to Bath, but it became a trifle involved after that, a dark reference to the possible need of a second leaving Mr. Ringwood to infer that Ferdy felt there was a strong likelihood of Sherry's calling him out: a contingency which he explained as being due to the machinations of a mysterious agency whose name might be discovered on application to the Honourable Marmaduke Fakenham. It struck Ferdy, when he came to this portion of the missive, that it would be highly undesirable for Mr. Ringwood to make any such application, so he appended a terse postscript: "*Better not.*"

The composition of such a literary effort naturally made it necessary for the Honourable Ferdy to seek a little stimulant. Fortunately, there was some brandy in one of the decanters on the sideboard. Ferdy poured it into a rummer, drank it off, and then, for he was very meticulous in all matters of good *ton*, added a second postscript: "*Took a glass of brandy*."

He departed from Mr. Ringwood's lodging, feeling that no action befitting a man of honour had been left undone; and, the brandy having made him pot-valiant, betook himself to Half Moon Street. The house was in darkness, and it was some time before he could obtain a response to his insistent knocking. It seemed to him a very peculiar circumstance that no one should answer the door in Sherry's house, and he was just wondering whether he could have made a mistake in the number when a window was flung up on the second floor, and Sherry's voice, rather sleepy and extremely irate, asked who the devil was there.

Ferdy gazed up at the vague outline of his cousin's head and said: "Hallo, Sherry, dear boy! What the deuce are you doing up there?"

"Is that you, Ferdy?" demanded Sherry wrathfully. "What the deuce are *you* doing down there, waking me up at this hour of night?"

"What, you ain't asleep, Sherry, surely?" said Ferdy incredulously. "Night's young! Come to have a chat with you. Very important."

"Oh, the devil! Dead-beat again! What a curst nuisance you are, Ferdy!" said Sherry, exasperated.

He withdrew his head from the window, and in a few minutes had opened the front door to admit his cousin. Ferdy walked in, smiling affably, but declined an offer of the spare bedchamber. "Going back to White's when I've had a word with you, Sherry," he said. "Engaged with some friends. What made you go to bed?"

"Dash it, it's past one o'clock!" replied Sherry. "Besides, I'm going to Bath to-morrow."

"Nothing in that," said Ferdy. "I'm going to Bath too, but I don't go to bed at one o'clock. Why should I?"

"You're foxed. You ain't going to Bath."

"Yes, I am. Came to tell you. Taken a fancy to go with you."

Sherry stared at him narrowly, holding up the candle he was carrying. "Why?" he asked.

"Fond of you, Sherry. Don't know why, but there it is. Always was. If you go to Bath, I'll go to Bath."

"Now I know you're foxed!" said Sherry, quite disgusted.

"No, I ain't. Fond of Gil too. Not the kind of fellow to leave my friends in the lurch. You driving down?"

"Yes, but——"

"Take me up in Cavendish Square. Ready for you any time."

"I don't mind taking you up if you really mean it," said Sherry. "In fact, I'd as soon have company on the way as not, but it's my belief you'll take the best part of to-morrow to sleep this off! If you won't go to bed, I wish you'd go home!"

"Not going home: going back to White's," said Ferdy. "Care to join us, dear old fellow?"

"No, I would not!" replied Sherry, opening the door for him.

"Quite right! Not dressed for it!" Ferdy agreed. "See you to-morrow!"

Contrary to Sherry's expectations, when he drew up in Cavendish Square at noon that day he found his cousin not only perfectly wide-awake, but prepared for a journey. Ferdy had had time to think of several reasons to account for his desiring to go to Bath, and although his cousin believed none of them, he was far from guessing what the true reason was. He had a suspicion that Ferdy's activities in London might have made it expedient for him to withdraw from the metropolis for a time, but as he took only the most cursory interest in Ferdy's affairs, he forebore to question him very strictly.

The winter being unusually mild, no particular discomfort was suffered during the journey, which, as Sherry had prophesied, took them two days to accomplish. The cavalcade, consisting as it did of one large travelling coach, two chaises, bearing servants and baggage, and one sporting curricle, was imposing enough to procure for the dowager the most flattering degree of attention at every halt made on the road. Landlords bowed till their noses almost touched their knees; waiters ran out with offers of cordials; chambermaids dropped curtsies; and ostlers fell over one another in their anxiety to be the first to serve a cortege the style of which promised unusually handsome gratuities.

They entered Bath towards evening on the second day, the dowager's coach bowling along considerably ahead of the curricle, which had stopped for an unseasonable length of time at a certain hostelry a few miles outside the town. Lady Sheringham had hired a palatial suite of apartments on the Royal Crescent, so Sherry, sweeping into Belmont from Guinea Lane, bore sharp right into Bennet Street, which led into the Circus, past the New Assembly Rooms. It was in the middle of this crowded thoroughfare, just as the nicest precision of eye was required to negotiate the passage between a hackney carriage, drawn up on the left of the road, and a perch phaeton being driven towards him by a down-the-road looking man in a many-caped greatcoat, that Sherry caught sight of his wife, walking along with her hand on Lord Wrotham's arm.

A violent expletive broke from him, and an equally violent start. He jerked his head round, heedless of the phaeton, and the next instant the wheels of both vehicles were locked, and much more violent expletives were issuing from the lips of the down-the-road man.

Since all the horses were plunging in sudden fright, and there was an ominous sound of splintering wood, Sherry was obliged to give his attention where it was most urgently required. By the time the carriages had been disengaged, thanks largely to the efforts of Jason, who had lost not a moment in leaping down from his perch, and running to the heads of his master's pair, Hero and George had disappeared into Russel Street. Sherry, paying no heed at all to the justifiably incensed remarks being addressed to him by the phaeton's owner, thrust the reins into his cousin's hands, and, with a brief admonition to him to "settle with this fellow," sprang down from the curricle, narrowly avoided being knocked down by a tilbury, fell foul of a couple of chairmen, whose load was impeding his passage, reached the other side of the street, and set off with great strides towards Russel Street. He was too late. When he reached the turning there was no sign of his quarry, and after taking a few paces up the street he paused, realizing the futility of hunting through all the roads in the vicinity. He turned and went back, becoming aware on the way that his singular behaviour had attracted no little attention to himself. He found, too, that he was still carrying his driving-whip, and had the sight of Lord Wrotham, bending solicitously over Hero, not filled him with murderous rage he must have grinned to think of the comic spectacle he presented.

He found Ferdy making his apologies with winning grace, and offering, on his behalf, to pay for the necessary repairs to the phaeton. The phaeton's owner was already a little mollified, and everything might have been settled comfortably over a third of daffy, as Ferdy was on the point of suggesting, had not the Viscount nipped such friendly overtures in the bud by scowling upon his victim, offering him the curtest of apologies, handing him his card, climbing into his curricle, and driving off without another word.

"Really, Sherry, dear old boy!" expostulated Ferdy. "No need to go off like this! Very pleasant fellow!"

"Did you see who that was?" Sherry demanded.

The late accident had temporarily put everything else out of Ferdy's head, but these words recalled him to a sense of his own surprise. "Yes, by Jove!" he exclaimed. "Dashed if I could believe my eyes! George! You see him too, Sherry?"

Sherry audibly ground his teeth. "Do you think I'm blind? I saw him, and what's more I saw who was walking on his arm! My wife!"

"Lady Sheringham?" said Ferdy cautiously.

"Yes, you fool!"

"Now you come to mention it, Sherry, dear boy, I saw her too," said Ferdy. "Didn't care to draw your attention to it."

They had by this time traversed the Circus and were halfway down Brock Street. "So *that* was why—!" Sherry muttered. "It is George I have to thank for—! By God, let me but get my hands on George!"

Ferdy, perceiving that it could only be a matter of minutes before a most unwelcome question would be hurled at him, said in a desperate attempt to avert suspicion: "No wish to pry into your affairs, Sherry!

Take it you wasn't expecting to see Lady Sherry? Very extraordinary business!"

Fortunately for him, the Viscount's mind was so taken up with the thought of George's duplicity that he paid no heed to this. The curricle swept into the Royal Crescent and drew up outside one of the houses, behind the chaises, which were being unloaded by a bevy of hirelings. Jason jumped down and went to the horses' heads. As his master descended into the road, he said in a stupefied tone: "So help me bob, guv'nor! That were the Missus!"

"Jason, hold your tongue!" the Viscount said angrily.

"Chaffer and daylights close as a oyster, me lord!" promptly replied the Tiger, his sharp countenance alive with curiosity.

The Viscount strode into the house, leaving his cousin to follow at his leisure. The entrance hall was a litter of trunks and bandboxes; his lordship picked his way none too carefully through them and ran up the stairs to the parlour on the first floor. Here he found Miss Milborne directing a couple of abigails where to take various packages that strewed the room. She smiled at Sherry, and said: "Your Mama has the headache, and has gone to lie down on her bed before it is time to dress for dinner. I am sorry we are still in such a pickle, but I will have all in order in——Why, what is the matter, Sherry?"

The Viscount waited until the two abigails had loaded themselves with impedimenta, and then firmly shut them out of the room. With his hand still on the door-knob, he said grimly: "Do you know whom I saw in Bennet Street?"

She looked a startled enquiry.

"George!" said the Viscount, flinging the name at her.

"Oh!" she exclaimed, blushing a little. "Oh, indeed!"

"Yes!" returned his lordship. "But you need not look so smug, Bella, for he has not come to Bath on your account! He was strolling along, as bold as brass, with my wife hanging on his arm!"

"*Oh!*" gasped Miss Milborne, in quite another voice. "Oh, Sherry, no!"

"He was, I tell you!" said the Viscount, taking a few hasty paces about the room and kicking an offending bandbox out of his path.

Miss Milborne clasped her hands together and said in a strictly controlled tone: "I told you—I *told* you, Sherry, that he had a marked partiality for Hero! It was the first thing that sprang to my mind when I learned of her having left you. But that he could have—all this time—— Oh, it is too base!"

"Only wait until I come upon him face to face!" Sherry said through his locked teeth.

She covered her eyes with one hand. "I was never more shocked in my life! I do not know what to say! You do not think—might it not be possible that he met Hero in Bath by chance?"

"No doubt that is what he will try to make us believe!" Sherry said, with a savage little laugh. "But it is doing it a trifle too brown! Now I know why he was so urgent with me not to come to Bath! Now I see it all! Why, he must have posted here ahead of me the instant he was apprized of my having taken the resolve of coming with my mother!"

"And she!" Miss Milborne said throbbingly. "Oh, I had not thought it of her!"

"Yes, you had!" retorted the Viscount, rounding on

391

her. "It is precisely what you did think, Bella! And there's not a word of truth in it, and if you dare to say it again I'll choke you!"

"Pray do not be thinking you can talk to *me* like that!" said Miss Milborne, bristling. "*I* am not your unfortunate wife, thank heaven!"

"If you are thanking heaven for that, then at last we are of one mind!" the Viscount threw at her. "This is your fault! If you had not played fast and loose with Wrotham, this would never have happened! By God, whenever I think of the way he did his possible to dissuade me from coming here, and——" He stopped short. "Yes, by Jupiter!" he said. "And Ferdy too! *Ferdy!* He knew! Well, that's one of them at least I can get my hands on! Cousin Ferdy has a trifle of explaining to do!"

He left the room precipitately as he spoke, and went down the stairs in several perilous bounds. But although his cousin Ferdy was not generally held to be quick-witted, he had a lively sense of self-preservation, and he had not waited for this inevitable moment. There was no sign of him in the house, or even outside it, and a furious enquiry of Bootle elicited the information that Mr. Fakenham had bethought himself of some urgent shopping that must be done without the least loss of time, and had gone off some ten minutes earlier. Sherry knew that he had formed the intention of putting up at the York Hotel, and instantly betook himself to his hostelry. He drew blank. Mr Fakenham's man and Mr. Fakenham's baggage had certainly arrived there, but Mr. Fakenham had as yet put in no appearance. The Viscount, growing steadily more wrathful, waited for some time in the coffee-room, but when it became apparent that his cousin had no immediate intention of emerging from whatever place of hiding he had found, he went back to the Royal Crescent, leaving a message with Ferdy's valet, which was calculated to terrify Ferdy into an instant flight for London.

The first thing which met the Viscount's eyes upon his return to his parent's lodging was a neat oblong of pasteboard lying on the table in the hall. He glanced cursorily at this, and his temper was by no means improved by the discovery that it bore Sir Montagu Revesby's name, in flowing copperplate characters. He passed on upstairs to change his travelling dress for raiment more suited to his mother's dinner-table. His sense of filial duty fell short, however, of the stockings and knee-breeches which she was old-fashioned enough to consider *de rigueur*; he compromised with a pair of exquisitely fitting pantaloons, strapped tightly under his feet; and one of Stultz's best coats of superfine cloth. His parent, who seemed to be in excellent spirits, welcomed him into the dining-room with a fond smile, and, when he offered a curt apology for his tardiness, said that it did not signify. He took his place at the end of the table, saying disagreeably, as he did so: "I saw that that fellow has wasted no time in calling upon you, Bella!"

"If you mean Sir Montagu," returned Miss Milborne composedly, "he was so obliging as to wait on us to discover if there were any service he could render us. We are already indebted to him for the flowers we found awaiting us."

"Yes, indeed!" agreed Lady Sheringham. "Such a delightful man! His air so distinguished: everything about him proclaiming the gentleman! I am sure he said everything that was kind and civil, and only fancy,

Anthony, he was able to give me some excellent advice about the treatment I should seek! It seems that there is a Dr. Wilkinson, who has lately acquired the Abbey Baths, who Sir Montagu thinks would do me a great deal of good. The Baths are private, you know, and it seems that this Dr. Wilkinson has a most interesting scheme in mind for the erection of a Pump Room in Abbey Street, where one may be able to drink four different waters! Conceive of it! Then, too, the doctor is a great advocate for the Russian method of Vapour Baths, which I had not before heard of, but which I am sure would benefit me excessively. I do not know when I had been so pleased with anyone! Sir Montagu spoke, too, of you, with the most flattering degree of affection, dear Anthony."

"I'll thank him to keep his affection for those who may value it!" replied his lordship unequivocally. It was apparent to him that Sir Montagu had not been slow to sum Lady Sheringham up, and had spared no pains to ingratiate himself with her. The idea of Revesby's having the effrontery to come to a house where he was known to be lodging gave him a passing twinge of annoyance, but as he had a far greater cause for annoyance weighing upon him, he did not waste more than a moment or two's thought upon it. He noticed that Miss Milborne had quite recovered her composure, and was able to eat her dinner with a tolerably good appetite. He himself tasted and rejected various dishes, and bore little part in the discussion between the two ladies of plans for the immediate future. He did indeed wonder that Miss Milborne could so calmly talk of the several acquaintances she had at present sojourning in Bath, of taking out subscriptions to the Balls at the Assembly Rooms, of visiting the best circulating libraries, and of a dozen other such irrelevant trifles.

As soon as dinner was over, he excused himself from joining the ladies in the parlour, and demanded of the butler if his Tiger had returned from the errand on which he had despatched him.

Jason was waiting downstairs, and was at once sent for. He grinned cheerfully at his master and announced that Lord Wrotham, whom he described as a peevy cull, was putting up at the White Hart, in Stall Street. The Viscount then changed his footwear for a pair of gleaming Hessians, called for his hat, and his drab Benjamin, and left the house.

...rat, and as it died the noise all through
the building...

As soon as there was any sign he edged nearer and
found the knife in his pocket, and just ahead of him
while it lit... her had stripped from the crowd of
watchers and despairing him.

There was a thud downstairs... and here he came and
for the ground and dilly at his wrist and announced
this there. A pointed knife he stood there in a ferop... ...
all was poking up at the... there then all started there.
The World... time... he... here to where for a... here one
at some... he now... called in the... ... then this day bow
hand... and felt the knife back, as... ...

CHAPTER 22

Lord Wrotham had arrived in Bath a day ahead of Sherry, and had stayed only to remove the travel stains from his person at the White Hart before repairing to Upper Camden Place. He was out of luck, the day being Wednesday, and Lady Saltash and her young friend having gone to attend the weekly concert at the New Assembly Rooms. George was obliged to wait until the following morning before delivering his warning to Hero. He found her at home then, winding wool for her hostess, and as soon as he was announced, she flew up out of her chair, and ran forward to greet him, with both her hands held out, and such an expression of joy in her face that Lady Saltash raised her brows a trifle. But Lady Saltash was shrewd enough to perceive that the welcome bestowed on this handsome young blood was sisterly in its nature, and she condescended to allow George to kiss her gnarled hand, and lost no time in putting him in his place, by recalling under what circumstances she had last met his Mama, how she had been an intimate friend of one of his more formidable aunts, and what she had said to his father when that deceased gentleman had scandalized his

397

well-wishers by mortgaging his estates. She ended by drawing a vivid word-picture of George himself at his christening, and in this masterly fashion contrived to make that dangerous and dashing blade feel much younger and less important than he had done for years.

"But, George, what brings you here?" asked Hero, smiling mischievously up at him. "It is not at all the sort of place for you! They do not allow hazard in the Rooms, you know, and nobody waltzes, so how will you go on?"

"I know: deuced slow place!" George agreed. "But I did not come for that! Kitten—Lady Sheringham, I mean"—he corrected himself, a guilty eye on Lady Saltash.

"No, no, don't call me that! I am known as Miss Wantage here, but please call me Kitten! It seems so long since anyone did!" Hero said, a catch in her voice.

He pressed her hand in a very feeling manner. "But you are well? You are tolerably comfortable?"

"Yes, indeed! Dear Lady Saltash has been so kind! But you have not told me why you are here?"

"Kitten, it's the deuce of a coil, and I did not know what you would wish me to do! Gil must needs go off to Melton, just when he was most wanted, and there was no sense in consulting Ferdy."

"George, nothing has happened to Sherry?" Hero cried.

"No, nothing. But he is even now upon his way here!"

Such a light sprang to her eyes, such a vivid colour into her cheeks that if he could have brought Sherry into her presence there and then he would have done it. "To—find—*me*, George?" she faltered, looking beseechingly at him.

He was obliged to shake his head. There was a long silence. Hero broke it. "No. I quite see. But—but it seems very odd of Sherry to be coming here, if it is not for that, because he cannot bear Bath."

"The thing is," said George, roughly, to conceal his overflowing sympathy, "that the dowager has taken a fancy to drink the waters, and nothing would do for her but that Sherry must escort her. She brings Miss Milborne with her."

"She brings—— Oh!" Hero said numbly. "*That* is why Sherry—— Yes, I see. It—it was very kind in you to come to warn me, dear George."

He stretched out his hand, and possessed himself of one of hers. "Kitten, there was no use in my trying to keep it from you! God knows I—— But I do not believe he cares a button for the Incomparable! He has not shown a sign of it in all these weeks! I own, when I heard that he had consented to come here I was instantly suspicious, and I taxed him with meaning to have a touch at her again. He denied it immediately: bade me remember he was a married man; assured me he had no notion of making love to her. For as soon as I knew Miss Milborne was to bear Lady Sheringham company I offered to take Sherry's place as their escort. He would not consent to it, but——"

"Was he so very set on going with them?" Hero asked wistfully.

He hesitated. "I hardly know—— Dash it, yes! There was no moving him. But it may well have been as he said: his mother would not have consented to the alteration."

"I don't think Sherry would have listened to Lady Sheringham if he had not himself wished to go in her party," Hero said. "You see, George, I know Sherry very well. And I know, of course, that if only he could divorce me Lady Sheringham would do all that lay in her power to marry him to Isabella."

"It is very true, but I do not believe it of Sherry. Dash it, Kitten, had he had any such notion he would not have stopped me on Piccadilly, which he did, only to tell me that this Miss Milborne was coming to Bath. Yes, by Jove, and he as good as told me also that it was I who had engaged her affections—for you must know that Mrs. Milborne's story was true: Severn did offer, and was rejected!"

"Oh, George, I am so happy to hear that!" Hero said impulsively. "If only the rest may be true! But why should Sherry come here, if you are right? You see, it is as I told you, the night I ran away: it was Isabella he really wished to make his wife, and he took me only because she would not accept him, and his mother had put him in a passion. I do not think he loves Isabella very much, but perhaps he is tired of—of everything, and willing to oblige Lady Sheringham."

"I do not know: I am not in his confidence. When you first left him, there was no coming near him. He was never at home: spent his time looking for you all over the country. But lately he has been kicking up every kind of lark, as though—— Not that that signifies! Plenty of people would tell you I have been doing the same thing myself, and the lord knows I had no pleasure in it! But what am I to do, Kitten? Do you wish him to know that you are here? I own I should be glad to be able to make a clean breast of the business to him, for I have not liked my part in it above half!"

"Oh, no, George, I beg you will not! If he is beginning to forget me—if he should not be pleased to know that I was here—I could not bear it! For he would feel himself bound to take me back, and I am not going to go back, unless—— But why do we talk like this? He does not come to Bath for my sake, but for Isabella's, and you know it as well as I do, George!"

"If I thought that——" he said broodingly, his hand clenching on his knee.

"It does not appear to me," interposed Lady Saltash dryly, "that either of you knows anything! Let me beg of you, my love, not to put yourself in a taking before ever that husband of yours has reached Bath! As for you, Wrotham—for I do not mean to stand upon ceremony with you!—you may escort us to the Pump Room, if you will be so obliging. I fancy the barouche is at the door already."

George expressed his willingness to be of service, took the front seat in the carriage, facing the ladies, and behaved in a very docile way until the arrival on the scene of Mr. Tarleton, who came up to them in the Pump Room, and greeted Hero with so much the air of a friend of long-standing that George's hackles rose instinctively. Hero made both gentlemen known to each other, and took the opportunity to whisper to Mr. Tarleton, when George went to procure her second glass of the famous water for Lady Saltash, that this was none other than the fire-eater she had told him about. Mr. Tarleton, who had a lively sense of humour, was immensely entertained, and he thanked Hero for her warning, and said that he would take good care not to incense so dangerous a young man. George, who had been keeping such a vicariously jealous eye upon Hero that he made himself very unpopular by forgetting to tip the pumper, soon rejoined them. Closer scrutiny of Mr. Carleton informed him that this pleasant person was no longer in his first youth, and he unbent a little towards him. For his part, Mr. Tarleton, quite as suspicious as George, but better able to hide it, could not detect in his manner towards Hero any trace of the lover. Lady Saltash, seated at a little distance, observed the trio with cynical enjoyment. Just such a situation as her mischievous nature delighted in appeared to be brewing.

When she and Hero were once more seated in the barouche, taking a turn about the town before going back to Camden Place, she said with the forthrightness which made her rather disconcerting: "Now, my love, I should be glad if you will inform me what you mean to do next?"

Hero shook her head hopelessly.

"You don't know. Nothing could be more disastrous! But perhaps you know whether or not you are willing tamely to relinquish your husband to this Beauty I hear so much about?"

Hero turned her face away, and stared blindly out of the window. "Oh, ma'am, pray do not ask me! I have—I have such *wicked* thoughts of poor Isabella!"

"Excellent! I am happy to perceive that there is some spirit in you! Well, let me tell you, my child, that if you mean to make a push to keep Anthony you should show yourself very well able to do without him. Do not be making sheep's eyes at him, and begging his pardon for having taken exception to his overbearing ways! *You* are the injured one, remember! and——"

"No, ma'am, indeed I am not!" Hero said earnestly. "It was all my fault for being so——"

"Do not interrupt me! I repeat, it is you who are injured, and if ever you hope to have the mastery over Anthony——"

"But, ma'am, you are quite mistaken!" Hero assured

402

her. "I never thought of such a thing! I only want to make him happy, and not to be such a tiresome wife!"

"You are besotted!" said her ladyship. "I have a very good mind to wash my hands of you! Only want to make him happy indeed! Yes! And if it would make him happy to divorce you and marry this Milborne chit, you will help him to do it, I dare say!"

Hero thought this over. "No, I won't!" she said suddenly. "If Isabella loved Sherry, I would try my best not to be selfish, but she doesn't love him, and if she is encouraging him now to follow her about in this odious way, it is just because Severn did *not* come up to scratch, whatever she may have told Sherry! And I know all the gentlemen who would like to marry Isabella, and Sherry is by far the most eligible, now that Severn is out of the running—or he would be, if I did not exist—and he shall *not* be sacrificed to Isabella's horrid ambition!"

Lady Saltash's eyes narrowed in amusement. "Now you are beginning to talk like a sensible woman!" she said. "And pray how do you mean to rescue him from this designing beauty's toils?"

"Well, I don't know," Hero confessed. "Of course, if I were to return to Sherry, she couldn't marry him, could she? But I do not at all know that he wants me: in fact, I have a great fear that he does not; and so that would not make him happy in the least. And, oh, dear, ma'am, when I recall how lovely Isabella is, besides being an heiress, and so well-bred, and never doing the wrong thing, and in every respect all that a wife should be, I can't conceive how Sherry's affections could fail to reanimate towards her!"

"It is my belief," responded her ladyship calmly, "that Sherry never had the smallest real affection for her. Very pretty all this talk of his having married you in a fit of pique! I am reading of such things for ever in trashy novels, but in all the course of my life I have not yet observed it to happen! A man whose affections had been seriously engaged would not have relinquished his suit as easily as Sherry seems to have done, my dear, depend upon it! The truth is that he was not in love with either of you. What his sentiments may now be I do not pretend to say, but it is in the nature of nine men out of ten that what may be theirs for the picking up they are much inclined to despise, and what seems to be out of reach they instantly and fervently desire. Now, you do not know whether Anthony loves you or not, and very likely he does not know either. Drop into his hands like a ripe plum, and I dare say you may never know, for I do him the justice to assume that he would receive you again with a good grace. He was never a bad-natured boy: indeed, I used to think he had a great deal of sweetness in his disposition, would someone but encourage him to show it! If you wish to know how you stand with him, let him think that you have no particular desire to return to him! If he wants you, he will move heaven and earth to win you; if he does not—well, then you may make him happy in whatever foolish fashion you choose!"

Hero, who had listened to this with the greatest attention, turned it over in her mind before replying. She said slowly, at last: "It will be very hard, but perhaps, in the end, it would be for the best. I do understand what you mean, dear ma'am. Only, when George told me that he was coming here, I thought—I could not help thinking that it was because some chance had informed him that I was with you. And I could not help indulging the hope that he did love me after all."

"Yes, my dear," agreed her ladyship, with a certain amount of dryness. "That would have put quite another complexion on the affair. But it does not appear that he has the least notion of your being with me."

"No," Hero said sadly.

Lady Saltash left it at that. Shortly after noon, Mr. Tarleton came to Camden Place by appointment, in his curricle, and took Hero up for a drive to Kelston. It struck him that she wore rather a sober face, and he rallied her on it, accusing her of finding Bath a tedious place and himself a great bore.

"Oh, no, that I certainly do not!" she said quickly.

"I am persuaded you think me a dull dog, with one foot in the grave, and not a spark of romantic fervour in my whole composition!"

She laughed. "No, how should I be so foolish? I dare say you could be excessively romantic, if you wished to be, and as for having one foot in the grave, pooh!"

"But I fancy you did think so, when first we met?" he said quizzically.

She coloured. "Yes, it is true, but that was before I became properly acquainted with you."

"Tell me, Miss Wantage, do you consider me past the age of thinking of marriage?"

She looked up. "No, indeed! Why, have you some such notion?"

"Yes," he replied.

Her dimples peeped. "Then, of course, you must become romantic, Mr. Tarleton! Females are so silly, you know, that they much prefer romance to solid worth!"

He pulled a grimace. "Solid worth! Of all abominable phrases! Do you remember telling me once that you thought runaway marriages the best? Are you still of the same mind?"

She stifled a sigh. "Yes. That is, it is the only kind of marriage for me. I do not think it would suit you, however! Do you think I shall ever be able to drive a team, Mr. Tarleton?"

"Yes. I would willingly teach you."

"I never met anyone I dealt with so extremely kind as you!" she said, laughing. "But I am sure I should not be allowed to! I expect it is not the thing at all."

"Who cares?" he returned. "I am not such a prosy old fellow as to be for ever thinking of what is the thing, I assure you!" He glanced down at her profile. "You have never told me anything about yourself, Miss Wantage. I collect you are not related to Lady Saltash?"

"No," she replied.

"Forgive me if I seem to you to be impertinent! But I see you living a life that must be unsuited to one of your youth and natural spirits, and I——"

"Lady Saltash is everything that is kind!" she said. "Indeed, I am under no inconsiderable obligation to her, and if I have seemed to you to be ungrateful——"

"Ungrateful! No, indeed! I have been much struck by your constant attentions to her. I have the greatest regard for Lady Saltash, but I cannot believe that you are happy in Camden Place."

She was silent, her colour much heightened. After a short pause, he continued: "Do you mean to remain permanently in your present position?"

She started. "Oh, no! It would be impossible, for I have not the least claim on Lady Saltash! Already I feel that I have trespassed on her kindness for too long. I do not—I am not perfectly certain what I shall do, but you must know that I was trained to become a governess, and—and it was with the object of finding an eligible situation in some seminary that I came to Bath."

"A governess! You!" he exclaimed. "You are not serious! You cannot mean me to believe that you wish for such an existence!"

A rather melancholy smile trembled on her lips. "Oh, no! I shall dislike it of all things! In fact, I once said that I would do anything rather than become one! But if I do find such a post perhaps it will not be so very bad after all."

"Have you no relatives to provide for you?" he asked. "You are so young! Surely there must be someone—a guardian, perhaps—whose business it must be to take care of you?"

"No, there is no one—at least, I have a cousin who gave me a home when my father died, but she could not house me for ever, you see, and to tell you the truth I did not like her, nor she me."

"I had not imagined that this could be so," he said, in a moved tone. "I had thought——This alters things indeed!" He smiled, as she looked up enquiringly, and said: "No wonder you dream of romance and adventure! You should be called Cinderella, I think!"

Her mouth quivered. She replied: "It is odd that you should say so. I have sometimes thought that too. You do not know the whole, and I cannot tell it to you just now, though perhaps one day I may. I—I was very like Cinderella."

"Except that no Prince has yet come with a glass slipper for you to try on your foot!" he said.

She was silent, her attention fixed on the road ahead, her face still a little flushed. When she did speak, it was with a touch of constraint, and only to say that she fancied it must be time they were thinking of a return to Camden Place. He agreed at once, for he thought her embarrassment arose from maidenly shyness. He said gently: "Was it very dull and disagreeable in your cousin's house, Cinderella?"

She smiled at that. "Yes, odiously dull! And she has three daughters, and they are all of them quite shockingly plain, though perhaps not plain enough to be called the Ugly Sisters!"

"And did they go to parties while you stayed at home and swept out the kitchen?"

"Well, not quite as bad as that, for I was not out, you know! I do think they were not always very kind to me, but I dare say it was tiresome for them to be obliged to have me."

"I hope they may every one of them die a spinster!"

"Oh, no, how spiteful!" she protested.

"You dreamed of romance, and they made you a governess! I cannot forgive them! You must have your romance in despite of them! How would you like to be carried off, married out of hand, cosseted and cared for by a husband who would adore you—ah, the happy-ever-after ending, in effect? Is that not what you have dreamed of?"

"All girls do," she said, in a constricted tone. "At least, when they are very young and foolish, they do. But—but real life is not quite like the fairy-tales."

"But you were made to live a fairy-tale life, and I am determined you must do so!"

She raised her candid eyes to his face, and said simply: "Please do not, Mr. Tarleton! I know you are only funning, but—but I would rather you did not!"

"I will do nothing to displease you," he promised.

"Shall I see you at the Dress Ball at the Lower Rooms to-morrow night?"

"I—I am not perfectly certain. I believe not."

"Oh, that is too unkind!" he teased. "Did you not promise to let me put your name down for the minuet? I shall certainly do so before I leave Bath this evening. You will not be so cruel as to leave me without a lady to stand up with!"

She returned a light answer; he continued to talk easily on a number of trivial topics for the remainder of the drive; and set her down in Camden Place more enchanted than ever with her, and resolved upon a course of action fantastic enough to have appealed to the silliest damsel ever discovered between the marble covers of a circulating library novel.

It was when Hero was returning on foot from Milsom Street, later in the afternoon, that she fell in with George. She had been executing a commission for Lady Saltash, and he at once relieved her of her parcel, and insisted on escorting her back to Upper Camden Place. They had just crossed Bennet Street when Sherry's curricle swept round the corner from Belmont. His start, and the expression of frozen amazement on his face were not lost on Hero; and as it did not occur to her (or for that matter, to George) that his astonishment was due not so much to seeing her as her companion, the last shreds of hope that he might have come to Bath to search for her were banished from her mind. While Sherry was disentangling his curricle from the phaeton, she hurried on toward Russel Street, almost dragging George with her. Himself no mean whip, other considerations were momentarily lost with him in the contemplation of the wreckage Sherry had caused.

"Well, of all the cow-handed things to do!" he exclaimed.

In the midst of her misery Hero could not help laughing, although a little shakily, at the accident. "It was so like Sherry!" she said. "And I know he will say it was all the poor man's fault! Oh, George, he did not think to see me here! You were right. I never saw him look more shocked! Oh, dear why was I ever born?"

"Did you see who was with him?" George demanded. "Ferdy! He must have told him he was coming here, just as he told me! I must say, I had not thought Ferdy would have had sense enough to have come along too. Depend upon it, he will be calling Camden Place within the hour! But what the deuce is to be done now, Kitten? The mischief is in it that he has seen me with you, and he will ask me for your direction. What would you have me say to him?"

She was unable to make up her mind; but when they reached Camden Place, Lady Saltash took the decision out of her hands, and instructed George to furnish Sherry with the information that Hero was at present residing with her.

Hero, who had been walking about the room in some agitation, paused to interject in a tone of strong resolution: "George, if he should ask you if I am happy, you are to tell him that I have no time to be anything else, for I am for ever going to parties, and balls, and concerts! And tell him that I am become Miss Wantage again! And should you mind very much, dear George, telling him that I have a great many admirers in Bath? And if you dare to let him guess that I miss him quite dreadfully I will never speak to you again as long as I live!"

George promised to obey her instructions to the letter; but he looked a little concerned, for he had never seen her face so ravaged. However, Lady Saltash appeared to approve of the commands laid upon him, so he thought he could not do better than to carry them out. Having a lively curiosity to see Ferdy, and being convinced that that young gentleman would shortly arrive in Camden Place, he lingered in Lady Saltash's drawing-room. He had not long to wait; within a surprisingly short space of time a hackney carriage set Ferdy down at the door. His fawn-like countenance bore such a hunted expression that even Hero could not help laughing, as she joined George at the window to watch the arrival.

But no stress of circumstance ever made Ferdy forget his exquisite manners, and when he was ushered into the room a minute later, nothing could have been more polished than his bow, or more graceful than the salute he bestowed on Lady Saltash's hand.

"Well, young man," said her ladyship caustically, "you look like a rabbit with a savage dog after it! Is Sheringham hard upon your heels?"

"Thank God, ma'am, no!" he replied earnestly. "Very near thing, though! Greatest presence of mind needed!"

"Not to mention absence of body, I collect!"

He raised Hero's hand to his lips. "Lady Sherry! Your very obedient! No wish to alarm you, but we are in the basket! Dashed unfortunate you should have been in Bennet Street just then! Poor Sherry cast into such a pucker! Had no notion you was in Bath, you see. Poor fellow was clean floored! Drove the curricle slap into a very pretty sort of a perch phaeton, and left me to make his apologies while he dashed off to catch up with you. Didn't find you, but he will, Kitten: you know Sherry! too game to be beaten on any suit!"

"Was he very angry, Ferdy?" she asked anxiously.

"Mad as fire!" he assured her. "Taken a pet at seeing George with you. Don't like to think George has been gammoning him all this time. Says he only wants to get his hands on him, so I thought best to come round on the instant and warn you, George."

"Good God, I ain't afraid of Sherry!" George said scornfully.

"No, no, George! Pluck to the backbone! All know that! The thing is, you don't want to have Sherry calling you out again!"

"Let him do so if he chooses!" George replied instantly. "I shall be ready for him, I promise you!"

"No, George, you shall not! I won't have Sherry killed!" Hero said quickly.

"That's right!" Ferdy approved. "Only set up the backs of people if you kill Sherry, George! Always get over heavy ground as light as one can! Besides, my cousin, you know! Fond of him!"

"Yes, that's all very well, but if he challenges me to fight I'm dashed if I'll refuse him satisfaction!"

"For my sake, George!" begged Hero, clasping his arm.

"Oh, very well!" he said. "Mind you, Kitten, I'd not do it for anyone else, and I shall find it mighty hard as it is! Did you come here to warn Lady Sherry, Ferdy?"

"Thought I should do so," Ferdy explained. "Gil away: couldn't prevail on Sherry not to go to Bath: didn't know you was here. You come to warn her too?"

"You are so kind to me, both of you!" Hero said warmly. "I am sure no one ever had such good friends! Indeed, I thank you, and I do trust, Ferdy, that Sherry is not very angry with you?"

"Too much on the fidgets to think whether I had anything to do with your being here," replied Ferdy. "Went into the house in the devil of a miff—Lady Sheringham lodging in the Royal Crescent, you know—don't know why: dare say he wanted to tell the Incomparable. Seemed to me the moment to go away. It ain't that I'm afraid of Sherry, but I don't know what I'm to say to him, and once he guesses I knew you was here, Kitten, he's bound to try to get the whole story out of me."

"We are to tell him the truth," George said.

Ferdy's eyes started at him. "Dash it, George, he'll tear us limb from limb! What I mean is, hiding his wife from him, bamming him we hadn't a notion where she was! Making a cake of him! Won't stand it: not my cousin Sherry! Couldn't expect it of him!"

"He won't tear *me* limb from limb!" replied George, his lip curling.

Ferdy failed to derive any consolation from this, and said, in an indignant voice: "What's that to the purpose? Very likely to tear *me* limb from limb! Never was up to his weight, besides I'm not handy with my fives. Beginning to wish I hadn't come to Bath. What's more, Sherry knows I'm putting up at the York, and I'll lay a monkey he's there now, ready to pounce on me the instant I step inside the place!"

"Nonsense! If I know Sherry, he's a deal more likely to try to run me to earth!" said George bracingly. "In fact, I think I'll go back to the White Hart now, for the sooner I clear this fence the better it will be for us all."

"George, you won't forget that you have faithfully promised me not to call Sherry out, will you?" Hero asked anxiously. "Do you not think Ferdy should go with you, just to keep you in mind of it?"

413

"No, dash it, Kitten!" expostulated Ferdy, looking more like a hunted deer than ever. "Bad enough as it is! Besides, it would take a couple of us to hold that pair off from one another's throats. Not a bit of use in my going! Only get hurt!"

At this point, Lady Saltash gave it as her opinion that Lord Wrotham would do much better without Ferdy's assistance. She earned Ferdy's undying gratitude by telling him that he might stay to dine in Camden Place; and told George that if Sherry showed any desire to come in search of his wife he was to inform him that she had gone to a private party, and would certainly not return home before midnight.

CHAPTER 23

It was nine o'clock, and the Abbey bells were just chiming the hour, when Sherry stalked into Lord Wrotham's private parlour at the White Hart. George had dined, and the covers had been removed, and a bottle of Old Red Port, and two glasses, set upon the table.

Sherry waited only until the waiter who had shown him up to the parlour had withdrawn before greeting his friend in a manner that in some slight degree expressed his feelings. "You black-hearted scoundrel, George!" he said fiercely.

Lord Wrotham, suppressing a strong inclination to retort in kind, tried what a soft answer would achieve. "Hallo, Sherry! Thought you would be coming to see me. Glass of port with you!"

"The only use I have for a glass of port is to throw it in your damned face!" replied Sherry, not in the least mollified.

Lord Wrotham laid a firm hand on the bottle. "No, you don't," he said. "And it's no use your trying to call me out, because I'm not going to meet you, and even if

I did you couldn't kill me! Probably wouldn't hit me at all. I don't blame you for wanting to try, mind you!"

"Oh, you don't, don't you?" Sherry exclaimed. "Very obliging of you, by God! What were you doing with my wife?"

"Escorting her home," answered George calmly.

"The devil you were! Met her by chance, I take it?" said Sherry, with awful sarcasm.

"I did, but if you mean wasn't I aware that she was in Bath, yes, I was."

"You dare to stand there coolly telling me you knew where she was——"

"Yes, but I own it was a curst trick to play on a fellow," admitted George. "I never have liked it above half, but I gave my word to Lady Sherry I'd not betray her, so there was nothing for it but to hold my peace."

Sherry was looking as black as thunder. "She told *you* where she could be found? She took *you* into her confidence? Wrotham, answer me this, or I'll choke the truth out of you!—Did she run away from me to *you*?"

"No, ran to Gil," replied George. "Ferdy and I had been dining with him. To be frank with you, Sherry, she told us the whole, and begged us to help her to hide from you. She was in a sad taking. In fact, I was within an ace of setting off to find you there and then, to call you to account!"

"You had better have done so!" Sherry said swiftly, a white shade round his mouth. "A precious set of friends I have! All these weeks—— Where is she?"

"She is residing in Camden Place, the guest of Lady Saltash," George said.

Sherry stared at him. "Lady Saltash! Gil's grandmother? Well, of all the——I little thought when I came here what I was to find! It passes everything, so it does! The guest of Lady Saltash! And tolerably well entertained, I collect? Not obliged to earn her bread! Not in any kind of straits!"

"Damn it, you should be glad of that!" retorted George.

"Glad of it! Of course I'm glad of it! But when I think—— And you knew! You, and Gil, and Ferdy! Calling yourselves my friends and aiding and abetting my wife to conceal herself from me, while I hunted high and low for her, and was gudgeon enough to picture her in want and distress! By God, it beats everything so it does! I'd like to tear your guts out and throw 'em to the crows!"

"Oh, take a damper!" said George impatiently. "Or go back to London, and tear Gil's guts out! It was his notion, not mine."

Sherry, who was striding about the room, said over his shoulder: "Walking along as cheerfully as you please, with her hand in your arm! Never even waiting to let me come up with her! The guest of Lady Saltash! A pretty fool you have made me look, between the four of you!"

"No, we haven't. No one knows the truth save ourselves. Lady Sheringham goes by the name of Miss Wantage here."

This piece of intelligence seemed, oddly enough, to enrage the Viscount more than ever. He appeared to have difficulty in catching his breath. George judged the time ripe for a second offer of refreshment. He poured out two glasses of port, and handed one to his afflicted friend. Sherry took it absently, tossed off the wine, and regained his power of speech. Fixing George with a smouldering eye, he said: "I take it my wife ain't wearing the willow for me?"

"No," said George, following out his instructions. "She was devilish upset at the start of it all, but she seems to be in famous shape now. Likes Bath, you know. Likes the balls, and the concerts, and has made friends here. Very taking little thing, Kitten: I fancy she is quite the rage in Bath."

This information did not afford the Viscount any gratification. He ground his teeth. "She is, is she? And I thought——!" His feelings again overcame him, and he resumed his pacing about the room. He was about to speak again when a distant medley of sound which had been vaguely irritating him since his entrance into the room more forcibly intruded upon his ears. "What the devil is that infernal howling?" he demanded.

"Devilish, ain't it?" agreed George. "It's the Harmonic Society. They meet here every week. Wouldn't have come if I'd known. They sing glees."

"What!" Sherry exclaimed incredulously. "You mean to tell me they come here just to kick up that curst caterwauling din every week? Well, there's a horrible thing! Bath! That's Bath for you!"

"You'd think it was enough to put the shutters up at this place, wouldn't you?" said George. "Gave me a nasty start when they first struck up, I can tell you."

Both young gentlemen brooded silently for a moment or two over a state of society that could permit such atrocities. A pause in the musical activities in the distance recalled Sherry to more pressing matters. He cast George a measuring glance, and said: "How often have you been here since Kitten left me?"

"Dash it, Sherry, what kind of a fellow do you think I am?" said George indignantly. "I never came near the place till I heard you was on your way! Then I had to warn Lady Sherry. You'd have done the same in my shoes!"

"Had to warn her!" ejaculated Sherry. "As though I had been a regular Bluebeard! If that don't beat all!"

"Well, you scared her into running away from you," said George unkindly.

Sherry picked up his curly-brimmed beaver, which he had flung into a chair, and carefully smoothed its nap. "I've nothing more to say to you!" he announced "I'm going to see my wife!"

"It's no use your going there to-night," said George. "She's gone to some party or another. They don't expect her back until after midnight."

"Gone to a party!" repeated the Viscount, stupefied. "She must have known I should seek her out immediately, once I had seen her here!"

"Dare say she did," responded George coolly. "I fancy she don't want to see you, Sherry."

The Viscount's blue eyes stared into his dark ones for one dangerous minute. Then Sherry turned sharply on his heel, and strode out of the room.

He made no attempt to prove the truth of George's statement, but returned to the Royal Crescent, seething with so many conflicting emotions that he scarcely knew himself whether anger, relief, or anxiety was paramount. His temper was not improved by finding a party, consisting of two young ladies with their brother, sitting in his mother's private parlour, chatting in the most animated style with Miss Milborne. His aspect was so forbidding as to daunt Mr. Chalfont, but the ladies were not easily daunted, and merely thought him a remarkably fine-looking man, and would have done their best to have captivated him had he allowed them the least opportunity for the display of their charms. He excused himself almost at once, and went off to brood in the solitude of his own apartment.

The result of this period for reflection was that every other feeling gave place to the overmastering desire to see Hero at the earliest possible moment. He was knocking on the door of Lady Saltash's house at an unconscionably early hour next morning, only to be denied admittance by a portly butler, who informed him that neither her ladyship nor Miss Wantage had as yet come downstairs. His look of austere surprise made Sherry flush and retreat in disorder. He had been on the point of announcing his intention to go up to Hero's bedchamber, quite forgetting that no one in Bath knew her to be his wife, and the realization of the scandalous comment he would thus have occasioned in Lady Saltash's household shook him temporarily off his balance, so that he went off without leaving his card.

By way of passing the time, and giving a little relief to his feelings, he called on his cousin, at the York Hotel, and favoured him with a pithily worded opinion of his morals and character. Ferdy, who was partaking of a continental breakfast in bed, made no attempt to defend himself, but uttered a few soothing noises, and said it had all been Gil's fault.

"You may think yourself devilish lucky I don't haul you out of that bed, and give you a leveller!" said the Viscount, eyeing him in a frustrated way. "Very lucky indeed, let me tell you!"

"Assure you, dear old boy, I do!" Ferdy said winningly. "Very glad you don't mean to do it! Always bellows to mend with me if I have a set-to with you!"

"Chicken-hearted!" the Viscount taunted him.

"Anything you like, Sherry!" Ferdy said.

The Viscount gave it up, laughed, and consented to join his cousin in a cup of coffee.

He was in Camden Place again by half-past ten, again to be refused admittance. The ladies, said the butler, were not at home. This time the Viscount produced his card, but although the butler bowed in a polite way he did not relent towards his lordship.

The Viscount then had the happy thought of repairing to the Grand Pump Room, where he ran straight into his mother and Miss Milborne, who were the centre of a chattering group of persons. Lady Sheringham immediately claimed his attention, and made him known to her new acquaintances. One of the Misses Chalfont said that she felt herself to know his lordship already, and received a frosty look for her pains. The Viscount then perceived that Sir Montagu Revesby made one of the group, and favoured him with the coldest of bows, deliberately turning his shoulder when Sir Montagu said smilingly: "I am delighted to see you again, my dear Sherry!" The elder Miss Chalfont then attached his lordship firmly to her side, and asked him if he did not consider the weather clement enough for an expedition to Wells. He replied briefly: "No."

"Cruel!" said Miss Chalfont, making play with a pair of fine eyes. "I have made up my mind I will go there, for I quite dote on cathedrals, do not you, my lord?"

"Cathedrals?" said the Viscount, varying his response. "Good God, no!"

"I am sure I do not know how it will answer, this notion the girls have taken to go to Wells," interposed

Lady Sheringham. "But if dearest Isabella should like the drive, I know you will be pleased to take her in your curricle, Anthony."

"Nothing, ma'am, would afford me greater pleasure," replied the Viscount, casting a darkling glance at Miss Milborne, "were it not that I shall be otherwise engaged."

"Oh! naughty!" cried Miss Chalfont. "You do not know which day we mean to go!"

"I shall be engaged for the whole of my stay in this cur—in this place," responded the Viscount.

The dowager, much scandalized by this disobliging speech, showed a tendency to argue the point, but Miss Milborne intervened, saying that she had no notion of going for such a long drive at this season of the year. Through the ensuing babel of protests, Sir Montagu's voice made itself heard, gallantly offering to drive Miss Milborne in his curricle, wherever she should like to go. She thanked him civilly, but returned no positive answer. Miss Chalfont's questing eye alighted at this moment on a newcomer to the Pump Room, and since he was quite the most handsome young man who had yet come in her way, she withdrew her attention from Sherry, who lost no time in making his escape. Lord Wrotham, coming up to the party, fell alive into Miss Chalfont's clutches, and was granted nothing more than an excellent view of the Incomparable's profile for the following quarter of an hour. When he at last found an opportunity to approach Miss Milborne, she behaved to him with chill civility, and affected not to hear his urgent request for some private speech with her. He was about to press the matter when he caught sight of Hero, leading Lady Saltash to a chair, and attended by Mr. Tarleton, and the Honourable Ferdy

Fakenham and a third gentleman who was a stranger to George. He got up quickly, said: "Pray excuse me!" to Miss Milborne, and made his way across the room to warn Hero that Sherry was present. Miss Milborne gazed after him with a wooden countenance, and a bosom swelling with indignation.

George had hardly reached Hero's side when Sherry bore down upon them. His eyes were fixed on his wife's face, and he would no doubt have ignored everyone else had he not been brought sharply to earth by Lady Saltash, who said compellingly: "Well, Anthony? How do you do?"

He was obliged to pause by her chair, to take her hand, and to answer her questions. After asking him how his mother did, she said in a significant tone: "You are acquainted, I believe, with Miss Wantage?"

Sherry stammered that he rather thought he was, and as one in a trance shook hands with Hero. She did not meet his eyes, murmured a conventional greeting, and swiftly disengaged herself. Turning to Lady Saltash, she said: "Are you quite comfortable there, dear ma'am? You will not mind my leaving you?"

"No, no, child, be off with you!" Lady Saltash replied. "I know very well you are agog to go! I only wish you may not come to grief one of these days! Mind you have a care to her, Mr. Tarleton, and do not be letting her spring your horses in the middle of Bath, which I dare say she is quite capable of doing! Sit down beside me, Sheringham, and tell me all the London gossip!"

"I beg you will hold me excused, ma'am!" Sherry said. "If Miss—Miss Wantage wishes to drive, I should be happy to take her in my curricle, for I have the greatest desire to renew my acquaintance with her!"

"But Miss Wantage is promised to me," said Mr. Tarleton gently.

He encountered a look that startled him. The Viscount, controlling himself with a visible effort, said: "I shall be much obliged to you, ma'am, if you will afford me the favour of a few minutes' conversation with you, alone!"

Hero, terrified of a scene in public, conscious that her mother-in-law had perceived her, and was staring at her as though she could not credit her eyesight, said hurriedly: "Some other time, if you please! Indeed, I am engaged with Mr. Tarleton this morning!"

She put her hand on Mr. Tarleton's arm as she spoke, nipping it compellingly. He instantly sketched a bow to the Viscount, and led her out of the Pump Room. He felt that she was trembling, and laid his hand over hers, saying: "Do not be alarmed! Who was that ferocious young man? I did not properly catch his name."

"Lord Sheringham," she replied in a shaking voice. "You will think it very odd of me, and I cannot explain it to you, but I have a particular desire not to be alone in his company!"

Mr. Tarleton assured her she need have no fear of this. Sherry's slightly rakish air, coupled with Hero's words, conjured up an abominable vision of attempted seduction, rapine, and violence. He felt a burning desire to protect Hero, and, had Sherry attempted to pursue her, would undoubtedly have done his best to have knocked him down.

But Sherry was fully alive to the consequences of forcing an issue in public, and he did not pursue her. Instead, he turned to Lady Saltash, and asked her to inform him when he might have the honour of calling upon her. Lady Saltash, hugely tickled by the whole situation, said affably that he might call at any hour that suited him, only they were such gadabouts, she and Miss Wantage, that she could not promise that they would be at home. The Viscount, no fool, bowed formally and registered a grim resolve to be even with her ladyship one day before he was much older. He then retired to his mother's side, and asked her if she was ready to go. It had occurred to him that it might be as well to put her in possession of the facts of the case.

She received them much as might have been expected, exclaiming against Hero's effrontery, and taking care to point out to her son that the designing hussy had lost no time in attaching another unfortunate victim to her apron strings. She professed herself to be more than willing to speak of her as Miss Wantage, adding that she had never thought of her as anything else.

Shortly after they had reached the Royal Crescent, Miss Milborne joined them, having been escorted to the door by Sir Montagu. Lady Sheringham greeted her with a sort of moan, begging her to say at once if she had seen "that shameless creature" flaunting herself before their eyes in the Pump Room.

Miss Milborne replied; "Dear ma'am, she was hardly flaunting herself! I did indeed see her, and I own I was excessively shocked to think of you and Sherry being put into so awkward a situation! I wonder Hero should do such a thing! What everyone must think——!"

"It's no such thing!" snapped Sherry. "She is known here as Miss Wantage, and in any event I care nothing for what a parcel of Bath nobodies may think! What makes me as mad as Bedlam is that George, and Gil, and Ferdy all knew she was here! Have known it from the outset!"

"We guessed as much, did we not?" said Miss Milborne coldly. "Lord Wrotham appears to be so assiduous in his attentions that I am sure I should not wonder at anything I heard. Dear Lady Sheringham, if you do not dislike it, I own I have a great fancy to see Wells. The scheme is that we should go in three carriages—a party of six, you know—to see the cathedral to-morrow, whle this mild weather continues. Miss Chalfont assures me that we may do it easily in the daylight, and be back again in Bath in excellent time for dinner. Sir Montagu Revesby has been so obliging as to offer me a seat in his curricle; Mr. Chalfont will be of the party, with a friend of his; and both his sisters, of course."

"If you take my advice, Bella," struck in the Viscount, "you will not go jauntering about the country with Revesby!"

"Thank you, Sherry, you are very good, but since my Mama sees no objection to Sir Montagu, I do not know why you should."

"I am sure Sir Montagu is everything that is most unexceptionable," said the dowager. "Only if you are set on going, my love, I wish I might prevail upon Anthony to escort you, for I am sure you would be more comfortable with him."

"On the contrary, ma'am, I should not be at all comfortable with him, for of all things I most abominate a man in a fit of the sullens!" said Miss Milborne acidly.

"Take care!" retorted the Viscount. "If you set up my back I'm dashed if I'll gallant you to the Lower Rooms to-night!"

"Good gracious! do you mean to do so?" said Miss

Milborne. "I assure you I had not the smallest expectation of your being willing to go to the ball!"

"Well, I am willing, and what's more I've paid for a subscription which gives me a couple of ladies' tickets as well, so if you and my mother choose to go this evening, you may do so," said his lordship gratefully.

"I must say that was very prettily done of you, Anthony!" approved his parent.

"I want to see my wife," responded his lordship. "And I can tell how it will be if I call in Camden again!"

"She will surely not be present!" exclaimed Lady Sheringham. "She would not have the effrontery!"

"I know of no reason why she should not go anywhere she chooses!" retorted Sherry, firing up. "And as she has her name down to dance the minuet with some fellow of the name of Tarleton, and is engaged to George for the first cotillion, I assume that she certainly has the intention of being present!"

So indeed it proved. The jealous look in Sherry's eyes at the Pump Room seemed to indicate that Lady Saltash's advice had been sound. It had set Hero's heart fluttering, until she remembered that she had seen that look in his eye once before, when she had kissed George, and it had not then appeared to betoken anything more than a dog-in-the-mangerish spirit. Between joy at seeing him again, hurt that he should have come to Bath in Isabella's train, hope that he might be desirous of having his wife again, and fear lest he should not, she knew not what to think. To go to the ball, and perhaps to see Sherry gallanting Isabella there, must give her pain; to stay away, and so miss the dear sight of him, was unthinkable; and mixed up with all this was a wish, born of pride, to conceal her unhappiness from him, even to make him think that she did very well without him. So she had permitted Mr. Tarleton to put her name down for the minuet, and had engaged herself to dance the first cotillion with George, and the second with Ferdy. To Mr. Tarleton was to fall the privilege of taking her in to tea. She had not made up her mind about the country dances. Sherry never stood up for them, voting them a great bore, but if he should break his rule and solicit her hand, she did not think that she would be able to refuse him.

Those meaning to take their places in the minuet were obliged to present themselves in the ballroom not later than eight o'clock, so Lady Saltash's party arrived at the Lower Assembly Rooms considerably in advance of Lady Sheringham's. The minuet had started when Sherry escorted his ladies into the room, and installed his mother on one of the upper benches. Hero, gracefully performing her part in the dance, could not help reflecting that it was something new for the Incomparable to be obliged to sit at the side of the room while other, and much less dazzling, females took the floor. Then she scolded herself for such an ill-natured thought, acknowledging that the Incomparable was only sitting out because there had been no time for her to set her name down for the minuet. She was looking quite superb to-night, too, dressed in a cloud of primrose gauze, her tawny locks exquisitely cut and curled, her skin almost unbelievably white. As Hero watched her, she looked up at Sherry, standing beside her chair, smiling rather mischievously. Some quality of intimacy in that smile, something in the way Sherry bent to hear what was being said to him, stabbed Hero. He too smiled, and nodded, and uttered some remark which made Miss Milborne laugh, and lift an admonitory finger. Then the movement of the dance made it necessary for Hero to turn her back on them, and she took care not to glance in their direction again. Instead, she embarked on a playful flirtation with Mr. Tarleton. This was not missed by Sherry, who no sooner saw who her partner was than he said, quite unreasonably, that he might have known that that fellow would turn out to be Tarleton.

As soon as the minuet ended, and while the couples were still moving slowly off the floor, a young gentleman came up to Hero to beg her to dance the first country dance with him. She accepted, people began to take their places for it, and by the time the Viscount, threading his way across the room, reached his wife's side, her new partner was leading her into the set. He was so nettled that he went straight back to Isabella, reaching her a bare instant before Sir Montagu Revesby, and saying savagely: "Come and stand up with me, Bella! I'm dashed if I will give my little wretch the pleasure of seeing me propping the wall, as George does!"

"But you never stand up for the country dances!" Isabella reminded him.

"I'll stand up for this if it kills me!" swore his lordship.

Hero's set was already made up, and he was obliged to join the second set. This was not what he wanted, but Miss Milborne could only be thankful, since the prospect of standing up with a gentleman who was bent on catching the eye and ear of another lady in the same set was not one which she could view with anything but misgiving.

Hero, of course, saw his lordship lead out Miss Milborne, and she at once felt that her cup was full. She would have liked to have fled from the ballroom to indulge in a hearty bout of tears, but since she could not do this became extremely animated instead, and laughed and talked, and presented all the appearance of a young lady who was enjoying herself prodigiously. The Viscount, marking this callous behaviour, promptly imitated it; and as Miss Milborne had just seen Lord Wrotham's striking figure in the doorway she had no hesitation in encouraging her childhood's friend to flirt with her as much as he liked. Since his more extravagant sallies were interspersed by comments, delivered in a furious undervoice, on his wife's shameless conduct, she was in no danger of over-estimating the worth of the compliments he paid her.

Whatever might have been the Viscount's intentions when the dance ended, they were frustrated by the descent upon him of Mr. Guynette, the Master of Ceremonies. Mr. Guynette was well accustomed to handling reluctant gentlemen, and before his victim was aware of what was happening, he had presented him to quite the plainest damsel in the room, a circumstance which should have brought home to his lordship the unwisdom of neglecting to write his name in the Master's subscription-book. Common civility obliged Sherry to ask the plain young lady to stand up with him, and as she had no hesitation in accepting the invitation, he was condemned to another half-hour of purgatory. The first cotillion followed, which Hero danced with George; and then everyone went in to tea. Isabella had by this time collected the usual court round herself, of which the most prominent member seemed to be Sir Montagu; Hero and Mr. Tarleton were seated at a table which had no vacant place when the Viscount succeeded in edging his way into the crowded tea-room; so the end of it was that his lordship was forced to join several unpartnered gentlemen by the buffet. Here he found Lord Wrotham, who was wearing his well-known thunder-cloud aspect; and such was the state of his mind that he forgot that he had parted from Wrotham on the worst of bad terms, and hailed him thankfully as a kindred spirit.

"Of all the abominably stupid evenings!" he ejaculated. "It is ten times worse than Almack's!"

"I should like to know," said George, eyeing him broodingly, "what the devil you meant by telling me it was I who had engaged Miss Milborne's affections?"

"Never told you any such thing!" replied the Viscount. "Not but what she as good as told me so. What's put you in a miff?"

"I begged to be allowed to take her in to tea, and she said she was promised to Monty. I stood up with her for the second country dance, and she behaved as though she had never met me before in her life!"

"Well, let that be a lesson to you not to dance attendance on my wife!" said Sherry, with asperity.

"She cannot think that there is anything beyond common friendship between Kitten and me!" George said.

"Who asked you to call my wife Kitten?" demanded the Viscount belligerently.

"You did," replied George.

"Oh!" said Sherry, dashed.

"I will not believe the Incomparable could credit such nonsense!" George declared, flushing. "Why, what reason have I ever given her to think that I would so much as look at another female?"

"Well, upon my word!" exclaimed Sherry. "If that don't beat all! If kissing my wife at the Fakenhams' ball isn't reason enough——"

"She knew nothing of that!"

"Oh yes, she did! Kitten tried to persuade her to beg you not to meet me!"

"Good God!" George uttered, turning pale. "Then was that why——I must speak with her!"

"You won't do it here," said Sherry, with gloomy satisfaction. "Come to think of it, a pretty pair of cakes we must look, you and I, running after a couple of females who won't have anything to do with us! And nothing to drink but this curst tea!"

"She will have Monty!" George said heavily.

"Not she!"

"She is going in this curricle on some damned expedition to-morrow. She told me so. I will not waste my time here any longer. I shall go back to the White Hart. They have a very tolerable Chambertin there."

"Dashed if I won't come with you!" said Sherry.

"You cannot. You are escorting Lady Sheringham and Miss Milborne."

"I'll come back in time to take 'em home," said Sherry. "unless——By Jove, I might force Ferdy to give up his place in the cotillion to me!"

"What's the use of that?" George said. "I've done much the same thing before now, but the fact of the matter is a ball is no place for private conversation. You are for ever being separated by the movement of the dance and it all ends in a quarrel."

"Well, I dare say you may be right," Sherry said. "And if I bore Kitten off——"

"You can't do that!" George said, shocked. "Devilish strict at these balls! What's more, if she refused to go with you, you'd look a bigger cake than you do now."

"Yes, my God, so I should!" agreed Sherry. "I was a fool to have come! Let us go, George!"

So the two ladies who had spared no pains to demonstrate their indifference to their lordships had the doubtful pleasure of seeing them withdraw from the festivities. They should have been gratified to find their hints so well understood, but gratification was not the emotion uppermost in either swelling bosom. After seeking a certain amount of relief in pointedly ignoring one another for the next hour, each lady developed the headache, and discovered in herself an ardent desire to go home.

refused to go with you, you'd look a bit... something
they'd do now.

'Yes, my God, so I should!' agreed Sherry. 'I was a
fool to have asked I at us go [to] Chester.'

So the two ladies who had spared no pains to demonstrate their indifference to their lordships had the
doubtful pleasure of watching them withdraw from the
assembly. They should have been gratified to find their
plan so well understood, but gratification was not the
emotion uppermost in either swelling bosom. After
savouring a certain amount of relief in potentially taunting
one another for the next hour, each had developed the
headache and discovered in herself a great desire to go
home.

CHAPTER 24

Hero, who had passed a sleepless night, arose next
morning with a headache indeed, and with suspiciously
swollen eyes. Lady Saltash took one look at her, and
sent her back to bed, recommending her to glance in
her mirror, and decide for herself whether she wished
to show her husband, or anyone else, that woebegone
face.

"Oh, ma'am, do you think he will come this morning?" Hero asked. "I am persuaded he is thinking only
of Isabella! When I saw him stand up with her for
the country dance—*Sherry!* —I felt ready to sink!"

Her ladyship laughed. "Why, what else should a man
of spirit do, pray, when you was flirting so scan-
dalously with that boy out of the nursery? Silly puss!
The affair is going on famously! Sheringham scarcely
took his eyes off you the whole time he was in the
Rooms!"

Hero's lip trembled. "He left while we were having
tea. I thought——I wondered if perhaps he would
come up to me after tea, and make me dance with him,
but—but——"

"I dare say! And carry you off willy-nilly, perhaps? At a Bath Assembly! Unheard of!"

Hero smiled faintly. "I don't think he would care for that. It would be just the sort of thing Sherry would do, if he wanted to. Only he didn't want to. If—if he should come here this morning, ma'am, would you perhaps be so very obliging as to see him, and—and discover, if you are able, what his sentiments truly are?"

"Make yourself easy, my love; I will see him," promised Lady Saltash.

But her ladyship was not called upon to see him. He did not come to Camden Place that morning, for Mr. Ringwood had arrived in Bath by the night-mail.

The mail-coach having run punctually, he was set down at the White Hart a few minutes after ten o'clock, and found Lord Wrotham breakfasting. He joined him at this meal, as soon as he had shaved, and changed his travelling-dress; and listened in stolid silence to the slightly disjointed account his lordship gave him of the imbroglio which seemed hourly to be growing more complicated. A considerable part of George's recital was naturally concerned with the behaviour of the Incomparable, but Mr. Ringwood paid little heed to this. When he had heard George out, he grunted, and said: "Pack of gudgeons!"

"Who?" demanded George.

"You, and Sherry, and Ferdy," replied Mr. Ringwood. "Dashed if I don't think Ferdy's the worst of you! Take a look at that!"

He handed over Mr. Fakenham's letter to him, which George perused in gathering amazement. "Bosky, I dare say," he remarked. "Who's this fellow he believes to be at the bottom of Sherry's coming to

436

Bath? That's all a hum! I don't know why he came, but there wasn't any plot about it. And how the devil does Duke come into it?"

"Lord, I don't know!" said Mr. Ringwood scornfully. "You don't suppose I wasted my time asking him for the name of a fellow I'm not interested in, do you?"

"No, but I'd give something to know why Ferdy thinks someone is behind it all," said George, pondering the problem. "Hasn't said a word to me about it. Couldn't be Revesby, could it? Don't see how Ferdy came to forget his name, if it was. I'll ask him."

"You may do as you please: I'm going off to see Sherry," said Mr. Ringwood. "Where is he lodging?"

"In the Royal Crescent. He's in the devil's own temper, I warn you, Gil!"

"There ain't the least need to warn me," said Mr. Ringwood.

"If you haven't been able in five years to call me out, it ain't likely Sherry will!"

He then pulled on his Hessians, which his man had lovingly treated with Spanish Blue King Polish, shrugged himself into his greatcoat, tucked a malacca cane under his arm, and set off for the Royal Crescent.

He found Sherry just about to leave the house, to pay a morning call in Camden Place; but at sight of him Sherry abandoned this immediate intention, and pounced on him with something of the growl of an infuriated tiger.

"The very man above all others I wish to see!" Sherry said menacingly. "You have the devil of a lot of explaining to do, let me tell you! Come upstairs!"

"I'm going to," replied Mr. Ringwood. "But as for

explaining, seems to me you have some of that to do!"

"I like your curst impudence!" gasped Sherry. "What in Hades have I to explain?"

"Well, you may begin by explaining what the deuce brought you to Bath," said Mr. Ringwood, following him up to the parlour. "If Lady Sheringham is at home——"

"She ain't," interrupted Sherry. "Gone off to see some curst doctor or other. And the Incomparable set out for Wells a couple of hours ago, so you needn't fear you'll be obliged to do the civil to either of 'em!" He flung open the parlour door and ushered his friend into the room. "Now, then, Gil! A pretty way you have dealt with me all these weeks! What in thunder possessed you to hide my wife from me, and bam me into thinking you knew no more than I did where she was? By God, if I were not so well-acquainted with you, I might have a very fair notion of what your intentions were towards her, so I might!"

"You'd have to be uncommonly disguised to fancy I should take your wife to live with my grandmother if I'd any dishonourable intentions!" retorted Mr. Ringwood.

"There is that, of course," Sherry admitted. "All the same, Gil, I don't understand what game you are playing; and when I think of your gammoning me when you knew I was half out of my mind with anxiety over Kitten——"

"Point is, I didn't know it," said Mr. Ringwood. "Come to think of it, I still don't know it."

Sherry stared at him. "Are you mad?" he demanded. "What kind of a fellow do you take me for, in God's name? My wife leaves me, and you don't know whether I'm anxious?"

"Thought you would have been glad to know she was in good hands," said Mr. Ringwood painstakingly "but didn't know whether you cared much that she wasn't living with you any more."

"Not care!" Sherry exclaimed. "She's *my wife*!"

Mr. Ringwood polished his quizzing-glass, paying the greatest attention to the operation. "Going to be frank with you, Sherry," he said.

"By God, I shall be glad of it!"

"Don't fancy you will, dear boy, when it comes to it. Very delicate matter: wouldn't mention it if I hadn't got to. I know she's your wife: came to the wedding. Point is, that was a devilish queer business, your marriage, Sherry. Never pretended you was in love with Kitten, did you?"

Sherry flushed, tried to speak, and failed.

"Good as told us all you wasn't," pursued his friend. "Not that there was any need: plain as a pikestaff! Something else plain as a pikestaff, too, but whether you saw it is what I don't know, and never did. Tried several times to give you a hint, but it didn't seem to me you took it up. Thought the world of you, did Kitten. Wouldn't hear a word against you: wouldn't even admit you can't drive well enough for the F.H.C. That shows you! Always seemed to me she only thought of pleasing you. If she took a fancy to do something she shouldn't, only had to tell her you wouldn't like it, and she'd abandon it on the instant. Used to put me in mind of that rhyme, or whatever it was, I learned when I was a youngster. Something about loving and giving: that was Kitten! Mind you, I don't say you wasn't generous to her, encouraged her to spend what money she liked, and——" He stopped, for Sherry had flung up a hand. "Well, no sense in going into that. Dare say you know

439

what I mean. Dashed if I knew what to make of it all! Then you had that turn-up with her over the race she meant to engage in, and she came to me, because there was no one else she could turn to. Sat in my room, with that curst canary I once gave her, and the drawing-room clock, and cried as though her poor little heart was breaking. Don't mind telling you, I was dashed near calling you out for that, Sherry! Seemed to me you'd been a curst brute to the poor little soul! But she never blamed you: stuck to it everything had been her fault from the outset. Said something which made me think a trifle. Said you had never loved her, and it was the Incomparable you had really wished to marry."

"No!" Sherry interjected, in a strangled voice.

"I must say, I never thought you cared a button for the Incomparable," agreed Mr. Ringwood. "Thought maybe you cared more for your Kitten than you knew."

Sherry had gone over to the window, and was standing with his back to his friend. He said curtly over his shoulder: "I did."

"That's why I brought Kitten down to my grand-mother, and made Ferdy and George keep it from you they knew where she was. Thought if you felt you had lost her, it might make you think a trifle." He paused, and glanced across at the Viscount. "Wouldn't have betrayed her in any event, you know. At one time I'd a strong notion it was all going to be for the best. Haven't been so sure of it lately. Don't know why you're setting Sheringham House in order, for one thing."

Sherry wheeled round. "You fool, for Kitten, if ever I should find her! Do you suppose I have not had time to think as well as you? I see now what I ought to have done! I thought I could continue in the same way, even though I was married: had no notion of settling down! Well, I know now that it's not possible, and, damn it, I don't desire it to be! I thought, if I could find Kitten, we would start afresh: try to be more the thing! If I had not thought she might return there, I would have got rid of that curst house in Half Moon Street long since! God knows I have grown to hate it! But how could I do so? Suppose she had come back, only to find the shutters closed, or even strangers living there? I had to stay, though it has been like a tomb to me!"

"I see," said Mr. Ringwood. "Shan't deny your setting Sheringham House in order looked to me as though you had different ideas in your head. When Severn fell out of the running—— Well, couldn't help wondering a trifle, Sherry!"

"If you mention Bella's name to me again, Gil, I am likely to do you a mischief!" Sherry warned him. "I never cared the snap of my fingers for that wretched girl, and if you are not assured of that, ask her! Why, God save the mark, she may be a beauty, but give me my Kitten! Bella, with her airs and her graces, and her miffs, and her curst sharp tongue! No, I thank you! What's more, no man who had lived with Kitten would look twice at the Beauty!"

"Then why the devil did you come to Bath, which we all know you can't abide, only to be near her?" demanded Mr. Ringwood, exasperated.

"To be near her? My God, is that what you think? You must be crazy! Nothing would have induced me to have come here, but one circumstance! When my mother asked me to go with her, I would not listen. Yes, and I told Bella if she thought she had the power to persuade me she was mightily mistaken! But something she said—or I said: I don't recall precisely what it was—made me remember that it was to Bath that Bagshot woman had the intention of sending Kitten, to become a governess. I made sure I should find her here, in some seminary in Queen's Square, and that is all the reason I had for coming to a place I never mean to set foot in again if I live to be a hundred!"

Mr. Ringwood sat staring at him. "So that is how it was!"

"Of course that is how it was! And I saw Kitten with George almost the very instant I entered the town, and if I could have come up with him then, I'd have murdered him in cold blood! I have been trying ever since to get two words with Kitten alone, but she will not receive me in Camden Place, nor do more than accord me the civility of a stranger when we meet in public!"

"Upon my soul, Sherry, if ever there was a born fool, you are he!" exclaimed Mr. Ringwood. "How the deuce was Kitten to know you had come here to search for her? Depend upon it, she believes you came only to be near Miss Milborne, and had not the least expectation of seeing her! I do not wonder that she will not speak to you!"

"But she could not think—she *could* not think——!" stammered Sherry.

"She!" said Mr. Ringwood witheringly. "Seems to me it's you who can't think, Sherry! Damme if ever I knew such a fellow! It's a very good thing I came down here, for a rare pucker you have got yourself into! What's more, I'm not sure it ain't too late to get you out of it."

"What do you mean?" Sherry said quickly, fixing his eyes on his face.

Mr. Ringwood met that look squarely. "Said I'd be

frank with you, dear boy, didn't I? Well, I've been hearing lately from my grandmother that there's some fellow or other paying Kitten attentions."

"There is!" Sherry said grimly.

"The old lady didn't seem to think there was much to it yet, but she gave me a hint you'd do well to step in before it was too late. Matter of fact, I was about to write to Kitten to tell her I thought it was time she gave me leave to tell you the truth, when you went off in your mother's train. From what I can make out, he's a very tolerable sort of a fellow, with a nice little property, easy address, and that kind of thing. Devilish taken with Kitten, ready to do anything in his power to please her."

Sherry was just about to favour him with his own impressions of Mr. Tarleton when the justice of this description struck that innate honesty at the bottom of his nature. "Yes, damn him!" he said bitterly. "I suppose he is a tolerable sort of a fellow. Dare say he'd be a dashed sight kinder to Kitten than ever I was."

Mr. Ringwood rose from his chair. "Best thing for me to do now is to go round to Camden Place and see Kitten," he said. "Do what I may to unravel this curst tangle you've made!"

Sherry grasped his hand. "Gil, you're the best friend a man ever had!" he declared. "You'll tell her it was to find her I came here, won't you? Tell her I've been fit to blow my brains out any time since she left me! Beg her only to see me! Tell her——"

"Don't put yourself about! I'll tell her everything!" promised Mr. Ringwood.

But when he arrived in Camden Place, Hero had dropped into a sleep of exhaustion, from which Lady Saltash refused point-blank to rouse her. Mr. Ringwood had to deliver his messages to her instead, which, however, she assured him, would answer quite as well. When he had told her the whole, she nodded, and remarked that she would have expected Sheringham to behave in just such a stupid fashion.

"He deserves to be kept on tenterhooks, and if I had my way he should be," she said severely. "However, it is high time this nonsensical situation was put an end to, for if I do not mistake the matter, my friend, Jasper Tarleton, has lost his heart more entirely than I was prepared for." She considered for a moment, drumming her fingers on the table under her hand. "You may tell Sheringham, from me, that if he chooses to dine in my house to-night, he will not find me at home. I am dining with some friends in Laura Place, and it is not the sort of party to amuse his wife. He may come round at seven o'clock precisely. I shall keep the child in bed for the rest of the day, for I have not the least notion of letting her show Sheringham a wan face, I can tell you!"

"But will she consent to his coming, ma'am? Are you positive ot that?" Mr. Ringwood asked anxiously.

She gave a dry chuckle. "Oh, she will consent, never fear!"

"Beg pardon, ma'am, but you'll not fail to deliver Sherry's messages to her, will you? Can't but see that he has given her a great deal of cause not to be wishful of seeing him!"

"Tell him so!" recommended her ladyship. "And you need not tell him that she is ready to fall upon his neck, Gilbert! Let him come in a humble frame of mind! I dare say it will be for the first and very likely the last, time in his life!"

Mr. Ringwood promised that he would say nothing

to Sherry that would puff him up in his self-esteem, left his compliments for Hero, and went back to the Royal Crescent.

This time, the dowager having returned from the Cross Bath, Sherry took him into the dining-parlour on the ground-floor and eagerly demanded to know how he had sped. His face fell when he heard that Mr. Ringwood had not had speech with Hero herself, but his spirits rose mercurially when he learned that he would find her alone that evening, and he wrung Mr. Ringwood's hand fervently, quite forgetting that there had ever been a moment when he had not been in perfect charity with him.

As for Hero, when her hostess recounted to her the morning's interview with Mr. Ringwood, her feelings so far overcame her that she bounced up in her bed, cast her arms round Lady Saltash, and ruthlessly hugged her, to the gross disarrangement of her ladyship's second-best wig. Called to order, she at once became very docile, even promising to remain quietly in her bed during the afternoon, if Lady Saltash would but instruct her cook to prepare for dinner all Sherry's favourite dishes. She then lay and watched the clock until she could bear it no longer, when she rang for her maid, and had herself dressed in a gown Sherry had once commended. She flitted restlessly about the house after that, until Lady Saltash complained that she gave her the fidgets. Bath hours not being as late as those fashionable in London, her ladyship set forth for her dinner-party at six o'clock, prosaically reminding her protegee not to forget to see that Pug had his usual run.

It was Hero's custom to lead this animal out to take the air for a few minutes before Lady Saltash's dinner-hour; and when Lady Saltash had driven away in her barouche she thought that she would fill in the lagging time in this fashion. Accordingly, she put on her hooded cloak, took Pug's leash in her hand, and let herself out of the front door. It was growing dark by this time, but there was still light enough to make a short walk round the Upper and Lower Place unobjectionable. It was, besides, so select a neighbourhood that there was little or no fear of her meeting any undesirable persons. She tripped along, Pug snorting at her heels, her thoughts winging ahead to the magic hour of seven o'clock. So lost in these thoughts was she that she barely noticed a vehicle drawn up in Lower Camden Place. She did indeed perceive its outline, vague in the gathering gloom, but she did not even wonder at it until there suddenly loomed up before her the figure of a man in a caped greatcoat and a tall beaver hat. She gave a gasp then of fright, but she had no time to do more before she was caught up into a strong embrace. She made a frantic attempt to free herself, and tried to cry out. Her captor prevented this by setting his lips to hers and passionately kissing her. She had a glimpse of a loo-mask covering the upper half of his face, and quite suddenly she thought that she knew who it was who had waylaid her, and she got an arm free, and flung it up round his neck, returning his embrace with the utmost fervour. The sound of leisured footsteps approaching in the distance made the masked gentleman sweep her off her feet, bear her in three swift strides to the waiting post-chaise, and toss her up into it. Since she was still unconsciously clinging to Pug's leash, this lethargic animal was swung up willy-nilly after her, and had much ado to scramble into the chaise before the door was shut on him.

Hero, tumbled without ceremony on to the padded seat, picked herself up as the chaise moved forward, and found that she was laughing and crying together. The sight of the indignant Pug, panting on the floor of the chaise, effectually dried up her tears.

"Oh!" she gurgled. "Oh, you horrid little dog, how *like* Sherry to have thrown you in on top of me!"

Mr. Tarleton, meanwhile, riding behind the chaise, was congratulating himself on the success of his outrageous plan to abduct the lady he desired to make his wife; and Sherry, already dressed for dinner with his wife, was seated at his dressing-table, impatiently assuring Lord Wrotham that no foreigner, Greek or otherwise, had had any finger in his having come to Bath.

"Well, I can't make it out!" George said. "No making head or tail of what Ferdy says! Seems this fellow was at Eton with him. Never knew there was any Greeks there, did you? Sounds to me like a devilish rum customer, too. Always creeping up behind a man, and giving him a start. He says Duke knows him."

"He may do so, but I don't!" replied the Viscount. "I wish you will stop teasing me about it, and go away! Go and do the civil in the parlour! Dare say Isabella may be there by now. You'll find Gil, too. Came to pay his respects to my mother, poor devil, and she's had him buttonholed this past hour, listening to what some curst doctor has told her about Russian Vapour Baths."

"I own, it was in the hope of seeing Miss Milborne that I called," said George ingenuously. "The thing is, though, that your mother don't like me above half, and I'd as lief you came in with me to make all smooth."

The Viscount, who was putting the finishing touches

to his cravat, said that he was a cowardly fellow after all, but if he would wait a moment, and not prate of mysterious Greeks, he would do his best for him. But even as he spoke, a knock fell on the door, and, when he called Come in! the dowager entered, clasping, ominously, her vinaigrette. She acknowledged Lord Wrotham's presence by a slight inclination of her turbaned head, but addressed herself to her son.

"Oh, Anthony, I am so thankful you are not yet gone out! I am in such anxiety over dearest Isabella, and fear that some mishap may have occurred! She assured me she should be home by five o'clock at the latest, and here it is, half-past six already, and no sign of her! And, as though that were not bad enough, I am quite overset by having this instant received Mr. and Miss Chalfont, who called here to set down Isabella's scarf, which she was so careless as to drop in the inn at Wells. My dear Anthony, it appears that she and Sir Montagu set out to drive back to Bath by a different road quite half an hour ahead of the others in the party! What can have become of them? When the news was broken to me, I had such an attack of palpitations that Mr. Ringwood—so very obliging of him! such a gentlemanly man! Oh, there you are, dear Mr. Ringwood! Well, I am sure——! As I was saying, he was obliged to summon my abigail, with some hartshorn and water to revive me! For, you know, I am responsible for dear Isabella, and how I should ever be able to face her Mama if any accident were to befall her—— There is nothing for it, Anthony, but for you to set out instantly in search of her in your curricle!"

"Oh, isn't there, by Jove!" said the Viscount. "No, I thank you, ma'am! I warned Bella not to go jauntering about the country with that fellow, and if she would not heed me she may take the consequences! I am dining with my wife in Camden Place at seven o'clock, and you may judge how likely I am to break that engagement for any start of Bella's!"

George, whose expressive eyes had been fixed on the dowager's face throughout her speech, stepped forward at this point, saying in a low, vibrant voice: "You may leave the matter in my hands, Lady Sheringham! This concerns me more nearly than Sherry! I shall set forth on the instant, and you need have no fear that I shall not only restore Miss Milborne to you, but I shall certainly call Revesby to answer for whatever carelessness or—or villainy he has committed!"

He bowed briefly and strode towards the door, such a look of ferocity in his face that Mr. Ringwood protested. "No, really, George! Really, I say! Ten to one it is due to some trifling accident, and they will arrive here at any moment! Dash it, Monty would not—*George!*"

Lord Wrotham, casting him no more than a contemptuous glance, vanished from the room. Mr. Ringwood turned to Sherry. "Think I'd better go after him, dear old boy!" he said. "You know what he is! Don't like Monty, but can't let George murder him—for that's what it would be: sheer murder! Very obedient servant, Lady Sheringham! Wish you good fortune, Sherry, dear old boy!"

The dowager sank down upon a chair, quite overcome by the sudden twist of events. She raised her handkerchief to her eyes and was just about to bemoan her son's approaching reconciliation with his wife when a servant came to the door to announce the arrival of the Honourable Ferdy Fakenham, who had been invited to dine in the Royal Crescent. The Viscount, glad to escape a more than ordinarily foolish jeremiad from his parent, bade the man invite Ferdy to step into his room, and turned his attention to the far more pressing problem of the choice of a fob to finish off his toilet.

Ferdy, upon his entering the room, was at once regaled by his aunt with a tearful account of the disasters which, she was convinced, had overtaken them all. He shook his head and said that Monty was a Bad Man, and there was no saying where the havoc created by that old Greek fellow would end. This attracted the Viscount's interest, and he was just going to demand an explanation of his cousin when Bootle entered the room, looking offended, and informing him that Jason, whom he freely designated a Varmint, insisted on having instant speech with him.

"What the deuce can he want?" said his lordship. "Where is he?"

"Here I be, guv'nor!" responded the Tiger, diving under Bootle's arm. "Out of breath I be, what's more, loping after a rattler fit to bust meself!"

"You're boozy!" said his lordship severely.

"I ain't! You send that fat chub off, and I'll tell you something as you had ought to know! Yes, and don't you go putting your listeners forward t'other side of the door!" he added.

Bootle was so much affronted by this admonition that he stalked from the room without another word, shutting the door with meticulous care behind him. The Tiger looked at his master, real trouble in his sharp eyes. "It's the missus!" he blurted out.

The Viscount dropped the fob he had selected. "What?" he said quickly. "What has happened?"

The Tiger shook his head sadly. "Piked on the bean, guv'nor!" he said simply.

"*What?*"

"So help me bob, guv'nor, it's Gawd's truth! Loped off with that well-breeched swell I seed her with t'other day!"

The Viscount had the oddest impression that the floor was heaving under his feet. He put out a hand to grasp the edge of his dressing-table, saying hoarsely: "It's a lie!"

"I'll wish myself backt if ever I told you a lie, guv'nor!" Jason said earnestly. "Nor I wouldn't tell no lies about the missus! Fit to nap my bib, I be!"

In proof of this statement he drew the sleeve of his jacket across his eyes and sniffed dolorously. The Viscount, white as his shirt, said: "How do you know this, rascal?"

"Seed her with my werry own daylights, guv'nor." He shifted uneasily from one foot to the other. "I was waiting in Camden Place, that Maria—the saucy mort what is maid to the missus—whiddling the scrap to me that the missus takes the dog what belongs to the old gentrymort for a walk every evening. Seemed to me if I was to go and tell the missus as how we miss her mortal bad—but I never had no chance to open me bone-box! There was a rattler a-standing in the road, and this cove as you knows of, guv'nor. So I lays low, and keeps my daylights skinned. And along comes the missus with the dawg on a string. Then I seed that well-breeched swell put a mask over his phyz, and I'm bubbled if he didn't catch hold of the missus and start a-kissing of her! And afort I could get my breath he threw her into the rattler and jumped on a niceish piece

451

of blood, and the whole lot starts off!"

The Viscount started forward. "You damned little fool, did you do *nothing* to aid her ladyship? You watched her being forcibly carried off, and you——"

"Guv'nor, it ain't no use bamming you: she weren't carried off, not agin her will she weren't! For I seed her put her arm round the cove's neck, hugging him like you never saw, and she didn't struggle, nor let a squeak, not once!"

"I knew it!" declared the dowager.

"No, dash it, ma'am, can't have known it!" Ferdy expostulated, much moved by the stricken look on his cousin's face. "Sherry, dear old boy! Depend upon it, all a hum! Kitten wouldn't go hugging fellows in masks! Might kiss George, but not a fellow in a mask! Wretched Tiger of yours has shot the cat!"

Sherry shook his head dumbly. Jason said: "I ain't shot the cat! What's more, I loped after that rattler—ah, right through the town, I did, *and* I know the road that leery cove took, and it ain't the road what leads to his own ken, neither! Gone off with the missus on the Radstock road what leads to Wells, he has, but he won't get far, not if I know it, he won't!"

Sherry raised his head. "Why won't he?"

"Acos I forked the cove while he was a-waiting for the missus," said Jason sulkily. He added in a defensive tone: "You never telled me not to fork that cull, guv'nor, and if he's a friend of yourn it's the first I heard of it!"

Sherry was regarding him intently. "What did you steal from him? Come, I'm not angry with you! Answer me!"

Jason sniffed, and reluctantly produced from the breast of his jacket a bulging wallet, and a purse with a

452

ring about its neck, both of which he handed over to his master. The wallet was found to contain, besides a handsome number of bank-notes, a special marriage-licence, and several visiting-cards, inscribed with Mr. Tarleton's name and direction; and the purse held some guinea and half-guinea pieces.

Sherry restored the notes to the wallet with a shaking hand. "He may have some loose coins in his pockets, but you are right!" he said. "He won't get beyond the first stage, if he's travelling with hired horses. He doesn't know the truth: he thinks she is free to marry him, of course. You are positive he took the Radstock road, Jason?"

"Take my dying oath he did!" responded the Tiger.

"Wedding at Wells—yes, very likely! Get my curricle round to the door as quick as you can now! Off with you!"

"Anthony!" intoned the dowager, rising from her chair as Jason sped on his errand. "Will you not listen to your Mother? Do you need further proof of that wicked girl's——"

"I beg you will say no more, ma'am!" he interrupted, with a look so stern that she quailed. "Mine is the blame—all of it! I have come by my deserts, and I know it, if you do not! My folly—my neglect of her, my damnable brutality have led her into this flight! Lady Saltash must have compelled her to consent to my visiting her to-night, and rather than meet me——" He broke off, his lip quivering. "But she must not—I cannot let her run off with this man before I've—before I've arranged to set her free! I must find them—explain the circumstances to Tarleton—bring her back to the protection of Lady Saltash!"

Ferdy, who had been lost in profound meditation,

looked at him earnestly. "Sherry, dear old boy, you know what I think? All a mistake! Ten to one that fellow of yours don't know what he's talking about! Might have taken Kitten to a masquerade. Mask, you know."

"Ferdy, I was to have dined with her!" Sherry said in a voice which cracked.

"Must have forgotten that. Dash it, deuced easy to forget a dinner engagement! Done it myself. Mind you, quite right to go after her! Not the thing to be driving about with a fellow in a mask: ought to have warned her! But no getting into a miff, Sherry, and frightening the poor little soul half out of her wits!"

"No, no! Though how I am to keep from choking the life out of that Tarleton fellow—— But I shall do it, never fear!"

Ferdy took a noble resolve. "Tell you what, Sherry: I'll come with you," he said. "Dash it all; not one to leave my friends in the lurch!"

CHAPTER 25

Hero, flung up into the post-chaise with so little ceremony and jolted and bounced over the streets of Bath, had not the smallest notion whither she was bound, or why Sherry had not entered the chaise with her. She pulled a rug, which she found on the seat, over her knees; settled herself in a corner of the vehicle, holding on to one of the straps which served as armrests; and awaited eventualities in a state of pleasurable expectation. Had she but known it, her abductor, not so far gone in romance that he had lost quite all his common sense, had had a very fair picture of what would be the result of trying to make love in a form of vehicle nicknamed, not without good reason, a bounder. The road from Bath to Wells, particularly at this season of the year, was pitted with holes: Mr. Tarleton thought that romance would have a better chance of surviving if he postponed his love-making until Wells was reached.

This cathedral town lay rather more than eighteen miles from Bath, across the Mendip Hills. Mr. Tarleton had booked a room for his prospective bride at the Christopher, and another for himself at the Swan, for although his anxiety to bring adventure into Hero's drab life might have led him to an act which he did not like to think about very closely; his naturally staid disposition made him paradoxically careful not to incur any more scandal than might be necessary. Indeed, he had prudently hired his chaise and pair from a hostelry where he was unknown, and was sometimes conscious of a craven hope that the truth about his marriage might never be made public property.

This consideration made him decide to change horses at the little village of Emborrow, lying at the foot of the Mendips, rather than at Old Down Inn, which, lying twelve miles beyond Bath, was the usual stage. By the time they had reached this place, the moon was coming up brightly, and the going was consequently easier.

The chaise pulled up in the small yard belonging to the one hostelry of any size, and an ostler shouted for the first turnout. At the same moment, one of the windows of the chaise was let down, and Hero looked out, her eyes dancing in the mingled lantern and moonlight, her lips parted in a roguish smile. "Of all the absurd, delightful starts!' she began, her voice quivering with amusement. Then she broke off short as her gaze encountered, not Sherry's beloved features, but Mr. Tarleton's wholly unexciting countenance. A look of startled dismay entered her face; the colour receded from her cheeks; she uttered, in repulsive accents, one word only: "*You!*"

Mr. Tarleton had been prepared for maidenly indignation, but not for this, and he was slightly staggered. He stepped up to the chaise and said, looking up at the blanched face at the window: "But, my sweet love, whom else should it be?"

"Oh!" wailed Hero, her face puckering like a baby's.

"Oh, I thought you w-were Sh-Sherry!"

Mr. Tarleton's brain reeled. "Thought I was whom?" he said numbly.

"M-my husband!" wept Hero, tears rolling one after the other down her cheeks. "Oh, how *could* you play such a c-cruel trick on me?"

If the floor had heaved under Sherry's feet, the universe fairly rocked about the unfortunate Mr. Tarleton. For a moment he could only gaze up at Hero in uncomprehending amazement. He repeated in bemused accents: "Your *husband?*"

Only heart-broken sobs answered him. He became aware of a postboy at his elbow, and pulled himself together with an effort. "I beg of you, ma'am——! Pray, do not——! Here, you, what's the figure?"

The post-boy who had driven the chaise from Bath told him eighteen shillings, reckoning the hire of the chaise-and-pair at the rate of one-and-sixpence a mile, and Mr. Tarleton, anxious to be rid of him, dived a hand into his pocket. It was then that he discovered that not only his purse, but his wallet also, was missing, and that all the loose cash he carried in the pockets of his breeches amounted only to six shillings and ninepence. Never was an eloping gentleman in a worse predicament! Never had he expected to regret with such bitterness having hired his coach from an inn where his name was unknown! One glance at the post-boy's face was sufficient to inform him that he would not be permitted, without a most unseemly brawl, to travel upon tick. He was not even known at the inn. There was nothing for it but to turn to his weeping victim, and as he did it his sense of the ridiculous threatened to overcome more poignant emotions.

"My dear, pray do not cry so! I promise you I will set

all to rights! The only thing is—— Miss Wantage, it is the most absurd of predicaments to find oneself in, but I have been robbed of my purse, and here is this fellow expecting to be paid for his services. Are you able to lend me a guinea?"

Hero raised her head from the window-sill to reply: "Of c-course I am not! I have not my p-purse with me!"

"Oh, my God!" muttered Mr. Tarleton. "Now we *are* in the basket!"

"I wish I were dead!" responded Hero.

"No, no, don't do that! Heavens, what a coil! But how could I have guessed—— My dear child, you cannot stay there! Do, pray, come down, and into the inn! Really I don't know whether I am on my head or my heels!" He mounted the steps, which the ostler had helpfully let down, and opened the door of the chaise, only to have his entrance to the vehicle hotly disputed by Pug. He recoiled exclaiming: "Good God, what possessed you to bring that creature?"

"It was your fault!" Hero said, from the folds of her handkerchief. She blew her nose defiantly. "I did not want to bring him, and oh, I thought it was j-just l-like Sherry to throw him in on t-top of me!'

"Don't, pray don't begin to cry again!" implored the harassed Mr. Tarleton. "We shall have the whole stable-yard about us in a trice. Only come inside the house, and I will set all to rights!"

"No one can set all to rights, for I am utterly ruined!" declared Hero. "My husband was c-coming to dine with me, and I shall not be there, and he will never, never speak to m-me again! And if he finds out this dreadful scrape you have put me into it will be worse than all the rest!"

Mr. Tarleton took her hand and helped her to alight

from the chaise. "He shall not discover it. We will make up some tale that will satisfy him. But who—why—— No, come into the inn, where we can be private! As for you, fellow, you must wait! Go into the tap-room and order yourself a glass of flesh-and-blood at my expense! And here's a crown for you to keep your mouth shut!"

The post-boy pocketed this douceur, but warned his client not to try to lope off without paying him for the hire of his horses. Mr. Tarleton somewhat testily demanded to be told how he could do any such thing in his present pecuniary circumstances, and led Hero into the inn. Here he peremptorily ordered the landlord to show the lady into a private parlour. When this had been done, and the landlord had rejoined him in the deserted coffee-room, he explained, with what assurance he could muster, that he had been robbed of his wallet and purse. The landlord was civil, but palpably incredulous, so Mr. Tarleton haughtily said: "Here is my card, fellow!" Almost immediately after this he was obliged to correct himself. "No, curse it, that's gone with the rest!" But my name is Tarleton—of Frensham Hall, near Swainswick! You will have heard of it! I am escorting a—a friend to Wells—at least, I was doing so, but it so chances that she has discovered that she has left behind her in Bath a most important—er—package, and we are obliged to return there with what speed we can muster. Do me the favour of paying off that post-boy—or no! Better still, let one of your own boys or their cads lead the horses back leer, and let my post-boy drive us back to Bath with a fresh pair! You and he may thus be assured of receiving your money. Meanwhile——"

The landlord, who had been thinking, interrupted at

this point. "Begging your honour's pardon, if you live at Frensham Hall, how do you come to be travelling to Wells in a hired chaise?"

"What has that to do with you, fellow?" said Mr. Tarleton, colouring in spite of himself.

"I don't know as how it has aught to do with me, sir, but what I was thinking was that it seems a queer set-out to me that a gentleman wishful to travel only to Wells wouldn't drive in his own carriage—ah, and at a more seasonable time o' day, what's more! Not being wishful to give offence, sir, you understand."

"I am well known in Bath," Mr. Tarleton said stiffly. "Yes, and they know me at the Old Down Inn, so you may satisfy yourself only by sending to enquire there if a Mr. Tarleton has ever changed horses with them."

"Yes, and when I've sent one of my boys a mile and a half up the road to make them enquiries, who's to say you *are* this Mr. Tarleton?" retorted the landlord. "And if you're so well known in Bath, how comes it that post-boy don't seem to reckernize your honour? That's what I'd like to know!"

Mr. Tarleton had the greatest difficulty in maintaining his control over his temper. After a moment's struggle, he succeeded in choking back the angry words which rose to his lips, and managed, after a most wearing argument, to persuade the landlord to have a fresh pair harnessed to the chaise, and to prevail upon the post-boy who had brought him from Bath to take him back there as soon as he should have had time to refresh himself, which the landlord assured him he would certainly insist upon. Mr. Tarleton then gave up his gold timepiece and his signet-ring as pledges, ordered coffee to be sent immediately to the parlour, and made haste to rejoin Hero.

460

He found her seated by the fire, clasping Pug in her arms, and looking the picture of tragedy. Such a look of reproach did she cast upon him as he entered the room that he exclaimed: "How could I tell? I thought you would like it! And when you kissed me—— Good God, was there ever such a hideous coil?"

"Never, never!" Hero said, with whole-hearted fervour. "I cannot imagine why you should suppose that I should want you to run off with me! And to bring this horrid little dog, too!"

"But, my dear, surely you were aware that I have been head over ears in love with you these weeks past!"

Her face showed him plainly that she had been aware of no such circumstance. "In love with me? But you might be my——I mean—I mean——"

"No, I might not!" he said, nettled. "Not your father, if that is what you were about to say! But how came you to be living with Lady Saltash, under the name of Miss Wantage? Who is your husband? Do I know him? Is he in Bath now?"

"Yes, oh yes! He came there in search of me, because we had had a dreadful quarrel, and I ran away from him, only I never knew it, and I thought he came on Miss Milborne's account, and that is why—— Oh, he must not find out what has happened to-night! It is much, much worse than all the other scrapes I was in!"

"Good God!" said Mr. Tarleton blankly. "But who is he?" An appalling thought dawned on him; he looked across at Hero with the grimmest foreboding, and asked: "Not—— I do devoutly trust!—not the ferocious young gentleman of the Pump Room?"

"He is not ferocious!" replied Hero, flushing indignantly. "He is the dearest and best person in the world! It was just that he was in a very bad temper, because I went off with you! And when I think that he called Lord Wrotham out, only for kissing me once, I am afraid he will be in a much worse one if this should come to his ears! Oh, I do hope there may be some way of preventing his discovering it!"

"Indeed, so do I!" said Mr. Tarleton frankly. "In fact, to be honest with you, my dear, my knees are already knocking together so that I wonder you do not hear them!"

She was obliged to smile at this, but relapsed almost immediately into gloom. "It doesn't signify. What must he think when he finds no one in Camden Place at seven o'clock! Oh, do you not see that he will suppose I did not wish to meet him, and he will be so hurt, and so angry, and how can I ever explain that it was not my fault? I am utterly undone!"

"Let me think!" begged Mr. Tarleton, sitting down by the table and clasping his head between his hands. "You have set my brain in such a whirl——! You could not tell him that you had gone to dine with some friends, I suppose?"

"No, I couldn't!" said Hero, quite crossly. "He was coming particularly to see me, and oh, we were to have had buttered crab and a n-neat's tongue with c-cauliflowers!"

Mr. Tarleton looked somewhat taken aback by this, and suggested feebly that such mundane considerations were of small consequence.

"It is Sherry's favourite dinner!" Hero explained tragically.

"Well, never mind!" said Mr. Tarleton. "You will be able to give him many such dinners, I dare say, and really, my child, at a moment like this to be vexing yourself over——"

"No, I shan't, because he will be so angry that he will utterly cast me off, and I shall be left upon the world with only this odious little dog and a canary to love!"

"My dear Miss—— I mean, my dear Lady Sheringham, I feel certain that your husband would not use you with such undeserved harshness! Do, I entreat you——"

"Yes, he would!" averred Hero, wiping her eyes with a very damp handkerchief. "Any husband would, after such a scrape as this!"

"Upon my word of honour, I assure you the man who could do so would be the veriest Monster!"

Hero instantly took exception to such a term's being applied to her beloved Sherry, and Mr. Tarleton was only rescued from a morass of retractions and attempted explanations by the entrance of the waiter bearing the coffee he had ordered. While the waiter slowly and carefully arranged the cups on the table, he left the door into the adjoining coffee-room ajar. Sounds betokening some fresh arrivals to the inn reached the ears of the couple in the parlour. A voice which made Hero stiffen in her chair said with something less than its usual suavity: "Be so good as to show us to a private parlour, and to send up some refreshment for this lady! There has been an accident to my carriage, and we have been obliged to walk to this place."

The landlord began to say that his only private room had been bespoken already, but he was interrupted by a fresh voice, glacial with arctic rage, but even better known to Hero. "I shall be glad of a cup of hot coffee —*hot*, if you please!—but I prefer to drink it here, in your public room; and while I am doing so I shall be obliged to you if you will have horses harnessed to a

463

chaise to convey me instantly to Bath."

Hero gave a gasp and sat bolt upright in her chair, round-eyed with astonishment. The landlord was heard to explain apologetically that he kept only one chaise, which was out on hire at the moment.

"I do not care what kind of a vehicle I ride in, but a vehicle I must and will have!" announced Miss Milborne. "Whose is the chaise standing in your yard, pray?"

"It is hired by the party in the parlour, ma'am. Indeed, I have nothing to offer but my own gig, and it would not be suitable!"

"I thank you, it will do excellently, if you will be so good as to hire it to this—this gentleman!" said Miss Milborne in bitter accents.

The waiter, having arranged the table to his satisfaction, withdrew at this point and closed the door behind him. To Mr. Tarleton's surprise, Hero rose up from her chair, pushing Pug from her lap as she did so, and tiptoed to the door and tried to peep through the keyhole. She could see very little, so she set her ear to the crack instead and listened with an intent face to what was going on in the coffee-room. When Mr. Tarleton would have asked what in the world she was about, she lifted an imperative finger and hissed: "Sh!"

Apparently the landlord had withdrawn to carry out Miss Milborne's orders, for Sir Montagu's voice was clearly heard to say: "Now, my dearest Miss Milborne, let me assure you that you are entirely mistaken! Come, do not let us quarrel! The most unavoidable and unfortunate accident——"

"If you attempt to lay a finger upon me, sir, I shall scream at the top of my lungs!" interrupted Miss Milborne.

"But, my dear ma'am, only listen to me! I should not dream of touching you! But——"

"No! And no doubt you did not dream of trying to force your most unwelcome caresses upon me, and *mauling* me in your arms as though I had been the sort of vulgar wretch you are plainly accustomed to dealing with!" retorted Miss Milborne. "No doubt, too, you would have been so obliging as to have unhanded me without the inducement of a pin's being stuck into you!"

At this Hero's eyes began to dance, and she gave a smothered choke of laughter.

"If," Sir Montagu was saying, "if, in the intoxication of finding myself alone in the presence of one for whom I cherish the most passionate devotion, the most——"

"I beg you will spare me any more of these transports!" said Miss Milborne. "If passionate devotion led you to suggest to me that since we were stranded in so remote a hamlet there was no help for it but for me to become betrothed to you, I can only trust that I may never encounter such devotion again! I do not know by what means you may have contrived the accident to your carriage, but I am no longer in any doubt as to why you were so desirous of driving me back to Bath by another route than the post-road! You sought, sir, to entrap me into marriage with you, since you were aware that you had no hope of winning my hand by more gentlemanly methods. But you were much mistaken in my character if you supposed that I was so weak and foolish a female as to submit to your infamous proposals!"

Hero, who had listened to this speech with a rapt look of concentrated thought on her face, now left the

465

door and ran to Mr. Tarleton's side. "I am saved!" she whispered joyfully. "It is Isabella Milborne, and the most odious man imaginable! I have known Isabella all my life, and I know she will help me out of this tangle! And I dare say she may be very glad to see me, too, because she may drive back with me in the chaise, and she cannot wish to sit perched up in the landlord's gig, you know. It is not at all the style of thing which would suit her. Do you remain in this room, Mr. Tarleton, while I arrange it all!"

"But, Lady Sheringham, consider a moment!" he said urgently. "Are you sure——"

"Yes, yes, and in any event, how could I leave poor Isabella to Sir Montagu's mercy?"

"From what I have been privileged to hear, I should judge poor Isabella to be very well able to protect her virtue!" said Mr. Tarleton dryly.

"Yes, was it not famous to hear her giving him such a set-down? She is a most spirited girl! But it cannot be very comfortable for her, I dare say! Pray hold Pug's leash, dear sir!"

Mr. Tarleton, on whom the events of the evening were beginning to leave their mark, accepted the leash meekly, and, with some misgiving, watched his companion open the door and walk into the coffee-room.

Miss Milborne, who was standing by the fireplace, holding one foot, in a mired half-boot of orange-jean, to the glow, turned her head and uttered an exclamation of astonishment. "Hero!"

"Yes, it's me," said Hero, with a fine disregard for grammar and the sunniest of smiles. "Poor Isabella, how muddied you are, and how odious for you to be in such a fix! Do pray, come into the parlour! There is not the least need for you to hire the landlord's gig, for I

466

will escort you back to Bath in my chaise!"

"But how is this?" stammered Miss Milborne, in the greatest bewilderment. "How in the world do you come to be here, and at such an hour? Oh, Hero, what fresh scrape have you fallen into?"

"Well, I must say, Isabella, I think it is the outside of enough for *you* to be accusing *me* of being in a scrape, when you are in a much worse one yourself!" said Hero. "I cannot conceive how you come to be driving about the country with Sir Montagu Revesby, for I am sure it is not at all the thing!"

"Sir Montagu and I," said Miss Milborne, colouring, "have been on an expedition to Wells, in company with some friends of mine!"

"Well, where are they?" asked Hero reasonably. "You must know, Isabella, that I overheard all that has just passed between you and Sir Montagu, and although I quite see that it was not your fault that there was an accident to his carriage, there is no denying that you are in an awkward situation. And you may say what you please, but I am persuaded there is *one* person whom you would not wish to hear of this! For you are not so heartless as to give him such pain: I know you are not!"

Miss Milborne, who was tired, and cold, and more shaken than she had allowed to appear, felt sudden tears sting her eyelids, and covered her face with her hands, saying in a trembling tone; "Oh, Hero, do not! Pray say no more!"

Hero ran to her at once. "Oh, I am sorry! Do not cry, dearest Isabella! I did not mean to hurt you, indeed, I did not!"

Sir Montagu spoke, in his silkiest voice. "Very affecting, Lady Sheringham! And, pray, where is your

467

husband? Not here, I fancy! In fact, he has not been over-much in your company of late, I apprehend! You have been a most determined enemy of mine, have you not? I wonder if you will live to regret it? Do you know, I almost believe that you may? Is it too much to hope that we may be permitted a glimpse of the gentleman who is no doubt concealed in that private parlour?"

"No!" said Mr. Tarleton from the doorway. "It is too much, sir!" And with these words, he landed a useful right on Sir Montagu's jaw, and sent him crashing to the floor. "Get up, and I will serve you a little more home-brewed!" he promised, standing over Sir Montagu with his fists clenched.

Sir Montagu had had a trying day. He had failed both by fair means and foul to win an heiress's hand in marriage; he had had a businesslike scarf-pin thrust into the fleshy part of his arm; he had been obliged to tramp three miles down miry lanes beside a lady who maintained a stony silence throughout the trudge, and the yokel whom she had bribed to guide them to the nearest posting-inn; he had been confronted then by the very person to whom he attributed the greater part of his misfortunes; and finally he had been knocked down painfully and ignominiously by a complete stranger who seemed to be only too ready to repeat the performance. Between rage and the natural fright of a man to whom physical violence was at all times horrible, he lost his head. His walking-stick had clattered to the floor, with the chair across which he had laid it, and which he had wildly clutched in his fall. He reached out his hand for it, dragged himself up, fumbling with the carved ivory handle and, as Mr. Tarleton squared up to him purposefully, tore the concealed blade from its innocent-seeming sheath and thrust at his assailant. Mr. Tarleton was just too late to avoid being touched. He saw the thrust coming, and dodged it, so that instead of entering his chest, it tore through the sleeve of his coat and gashed his upper arm. The next instant he had closed with Sir Montagu, twisted the sword-stick from his grasp and floored him again. After that, he stood panting, and instinctively trying to grip his own arm to stop the blood which was flowing copiously, staining his sleeve a horrid colour and dripping on to the floor.

The two ladies, who had been transfixed with dismay by these proceedings, started forward.

"Shame!" cried Isabella, her eyes flashing magnificently. "To draw steel upon an unarmed man! Dastard!"

"Oh, *poor* Mr. Tarleton!" said Hero. "And you did it all for my sake! I am excessively obliged to you, but I do trust you are not dreadfully hurt! Pray, let me help you to take off your coat immediately! Oh, landlord, is that you? Be so good as to bring me some water in a bowl as quickly as you can, and some brandy! And, waiter, pray help this gentleman to take off his coat, and the rest of you go away, if you please!"

"Good God!" said Mr. Tarleton faintly, becoming aware of the landlord, the waiter, an ostler, two post-boys, and a chambermaid. "What have I done! My curst folly! But when I heard him address you in such terms I could not help myself!"

"No, no, of course you could not!" said Hero, tenderly rolling up his shirt-sleeve and laying bare an ugly gash. "Oh, we must have a surgeon to this! Landlord—— Oh, he has gone! One of you, if you please, run for the nearest surgeon, and tell him there is a gentleman hurt in an accident!"

"For heaven's sake, no!" begged Mr. Tarleton from the chair into which he had been lowered. "The merest scratch! If you would but hand me one of those napkins, and assist me to twist it tightly about my arm!"

Isabella, who had been hunting in her reticule, produced a pair of scissors and began, with the aid of these, to tear a napkin into strips. Sir Montagu, appalled as much by his late madness as by the frightful consequences he saw clearly might result from it, had picked himself up and staggered to the far end of the room, holding a fast-swelling jaw and trying to think in what way he could avert retribution. The landlord came back with a bowl of water, and sharply ordered his hirelings to be off about their business. The waiter put a glass of brandy to Mr. Tarleton's lips; and Mr. Tarleton, who was feeling rather faint from so much loss of blood, swallowed the tot and leaned back in his chair with his eyes closed.

The landlord, thoroughly incensed by such irregular conduct in his house, dealt expeditiously with the wound, but stated his intention of summoning the village constable to take up both combatants. He was just adding a rider to the effect that the magistrates would know how to deal with so-called gentlemen who tried to cheat honest post-boys out of their fees, when the clatter of hooves sounded in the yard, the grating of wheels on cobble-stones, and an impatient voice called out: "Hi, there! Ostler! *Ostler*, I say!"

"Sherry!" shrieked Hero, and flew up from beside Mr. Tarleton's chair and sped forth into the corridor which led to the yard. "Sherry, Sherry!"

His Lordship had just sprung down from his curricle. He saw his wife in the shaft of lamplight cast through the open door, and strode towards her. "Oh, Kitten, thank God I have found you!" he exclaimed, holding out his arms. "You mustn't do this, my little love! I can't let you!"

Hero ran straight into his arms, and flung her own round his neck. "No, no, Sherry! I never meant to do it!" she sobbed. "I thought it was you, not Mr. Tarleton!"

"Oh, Kitten, if that isn't just like you!" he said unsteadily. "It ought to have been me! And if I hadn't been such a gudgeon—— Kitten, you little wretch, what a dance you have led me! Kiss me!"

The Honourable Ferdy Fakenham, observing with intense interest the passionate embrace being exchanged by two persons who appeared to be wholly oblivious of their surroundings, descended from the curricle, and with great dignity bade the equally interested Jason lead the horses into the stable, and see them well rubbed down. By the time this order had been reluctantly obeyed, Sherry was drying his wife's wet cheeks with his handkerchief, and Hero was smiling up into his softened face. "But, Sherry, how did you know?"

"Jason saw you. I thought—— I was afraid it was because I had given you such a dislike of me that you could not bear even to speak to me! I felt like blowing my brains out!"

"Oh, Sherry, no! How could I dislike you? I have loved you all my life!"

"Kitten, Kitten!" he said, folding her in his arms again. "I wish I could say the same! But it wasn't until after I had married you that I grew to love you so! What a fellow I am! But I found out when you ran away from me how dearly I loved you! You won't get the chance to run from me again, I can tell you!"

She laid her cheek against his heart. "Oh, and I have been so troublesome! And now this shocking scrape! I thought you would utterly cast me off!"

"It was my fault! All my fault!" he said vehemently.

Ferdy coughed apologetically. "Told you it was a mistake, Sherry, dear old boy! No wish to disturb you, but there are a couple of postboys peeping at you round the corner of the stable door."

"Let 'em peep!" said his lordship, but he tucked Hero's hand in his arm, and walked slowly into the inn with her. "Where's this felow, Tarleton? You little fiend, nicely you must have gammoned him! Dashed if I'm not sorry for the poor devil! But what the deuce did he mean by running off with you like that?"

"Oh, Sherry, I am much afraid it may have been because of something very foolish which I once said to him!" confessed Hero guiltily.

He gave a shout of laughter. "I might have known it! Lord, it's like seeing your last hope come first past the post to be pulling you out of a scrape again, brat!"

"Well, I am excessively relieved to hear you say so, Sherry, because, to tell you the truth, it is a worse scrape than you know. In fact, it is quite shocking, and the landlord says he will give us up to the constable; but perhaps if you will be so obliging as to pay the reckoning for poor Mr. Tarleton he may relent. He had all his money stolen from him, you see——"

"I know he had," grinned Sherry. "Jason forked him! That's how I managed to catch you."

"Oh, how clever of Jason!" Hero cried. "We must give him a handsome present!"

They had by this time reached the end of the passage which led to the coffee-room. Mr. Tarleton had succeeded in getting rid of the landlord, but to the Viscount the room seemed strangely full of people. His astonished gaze took in first Miss Milborne, then Sir Montagu Revesby, and lastly Pug, who, having been sleeping stertorously before the parlour fire throughout the late proceedings, had just waddled into the coffee-room, and now greeted his lordship with a wheezy bark.

It was characteristic of the Viscount that his mind was instantly diverted from the stirring events which had occurred that day. An expression of foreboding entered his face; he stared with repulsion at Pug, and demanded: "Where did that come from?"

"Oh, I brought him!" replied Hero happily. "It's Pug!"

"I knew it!" said Sherry. "No, dash it, Kitten! I don't mind Gil's canary—at least, I do, but I can bear it—but I'll be hanged if I'll have an overfed little brute like that in my house! If you want a dog, I'll give you one, but I warn you, it won't be a pug!"

"Oh, Sherry, will you?" said Hero. "Well, I do think I should like one. This isn't mine, you know. He belongs to Lady Saltash, and he is quite odious!"

"Well, why the deuce did you bring him?" Sherry asked. "Can't see what you can possibly have wanted with a dog when you were eloping!"

"No, and I did not in the least mean to bring him, but I was taking him for an airing when Mr. Tarleton abducted me, and somehow he got into the chaise too. Oh, Sherry, this is Mr. Tarleton!"

Mr. Tarleton had risen rather unsteadily to his feet, and now said with as much dignity as could be expected of a man half-in and half-out of his coat: "Sheringham, if I may have only one word with you alone, I fancy I can explain everything to your satisfaction!"

"Oh, you don't have to do that!" Sherry responded cheerfully, shaking hands with him. "I don't blame you for running off with my wife: did the same thing myself! Come to think of it, you owed me one, for it was my Tiger forked your wallet and purse. Meant to have brought 'em along with me, but what with one thing and another I forgot 'em. Hallo, you're hurt! How is this?"

Ferdy, who had been staring fixedly at the bowl of reddened water on the table, with the bloodstained napkin beside it, now nudged his cousin. "Know what I think, Sherry? Been a regular turn-up. Someone's had his cork drawn. Claret flowing copiously. If it was Monty's cork, good thing! Don't like him. Never have."

Sherry turned to look at Revesby, his face hardening. "I was forgetting that damned scoundrel was here!" he said. "By Jove, you're right, Ferdy! Someone's landed him a facer at last! Take a look at his jaw!"

"Very wisty castor," agreed Ferdy, nodding his head approvingly. "Dashed if this fellow, Tarleton, ain't a regular right one! Very obedient servant, sir! Happy to have met you!"

"Yes, but wait a bit!" Sherry said, his gaze taking in the unsheathed sword, and Mr. Tarleton's arm. "Something devilish queer about this! What's that sword-stick doing there? You don't mean to say——?"

"Ask Sir Montagu!" said Miss Milborne, who had been leaning her chin in her hand, and staring into the fire, quite divorced from these proceedings. "Ask him to tell you how he drew steel upon an unarmed man!"

"He did?" said Ferdy. "Well, of all things! You hear that, Sherry? Told you he was a Bad Man."

"Lord, I've known that any time these past three months! What I want to know is why he drew steel, and what he got that facer for! And another thing I may as well know, while I'm about it—not that I care much, but it'll save trouble, I dare say—is what the pair of you are doing here at this hour of night!"

Miss Milborne promptly favoured him with an exact account of her share in the evening's adventures. The Viscount remained unmoved." Well, I warned you not to go off with him, Bella," he said. "Might have guessed he would be up to some mischief. Dashed if it doesn't serve you right! A rare dust you have kicked up, and all to spite George, if I know anything of the matter! But that don't tell me how he came to have a set-to with Tarleton!"

"Oh, Mr. Tarleton very kindly knocked him down, because he said such horrid things to me!" explained Hero blithely.

"Oh, that was it, was it?" said his lordship, a martial light in his eye. "I'm much in your debt, Tarleton! And what, my buck, did you say to Lady Sheringham, before I choke it out of your lying throat?"

Sir Montagu, retreating, said hoarsely: "You will regret it if you touch me, Sheringham! If the events of this night were to become known——"

"No, Sherry!" exclaimed Ferdy, seizing his cousin's arm, and clinging to it desperately. "Promised you wouldn't get into a miff! Won't do a bit of good! Got to stop the fellow's mouth!"

"I'll stop his mouth so that he'll never open it again!" said Sherry savagely. "Damn you, Ferdy, let go! I'm going to tear that ugly customer limb from limb, and if there's anything left of him by the time I've done with him——"

"Not in front of ladies, dear boy! Shocking bad *ton!* Besides, it ain't necessary: George wants his blood, and dash it, why shouldn't he have it? Do him good, poor fellow! Put a bit of heart into him!"

"If there is to be any more fighting, I shall have the vapours, and so I warn you!" declared Miss Milborne. "I am sure I have had more to bear at Sir Montagu's hands than Hero, and if I am satisfied I do not know why you should not be, Sherry! And if, sir, you should be so unwise as to open your lips on the subject of this night's adventures, I shall have something to tell the world also! I imagine you would not care to have it generally known that you drew your sword upon an unarmed man!"

Sherry shook his cousin off. "Revesby," he said, eyeing Sir Montagu with a measuring glance. "I'd like to have the chance to pay off a certain score with you, but I fancy Ferdy's right, and it ain't necessary. Wrotham is searching for you, and he's likely to fetch up here at any minute. You're a dead man, Revesby!"

"George is searching for me?" said Miss Milborne faintly. "Oh, good heavens!"

"Went off in one of his pets as soon as he heard you wasn't home," said Ferdy. "Said he'd call on Revesby to answer for his villainy. Good God, I'm dashed if that Greek thing hasn't got after Monty too, Sherry! Very remarkable circumstance, 'pon my soul it is!"

"What the devil *is* all this about a dashed Greek?" demanded Sherry. "George was trying to tell me about him, but I'm hanged if I could make head or tail of it! All I know is, I'm not acquainted with any Greeks, and what's more I don't want to be!"

"It ain't a thing you're acquainted with, dear old boy. Duke knows what it is. Comes up behind a fellow

476

when he ain't expecting it. Thought it was after me, but it turns out to be Monty. Good thing."

"Yes, but what *is* it?"

Mr. Tarleton said, with a quiver of amusement in his voice: "I fancy he means Nemesis."

"That's it!" Ferdy said, looking at him with respect. "Nemesis! You know him too?"

"Well, it's more than I do!" declared Sherry. "What's more, whoever he is, he had nothing to do with my coming to Bath!"

"Not, 'he'," murmured Mr. Tarleton, who was beginning to feel his years. "Goddess of retribution. The daughter, according to Hesiod, of Night."

"Was she, though?" said Ferdy. "Well, by Jove! Daughter of *who?*"

"Night," repeated Mr. Tarleton.

Ferdy looked a little dubious. "Seems a queer start, but I dare say you're right. Come to think of it, devilish rum 'uns, all those old Greeks."

His cousin regarded him with a surprise not wholly free from disapproval. "Well, I never knew you was bookish before, Ferdy!" he said.

"Learned it at Eton," Ferdy said, with a deprecating cough. "Point is, thought the thing was after me. Turns out it was after Monty. Gave him that wisty castor, and set George on to his track. All the same, Sherry, not sure it is such a good thing, now I come to think of it. Don't want George to be obliged to fly the country. Tell you what: let Monty go before George arrives! Pity, in some ways, but there it is!"

Sherry had raised his head, and was listening to an unmistakable sound. "Too late!" he said, with a little laugh. "Lay you any money this is George!"

So indeed it proved to be. A bare couple of minutes

later, George came striding into the coffee-room, with Mr. Ringwood at his heels. He checked on the threshold. "Sherry!" he ejaculated. "Good God, you here? What the—*Kitten!*"

Mr. Ringwood put up his glass. "Well, upon my word!" he said, mildly astonished. "Devilish queer place to run into you people! Your very obedient, Kitten! You and Sherry come here on your honeymoon?"

Hero clasped both his hands tightly. "Dear Gil, I am so glad to see you again! I have been in such a scrape! I was carried off by poor Mr. Tarleton there, quite by mistake; and Isabella got into a scrape too, through Sir Montagu Revesby; but then Sherry came, and everything is all right and tight—I mean, everything has ended happily!"

Lord Wortham, fastening on to the one point in this ingenuous explanation which concerned him, looked round for his quarry, perceived him, and said: "*Ah!*"

Sir Montagu, a perfectly ghastly smile writhing on his lips, said: "Lady Sheringham mistakes—I can explain the most lamentable accident!"

"Yes?" said George, stripping off his driving-gloves, taking them in his right hand, and advancing upon Sir Montagu. You got Miss Milborne into a scrape, and you fancy you can explain it, do you? Not to my satisfaction, Revesby!"

"No you don't George," suddenly said Mr. Ringwood, grasping his lordship's right wrist. "By the looks of it, someone's been before you! Let be, man, let be!"

"By God, Gil, if you don't let me go——I've been wanting an excuse to call that fellow out these two months, and if you think you or anyone else can stop me now I've got it."

"George!" said Miss Milborne compellingly.

Lord Wrotham's eyes turned swiftly towards her.

"George!" said Miss Milborne again, rather pale, but meeting his gaze squarely. "If you call him out, I will not marry you!"

"Isabella!" uttered his lordship, trembling. "Do you mean—can you mean——?"

Mr. Ringwood let him go, but not before he had thoughtfully removed the gloves from his suddenly slackened grasp.

"Oh, George, for heaven's sake, take me home!" begged Miss Milborne, her admirably modulated voice breaking. "I'm so tired, and hungry, and I never cared a rap for that odious man, no, nor for Severn either, or Sherry, or anyone save yourself, and I'm sure I don't know why I care for you, for you are just as odious as any of them, only I do, and I will marry you to-morrow, if you like!"

"If I like!" said his lordship thickly, and enveloped her in a crushing embrace.

Mr. Ringwood, observing his attention to be distracted from Sir Montagu, touched that pallid gentleman on the shoulder, and nodded significantly towards the door. Ferdy, ever helpful, picked up his hat and greatcoat, and silently handed them to him. Sir Montagu clutched them thankfully, and made good his escape.

"And the best of it is," remarked Sherry, closing the door, and setting his shoulders to it, "he won't dare show his face in town for months, in case he should run into George, and George's feelings should get the better of him."

"Have you let that fellow go?" George demanded, turning his head.

"Yes, but really it is much better that he should go,"

said Hero soothingly. "For if you were to shoot him, you would have to leave the country, and then you could not marry Isabella. And he will not dare say a word about what happened to-night, because of what we might say about his wounding poor Mr. Tarleton. And besides that, if he spread a horrid scandal, I dare say Sherry would not mind my telling people about his baby, for he has one, you know, and he would not give its mother a penny to provide for it, and it is Sherry who has to do so, which is a great deal too bad, for it is not Sherry's baby! Indeed, I wish it was—at least, I mean I wish it was mine, because it is the dearest little thing!" A thought occurred to her; her eyes lit up; and she turned impulsively towards Sherry. "Oh, Sherry, do think——"

"Yes!" said his lordship hastily. "Yes, I do, Kitten, but not now, for the lord's sake!"

"Bad *ton!*" explained Ferdy kindly. "Not quite the thing! That fellow Tarleton present: very tolerable sort of a fellow, but almost a stranger! Talk it over later!"

"No, by God, you won't!" said his lordship forcibly.

"Eh?" said Ferdy. "Good heavens! No, by God, so I won't!"